MIDNIGHT FLIGHT

V.C. Andrews® Books

The Dollanganger Family Series
Flowers in the Attic
Petals on the Wind
If There Be Thorns
Seeds of Yesterday
Garden of Shadows

The Casteel Family Series
Heaven
Dark Angel
Fallen Hearts
Gates of Paradise
Web of Dreams

The Cutler Family Series
Dawn
Secrets of the Morning
Twilight's Child
Midnight Whispers
Darkest Hour

The Landry Family Series
Ruby
Pearl in the Mist
All That Glitters
Hidden Jewel
Tarnished Gold

The Logan Family Series
Melody
Heart Song
Unfinished Symphony
Music in the Night
Olivia

My Sweet Audrina
(does not belong to a series)

The Orphans Miniseries
Butterfly
Crystal
Brooke
Raven
Runaways (full-length novel)

The Wildflowers Miniseries
Misty
Star
Jade
Cat
Into the Garden (full-length novel)

The Hudson Family Series
Rain
Lightning Strikes
Eye of the Storm
The End of the Rainbow

The Shooting Stars Series
Cinnamon
Ice
Rose
Honey
Falling Stars

The De Beers Family Series
Willow
Wicked Forest
Twisted Roots
Into the Woods
Hidden Leaves

Broken Wings Series
Broken Wings
Midnight Flight

Published by POCKET BOOKS

V.C. ANDREWS®

MIDNIGHT FLIGHT

POCKET BOOKS

New York London Toronto Syndey Singapore

and

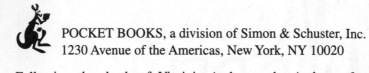 POCKET BOOKS, a division of Simon & Schuster, Inc.
1230 Avenue of the Americas, New York, NY 10020

Following the death of Virginia Andrews, the Andrews family worked with a carefully selected writer to organize and complete Virginia Andrews' stories and to create additional novels, of which this is one, inspired by her storytelling genius.

ISBN: 0-7434-2868-4

First Pocket Books hardcover edition October 2003

10 9 8 7 6 5 4 3 2 1

V.C. ANDREWS and VIRGINIA ANDREWS are registered trademarks of the Vanda General Partnership

POCKET and colophon are registered trademarks of Simon & Schuster, Inc.

Manufactured in the United States of America

For information regarding special discounts for bulk purchases, please contact Simon & Schuster Special Sales at 1-800-456-6798 or business@simonandschuster.com

Contents

MIDNIGHT FLIGHT

vi   Contents

Prologue

Just like someone rising to the surface of a pool filled with ink, I slowly awoke from what felt like a month-long coma. My eyelids flickered, but they were two tiny lead curtains slamming closed repeatedly until I managed with determined effort to keep them open. Shadows swirled and wavered and then gradually came into focus. However, the shapes they began to form made no immediate sense to me.

Something was roaring in my ears. For a moment I thought I was right beside a waterfall, and then as my eyes focused, I read the instructions on the back of the seat in front of me: KEEP YOUR SEAT BELT BUCKLED WHEN IN FLIGHT.

In flight?

I lifted my head and looked about. I was in a small airplane that had room for what looked like twenty or so people, and I wasn't just buckled in the seat. A thick, black leather strap was around my upper body, tightened just below my elbows, keeping my arms so close to my sides I could barely move my hands.

No one else was in the plane!

I had been in an airplane only once before in my life when Daddy and Mama took me to see Daddy's father in an old-age home in Richmond just before he died. I was only five at the time, but I never forgot being on a plane. Mama wouldn't let me sit by the window. She wanted me between her and Daddy so I wouldn't really think about being up in an airplane. Daddy thought she should let me sit by the window, but she wouldn't have it.

"I don't want no kid screamin' and cryin' 'bout being afraid. It's enough I agreed to go on this depressing trip," she declared.

Mama never cared about raising her voice in public, and the only way Daddy could stop it was by looking away and stopping the argument.

I wasn't afraid of being in a plane. Actually, I was fascinated with everything, especially the feeling of being lifted into the sky. When my heart started to pound, I closed my eyes and smiled to myself. It was better than the time Daddy had taken me on the Ferris wheel. However, when it came to my getting up to go to the bathroom, I was nervous. Daddy wanted Mama to take me and she was annoyed.

"She can go to the bathroom herself at home. She can go in a plane," she told him.

I went myself, and when I came back to my seat, I curled up and fell asleep. The next thing I knew we were getting off the plane in Richmond. Because I'd behaved well, Mama let me sit by the window on the way back. I couldn't stop looking at the clouds and the earth below where houses looked like toys. I thought to myself that this was the way God saw the world every day. He rode inside a cloud or on the back of the wind.

But this plane ride was different, so different. I felt I was being transported from one dream to another. Was this real? Or would I wake up any moment and realize it had all been a terrible nightmare?

I was so busy looking around that I didn't realize immediately how I was dressed. Gone were my clothes. Instead, I wore what looked like a thick, faded white nightgown created from an old potato sack. It was that coarse. Whatever was on beneath it didn't feel like my panties either. Where were my jeans and blouse? And my watch? Even the ruby ring Daddy had brought back for me from one of his sales trips was gone.

I squirmed in the seat and glanced down at my feet. I was wearing white stockings, the sort of stockings I saw nurses wear, and instead of my pink and white sneakers, I wore a pair of the ugliest-looking black shoes with thick heels I think I had ever seen.

What was going on?

"Hello!" I screamed.

The only response was the continually monotonous roar of the engines. Whoever was in the cockpit might not be able to hear me, I thought.

I looked around the plane again. How had I gotten here? Who had strapped me into this seat?

I struggled through the maze of blurred memories, desperately trying to understand, to remember, and then, as if a dam in my brain had broken, it all came rushing back over me, and as soon as it had, I wished it hadn't.

After Mama had left Daddy and me and I had been in trouble too often in Atlanta, Daddy had convinced

Mama's sister and brother-in-law, my aunt Mae Louise and uncle Buster Howard, to take me into their suburban home in Stone Mountain and enroll me into a better school. Daddy was on the road too much to keep an eye on me. Unfortunately, I got into trouble quickly with a boy there named Ashley Porter, who came from a wealthy white family, and then after Daddy had been killed in the car accident, I had decided to run off.

I had learned that Mama had been left in a clinic where she was being treated for substance abuse , and I was headed there. I was hoping she would be well enough to get out and go somewhere where she and I could start a new life. I was hoping she would be as excited about that as I was, but when I arrived at the clinic and went to see her, she was so confused. She just couldn't or wouldn't understand what I was telling her about Daddy being killed in a car accident and me being forced to live with her sister, Mae Louise.

Unbeknownst to me, while I was visiting Mama, the doctor at the clinic had called my uncle and aunt and my aunt called the police. The state police were sent to bring me back. I wasn't supposed to leave Stone Mountain for any trips since I was to go to court for hitting a boy named Skip Lester with a small desktop statue when he, Ashley, and the other boys had all ganged up on me. Girls from my new school tricked me into joining what they called a sting operation to permit the police to arrest Ashley, who had been spreading stories about them and me. He was going to be arrested for selling and using drugs. Of course, the girls were in cahoots with Ashley and his friends to trap me and have fun with me. I still couldn't explain why I was so stupid and gullible enough to believe them. That's how you get when you're so desperate to have friends. You can have only one friend, I concluded, yourself.

The state policeman who picked me up at Mama's clinic dropped me off at a roadside diner to meet my uncle Buster. I thought my uncle was just going to bawl me out without my aunt being present and then he was going to take me home. Instead, he left me there to be taken to what he called some special school for troubled teenagers like me, girls whose parents and guardians could no longer contend with them and their problems.

No one wanted to listen to my side of things, especially my aunt and my uncle. My uncle didn't even have the courage to tell me what he had secretly arranged to take place at the diner. He tricked and betrayed me. I went to the bathroom and when I came out, he was gone and so was my suitcase.

A man and a woman came for me in an ambulance, and when I resisted, they stuck a needle in my arm and gave me something that made me dizzy and confused. I passed out as I was being loaded into the ambulance. That was the last thing I remembered.

And that was what my aunt and uncle had done to me, and I was supposed to be the bad one in the family?

Now, here I was alone in this strange plane. Had I died? Had they given me something to kill me? Was this how people were really transported to the other world?

"Hey! Anyone! Please," I screamed. "Someone, help me!"

I twisted and pulled and tried to kick the seat. Frustrated and frightened, I went numb inside and the tears in my brain flooded and washed my screams onto my face.

Still, no one responded. I gazed out the window at the wing and the engine. It was twilight, that time when the earth became a giant sponge and absorbed all the light around it. The dark sky lying in wait came rushing in behind like a black velvet ocean. I saw some stars appear. Their growing brightness comforted me until we flew into a wall of puffy, gray clouds that whirled about like so much smoke.

Every nerve in my body grew tighter and tighter, threatening to snap. My throat was so dry and my shoulders ached, the fingers of pain stretching down from the base of my neck. I continued to struggle against the straps, but they were too thick and too securely fastened. All I was doing by struggling was irritating my skin. Helpless, I relaxed and closed my eyes, trying to keep a lid on my boiling rage. Whoever had done this to me was going to be sorry, I vowed. As soon as they unfastened these belts, they'd see. How dare they take my clothing and put me in this rag and these ugly stockings and shoes!

As best as I could, I wiggled my fingers and explored what I was wearing beneath. It felt like . . . like a diaper, firm as plastic on the outside like one of those special undergarments women who have bladder trouble wear.

What was going on? Who dared to undress me? Was someone playing some sick joke on me? How long have I been on this plane? Where was I being taken? I thought I was going to some school. Why wasn't there anyone else with me? What if something terrible had happened to me? What if I was being kidnapped to become someone's slave? Who would know? Would that satisfy my uncle and aunt? All they cared about was getting rid of me. Whatever happened to me wasn't important.

As I thought of these things, the rage began to boil over again. I tried to turn and press my body against the straps in hope of breaking loose, but nothing helped. They felt woven of steel thread. Beads of sweat popped out on the back of my neck and my forehead because of my efforts. It was another futile attempt. I was just wasting my energy, energy I might need the moment I was finally released.

Inside, my stomach was churning, grinding rocks of frustration into sand. I closed my eyes and, taking deep breaths, again tried desperately to calm myself.

"Get hold of yourself, Phoebe Elder," I muttered. "Easy. You'll get out of this soon. You've been in worse places."

No, I haven't, I thought.

I opened my eyes and looked at the closed cockpit door. Why wasn't anyone at least interested enough to see if I had regained consciousness?

"Damn you!" I screamed. I could feel the veins in my neck becoming embossed in my skin. I shouted and then just released a long, animal cry of pain.

As if my scream affected the plane, it bounced and then dropped. I balled my fingers into fists and pressed them against my sides, gasping. What was happening now? Were we crashing? The plane bounced again and again and then rattled. Looking out the window, I saw how we dropped lower and lower until we were out of the clouds. Way off in the distance, I could see the lights of some small city, but other than that, the landscape was dark, just like that pool of ink out of which I had imagined myself rising.

The plane continued to descend. Finally, I heard wheels being lowered and locked into place and then the plane touched down with a small bounce. It slowed and taxied until it turned. Wherever we were wasn't much of an airport. Maybe because of the angle I was at, I couldn't see any lights or people or cars. I heard the engines being shut down and the propellers slowing. When it all stopped, I waited in anticipation to see who would come out of the cockpit. The door did not open for so long, I began to think no one was flying the plane.

Then, the two pilots emerged. They looked so young to me, too young to be in charge of an airplane, but they had wings on their white shirts and gold-threaded bars on their shoulders.

"Where am I? Who did this to me? Why am I tied down?" I fired my questions at them in machine-gun fashion.

They looked at me, but neither spoke, making me feel as if I weren't really there. Instead, one of them undid the door and lowered the steps. I heard a woman outside ask if everything was all right.

"Just peachy keen," one of the pilots said, and the two left the plane. No one else had emerged from the cockpit. Who was in charge here?

"What about me? What is going on?" I shouted after them. I watched the doorway and then tried to kick at the seat in front of me. "What's going on, damn it!"

Finally, a young woman with short, dark brown hair appeared. She was as tall as I was, about five feet ten or so, and she was wearing a dark blue uniform jacket with brass buttons and a pair of blue slacks. I thought she wasn't much more than nineteen or twenty years old. She was wide in the hips and small on top with narrow shoulders, making it look like two different bodies had been slapped together when God was busy attending to other matters.

"Who are you? What's going on?" I demanded.

"Keep your voice down," she said sharply, and approached. When she drew closer, I saw she had a pudgy face with thick lips and wide nostrils. A streak of freckles burst down the bridge of her nose on both sides and over the crests of her puffy cheeks. She wore no makeup, not even lipstick, and a small, thin scar was on the left side of her chin.

"Where am I?" I asked as softly and as calmly as I could. First, I had to have some answers. Then I could take some action, I told myself.

"You'll see," she replied, and began to unfasten the straps.

"Who are you? Am I at some school? Where is this school that I had to be flown here?"

"You're wasting your breath asking me questions," she said, stepping back. "Get up and get out."

"What happened to my clothes? Why am I wearing this rag dress?"

Her untrimmed eyebrows lifted and I thought she smiled, although it was hard to tell because her lips were so stiff. She seized my right arm and tugged to get me to stand. When I did, I wavered for a moment and she had to grab my shoulders to keep me from falling.

"I'm so dizzy," I said. "They put me to sleep. Maybe they gave me something poisonous."

"Oh, you poor little thing," she said with exaggerated sympathy and sweetness. Then she snapped, "Walk!" She poked me at the base of my spine with her thick, right forefinger, which felt like the barrel of a gun.

I scowled back at her and made my way down the small aisle to the door. For a moment I was dizzy and nauseated again. Then I caught my breath and navigated the half dozen metal steps. The outside area was well lit, but all I saw was what looked like a building made of concrete. It had bland gray walls and a metal door with no windows on it. The front of the building had no windows either.

The first thing I noticed when I started down the steps was how hot it was. It was dark, but it felt like the middle of a summer day in Atlanta, especially in the poorer part of the city where we had lived. It wasn't true that people of African descent didn't notice the oppressive heat and humidity as much as white people.

"Where is this? It's so hot."

"Hell," I heard her say behind me. "Keep walking toward the building before I have you carried there," she threatened, and I continued slowly. Where had the two young pilots gone? Why wasn't anyone else around? I stopped to look and she gave me another shove to move me toward the building.

"Where are we going?"

"Just walk to the building and keep your mouth shut," she ordered.

Every time I turned my head to look around, she pushed me.

"Keep your hands off me," I warned.

"We've got a long night ahead of us. Move it," she commanded.

When we reached the door, she stepped ahead and opened it. The hinges squeaked as if it hadn't been opened for a hundred years. It was like opening a tomb. How could this be a school? Why was I being brought here?

"Go in," she said.

I hesitated and she reached out, seized my wrist, and

pulled me forward, driving me into the building with such force, I nearly stumbled and fell.

The inside was poorly lit by some weak overhead neon lights, but I could see it was just a dusty, empty warehouse or something. At first I didn't realize anyone else was there. They were both so quiet and so still. Then I saw a petite, rust-color-haired girl sitting on a stool in front of a desk on my right. Her hands were folded, the fingers gripping like the fingers of someone in pain. Her knuckles looked as if little white buttons had been sewn onto them. She was dressed in the same sort of one-piece rag I was wearing, and I could also see she had the same style shoes.

Sitting off on my left was another girl with styled pecan brown hair. Even though she, too, was dressed like me and the other girl, she held her head with a more arrogant air, her posture firm, but her arms folded under her breasts. I thought I could even make out a small smirk of impatience on her lips. Who were they? Was this concrete building supposed to serve as a classroom? Why was it so poorly lit then? A hailstorm of questions peppered my brain.

"Sit," my escort ordered, and pushed me toward the empty stool and desk at the center.

"What is going on? Why am I in here? This isn't any school. I'm supposed to be taken to a school. I want to know where I am," I demanded more loudly, my hands on my hips. My voice echoed in the tomblike building.

"Just sit and shut up," my escort blared. "The longer you act stupid, the longer this is going to take."

I looked at the other two, who glared back at me with an expression of annoyance that suggested I was making things harder for them as well. Reluctantly, I did what she said.

"Now what?" I snapped back at her.

She did finally smile.

"Now, it begins," she said, turned, and walked out of the building, closing the door behind her.

I was right about that door. It sounded like a lid being shut on a coffin.

1

Orientation

The moment we were alone, I turned to the girl on my left.

"What is this? Where are we? Why are we in this place?" I asked.

"Why are you asking me? How would I know?" she shot back at me. "What do I look like, information please?"

"Well, you were here before me so I thought you might know more," I threw back at her with just as unfriendly a tone.

"We got here only a little while before you did," the second girl said, somewhat softer. I turned to her. "So we don't know any more than you do. I'm Teal Sommers. That's Robin Lyn Taylor. She didn't tell me her name," Teal added with a smirk. "I heard one of those girls call her that." She leaned forward to glare past me at Robin Lyn.

"I'm not exactly in a party mood, you know, and I told you, I don't like to be called Robin Lyn. Just call me Robin. You, too," she ordered me.

"Yes, Your Majesty," I said, and Teal laughed.

Robin folded her arms and turned away. "Well, we're here together so I guess we'll have to talk to each other decently. Where y'all from?"

"Where y'all from?" Teal laughed. "I'm from Albany, New York. I was flown in here just a little before y'all were, I think. I'm very unsure about the time. They took my watch."

"Mine, too," I said, rubbing my wrist. "And my ring. Why did they do that?"

"Maybe they're jewel thieves. They took Robin's watch, too, right, Robin?"

"Big deal. I stole it. I'll steal another first chance I get," she said defiantly, looking at the closed door. "I'm supposed to be at a school, a special school. That's what the judge said," she shouted at the door. "Not some dumpy, smelly building."

"Judge?" I asked.

She spun her head around to me so fast, I thought it would just keep going in circles on her neck.

"What are you, a scholarship winner or something? Is that why you're here?"

I stared, confused.

"Hardly," I finally replied. "My uncle and aunt arranged all this without telling me anything about it. I was drugged, kidnapped, and brought here."

Robin started to laugh and stopped. "Did you say drugged and kidnapped?"

"I know exactly what she means. That's how I felt," Teal said. "My father arranged for me to be transported here. He was nice enough to tell me I was going to a

special school, but my parents didn't even let me take a
change of clothing. Daddy had a hired goon bring me to
the airport and to the plane. Next thing I knew, I was
flying away and no one told me where I was going.
They kept the windows shut, too. They gave me something to drink, and before I knew it, I was asleep, so I
was drugged, too. When I woke up, I was here and
dressed in this rag and these stupid clodhoppers as well
as this . . . diaper."

"I guess I shouldn't have expected anything better
from my aunt, but why did your father do that to you?"
I asked. Even though I had had some of my things when
Daddy brought me to live with Aunt Mae Louise and
Uncle Buster, I didn't feel much different except I knew
why they'd got rid of me. There was no surprise for me
there.

"He was, I guess I can safely say, at the end of his
patience with me. I was an embarrassment to my
mother, who sits at the head of the social table of high
society."

"What did you do?"

"I robbed a bank," Teal muttered.

"What?"

"I stole money from Daddy's secret safe, his and my
brother Carson's."

"And your own father sent you away for that?"

"Well, it was a little more, I guess," Teal admitted.

"I bet," Robin muttered. "Don't be fooled by her
sweet little face."

I turned to her. "What about you?"

"I didn't rob a bank, but I was part of an armed robbery of a supermarket where I worked," Robin said,
looking ahead. It was as if she were reminding herself
and not telling us. "This is supposed to be an alternative

to going to a real jail. My mother darling talked me into it, and like both of you, I was eventually put in a plane and the same things happened to me. I fell asleep and they took my clothing and brought me here."

She smiled and shook her head and then shouted at the closed door, "They're just trying to frighten us with all this . . . this horror-hotel stuff, but it doesn't scare me! Y'all just wasting your time! You might as well give me back my clothes!"

"What brought you here?" Teal asked me after Robin's screams died down.

"I ran away from my uncle and aunt where I was supposed to stay."

"So, big deal," Robin said. "I bet we've all done that one time or another."

"I was supposed to be in court for hitting this boy with a little brass statue."

"Did you kill him?" Teal asked, her eyes widening with interest.

"No, but I put him in the hospital. He was part of a group of boys trying to rape me."

"So why would they put you in jail for that?" Robin asked skeptically. "It just sounds like self-defense to me."

"There's more to it."

"I bet."

"Look," I said, turning on her, "I don't have to defend myself to you. In fact—"

Before I could say anything else, we heard the door squeal open, followed by the machine-gun *rat-ta-tat-tat* of stiletto high heels on the concrete floor.

Out of the dark shadows came a tall, elegant-looking woman, statuesque with a firm figure in a ruby-red skirt suit. She had highlighted golden brown hair, about the base of her neck in length, neatly styled. As she moved more into the light and drew closer, I saw she was an attractive woman with high cheekbones and a perfect nose. She was wearing a soft red lipstick, very understated. A girlfriend of mine, Louella Mason, who was determined to become a beautician, had told me when a woman wants to emphasize her eyes, she de-emphasizes her lips, but this woman looked like she didn't need anything special to make her eyes prominent. They weren't big as much as they were striking and intense.

She paused, looked at the three of us, and smiled so warmly, I felt like getting up and rushing into her arms. It was a smile that brought a ray of sunshine to a rainy day, and, boy, did I need some sugar now.

"Hello, girls," she said. "I'm Dr. Foreman. Welcome to my school."

"This is a school?" Teal piped up immediately. "It's more like someone's filthy basement."

Dr. Foreman turned to her and, holding her smile, said, "No, this isn't the actual school." She looked about and smiled as if she didn't see what we saw. She saw a beautiful lobby or something instead. "This is my orientation center. The school is some distance from here, but I like to meet my girls as soon as they are brought and introduce them to the way things will be as soon as possible. That way, if they don't accept what I say and don't do what I say, I can put them right back on the plane and ship them somewhere else where a far worse fate awaits them. Is this plan all right with you, Teal?"

I could see Teal was both impressed and intimidated that Dr. Foreman already knew which of us she was. Teal didn't answer. She just sat looking at her, her mouth slightly open. Dr. Foreman did not turn away immediately either. She held Teal's gaze, froze that now cold smile on her lips, and only after a few beats, slowly turned back to Robin and me.

"Now then, as I was saying, welcome to my school," she continued.

As if that was their cue, three young women, the one who had escorted me from the plane to the concrete building, and two others dressed similarly with their hair cut identically short, entered and took position just behind Dr. Foreman. They stood with military posture, their arms behind them, hands clasped, and looked forward, not at us, just forward and poised like guard dogs ready to pounce upon command. Foreman's rottweilers, all teeth and muscle, I thought.

"I created my school only five years ago, but I have, shall we say, graduated dozens of girls like you, releasing them back into society as productive young women, all of whom have kept out of any trouble with their families or with the law. Three are in fact law officers now themselves," Dr. Foreman said, smiling wider with pride. "Two are correction officers and one is a policewoman in a big city."

"Something for us to look forward to," Robin muttered. "A career as a policewoman."

Dr. Foreman looked straight ahead, but her body began to turn as if it were robotic, slowly, stiffly, her shoulders firm and straight.

"Right now, Robin Lyn Taylor, all you have to look forward to is getting yourself into more trouble and so deeply that you are eventually put away in a room without any hope of getting out. In effect, you have no future. The reason you have been sent here is to help you regain one. Until that happens, you, all of you,"

Dr. Foreman said, looking at Teal and me as well now, "are nonentities. You don't exist for your families. You don't exist for yourselves. All you've accomplished up until now is sharpened yourselves as thorns in the side of civilized society. With me, under my care, you will either develop the ability to have a future or you will be pulled out of the side of the civilized world and discarded like any nuisance. The choice is ultimately yours to make, but," she said, smiling warmly again, "we will do our best here to help you make the right choice. In the past, whenever you were given the opportunity to do what was right and decent, you all made other choices. We expect to correct that. We will help you.

"Someone, thanks to the mercy of our court system, has decided to give you this one last chance. Rather than sit here sulking and trying to think of wisecracks, you should begin to show some appreciation.

"But," she continued in a sweet, melodic tone, "I am the first to recognize that you are all here because you are all filled with defiance, anger, and most of all fear."

"Fear?" I muttered. I couldn't help it. It just slipped out between my lips. How could fear have brought us here?

"Yes, my dear Phoebe, fear. Antisocial behavior stems from a well of fear. You act out because you are defensive, slightly paranoid, I'm afraid. In your present way of thinking, the world around you threatens you. You believe everyone is against you and you're just naturally antagonistic to everything."

I guess she saw the lack of understanding in my face. She smiled, again so softly, I felt I could relax and listen to her for hours.

"Don't worry about any of that yet, my dear. You'll

see. You'll all see. That's what's so wonderful about my work," she said excitedly, "at least to me, especially the way it opens the eyes of my girls. For me," she said, her voice rising an octave, "there is nothing as satisfying as seeing one of my girls suddenly come to the realization she can be as good as anyone else out there, she can be productive and worthwhile. She can make friends and be liked and like others. Her heart can hold sunshine, even on rainy days."

She did make it sound wonderful. For a moment she paused with her face so radiant and full of happiness, I felt some hope seep into my hardened and crusty surface. She looked at me as if she could sense it and gave me a special nod, a little more of her smile.

"People are always asking me, 'Dr. Foreman, you were a successful and renowned college professor. Why did you throw away your classroom work, your publications, your lectures, put all your fortune into this school, and go off and surround yourself with the hardest sort of challenge: girls whom everyone has given up on, girls who would easily end up in penal institutions?'

"Well, the answer is you, my dears," she declared with her arms out as though she were about to embrace all three of us at once, "you and your awakening. Nothing is more satisfying to me than to bring someone back from the dead," she continued, her right hand over her heart, "for that is where you are now, in some cemetery of your own making, burying yourselves in your disgust, your fears, your dysfunction."

She grew stern looking again and took another step toward the three of us.

"Within the next twenty-four hours, fourteen hundred teenagers like yourselves will attempt suicide, twenty-eight hundred will get pregnant, fifteen thousand will try alcohol for the first time, and thirty-five hundred will run away from home."

She let those facts linger in the air between us for a moment. I glanced at Robin and then Teal. Neither seemed impressed nor seemed to care.

"But not you. No, not my girls. To me," Dr. Foreman said, looking up at the ceiling as if she could look right through to the heavens, "you will all be like Lazarus, rising from the grave."

"Does that mean you're God?" Teal asked, her mouth dripping with sarcasm.

I thought I was brave and tough, but this soft, pretty white girl who sounded like she had been born with a silver spoon in her mouth was sure nasty and unafraid, even after all that had been done to her, to us.

Dr. Foreman's eyelids fluttered. She had what seemed unflappable poise. That smile never faltered as she lowered her gaze at Teal like someone lowering the barrel of a cannon at a new target.

"For you and for the others, dear Teal, as long as you are here, that is exactly who I will be."

She waited a moment for her words to settle. Teal shook her head and looked away.

"Now," Dr. Foreman said, turning back to speak to all of us, "let me begin by explaining that you're not going to a school any way like the ones you have attended. First, my school is at my ranch. It's a working ranch and you will all participate in the daily chores."

"Oh, so we're really a form of cheap labor, is that it?" Robin complained.

"Hardly cheap, Robin. For your work, you will be given full room and board."

"Isn't my father paying you?" Teal fired at her. "I

shouldn't have to do any daily chores," she declared staunchly, her eyes burning with arrogance.

"Yes, in your case, the family is paying, but there is much more that will be given to you than you would get anywhere else for that amount of money," Dr. Foreman said calmly. The arrows and darts Teal shot at her with those fiery eyes seemed to bounce off an invisible wall of protection that surrounded her.

"Like what?" Teal demanded, refusing to step back. I saw how the girls behind Dr. Foreman glared at Teal. They all looked eager to get their hands around her neck and shake her head off her body.

"Like my expert treatment, my therapy sessions, my proven techniques," Dr. Foreman said to all of us and not just Teal. "It's off the charts when you start computing the costs, and even Teal here, who points out that her parents are paying the tuition, couldn't really afford the tuition if it were equated with the value you will all receive."

"Why are you so nice and generous to us?" Teal muttered, the corners of her mouth folding in.

"Why? I do this because I want to give back to the science that has been so good to me, as well as my deep desire to help young women in desperate need, to help them find what is spiritually good in them."

"Oh, brother," Teal muttered. "We're in a nunnery."

Dr. Foreman's rottweilers moved restlessly. She glanced at them and turned back to us.

"To continue"—Dr. Foreman glared at Teal—"at my school you will not find a staff of teachers to coddle and prod you into doing your homework, studying properly, and achieving. I will assign you all your work and you will have to master it all yourselves."

"Huh?" Robin said. "Did you say ourselves?"

"What are we going to study, basket weaving?" Teal asked with a crooked smile.

"You will be studying regular academic subjects, of course. We want you to qualify for high school graduation, to be able to pass exams, even be good enough to be admitted to institutions of higher learning, but you will be in a different sort of classroom. Life itself, you will see, will become the chief subject. You're all failing at that right now, and for now, that is far more important a subject than anything else."

"I don't get it. How are we supposed to learn anything without a teacher?" Robin asked. "It was hard enough to learn with one."

"Oh, you'll be surprised at what you can accomplish when you are left to your own initiative, Robin Lyn. Of course, you will all help each other. Cooperation in that regard is very important. I will want you all to fully understand how important it is to get along with each other, with others of different backgrounds. Out there, that's what you must do to be a contributing member of society.

"But, self-reliance is essential, too. We can cooperate with each other, but we can't become totally dependent upon others or we become a burden, don't we? That is truly what the three of you are right now, a burden. You'll either be cast off or you'll learn to walk on your own. Sink or swim," she said, her face now turning cool. When she called for it, that iciness seemed to emerge from within her, rise to the surface of her face, penetrate her eyes, tighten her lips, and make her look taller, more intimidating.

I glanced again at the other two. Despite the brave fronts they were putting on, I sensed they were just as anxious about all this as I was. I noticed as well that the three young women behind Dr. Foreman had grown still again, had barely moved a muscle since she had looked at them. How could they be so disciplined? They were three statues.

How much longer would we be kept here? I wondered. It was dank and musty, the air so stale my throat ached. Why did we have to begin in such a place anyway? The stool was uncomfortable. The lighting was dull. What was the point of having us sit at old grade-school desks? I was still tired and achy from my unpleasant trip. I couldn't wait to go to sleep in a bed and I had to go to the bathroom, but I was afraid to mention it yet. I didn't want to be the first one.

"To be sure you are making the right amount of effort at your schoolwork, you will be tested from time to time on your academic subjects, and if you don't pass, you will be given demerits," Dr. Foreman explained.

"Demerits?" Teal said, smirking. "What does that mean, we won't get our Girl Scout patches and medals?"

"No, my dear," Dr. Foreman responded. "Nothing that important. You are all as of now under my merit system. Since you have all been brought here as a last resort because of your antisocial behavior, you will all be beginning with a minus ten and have to work your way back up to zero before you can even hope to achieve rights and privileges."

That did sound threatening.

"What rights and privileges?" I asked.

"Well, for one thing, you will have to wear what you're wearing until you achieve the points to wear my school uniforms."

"What are we wearing? This is disgusting," Teal

complained. "Not only are these . . . these rags irritating my skin, they smell, and why do we have to wear diapers, for Christ sakes? I want my clothes back."

"Yes, I'm sorry about these transitional outfits. They do have that unpleasant odor." Dr. Foreman sounded sympathetic. She also made it sound as if there were no other choice. I finally saw the three rottweilers soften their lips into a smile.

"But why are we wearing diapers?" Robin asked.

"Because, my dear, you are being reborn. Unfortunately, none of you have shown enough maturity to be considered anything but infants, and until you do, that's how you will be treated," Dr. Foreman said firmly, losing the smile. Then she blossomed into another to add, "Believe me, my dear, you'll be grateful you have them on."

The slight smiles on the three young women behind her widened almost into laughter when she said that.

"That's cold," Teal said. "And disgusting. I feel like some old lady with bladder trouble. I want my clothing back. They were expensive, especially the designer jeans. You have no right to take them away from me. Why can't we all have our clothes back?" she whined, now sounding more like a spoiled child than a defiant teenager.

"I've already given that answer. One thing you will learn and learn very quickly here, Teal, is if I or anyone else has to repeat something to you, it's because you don't or won't listen, and that will result in a demerit."

"I don't care about any demerits. I want my clothing!" Teal shouted back. Her voice echoed off the cement walls and then died as if her words were smashed to bits, the letters splattered and then raining down to the dank concrete floor.

Dr. Foreman took a step toward her. "Oh, but you will care, my dear. That will be one of the significant changes in you very soon," she said slowly, her voice so full of chill, I imagined the words turning to ice in the air between them. Even the cold smile disappeared.

"I want to go home," Teal cried back at her. "Right now."

"Do you? Unfortunately for you, for all of you, no one wants you back, Teal. In fact, I'm the only one who wants you."

"How long do I have to stay here, live on your ranch, and milk cows or whatever?" Teal was definitely someone who couldn't stand being bossed around.

"That's entirely up to you," Dr. Foreman replied. "Now then, there will be no more questions." She turned to Robin and me. "No more questions from any of you. You will all just listen and you will do what you are told to do. Listen well, girls," she added, her cold smile returning to those lips. "Be keen, girls, be keen. Your comfort and happiness depend on it like they never have before."

She stepped back, glanced at the young women behind her, who looked excited about her firmness. I wouldn't admit it, of course, but they frightened me. I wondered if Robin's and Teal's hearts were pounding as hard as mine was now, despite the brave face masks they wore.

We were all brought here more or less against our will. Dr. Foreman was probably not wrong about that. We had no one out there to help us, no one to call, no one to come for us. I couldn't help feeling that I was dangling in space, holding on to a thin piece of spidery web that this strange woman, sometimes sounding nice, sometimes sounding scary, held at the other end. If she decided to let go, I, as well as Robin and Teal, would fall into some darker place. What else could we do but listen?

"Now, so there are no misunderstandings and no whining like we're hearing," Dr. Foreman said, glaring at Teal again, "let me be clear about what you should expect after you leave here. At my home you will find there are no radios, no magazines, no CDs, and especially no television for anyone until she has earned the right to leisure time. The only books permitted are the books related to your subjects, not that any of you look like you read very much," she added with a tightening at the right corner of her mouth.

"No one will have any phone privileges until she earns twenty merit plus points. That means no one can call you as well—not, from what I know of each of your histories, that anyone would want to call you."

"We really are like prisoners," Teal complained, and quickly looked down.

"Since that wasn't put in the form of a question, I will let it pass without penalizing you another demerit. If you are like prisoners, as you say, it's because you have imprisoned yourselves. You have put bars on your own windows and built the walls between yourselves and the rest of humanity. I am your best hope to remove those bars, to crumble those walls. Right now, you see me only as a disciplinarian, but in time, very soon, you will learn to appreciate what I have to offer you.

"It's a lot like Annie Sullivan and Helen Keller," she said, looking off. She smiled at some image of herself, and even that smile was disturbing enough to make my stomach feel as if I had just drunk a gallon of sour milk. "For in truth, you all can't really speak, can't really hear, can't really see. You're locked up inside your own troubled bodies, and I will free you. Yes, I will."

There was a long silence. My throat was dry. My stomach continued to churn and I felt the growing pressure of having to go to the bathroom. I trembled, but I had to ask. I raised my hand, hoping she would permit it.

"I said no questions," she declared.

"But . . ."

She raised her head and the very air seemed to freeze around us. If I uttered another sound, lightning might sizzle my brain, I thought. I bit down on my lower lip. She smiled again.

"I don't want to leave you thinking that all that awaits you is hard work, rules, and restrictions. We will have wonderful sessions together, my group therapy, during which time you will all have this, this terribly dark curtain of pain and anger lifted from your eyes. Believe me, girls, that will happen and you will be grateful. I've seen it so many times before on the faces of my girls. My girls," she repeated, her eyes glossing over as if she could see them all parading before her, hugging her like high school graduates at their diploma ceremony.

She was quiet again. We could hear a drip, drip, drip of something in the plumbing above and behind us. Her eyes slowly brightened, the gloss changing to a thin layer of ice. She stared at us so long, I felt uncomfortable and saw both Teal and Robin squirming a bit on their stools as well.

"Part of your work and your life at my school will be your confronting your own fears. One of the best ways to do that is to be out in nature. Nature has a way of tearing away all the conflicting, confusing things that have distorted our vision of ourselves. In nature you can make no rationalizations, no excuses, fall upon your knees and beg for mercy. You either become strong or perish. Everything out there teaches us that lesson and it's a wonderful lesson, one that we tend to forget in the world we call civilized. We'll help you regain that wisdom. Or, I should say, nature will."

Nature? I thought. What was she talking about, camping trips? Sleeping in a tent? Maybe Teal wasn't so off. Maybe this was like the Girl Scouts.

"Now then," Dr. Foreman said, pulling herself up and stepping back. "Unfortunately, I must conclude our little talk with a severe warning. Any signs of insubordination, even nasty looks and evidence of an attitude, will result in demerits. Profanity will be punished severely. If any of you get two demerits in one day, or fall two points or more below the minus ten I have generously given you, or finally do something so terrible that it is off the charts, she will be sent to our Ice Room to chill out, as you kids like to say these days."

Ice Room? What was that?

She looked around the cement room, once again as if she could hear my thoughts. "This place is a first-class hotel room compared to our Ice Room." She didn't make it sound like a threat either, but it clearly put the shivers into Teal and Robin as quickly as it did in me. Not describing it any further left it to each of our imaginations, and I was sure we each came up with our worst fears.

"And now, my dears," she said again, sounding as if we were all at a grand tea party, "it's time for you to be introduced to your buddies. They are three of my graduates, three of whom I am very, very proud. They have earned the right to assist me."

The girls beamed with joy at her compliments and gazed at her adoringly. I didn't know why yet, but it made my nerve endings sizzle to see the way they all looked up to her. I had the feeling she could ask one or all of them to open their wrists, and they would instantly obey.

As Dr. Foreman continued, she looked at them with a mother's pride. "I call them your buddies because they are here to give you the benefit of their experience. They will be in charge of your daily life, your daily development, and since they have experienced my school firsthand, they have real insight into what goes on in a new girl's mind. Depend on them, listen to them, and most of all, obey them."

She turned back to us. "Even though they are your buddies, you are to treat them as respectfully and obediently as you would me. In order to establish that, and to help you understand how far they have grown and what they have become now, you are to address them only as *m'lady,* for that is truly who they are, ladies."

Teal couldn't help a guffaw, her laughter spurting out of her lips like something she was unable to keep from coming up. It was like a small explosion.

"If you don't tighten your lips this instant," Dr. Foreman snarled at her, "you'll be starting at a minus fifteen with the Ice Room as your initiation to my school."

Teal's smile evaporated.

After a long silence, Dr. Foreman stepped to the side and introduced M'Lady One, who was the young woman who had escorted me off the plane. She stepped forward and waited, still at attention. M'Lady Two, who stepped up beside her, was a far more attractive woman with light brown hair, a perfect nose, and a far more feminine mouth. She wasn't as tall, perhaps only five feet five, but because of her firm military posture, she didn't look much shorter. She had a nice figure, well proportioned, that couldn't be disguised even in the blah uniform.

M'Lady Three was the stoutest and shortest. I thought she was barely five feet tall. She had shoulders like a football player and hard, sharply cut facial features. Her dark eyes were too far apart and her short, dull brown hair was trimmed farther back on her forehead than that of the other two. When she opened her mouth, I saw she had crooked teeth, especially on the bottom.

"A new student does nothing without permission until she is told she may do so," M'Lady One recited.

M'Lady Two continued, "That means even going to the bathroom. A new student does not speak unless given permission to do so."

M'Lady Three picked up immediately when M'Lady Two stopped. She had the deepest, coarsest voice. "A new student learns that in the real world nothing comes to you because it's supposed to come to you. You earn everything; you are entitled to nothing. This is reality. Therefore, we will have reality checks periodically to determine whether or not you have earned what you want, what you have."

"This means everything," they all recited. They spoke like some chorus that had performed these speeches many, many times, all speaking without much emotion, except for the underlying and continuous threat.

"A new student knows that complaints earn demerits. Cheating, laziness, slacking off, any of that earns demerits," M'Lady Two said.

"And demerits put you in the Ice Room," they all chorused.

"Thank you, m'ladies," Dr. Foreman said. They looked at her as if they were desperate for approval, then they stepped back.

I raised my hand and she looked at me so long, I thought she was going to simply ignore it. Finally, she asked me what I wanted.

"I need to go to the bathroom," I said.

The three buddies smiled simultaneously as if they were of one face.

"After all this, that is what you ask? Have you heard nothing?"

"But I need to go," I cried, now unashamed to admit it.

"Your needs are no longer what is of primary importance. We are now going to think first of the group's needs."

"But . . ."

"You're here because you are selfish, and that will be the first demon we will destroy. I promise you that," Dr. Foreman said. "Now then, I have one more request of you all that you must fulfill before we can go any further."

She turned to the buddies and each stepped forward, M'Lady One coming to me, M'Lady Two going to Robin, and M'Lady Three to Teal. They handed each of us a small composition notebook and a pen.

"What is this?" Teal muttered. "Homework, already?"

"That's a demerit," Dr. Foreman said, pointing at her with a long, thin finger. "You didn't have permission to speak. One more and you're in the Ice Room."

Teal looked away. I could see, however, that she was fighting back tears, tears of rage and fear.

"Now then," Dr. Foreman said, "as a second part of your orientation, I want each of you to write her story. Tell me everything you can about yourself, what you remember as a child, where you lived, the friends you had or thought you had, the teachers you remember. I am very interested in how you see yourself, what you expect you will eventually do with your life. I want the notebooks filled with details, exact details of every thing you remember as important to you. I am particularly interested in your fears, so I want you to give lots of thought to that. All of us, including me, have something we fear. It's natural or, perhaps, it's something we have inherited or developed because of who we are, where we have lived, whom we have known. Don't dare leave that out.

"If you lie and I find out you have lied in this introductory history, you will be fined ten full demerit points. Remember, I know much about you. This is both a test of your veracity and a chance for you to think about yourselves."

We looked at each other in disbelief. Write our histories? Surely, this was a joke.

"I see you are not taking me seriously," Dr. Foreman said. "I assure you that you will all remain here until you are all finished. Until then, no one will get anything to drink or eat, nor will anyone"—she centered on me—"use the bathroom. That's academic anyway since there is no bathroom," she added dryly.

I felt my face flush. No bathroom? Reminding me I had to go built the pressure inside me. I felt myself breaking out into a sweat, my heart pounding. Didn't the other two have to go? If they did, they didn't show it.

"Finally, let me remind you that no one is to speak to

anyone during this exercise. One of your buddies will monitor you, and should anyone speak, you will all remain here one hour longer for every word uttered."

Then, as suddenly as she finished speaking, she smiled warmly at us and in loving tones said, "Welcome, girls. Welcome to my school. I truly hope this will be a lifesaving experience for you all."

With that she turned and walked out, her heels clicking and echoing around us until she was gone and it was deadly silent.

It was as if all clocks had stopped. Nothing beat anymore.

Not even our own hearts.

2

Dr. Foreman's
Funny Farm

~

Two of the so-called buddies left with Dr. Foreman, but M'Lady Three remained behind, her arms folded, her back against the door, glaring at us, the corners of her mouth dipped with annoyance at what I was sure she considered baby-sitting duty.

"This is so stupid," Teal muttered.

"Did someone speak?" M'Lady Three chimed. Like a hungry cat she was so eager to pounce.

We all looked down ashamed of our fear. That was when I saw that someone probably feeling as desperate as we did had carved the word *help* into my old desk. I felt like adding my own cry of rage. I would carve in *betrayed*. When I looked up again, I saw Robin open her composition notebook and begin writing. She shrugged at me as if to say, what else can we do? Humor her. Teal, on the other hand, remained stubborn, her head in her hands, the notebook still closed. I opened mine.

My life story?

Where do I begin? I was born in Atlanta. My daddy was an auto garage tool salesman and my mama worked as a waitress in one dump after another, drinking up most of what she made and sometimes not coming home until morning. It was one thing to remember it all, to think about it, but another to actually put it in writing. It made me more angry than ashamed to see it in black and white. Perhaps that was Dr. Foreman's purpose: to get us to hate who we were, who we are. I suppose I couldn't blame her. Why else would we work on changing ourselves?

It was funny though how tears came into my eyes after I began to describe our apartment in that rat-infested building, described my room, the crippled kitchen with the stove that worked when it was in the mood, and the living room with the threadbare rug where Daddy sat and watched television alone so many nights. Why would I cry over and long for a return to the life I used to hate? Why would I want to be back in that two-by-four room of mine where I could hear pipes groaning at night like someone with a bellyache, and people in other apartments yelling at each other and clawing the walls the way prisoners going mad might?

I wasn't in a good place to grow up. Even as a little girl, I knew bad things happened in our building. Someone I only knew as Mr. Rotter died of a drug overdose in the apartment directly below ours. It was the first time I saw a dead person. I stood on the stairway and watched them taking him out on a stretcher, the sheet over his whole body. The police said the apartment stank. He had been dead for nearly a week, but he had no relatives in Atlanta. Only in his midthirties, he was already dead.

That was when I first understood what Daddy meant when he said we were living in a cemetery. The doors of the apartments should look more like tombstones and read their names and *born in 19__; died in 20__. Rest in peace because that's the only peace you'll have.*

No wonder I didn't want to come home nights or stay there on weekends. No wonder I took advantage of Mama being at work and staying out to all hours and Daddy being on the road, away from home. I shouldn't have been blamed for that. Anyone living like I was living, seeing the things I saw, would have done the same thing.

The only excitement and happiness I had were what I had with my friends. So we smoked and shoplifted and drank at parties. So what? We didn't hurt people badly, did we? Well, maybe we hurt ourselves somewhat, but we weren't on anyone's Most Wanted list. Teachers barely tolerated us, were happy when we didn't bother them, and swept us along like so much dust from one room to another, one teacher to another, as if everyone was to share the burden.

Yes, I wrote in the notebook, it's true I did get arrested more than once. I was put on probation. I did violate it and I was in danger of going to a real prison. Yes, I knew why Daddy felt he had to place me with my uncle and aunt after Mama ran off with someone and deserted us, but I also knew my aunt and uncle never wanted me and were surely relieved when I got myself in new trouble and ran away. My aunt could claim she was right about me: I was hopeless and now she had a good excuse for getting rid of me forever.

I described it all, how I was cornered into hurting that boy, how I was arrested for it and decided to run off, how disappointed I was in Mama when I found her in that clinic, and how betrayed I felt when my uncle tricked me and got me taken here. I was never as mean to anyone as they were to me, I wrote. I don't deserve this.

As to my fears, I couldn't come up with much except what I had feared when I was a little girl and could actually hear the rats scratching their way through the walls, visiting different apartments as if the whole place were a mall for rats who could shop in this one's kitchen cabinets and then another and pass the news on to the world of rats out there: *Come to Phoebe Elder's home. Her mother is a slob. Lots to eat on the floor and counters, and she's so out of it nights in a drunken coma, she won't even know we're there.*

I used to curl up in my bed, wrapping the blanket so tightly around myself it was a wonder I didn't smother to death. Some nights I sobbed myself to sleep. Some nights I woke up positive a rat had crawled over my legs or sniffed my hair. I would throw off my blanket and turn on the lamp, but thankfully, I never saw one in my room. That didn't mean I didn't believe they had been there, however. I imagined their tiny footprints everywhere, and sometimes, I was sure I saw a pair of beady little eyes watching me from some crack in the wall.

I had no idea how much I had written in the notebook when I raised my head. I saw Teal had given in, and she and Robin were still reluctantly at it themselves. Then I heard the door open and saw M'Lady Two hand M'Lady Three a tumbler of ice water. Teal and Robin also watched her drinking it. She seemed to take longer and slurp it for our benefit. She spilled what she hadn't finished on the floor and looked at us with a smile so spiteful it made anger simmer my blood into a rolling boil.

I squirmed in my seat. My need to pee had become

impossible to ignore. Soon there would be no way to keep it from happening. It brought new tears to my eyes, tears that escaped my lids. I embraced myself and rocked as I moaned.

M'Lady Three got up and walked toward me. "What's wrong with you?"

"I have to pee, badly."

"So pee. You're wearing a diaper. We'll change you afterward."

I looked up at her in shock. I could see she was serious. It put me into a small panic, and when I looked at Teal, she seemed angrier about it than I could be. Then she nodded at me, her eyes small, urging me to call her bluff. Only I knew it wasn't a bluff. Robin looked down, ashamed for me.

M'Lady Three turned back to the door and then I let it go. It dripped off the chair. She looked back, smiling. Then she opened the door and shouted, "Get up a diaper. Baby One had an accident."

I heard some laughter outside.

I was crying harder now, the tears of shame and rage sliding off my cheeks as if my skin had turned to ice, my fists at my sides, my nails digging into my palms.

"Bitch," Teal shouted at M'Lady Three.

Her smile faded. "One word without specific permission. One extra hour for all of you to spend in here," she pronounced like a judge laying the death sentence on some convicted murderer.

M'Lady One returned with a new diaper for me. Teal and Robin watched with disgust and rage. Then Teal stood up and just let go. Robin smiled and did the same. M'Lady One and M'Lady Three looked at each other, then M'Lady Three smiled back at Teal and Robin.

"Gee, girls, sorry," she moaned as if she really cared,

"but we had only one extra diaper." Her phony smile
vanished. "Now sit down and shut up," she snapped at
them. Their faces of defiance quickly changed into
faces of disgust and panic. "Sit down or we'll keep you
here two more hours for every minute you're standing."

Without any other choice, they did what they were
told, both grimacing with discomfort. I returned to my
seat and held up my completely filled composition
book. M'Lady One took it and flipped through the
pages. Then she took the pen and left.

Robin and Teal started to write faster, the need to get
out of here that much greater.

M'Lady Three shook her head and smiled at them
gleefully. "That's better, girls. The faster you all learn
that obeying orders makes things easier for you, the
better off you'll be."

When Robin and Teal were finished, they lifted their
notebooks and M'Lady Three took them, checked
them, and went to the door. She handed them to
M'Lady Two and looked at us.

"After your hour's punishment, we'll be learning the
school prayer," she said, and left.

"I'm taking this off," Robin said, standing immediately and removing the wet diaper. Teal did the same.

"They're crazy. That doctor's crazy. I'm not staying
here," Teal vowed.

"Really? What do you intend to do? Catch a cab
home?" Robin asked.

"I don't know. Something."

"You better not let them hear you talking or they'll
tack on more time," I warned them.

"Don't tell me what to do! I don't give a damn! I
won't . . ." Teal stopped and slammed her lips shut
when she heard the door opening.

M'Lady Three returned. "Lucky for you two, we found two extra diapers," she sang. She gave one to Robin and one to Teal. "Put them on and keep quiet," she ordered, and left again.

I watched them change. We all walked about like caged animals, looking at each other as if one word would set us clawing ourselves as well as the walls, then we glared at the door. Teal tried it and of course it was locked.

"What if they just leave us here forever? Who would even know?" Robin queried. "There's no other way out."

Teal and I looked at each other.

"My parents would eventually find out. They can't do that. They wouldn't dare. My mother would sue the panties off that Dr. Foreplay or whatever she calls herself," Teal said.

"Right, your parents are worried sick over you. That's why they had you sent here."

"Shut up. You don't know anything about me or my family."

"Who wants to?" Robin mumbled.

All I could think about was getting out of here. Soon we'd be at each other's throat, but the hands of whatever clock we were on were arthritic or something. It seemed like much longer than another hour before the door opened and the three so-called buddies returned.

"Everyone stand in front of her desk," M'Lady One ordered. We did so, all of us thinking the same thing: we'll do anything to get out of here. "Okay, here is the school prayer. You are to recite it every morning and you are to recite it until you get it perfect. We'll stay here as long as we have to until all three of you have it memorized."

M'Lady Two came forward. "Repeat after me. 'I am nothing. I am less than nothing. I am a burden to my family and to my country. I must hate myself to death and I must change. I must thank Dr. Foreman for every punishment I receive.' "

Teal grimaced. "That's a prayer?"

"It's stupid," Robin agreed.

"Suit yourselves, girls. We're comfortable," M'Lady Two said, and started out.

"Wait a minute!" I cried.

She paused.

"I can't stand it in here anymore."

She looked at Robin and Teal.

"All right. How does it go again?" Teal asked.

M'Lady Two smiled and repeated it for us. None of us got it right the first time, so she repeated it and again we mumbled it as accurately as we could. They demanded we speak louder. Teal made an error and we were stopped and told to start again. I thought she wasn't going to do it, but she did and, of course, made a small mistake. All three of us were tired and groggy and uncomfortable. It was so hard to concentrate on words we hated anyway. Finally, we had it right almost to the end, when I left out a word and they jumped on me. Again we recited it and again one of us made a small error. Eventually, we had it perfect and they agreed we had done so.

"Orientation is over," M'Lady Three declared, slapping her hands together. "We can move out and take you to Dr. Foreman's School. Remember," she added before we started, "no talking without permission."

We marched out of the room. I don't think I was ever happier to leave a place than I was leaving there. Even the hot evening air seemed a relief. A dirty, white, windowless van was parked in front of the building. The rear doors were opened and we were told to climb in. There was nothing to sit on, just the metal floor of the van. A solid wall separated the back of the van from the driver. All three of us hesitated. It smelled like some farm animals had been transported in it only minutes ago. The odor of animal manure was strong.

Teal raised her hand.

"What?" M'Lady Three asked. We understood now that M'Lady Three was assigned to Teal; M'Lady Two to Robin, and of course, M'Lady One to me.

"There are no windows in there. How long is the trip? We'll suffocate."

"The trip is as long as it takes to get to the school. Get in. It will be longer if you waste time. We might," M'Lady Three said, smiling at the other two, "take you on a detour if you don't behave."

Teal looked at the two of us and then gazed around and into the darkness. Would she try to bolt and run? I think she realized she had no idea in which direction to go and the chances of her outrunning them were slim. Defeated, she climbed into the van and sat with her back to the side, her arms folded. I did the same, sitting across from her, and Robin got in and sat next to her. They closed the doors on us and we were in total darkness.

That wasn't the only problem. Teal was right. Once the doors were closed, we had little fresh air, the odor was nauseating, and the van walls felt like the walls of an oven.

"We'll die in here if we have to stay in here long," Teal moaned.

"Keep your voice down," Robin said. "Whisper. Who knows what else those sadistic creatures will do to us if they hear us talking."

"If I wasn't so tired, I'd choke one of them," Teal claimed.

"They don't look like they're afraid of that, especially your buddy," I told her. "I think she's a former football player or bouncer from some bar."

Robin grunted her agreement. We heard the van's engine start, then the van pulled away. It was smooth for a while, but not five minutes into the ride, it suddenly became quite bumpy, and for us to bounce sitting on this metal floor was not easy. It was at times painful. We all screamed and shouted complaints, but whoever was driving didn't hear us or care. The van jostled and shook us as it went along. At times, the driver turned so hard and sharply, we were thrown from side to side. Finally, the ride became a lot smoother.

"I'm going to strangle my mother darling when I get away from here," Robin vowed. "She just wanted to get me out of her hair while she tries to become a famous country singing star. She didn't care where I was sent. Just go, she told me. I'm better off. What she really meant was *she* was better off. She could party and carry on without worrying about me."

"What did your father have to say about it?" Teal asked.

"I don't have a father. Mother darling got pregnant when she was a teenager and my grandparents made her have me as a punishment. They are very religious and we had to live with them. Mother darling's not sure who my father is. The best she can remember is she was at a party where she had sex with three guys."

"Three in one night?" I asked.

"That's what she claimed."

"Some mother," Teal said.

"I didn't exactly have a choice, you know. From the sound of things, you're not that much better off."

"Yeah, well, at least I'm sure who my father is," Teal said.

"Doesn't sound like he wants to be your father," Robin batted back.

"How come you don't get along with your parents?" I asked Teal. Talking at least passed the time and stopped me from thinking about the horrible ride.

"They had me late in their marriage. I was an accident for sure," she replied bitterly. "I have a brother who's much older and he's by far the favorite. He works with my father in his business. No one had any patience for me. I'm sure they're just as happy to get rid of me as Robin's mother was to get rid of her."

"She'll be sorry," Robin swore. "If she ever does become famous, I'll tell the world how Mother darling treated me."

"Why do you call her 'Mother darling'?" Teal asked.

"Just to annoy her. You've heard of *Mommie Dearest*, right?"

"Yeah," Teal said so vaguely I was sure she hadn't. I hadn't but I didn't say so. What difference did it make? I thought.

"My daddy wouldn't have put up with this," I told them. "He was hoping to take me back as soon as he got himself a position where he didn't have to be on the road all the time."

"Sure he was," Teal said.

"He was!" I insisted. "If he didn't get himself killed, my aunt and uncle would never dare to do something like this to me."

"What about your mother?" Robin asked.

I told her about how she had deserted us in Atlanta

and how I had gone looking for her in hopes of our starting a new life.

"Get real, girl," Teal said. "Those kinds of dreams are for girls who still believe in the tooth fairy."

"I'll choose my own dreams, thank you," I said, but not with a great deal of confidence.

They were both quiet for a while, thinking. I guess in our secret heart of hearts, we were all longing for someone who would care enough about us to keep such cruel things from happening to us. Those kinds of people were just impossible to find for the three of us, I thought.

The van continued to ride over smoother roads. After a while, especially because of all we had already been through, the monotonous sound of the engine and the squeaks and moans in the metal were hypnotizing. We were all having a hard time keeping ourselves awake.

"I'm tired," Robin said. "I can't believe how tired I am. I feel like I just went through a torture chamber."

"I hate to think what awaits us at Dr. Foreman's funny farm," Teal said.

We were all silent again, each of us thinking about that, I'm sure. I know I managed to drift off for a while, but when I woke, I was sore and achy all over. I heard the other two rustling about. Finally, we felt the van turn sharply, speed up, bounce hard, then come to a stop. I didn't know about the other two, but I was sweating so much, I thought I would slide out of the van.

The door was opened and we saw a pole light shedding illumination on what looked like a gravel driveway. M'Lady One was there at the opened doors.

"Get out," she ordered.

We crawled to the doorway and climbed out of the

van. Across from us was a long, two-story, pitch-roofed, pink-stucco Spanish colonial house with an upper-level, full-length porch. The railings looked quite fancy. I could see the six doors that opened onto the porch. I imagined each one opened onto a room, and I hoped each of us was to have one of those rooms. All I could think of was dropping my head on a pillow and curling up on a soft mattress.

"All right, follow us," M'Lady One ordered. "This way." She started around the van.

Why weren't we going directly into the house? I wondered. We were all so tired. Surely they were tired, too. There just couldn't be more to this orientation. The three of us stumbled after them. Robin kept looking from side to side like someone who wanted to break loose and run, but all I could see through the darkness was a corral, another barn, and a large shed. There was no road and there were definitely no other houses anywhere nearby. There were no cars going past and no sign of any road. Just a mountain range in the distance, silhouetted against the blue black sky, now dazzling with stars.

Where were we exactly? I had no sense of direction, but because of how long it had taken me to get here by plane and van, I was sure I was at least halfway across the country. It was a frightening thought, to realize I was so far from anywhere and anyone I knew. Vaguely, I wondered what my old friends were doing at this moment. I envied them for being asleep in their own beds. I even envied the ones I knew shared beds with younger brothers or sisters.

We were directed off to the right and brought to what was outside showers. There were no stalls, just three showerheads over a concrete floor.

"Get undressed and take your showers," M'Lady Three commanded.

"This is a shower?" Teal muttered.

If M'Lady One heard her, she chose not to acknowledge it. "You take a shower every night before going to bed at Dr. Foreman's School."

We were each handed a bar of coarse soap, a stiff brush, a towel, and a small kit that included our toothbrush, toothpaste, and a supply of tampons.

None of us moved to undress, however.

"Well?" my buddy said, glaring into my face. "Let's get started. We don't have all night."

"Right out here, like this?" I asked, looking around. It seemed deserted, but it was still getting naked in full view of anyone.

"Always ask before speaking," she reminded me. "Yes, right out here like this. Do it! You all stink and the stench will keep you awake and bother others."

Others? I thought. What others?

Robin began to take off her sack, then undo her shoes and lower her socks. I followed, but Teal looked like she was going to be defiant.

"You won't go to sleep until you do this," her buddy told her.

She started to undress.

The water was a shock. It wasn't just cold; it was freezing. Every time we tried to get out from under, they pushed us back and shouted, "Scrub!"

I did it as fast as I could. Eventually, the other two did the same, but it wasn't good enough for our buddies. They told us to do it again and scrub harder. The bristles of the brush were stiff and painful. Finally, we were told to step out and turn off the water. Even in the darkness, I could see how red and irritated Robin's and Teal's skin were. We dried off quickly and put the degrading outfits on to keep ourselves warm again, despite that the sacks stank and would defeat the purpose of the shower. I was afraid to point it out, however.

"Let's move it," M'Lady Three commanded. She still did not lead us toward the house, however. Instead we were taken to an area off to our right where the three of us saw our clothing piled, shoes and all.

A sweet feeling of relief settled in me, as well as the other two.

"Finally," I heard Teal whisper.

"No speaking," M'Lady Two screamed.

We stood there obediently, waiting for the order to fetch our clothes. To our surprise, M'Lady Three went instead to a large open barrel beside them. She lit a match and dropped it into the barrel. Instantly, a flame shot up. Something very flammable was in the barrel.

"Okay, girls," M'Lady One said. "Take those clothes and throw them into the barrel."

"What?" Teal couldn't contain herself. "Burn my clothes? Why?"

Out of the shadows as if she were formed from darkness came Dr. Foreman.

"I know this seems hard to you, girls, but it is a very, very important first step. What we are doing here tonight is burning away the old you and beginning your rebirths. This isn't just symbolic. It has a great deal of psychological importance."

The fire crackled in the barrel.

"But that's not the old me. That's my clothing, my designer clothing!" Teal exclaimed.

For a long moment, no one spoke. Then Dr. Foreman stepped a little closer.

"We'll stand here all night if we have to," she

warned. "It is essential to my system, my process, that you all participate in your own rebirths."

"This is really crazy," Teal muttered.

"I'm so tired, I don't care about anything anymore," Robin declared, and went to the clothes.

"Don't throw mine in there," Teal screamed at her.

Robin picked out her own things and began to toss them into the barrel. I followed after her and did the same. Finally, Teal, standing alone, went to the remaining garments. Then, like someone giving up the most precious jewels, dropped them into the barrel.

"Good," Dr. Foreman said. "You're all beginning well. I'm proud of you girls, and to show you my appreciation, I'm giving you all plus five points. You're now that much closer to receiving comforts and privileges. M'ladies," she said, turning to the buddies. "Show them to their sleeping quarters."

Thank God, I thought. I followed along, my head down, not realizing where we were going until Teal moaned. We were standing at the barn.

M'Lady Two opened the door. We could see it was well lit within.

"Home sweet home, girls," she said, standing back.

"Home! What are you talking about? This is a barn," Teal moaned.

"Demerit," M'Lady Three said. "Even though Dr. Foreman rewarded you with five plus points, you have one demerit from before and now a second. Two demerits in one day qualify you for the Ice Room. Dr. Foreman must be immediately informed. You could go right to the Ice Room."

I raised my hand.

"Very good, Phoebe. Permission to speak. Speak," M'Lady One said.

"Can't you be a little bit understanding? We're confused and tired and this looks like a barn."

"It is a barn and we're not here to be understanding. You were given the rules and you must obey them. It's what we had to do and what we did." M'Lady One looked at M'Lady Three. "It's up to you," she told her. "What do you want to do about Teal?"

"I'll let this one slip, but consider it the one and only time I will," M'Lady Three told Teal.

We were then ordered to enter.

Before us were five wooden cots lined up beside each other. Two had mattresses, pillows, and blankets on them. The other three were just bare.

"Those three are yours," M'Lady One said, pointing to the bare ones.

Robin raised her hand.

"Permission to speak," M'Lady Two said.

"There are no mattresses or anything on them."

"You have to earn that," her buddy replied.

"But . . . how . . . ?"

"Reality checks, remember? You earn the points and then you are rewarded with comforts. It's how it works. Here we earn everything we have, even every morsel of food we eat. Whoever doesn't do her share, doesn't share. That includes water as well as food."

We all looked about despondently. The floor literally had straw over it. The place smelled like a real barn. The four windows had no curtains over them. The walls were bare and there wasn't much of an interior or any other furniture. Only by the two beds that had mattresses, we saw what looked like two small wooden chests.

Teal raised her hand.

"What?"

"Who sleeps on those?" she asked.

"Those are Gia Carson's and Mindy Levine's beds. They've earned enough points to have an hour's recreation time in the library where they can read approved books and listen to approved music. They will be back here momentarily. I now advise the three of you to go to sleep."

"I'm sure my father didn't pay all that money for me to sleep in a stinking barn," Teal declared.

M'Lady Three stepped up so closely to her, their noses almost collided. "Okay, you're not sleeping in the barn. I'm sick of your whining. You've just lost the privilege."

"Privilege?" Teal started to laugh. "You call sleeping in a barn a privilege?"

M'Lady Three nodded at the other two buddies, who then picked up a bunk and carried it out the door.

"Follow them," Teal was told. She looked to us desperately for some help, but neither Robin nor I had the courage to say a word. With her head down like a flag of surrender, she walked out of the barn. I would never have thought sleeping in a barn was so great, but it had to be to be better than being out there, I thought.

At the door, M'Lady Three turned to Robin and me. "Go to sleep. You'll need every moment of rest you can get, believe me."

She left, closing the door behind her.

"Any moment I'm going to wake up. Tell me that's true. Tell me I'm in a dream, a nightmare, and it's coming to an end," Robin muttered in the tone of a prayer.

I just shook my head and sat on the first bare wooden cot. The surface was hard, but I didn't care.

"I'm so tired," I whispered.

The lights in the barn flickered in warning that they would soon be out, then the door opened and two girls entered. The first was a diminutive girl with a mop of hair the color of black licorice. She had large, dark, haunted eyes with a small, delicate nose and thin lips turned down in the corners. Each girl was dressed in a pair of blue coveralls with a faded white short-sleeve shirt that looked more like a man's shirt than a woman's. They wore the same ugly shoes, too.

The second girl was tall and thin with hair so pale yellow it looked almost white. It hung down like dead straw over her ears, the bangs nearly over her eyes. My immediate thought was she was anorexic. Her wrists were slim and bony. I imagined that a strong handshake could shatter them. Her cheeks were sunken. The skin on her face was so taut it was transparent. Once, she must have had a pretty face, I decided. She had high cheekbones and a nearly perfect nose, but when she glanced our way, she never changed expression or in any way showed that she saw us. She looked more like someone dazed, moving in her sleep.

Both girls diverted their eyes to the floor and moved so softly, I had the sense they were floating in, gliding toward their bunks. They said nothing to each other, did nothing to indicate they were aware of each other.

Robin looked at me with quizzical eyes and shrugged.

The girls, still ignoring us, began to take off their coveralls and their ugly shoes, caked with mud. They did everything with great care as if they were performing a delicate lifesaving operation: folding their coveralls neatly and placing them in the chests beside their bunks, rolling their white stockings down and then again taking great pains to fold them perfectly as well and placing them in the trunks, all the while moving like two people in a hypnotic state.

Neither girl wore what we called diapers. They had ordinary-looking panties and both had bras over what looked to me like quite underdeveloped breasts. How could two such fragile-looking girls have gotten in the sort of trouble that would send them to a place like this? I wondered.

Because the door of the barn was still wide-open, neither Robin nor I risked speaking to them. They didn't seem to care anyway. They still showed absolutely no interest in us. We watched them with fascination, however, as they both got under their blankets and lowered their heads to their pillows.

I felt like someone in a desert watching someone drinking a glass of cold, sparkling freshwater. Those bunks looked so comfortable. How rich they were to have an actual pillow, a soft mattress. When I glanced at Robin, I saw a similar covetous expression on her face.

M'Lady Two stood in the doorway.

"Lights out, girls," she announced, and although I didn't see her throw any switch, the lights snapped off. It took a few moments to get used to the darkness. The starlight coming in through the four windows helped.

"Hey!" I chanced, calling to what I thought now were lucky girls. "Who are you? How long have you been here? Is this the only place for us to sleep?"

Neither responded.

"I'm Robin and that's Phoebe," Robin added. "What are your names?"

Silence remained.

"What's wrong with you?" I asked. "No one's here. Can't you talk?"

"We're not going to bite you," Robin said. They didn't budge. "You believe this?" she asked me.

"No. They're just being brats. What's your damn

name?" I asked sharply, raising my voice a bit too loudly.

Suddenly, the door of the barn swung open and the lights went on.

M'Lady One was standing there.

"Who's talking?" she demanded. "Well, who is it? Confess or I'll hold you all accountable."

The smaller girl sat up and pointed at me.

"She talked," she accused.

My mouth dropped. How could she do that, squeal on me?

"Sure. It just had to be my girl," M'Lady One muttered unhappily, "and after I thought she was beginning to do well." She entered the barn and approached me.

I turned away and looked down, but she kept coming.

"When lights are out, you go to sleep," she said, hovering right over me. I kept my head down. "Are you just stupid? Or are you just a hard case? What do you need to convince you we're serious about the rules here? Well, which is it, stupid or defiant? Answer immediately when you are asked a question," she bellowed.

I turned slowly. I was tired. I ached and I was afraid, but I couldn't help myself. I looked up and into her face as bravely as I could manage.

"I'm not stupid. This place is stupid."

She raised her eyebrows and then smiled. "Really? What do you find stupid? Surely, not your buddies," she said, and M'Lady Two entered the barn. She walked up beside M'Lady One and put her hands on her hips.

"What's the problem now?" she asked.

"My little sister here says this is all stupid. I'm trying to find out what exactly is stupid."

I looked at Robin, who immediately looked down at the floor when they turned to her as well.

M'Lady Three entered. "What's going on? I'd think everyone would be quite tired by now."

"We're about to hear a critique on Dr. Foreman's School," M'Lady Two told her.

"Well, Phoebe bird, what's your answer? What exactly do you find stupid?" my buddy repeated.

"The whole thing," I said. "Making us sleep on a hard wooden cot and making us earn food and water and wear these, these stupid sacks with diapers."

"She doesn't like her clothes," M'Lady One told M'Lady Two as if that were an amazing thing to hear me say.

"Well then," M'Lady Two said, "she shouldn't have to wear them."

"Exactly my thoughts," my buddy replied.

Before I could respond or move away, they seized my wrists. M'Lady Three stepped up. I screamed and struggled, but they were so strong. They got me down on the wooden bunk and M'Lady Three took hold of my sack and drew it up and over my head. In moments they had it off me and I was naked, but for the diaper, socks, and shoes. I knew how ridiculous I looked. I cried and screamed and they released me and stepped back. Immediately, I covered my breasts with my arms and sat up.

"Now, are you happier?" my buddy asked.

"No. Give it back to me," I cried.

"This . . . what did you call it . . . stupid sack? We don't want you to feel stupid."

She turned and the three started out.

"Wait!" I cried. "I'm sorry. Please. Give it back. I can't lie here like this."

They paused and looked at each other.

"Think she's sorry?" my buddy asked the other two.

"It's hard to tell. She looks sorry, but she looked sorry from the moment I set eyes on her," M'Lady Two said.

"Okay, let's see how sorry she is. Step outside," my buddy said.

I looked at Robin. She wore an expression of abject terror and avoided looking back at me. The other two girls remarkably were as they had been, their eyes closed, still on their backs. They hadn't turned or budged to witness any of it.

"Why?" I asked.

"Yours is not to question why," my buddy said.

"Yours is but to do and die," the other two recited.

I walked slowly behind them out of the barn. The first thing I saw was Teal lying on her side on her bunk. She must have tried to run off or something because I saw her feet were shackled to the cot. She was folded in a fetal position, her eyes closed, but her body shaking. It wasn't warm anymore. In fact, it was cold. I shuddered as well.

"Over here," my buddy ordered, placing me in the pool of illumination thrown down by a pole light.

I did as she said.

"Arms at your sides, face forward. Do it!" she screamed at me, and I did. I felt myself shaking harder and harder. "Okay, now recite the school prayer. Go on. Recite it and do it loud enough for them to hear inside. Do it!"

I started, trying desperately to remember it, but stumbling over words. Each time I did, one of them stepped close to me and shouted in my ear, "Wrong! Start again. Wrong!"

I don't know if I ever got it completely right, but eventually, I did recite it close enough to satisfy them. My buddy, M'Lady One, handed me the sack.

"Okay, put it back on."

I took it.

"Don't we get a thank you?" M'Lady Two asked.

"Thank you," I mumbled.

"We didn't hear you," my buddy said.

"Thank you!" I cried. I dressed quickly before they could change their minds and put me through something equally terrible.

"Get back inside and go to sleep. Another infraction of the rules and you'll go to the Ice Room," my buddy added.

I glanced at Teal. She hadn't dared turn to look at me. She was still shivering, but not as much. Sleep was overtaking fear and anger, I thought.

As I started toward the door of the barn, I glanced to my left because I saw something moving in the shadows. The silhouette became clearer and I realized it was Dr. Foreman. I cringed inside. She had been standing there all the while, watching them torture me. How could she let them do these things to us? A part of me wanted to call out to her, call out to that sweet smile of welcome she had first given us in orientation and ask her what had happened to that, but I was too afraid to do it. In a moment her silhouette seemed to merge with the shadows anyway and she was gone. I wasn't even sure she had really been there.

I entered the barn and went quickly to my bunk. The two girls were still asleep and Robin was on her side with her back to me. I lay down with my back to her. The lights went out again and the door was closed. I heard it being locked and it occurred to me that they had never told us where the bathroom was. What if we have to get up and go? I wondered. Were we supposed to just do it in our diaper again?

"Robin?" I whispered.

I listened, but heard nothing from her. Perhaps she had finally fallen asleep out of the same exhaustion I felt, or perhaps she was simply too terrified to utter a sound. I couldn't blame her.

Suddenly I heard the cry of something wild, a coyote, I thought. There was another, then another. It sounded like a whole pack of them out there in the darkness. They sounded like a pack of vampires. I wondered how Teal was doing and shuddered thinking about it. Sleep would be a hard-won prize tonight.

The long journey that had begun with a disappointment and a betrayal was finally over, I thought.

I was here.

This was my first night at Dr. Foreman's School for Girls.

And all I could think was I was right about that plane ride I took. Surely it must be the way the dead are taken to their afterlife.

I'm in hell.

What else could it possibly be?

3

Three New Squaws

Even if our buddies weren't there to whip us with their screams in the morning, the blazing sunlight pouring through the unblocked windows lit up the inside of the barn so brightly, it burned through our thick walls of sleep and dreams, melting away any determination and resistance we had to awakening. There was no question either of us wanted to wake up in a place like this. Teal, who I imagined was used to sleeping into the midafternoon when she didn't attend school, was probably in utter shock out there.

Almost simultaneous with the glaring light exploding around us came the shouts of the m'ladies to rise. I groaned and looked at Robin. She was awake, but she just lay there staring up. I turned and saw that the other two girls, Gia and Mindy, were already dressed and outside. When did they do that? Did they dress and leave in the dark?

As soon as I sat up, my back felt as if all the muscles in it were tearing away from the bones.

"Stand up!" M'Lady Two screamed at Robin.

M'Lady Three lifted her bunk at the foot of it, then dropped it hard to the floor.

Robin cried out with pain. Reluctantly, she rose, groaning like someone in her eighties or nineties.

"What time is it?" she asked, rubbing her lower back.

"Did you speak? Did you say something without permission? I didn't hear anything, did I? Well?" M'Lady Two demanded, her nose so close to Robin's, I thought they would touch.

Robin shook her head.

"All right then," M'Lady Two said, standing straight. She turned so she was addressing me as well. "This morning you will be introduced to your chores first and then you will be taken to breakfast."

"This first breakfast is a gift since you have done little to earn the food," M'Lady One said. "Consequently, from this time on, whenever you approach a m'lady or any other student at this school, you are to say, 'Excuse me. I'm sorry.' Should you forget to do it, you will be given a demerit on the spot. Is that understood? Is it?" she screamed at me.

"Yes," I said. Robin nodded.

"March out," M'Lady Two ordered, and we did so.

The sunlight made me squint. I covered my eyes and gradually got accustomed to what I was seeing. How could it be so hot so early? I wondered.

I looked for Teal. She was standing by her bunk, wavering as if drunk, her head down. The shackles were off her feet, but still attached to the cot. I looked around. The other two girls were nowhere in sight.

"Okay, let's have it," M'Lady One ordered. Robin looked at me. Teal raised her head. None of us knew what she wanted. "The prayer!" she screamed. "Our morning prayer. Are you all as stupid as you are incorrigible? Recite."

We began.

"No mumbling. Loud," she commanded.

Teal, who now looked terrified of making any mistakes, did the best. Robin and I spoke a split second behind her, correcting ourselves.

"Not absolutely perfect, but passable," M'Lady One decided, just as M'Lady Three came toward us. She was carrying three shovels over her shoulder.

"Good morning, girls," she sang with exaggerated glee. "Isn't it a beautiful morning? This is one of your tools." She distributed the three shovels to us. Teal took hers as if the handle were made of steel wool, holding it as softly as possible with just the tips of her fingers.

"From now on, you are responsible for it," M'Lady Three continued. "We will show you where the tool shed is. You will put them away neatly with every other tool. When you open the tool shed door, wait a moment or two since rattlesnakes seem to find it comfortable in there and I know we're low on antirattlesnake venom."

Teal looked up sharply and then at the two of us. I saw Robin was having trouble swallowing. She looked like she would topple any moment. My heart was pounding like a jungle drum, sending warnings to every part of my body. My blood was in a panic, rushing through my veins as if it were looking for a place to hide.

"This morning you will join Natani. He is a Navajo Indian and the farm manager. You are to give him the same respect and obedience you give to any of us. He will explain your work to you and you will work for two hours before we go to breakfast. As you have been told, you haven't done enough to earn it, but you will be given this first meal anyway. However, I assure you, anyone who doesn't do her job adequately will not be given breakfast and will remain out there working until she does."

Robin raised her hand.

"Yes, you may speak," M'Lady Two said.

"Can I go to the bathroom first?"

"You all can go to the bathroom one at a time." She turned to her right to point at a narrow shack.

"What's that?" Teal asked. "I mean, permission to speak."

M'Lady Three nodded.

"What's that?"

"That's your outhouse."

"What's an outhouse?"

"It's your bathroom, stupid. Once again, I advise you to hesitate a moment or two after you open the door as rattlesnakes like to curl up and sleep around the toilet at night."

Robin froze, her eyes widening.

"We're not going to wait all day for you to go to the bathroom, girls. If you don't go now, you pee or whatever in your diapers. Move!" M'Lady Three screamed.

With great hesitation, Robin started for the outhouse and Teal and I followed behind. As we did, I started to look around more at our surroundings. Obviously we were somewhere deep in some desert. I could see cactus and brush, but outside of the immediate property, which was fenced in, there was no grass, just long, rolling, brown, crusty dirt in every direction. The sunlight wavered over it, making it look even hotter and drier. Mountains were way off in the distance.

To our right we could see dozens of pigs bumping and pushing at each other to get at feed. They slobbered through mud and their own excrement, their heads down, consuming themselves in eating. Farther to the right were four horses nibbling on hay. The gardens were on our left and from the looks of them were bigger than any other garden I had seen. I recognized cornstalks, but nothing else, not being much of a farmer or around farms ever.

Robin opened the outhouse door and jumped back. "Who wants to go first?" she asked Teal and me.

Both of us looked in. Toilet? There was nothing but what looked like a big pipe with a crude wooden seat around it. Instead of toilet paper, sheets of what looked like wrapping paper were beside it.

"Let's go, girls," M'Lady Three called. "Every minute you waste here, you have to make up at the garden, and that's how much longer it will be before you have any food."

Teal stepped in timidly. She started to close the door behind her and then screamed and jumped out.

"Something's crawling in there. I saw it!" she cried.

"It's more afraid of you than you are of it, whatever it is," M'Lady Three said, stepping up. "Either pee in your pants or go in and do it now."

"Oh, God!" Teal screamed, her hands pressed to her temples. "I can't stand this. I can't stand it!"

Her whole body started to shake. I looked at the three buddies to see what they would do, but they just stared at her, watching her cry and pound herself. She raged for a few more moments, then sank to the ground, sitting and sobbing with gasps like someone who couldn't catch her breath.

"I want to go home!" she cried. "I'll do anything, say anything, promise anything. Let me go home. Please."

M'Lady Two turned to Robin. "Are you going to the bathroom or not?" she asked as if seeing Teal's tantrum and fit was nothing out of the ordinary for any of them.

Robin nodded and went into the outhouse.

Teal fell on her side and closed her eyes. "I want to go home," she whispered. "I want to go home." She said it louder: "Please, let me go home."

"What happened to the tough rich girl whose father would be angry at us? I have news for you, girl. Listen to this headline. You've got a long way to go before you go home," M'Lady Three told her. "And all you're doing this morning by throwing this stupid tantrum is making that journey longer yet."

The door opened and Robin came out. She looked pale, but said nothing. I stepped in, quivering all over, and did my business. When I came out, Teal was sitting up and wiping her cheeks.

"It's all right," I told her. "There's nothing in there but some bugs and ants."

She grimaced, got up, and went in. When she came out, we were marched toward the gardens. I couldn't imagine working in this sun for two hours before we could get something to eat. Surely, this was cruel and these people would be held responsible for whatever happened to us. They would be sorry, I thought, and that thought of them all getting into big trouble gave me enough strength to walk on.

As we approached a new field, we saw Gia and Mindy hard at work turning over the earth. Now that we were outside with them, I could see how tan their faces were. It amazed me that Mindy was able to do any work being as thin as she was, but she seemed unstoppable, digging, turning, digging, without looking up. Gia worked the same way.

At first none of us saw the man we were told was called Natani. He seemed to rise up from the ground where he was squatting, emerging like an instantly growing, dark brown tree trunk. He looked our way, then he wiped his hands on the sides of his overalls and walked toward us. As he drew closer, I thought he was at least a hundred years old. Although his hair was black with barely a sign of gray, his face was a dried prune. He had a small build and was surely not more than five feet four inches tall.

"Here are your three new squaws," M'Lady Three told him, and laughed. "They are very delicate flowers so you will have your hands full keeping them alive."

He said nothing, but looked at us and nodded not to agree with her, but more to acknowledge us. He wore a pair of white muslin trousers, a calico shirt, a pair of buckskin moccasins, and a bandanna twisted and tied around his head. On his right wrist was a leather band fastened with buckskin lacing and decorated with silver and turquoise.

"I am Natani," he said to us. "I will show you how we grow what we eat, how we care for the animals that care for us and give of themselves to us, and how we must live side by side with what is wild and true."

He looked at the buddies to see if they had any more to say or any other instructions.

"If any of them give you any trouble, let us know," M'Lady One said in as threatening a tone as she could produce. Natani looked at her without expression, then turned and beckoned for us to follow him.

I watched Gia and Mindy working. They still seemed to have little or no interest in the three of us. To me they were like people who had suffered a lobotomy or something. Were we doomed to become like them?

"This is good ground," Natani explained, and waved his hand over the earth before us like a priest blessing it. "It can bring all our seeds and plants to blossom and feed them what they need. It has sun all day and there are no big rocks, just little ones to remove. Here we have little wind. We must turn the earth on its back and then again to soften it and make it welcome our seeds and the roots of the plants we introduce to it."

He nodded at three wheelbarrows full of plants.

"It is the same for us, for we want to be welcomed wherever we go to live and grow. There is much to learn from the earth and the wind, the sky, and even the rocks. Never turn your back on anything and never stop listening."

"Oh, brother," Teal said. "We're in the hands of some crazy Tonto. Next we'll see the Lone Ranger."

Natani did not look like he heard or understood, but something in his aged face told me he had.

"Let's just get this over with," I muttered. "I'm starving and thirsty."

"We will turn over the ground and then we will with trowels dig holes for our tomato plants."

"Just what I always wanted to do," Robin said. "Plant tomatoes. Like I didn't work hard enough on my grandparents' farm. They raised sheep, and talk about stinks," she said, holding her nose.

"Here we have goats," Natani said. "And we make cheese with the milk."

"Goats? I thought those were pigs," I said.

"Pigs, too."

He smiled wider and we could see he was missing some teeth. He spread us out and showed each of us how we should use the shovels and how to turn the earth. We started to do it, and Teal immediately cried about her hands.

"This is hard. I'll get blisters!"

Robin and I worked quietly, glancing every once in a while at Mindy and Gia, who stopped working and left the garden.

"Where are they going?" Robin asked jealously. "I didn't hear any bells ringing."

We worked on, Teal moaning the loudest, but soon all three of us were muttering to ourselves. I didn't think it was possible to get this tired and sore. Every once in a while, Natani would take the shovel from one of us and again demonstrate how to use it efficiently. He seemed to have magical hands, making it all look so easy.

At one point he knelt by Robin and picked up a rock. It glistened.

"She has waited a long time to see the sun again," he said.

Robin looked at me and shook her head. "She?"

Teal groaned and cried, "I'm going crazy. How is this a school? I nearly froze to death out there last night."

"What choice do we have at the moment?" Robin asked dryly. "It doesn't look like there's a bus station nearby."

"I don't care. The whole thing, this idea of this being a school, all of it is someone's idea of a sick joke. My parents probably arranged for all this just to scare me to death. Well, I'm not ashamed to admit they have. I just want to go home."

"Big deal what you want, what any of us want," Robin said.

Teal looked at her with a mixture of disgust and

anger. "You might be willing to hang around and take all this crap, but I'm not."

"Yeah?" Robin rested on her shovel. "And what are you going to do, call your daddy?"

"I might just do that and wave good-bye to you when they take me home."

Robin laughed.

Teal looked like she would go at her, but for the fact that M'Lady Two appeared and announced we could go to breakfast. My mouth was so dry from the heat and the dust, I couldn't swallow. We laid our shovels down, and like truly obedient puppy dogs, we followed her back to the main house. Outside the door, we were told to take off our clodhopper shoes and wash our hands in the springwater coming out of a pipe in an outside wall. We were also permitted to take a drink. Water had never tasted as good or as refreshing.

Suddenly, Dr. Foreman appeared in the doorway. She looked as elegant and composed as she had the first time we had met her. One thing was for sure—she never did any chores on this farm, I thought, not with those fingernails.

"Good morning, girls," she said. "I understand you've had a good beginning. There will be merit points waiting for you at the day's end if you continue to behave and follow our rules."

Robin raised her hand and Dr. Foreman nodded at her.

"Will they get us mattresses, pillows, and blankets?"

"They could. Let's wait and see, but you're thinking on the right track, Robin. That's good. That's reality. Now come in, take from the food table, and sit at the dining room table. One of Natani's nephews is our cook and he's very good."

We walked into the entryway and looked to our right where a table of fruits, juices, breads, cereals, and hard-boiled eggs were displayed. At the long dining-room table, Mindy and Gia ate quietly, neither looking up at us nor at each other for that matter.

M'Lady Two came up behind us. "Remember, when you meet each other, when you meet one of us, you say, 'Excuse me. I'm sorry,' " she instructed. "We'll be listening for it."

We were herded to the food table.

"Do not make a pig of yourself or you will sleep with the pigs," M'Lady Two warned.

All of us timidly filled our plates and poured ourselves some juice. Then we approached the table and Mindy and Gia looked up.

Robin said it first: "Excuse me. I'm sorry."

Teal and I recited it as well and we sat.

"After breakfast, you will return to the garden. There is no lunch. You will go from the garden and be oriented to your chores on the farm, and then you will be brought back here for your first therapy session. The initial one will be a group session. I like to think of them as get-well sessions," Dr. Foreman told us, wearing that friendly smile.

"Following all that, we will have a reality check and your buddies will give me their evaluations of your behavior. We will assign merit points as they were earned and you will be rewarded accordingly. Eat slowly, girls. Waste not, want not," she sang, and walked away. The buddies followed her out of the dining room and we were all finally alone and together.

"Why did you tell on me last night?" I demanded immediately of Gia.

She didn't look up, but Mindy did and said, "She

received two plus points for that. She's close to being able to make a phone call or receiving one."

"Golly gee, how lucky can a girl get," Teal muttered. "A phone call."

"You'll see how lucky that is after a while," Mindy told her confidently.

"How long have you two been here?" I asked.

"I've been here four months. Gia's been here seven," Mindy said.

"Seven!" Teal exclaimed. She looked at Gia. "How could you last here that long?"

"We manage. Like Natani says, a branch that doesn't bend, breaks. You learn how to bend," Mindy said. "It's that simple."

"Doesn't she talk, say anything except point out who has broken a rule?" Robin asked, nodding at Gia.

Gia looked up at us. Her eyes looked more ebony than mine perhaps because they were shining with such anger. However, it didn't look like anger directed just at us. She looked as though she was in a habitual rage, hated everyone and everything. A tiny, cold smile flowed into her small mouth that seemed to have forgotten how to smile.

"Oh, you're so smug and so smart now," she said. "You still think you're stronger than they are, or someone will come charging in here and save you and tell you it's all a big mistake. They can't do these things to you. You don't have to be here. You have rights. How dare they take away your rights? You'll get so you pray for it, but all you will hear in return are the yelping coyotes or Natani's drums when he is talking to the wind and the stars.

"You see this piece of bread?" she said, holding it up. "It's more important to me than your friendship. Think you'll never get that way yourself?"

She laughed a maddening, shrill laugh that put icicles under my breasts. Then she lost her energy again, and like a weakening lightbulb paled and lowered her head to continue eating.

None of us spoke. I saw that Mindy was staring at me curiously, waiting to see my reaction.

"I hope I never get like that," I said.

Gia nodded her head but kept it down and kept eating. "You're eating on our plates and out of our bowls," she muttered.

"What?" Teal asked.

Mindy turned to her. "Later today, they will take you to the pottery room in the cow barn and Natani will show you how to make dishes and bowls. They will be what you'll eat upon, and if you don't make it right, you'll eat off the table until you do. Remember, reality checks. Everything you have, you have because you've earned it, made it, provided for yourself."

"Oh, I hated doing that in school," Teal said. "Arts and crafts class. I never did any of it right. It's disgusting and so messy."

Mindy smiled at her. "Wait until you clean a pigpen or shovel cow manure and then tell me pottery work is disgusting."

Teal's lips began to tremble again. She looked as if she were going to go catatonic.

"Just eat. We don't eat again until dinner. You heard her," I advised her.

Robin nodded. "Phoebe's right, Teal. Stop worrying about it all. You'll make it bigger and bigger in your mind and only bring pain to yourself." Robin ate faster.

Teal did the same and we were all quiet again.

"Where you from?" Robin asked Mindy.

I thought she wasn't going to answer, but she finally

lifted her head as if it were made of stone and gazed at Robin across the table. "Nowhere. I'm from nowhere."

Before Robin or I could respond, M'Lady Two entered.

"Time to go back to work, girls. Take your dirty dishes to the sink. Mindy, you and Gia remain behind and wash them today. Tonight, Robin, Teal, and Phoebe will do the dinner dishes and silverware. Make sure the table is clean before you return to your farm chores.

"You three will return to the garden now and work until Natani says it's time to go to clean out the pigpen."

Mindy smiled at Teal, who glared back at her.

"Get up now!" M'Lady Two commanded.

We did so and Gia and Mindy began to clear the table.

"It's proper to thank each other for the food," M'Lady Two declared. "Do so."

Everyone mumbled a thank-you to everyone else.

"And don't forget to add, 'God bless Dr. Foreman,' " we were told.

We did so. Then we were marched out to put on our shoes and return to the garden.

Natani wheeled over the tomato plants, handling them as if they were babies.

Teal mumbled just that and he stopped and looked at her.

"They are babies," he said. "Everything is born, begins, matures, and grows old in the world. I'm sure you have heard, 'As ye sow, so shall ye reap,' have you not?"

"I have," Robin said. "My grandparents practically told that to my mother every day, and my grandfather told my grandmother the same thing every time my mother did something he didn't like, which was about always."

"Well, I haven't," Teal said. "I haven't heard anything that has to do with plants."

"Oh, it has more to do with people," Natani said.

Teal smirked at him.

"I know you are not happy," he said. "But you must remember that life's sorrows often bring great joys."

"Here?" I said. "What joys could we possibly find here?"

Natani looked out toward the sprawling desert. "Many years ago the Great Spirit made the sky and the earth and he put the animals on the earth. One day he decided to move the vulture bird to the desert to live. The vulture took one look about and said, 'What a forsaken, miserable place is this. It is hot and dry and full of poisonous creatures. What joy could I possibly find here? Why did the Great Spirit move me here?' And then he saw a dead desert rat and swooped down to gobble it up. After that he saw a coyote that had died when it had disturbed a rattlesnake, and he feasted on that. Then, he smiled as well as vultures could smile. He was full of joy because what better place is there for a vulture than the desert?"

"I'll remember that next time I come upon a dead desert rat," Teal muttered.

"Yes," Natani said. "I'm sure you will."

He began to show us how to plant the tomato plants and we worked at it until all were in the ground.

"When you eat your first tomato from the plant you have put in the ground, you will understand what joy is here," Natani declared. "Now we go to clean the pigpen."

"What difference does it make to a pig if his pen is clean or not?" Teal asked.

"Maybe nothing to the pig, but much to us," he said. "First, we will use what they drop as fertilizer. Second, we will keep them clean so they don't get diseases and smell bad."

"I can't believe I'm doing this," Teal moaned. "We had maids. I never cleaned my room. I never ironed or washed clothes in my life, and now I'm cleaning a pigpen." She looked around. "How far is the nearest city?"

"A lifetime," Natani replied.

"What's that mean?"

"It probably means if you ran off in any direction, you'd die," I said. "Is that what it means, Natani?"

He smiled. "One must learn to live within a small circle before he or she tries to cross the world."

"I just want to get home," Teal moaned. "Not cross the world."

"To go home is to cross the world," Natani told her.

We paused at the pen. Natani opened the gate and shooed the pigs away. Then he stood back.

"I'm going to vomit on the spot. I mean it," Teal warned.

"If you do, you'll clean it up," we heard, and saw M'Lady Three standing nearby. "Start shoveling. You have to go to the pottery barn before therapy today."

"Therapy? We'll need more than therapy at the end of this day," I muttered.

The three of us began to shovel the pig manure into a wheelbarrow. Natani would then take it around to the side of the garden and dump it in a pile while we filled another wheelbarrow. The stench made me dry heave so hard I thought my stomach would crack open, but we didn't stop because every time we tried to back away, we heard one of the m'ladies warning us about the Ice Room.

Where were Gia and Mindy? How come they didn't have to do this? I wondered.

A good hour or so later we found out. They were in with Dr. Foreman. We saw them leave the house and head toward the barn, both walking with heads down.

"What's with Tweedledum and Tweedledee?" Robin asked.

I shook my head. "Maybe they're finished with their chores and have free time."

"Free time? What good is it? What could you do here but twiddle your thumbs?" Teal asked.

"Don't worry about it. Free time is something you won't see for a long time," M'Lady Two replied, coming around the corner of the pigpen. "Pottery time," she declared, and led us to another barn where we passed cows in stalls and entered a room where there was a kiln, tables, and clay.

Natani was already at work at a table. We were told to sit around and listen to his instructions. He showed us how to mix the clay, how to keep it from being too wet, then how to shape our bowls and dishes. M'Lady Two stood back near the doorway watching us work. She wore a wry smile and seemed to enjoy Teal's discomfort. Natani was patient and focused. Once again, I thought he had magical hands. Everything seemed to come so easily to him.

"You must see the bowl and the dish here first," he said, pointing to his temple. "Then it will travel down into your fingers and it will be born through them."

Teal swung her eyes toward the ceiling, but said nothing. Every once in a while she moaned over the clay that was getting under her fingernails. Finally, we had each formed our bowl and our dish well enough to please Natani and he put them into the kiln.

"Let's go," M'Lady Two said. "Dr. Foreman is waiting for you."

Robin asked for permission to speak.

"What do you want now?"

"Can't we clean up, rest a moment?"

"Why? You're not going to a party, stupid. Follow me."

None of us moved with any energy. We dragged our-selves through the afternoon's hot sun and, once again, took off our shoes and washed our hands in the spring-water. We gulped water until our buddy told us to move and we entered the hacienda. M'Lady One led us into the house and brought us to an office with a long, brown leather sofa, an oversize leather chair, and a coffee table between them.

On an oversize dark cherrywood desk, papers were neatly arranged, with a computer on the side, the moni-tor lit with a screen saver showing spiraling solar systems twirling. The walls had plaques and frames, some with degrees in them, some with letters of com-mendation. The windows were shaded with blackouts and the room was cool and comfortable, obviously well air-conditioned. A large oval area rug with desert colors was on the floor, between the sofa and the desk.

"Sit on the sofa," M'Lady One told us. "Remember, no one is to speak until asked to do so. We'll be listen-ing."

We sat on the sofa; then she closed the door behind her as she left. For a moment, the three of us, so tired and exhausted, just sat quietly enjoying the cool air. Teal turned her hands over and looked at her palms. She grimaced sharply, looking like she might burst into tears. Robin closed her eyes and sat back. I lowered my head and stared at the floor.

"I'm running away from here tonight," I heard Teal whisper.

"You can't do that. You'll get lost and die out there," Robin said.

"I'll die here anyway," Teal replied, but not with as much conviction as someone who really believed she had no other choice.

We heard the door being opened and pressed our lips shut. Dr. Foreman walked in, smiled at us, and went first to her desk. She turned some pages of a document in front of her, then came around her desk and sat in the oversize chair, the document in her lap.

"So here we are," she said. "I thought it would be nice if our first session was together, the three of you and me, beginning as a group. How does everyone feel?"

For a moment none of us took the question seriously. How do we feel? How could we feel but miserable?

"I'm exhausted," Teal finally said. "I had a horrible night because I was forced to sleep outside chained to a cot, and it was cold, very cold. I don't know why I'm not sick with pneumonia or something, and I stink. We all stink. I want to go home. I'm sure my parents don't know what this place is like or they wouldn't have sent me here. When they find out, heads are going to roll."

Dr. Foreman had a face like a mask, I thought. Her eyelids barely blinked and those eyes of hers looked like they could bore holes into all three of us. Her lips remained firm, tight. Teal had to look away. She sucked in her tears and held her breath.

"Of course your parents, and your uncle and aunt in your case, Phoebe, know what this is like," Dr. Foreman began. "They were given our brochure and everything, every detail was explained to them. We don't take anyone here without all that being understood first. Agreements had to be signed. I can show you them, if you wish. Your parents want you here, Teal. Why do you suppose that is?"

Teal didn't reply. She kept her face turned away, her chin in her hand with her elbow braced on the arm of the sofa.

Dr. Foreman turned to Robin and me. "Anyone? Why do you suppose you were sent to me, to this school?"

"It isn't a school. It's a torture chamber," Teal snapped at her.

"Can you imagine what sort of torture you have put your families through?"

"Nothing as bad as this," Robin replied defiantly.

"That becomes a matter of opinion, doesn't it, Robin? The emotional and mental torture your families suffered was worse than anything to them or they wouldn't have turned to me in desperation, they and the courts that are frustrated with your behavior, that are ready to give up entirely on you. Tell me, any of you, why should your families have kept you? What did you give to them besides heartache? What do you give to anyone? What value are you to the world?

"Natani's cows give us milk, his pigs give us ham, his garden gives us vegetables, his pottery gives us dishes, his animals give us clothing. What do any of you do but take from the world around you, the world you spent your time damaging? Who will miss any of you?"

Maybe we were all just too tired, but when I shifted my tearful eyes toward Robin and Teal, I saw they were as pained and saddened.

"You were born, you hurt people, and you have been removed, just like some diseased rodent," Dr. Foreman continued, glancing at me. "You're going to lodge complaints? You dare to threaten? You don't know how ridiculous that sounds. Why should anyone listen to your complaints now? All your lives you never listened to anyone else's."

"What do you want from us?" Teal screamed, the tears streaming down her cheeks.

"What I want from you is what you should want from yourself. A rebirth, a complete change."

"I'll change. I promise," Teal followed.

"No. You can't promise that. You've promised it before and broken the promise. Now, you really have to do it, and to do it, you must truly come to hate who you are now and bury that person out there." Dr. Foreman nodded toward the windows.

"We might just do that if you keep torturing us like this," Teal shot back at her.

"Then that is what will be, but I don't think so. I think you'll change for the better. We're here to begin. Today, I want you each to tell me one thing that you did that you admit was shameful, something that in itself would almost justify your being here. I want to believe you when you tell me that, too, so don't just say anything. I know a great deal about each of you. I know what I would choose if I were any one of you." Dr. Foreman sat back. "Who wants to begin?"

Robin and I looked down. Teal turned away.

"No one is ready to begin her cleansing?"

"I didn't do anything bad enough to deserve this," Teal insisted.

Dr. Foreman looked at Robin.

"I'm here only because my mother darling wants to be free of me," she said.

Dr. Foreman turned to me.

"My aunt and my uncle hated having me. They jumped on the first opportunity to get me sent away."

Doctor Foreman nodded. "Okay. It's not unusual for you all to be like this right now, to not be ready. On rare occasion, one of my students will have insight immediately, but that's, as I said, rare."

"Students," Teal spit. "We're not students. How arc we students? We're trapped here and tortured. We're prisoners in some madhouse."

"I'm sorry you feel that way." Dr. Foreman sounded so sincere, really sorry, as if Teal had insulted her. I raised my eyebrows. Could she be serious? How else did she expect we would feel? Did she really believe all she was telling us?

She rose from her chair and went to the door.

"Girls," she said, and stepped back. All three buddies entered the office and looked at us. "My new students are not ready for any rewards yet. Therefore I am rescinding any positive merit points that they earned today. They'll begin again tomorrow."

"Does that mean we're sleeping on those hard cots again and still wearing these . . . these things?" Robin asked.

"If you're lucky," Dr. Foreman said, her eyes small, threatening.

"That's not fair!" Teal moaned. "We've done everything we were told to do. Look at my hands!" She turned the palms up to show the redness and puffiness.

"Why is it all right for you never to be fair and not for the rest of us? That's the world you created around you. Welcome home," Dr. Foreman said. "Now get up and follow your buddies out. I don't like wasting my time," she said sternly.

"What did you want us to say?" I cried with desperation, my arms out like some street beggar's.

She paused, her lips relaxing, her eyes brightening

with cold excitement. "I want you to tell me the truth and I want you to be truthful with yourself."

"What truth? I don't understand what you're talking about, what all this is," I said, shaking my head.

"Oh, but you will, Phoebe. Soon, you will," she said, smiling. "I have no doubt of that."

The buddies were all smiling, too, all of them confident we would fall into line. They were obviously enjoying this, enjoying seeing girls who were once like they were, girls who would be molded into whatever form Dr. Foreman had envisioned for us. Just as she had told Teal in that concrete building—she was playing God.

"Let's go, ladies," M'Lady Three sang.

With great reluctance, we rose and left that cool oasis, that comfort, and followed them back out to the still hot and glaring late-afternoon sun. When did it cool down?

We put on our shoes and followed our buddies away from the house, all of us shuffling along with exhaustion, looking like some ragtag, defeated army. The hot sun made the plains of the desert shimmer around us, the hot air wavering. I thought it wouldn't surprise me to see a mirage.

I looked back and saw Dr. Foreman standing in the doorway watching us.

She was smiling again and that smile was like a knife at my pounding heart.

And that was no mirage.

4

Betrayal

We were taken back to the garden and told to finish planting the tomatoes. M'Lady Two warned that if we didn't do our work well, we would be denied dinner. Sullen, but afraid to resist, the three of us began again. Natani had a way of appearing as if he just materialized out of thin air. None of us heard him approaching until he was there, standing behind us, observing, occasionally instructing again, and helping us get through it.

The sun was lower in the sky, now nearly completely behind a mountain in the distance. It was almost tolerable to be outside. As the glare lessened, I saw how badly burned both Robin and Teal were. Their cheeks were clown red, their upper arms especially looking raw. Neither realized it yet, I thought. When they turned their backs to me, I saw how crimson the backs of their necks were, too. They would surely be feeling miserable tonight, especially sleeping on those cots. When I looked at Natani, I saw him nod as if he could hear my thoughts.

"You must come with me now," he told Teal and Robin.

They looked at me. I shrugged as if to say, who knew what was next?

"I can't do anything else. I'm ready to die!" Teal moaned.

"You must come with me," Natani repeated.

None of the buddies were there to bully us, but we followed him around the far barn, carrying our tools. There we saw what looked like a dumpy old shack made out of logs and brush and mud. He pulled aside the blanket door and stepped back, urging us to enter.

"What is this?" Teal finally asked.

"This is my house," Natani said. "We call it a hogan."

We entered slowly. It wasn't much of a house. A thick blanket and a slim mattress were on the left. On the right was what looked like an ancient stove, the pipe up through the roof. We saw a drum and a pile of clothing beside it with two pairs of moccasins. Strings of beads hung on one wall.

"Where's the television set?" Robin joked.

Natani smiled. "My television set is out there." He indicated the door.

"Don't knock it," Teal muttered. "At least there are no commercials."

"Right now, I'd settle for commercials," Robin replied.

Maybe because we were all so tired and overwhelmed, we all became silly.

"And think of this: he doesn't need any cleaning lady," Teal said.

"And his electric bills must be very low," Robin added.

"He can't complain about the neighbors making too much noise. It won't do him any good," I said. "The neighbors are all animals."

Natani looked at us as if he had known us all our lives and expected us to be silly. He went to his stove where he had a pot of water simmering. Then he plucked a leather bag off the wall. The bag had fringes and a band of colorful beadwork on the bottom, as well as beads on its drawstrings. He opened it and produced handfuls of what looked like beans, which he dropped into the simmering water. He covered the pot and turned back to us.

"What are we doing here?" Teal asked. "Is that supposed to be our dinner tonight? Another sick joke of Dr. Foreman's, I bet," she said to Robin and me.

Could it be so? I wondered.

"No food, no. Soon, you will hear the sun," Natani said.

"Hear the sun?" Teal turned to me. "What the hell is he talking about now?"

"I think he means your sunburn."

As if speaking about it woke it, both she and Robin grimaced and then looked at their arms and felt the backs of their necks.

"Oh, Jesus," Robin moaned. "My skin feels like someone's holding a match to it."

"Mine feels like it was turned into cellophane. I think I can hear it crinkle," Teal added.

"You must sit," Natani said, indicating a place in his hogan. We did. Then he took his drum and sat with it between his legs.

"I'm in a tent with an old Indian man playing a

drum. Am I going crazy or am I going crazy?" Teal muttered.

"We're beyond crazy," Robin said.

Very low at first, Natani began to beat a rhythm and chant something.

"I thought we weren't permitted entertainment until we earned it," Teal joked through her lips, now twisting with some agony. The sun was speaking, just as Natani had predicted.

"This is starting to really hurt," Robin complained as she touched the back of her neck again. "Now that we're indoors, I see what he means about the sun talking. It's not talking; it's shouting."

Natani raised his voice and we all jumped. His chant became stronger, his drumming louder.

"Should we just run out of here or what?" Teal asked.

"Wait," I said. "I have a feeling he knows what he's doing."

"And you have sunstroke, too," Robin told me.

Abruptly, Natani stopped chanting and put the drum aside. Then he rose and went to his stove and the pot. He took it off the flame and stirred the contents. He poured the remaining water on the ground, then squatted in front of us and set the pot between his legs.

"These are beans from mesquite," he said. "They will keep the sun quiet."

"You're kidding," Robin said. "Mesquite. Isn't that a bug?"

"No, it's a plant," Teal said. "I know that much."

Natani dipped his fingers into the pot and came up with the dark, muddy mix.

Teal grimaced. "Maybe that will make it worse. Who told you it works?"

Natani smiled. "Many, many years ago, the coyote told us."

"The coyote? What coyote?" Robin asked.

"The coyote," he repeated, and urged her to give him her arm.

"You should let him do it," I said. "He lives here. He should know what works and what docsn't. You can be sure Dr. Foreman and her buddies won't care about your sunburn. I didn't see a nurse's office at this school."

"Quit calling it a school. It's a hellhole," Teal said.

Robin grimaced and then timidly leaned toward Natani. He began to wipe the mix over her shoulder and arm. He did the same with the other arm, then turned his hand to indicate she should let him get to the back of her neck. She closed her eyes and did so.

"How does it feel?" Teal asked.

Robin thought a moment. "Better, I think."

"Damn, I have to put mud all over me. It's not enough I have it under my nails," Teal complained, but offered her arms and her neck to Natani, who applied the mix on her. Then he put the remaining dark mush in a can and handed it to me.

"For later," he said, and I took it.

"Look at my hands!" Teal moaned, turning her palms up and then showing the blisters to us.

Natani nodded and rose. He went to his bag again and brought back another salve, which he applied to her hands and then to Robin's and mine.

"Natani!" we heard M'Lady Three scream. "Are those delicate flowers in there with you?"

"Go," he said, nodding. "You did good work today. Every day it will get easier, like a stream starting in a new direction. Soon, it flows freely."

"Just what I wanted to be all my life," Teal said, "a stream."

"Thanks," I said. Robin and Teal thanked him, too, and we left his hogan.

M'Lady Three was standing there with her hands on her hips. "Oh, you poor babies. Natani felt sorry for your delicate skin, I see."

"Didn't he do the same for you or weren't you as delicate?" Robin shot back at her.

Her face reddened. "That," she said, pointing at Robin, "will cost you a demerit, smart-ass. One more and you're in the Ice Room. Now get back to your bunkhouse. It's time to clean house."

We looked at each other. Clean house? How could we clean that barn? It had floor of straw and no real furniture. When we arrived, we saw that Teal's cot was still outside. Our other two buddies were waiting at the door.

Teal raised her hand.

"Speak," M'Lady Three said.

"Am I going to sleep out here again tonight?"

"Let's have you all decide." M'Lady Three nodded and M'Lady Two called Mindy and Gia out. "Teal here wants to sleep in the barn tonight. We're going to let you all vote. Of course, she can't vote, so it's the four of you. A tie means no."

Teal looked hopelessly at Gia and Mindy.

"Would you like to tell the voters anything before they decide?" M'Lady Two asked Teal. "You did insult their house last night."

Teal glanced at us, lowered her head, and then nodded.

"And what would that be, pray tell?" M'Lady Two asked.

Teal raised her head. "I'm sorry. I didn't mean to

insult the barn or any of you. Please let me sleep inside tonight," she begged.

The buddies looked self-satisfied. I, as well as Robin and Teal, I was sure, wished I could smother them.

"Okay, then," M'Lady Two said. "All in favor of Teal being permitted to return to the barn, raise your hands."

Robin and I lifted our arms quickly. Mindy and Gia looked as if they were still not going to vote for Teal, but after a second more, slowly lifted their arms.

"Well, then, Teal, you and your friends can bring your cot back inside. You all have an hour before dinner. You are to wash down your cots and wash the barn windows. Gia and Mindy have done their part. They brought the soap and water and the rags into the barn for you," M'Lady Three said.

Robin and I carried Teal's cot back into the barn and put it where it had been. Then, with the buddies watching us, we began to wash down our cots. We were all working like robots now, just moving thoughtlessly, doing what we had to do. When we finished the windows, we were told to bring the dirty water out and dump it. Then, we were rewarded with ten minutes of rest before dinner. I was afraid if I lay back and closed my eyes, I would fall right to sleep, even on the hard wooden surface of the cot.

"I mean it," Teal muttered. "I'm running away tonight. I'd rather die out there."

"You will," Mindy said. "You don't know anything about surviving in the desert. You would have to trek through miles and miles of brutal desert where there are scorpions, snakes, poisonous lizards, and devastating heat and dryness during the day, bone-chilling cold at night. You wouldn't know the first thing to do if you ran out of water or if you got bitten."

"Oh, and you do?" Robin snapped at her.

"I know some, but not enough to make me confident enough to try it."

"What about you?" Teal asked Gia. Gia looked up at us. "You want to run away? You want to get out of here? Give Dr. Foreman what she wants. That's your only escape."

"When are you getting out, smarty pants?" Robin asked.

"Soon."

We were all quiet. I knew I was thinking she might be right and she was lucky if it was soon. Robin looked defeated, too. Teal just looked angry.

"Okay, my little princesses," M'Lady One said from the doorway. "It's time to go to dinner. You all go to the pottery room first and fetch your bowls and your plates. When we see them on the table, we'll decide if they're good enough to eat upon. Move it!" she ordered, and we rose and filed out.

As we crossed toward the bigger barn, I could hear Teal muttering under her breath. She was losing it faster than Robin and I were, I thought. Soon, not even Natani's mystical medicines would be enough to save her.

Our bowls and dishes were on the table. They didn't look bad to me. I couldn't imagine anyone not approving of them. We carried them back to the house, set them down, removed our shoes, and washed our hands. Then we were permitted inside. Our food was already on the table to be served family style from large plates and bowls. I saw what looked like steamed vegetables, as well as mashed potatoes and slices of chicken. There was water to drink, but no bread and certainly nothing for dessert.

We set our bowls and dishes down and greeted Mindy and Gia with the "Excuse me. I'm sorry." I had forgotten about it, but Robin remembered and we did it.

Dr. Foreman entered the dining room. She was wearing a pink and white blouse and a skirt. Her hair was the same, but I could see she wore some lipstick. She stood there for a moment looking us over.

"Natani took care of two of them, I see," she said to the buddies, who smiled. "I hope you thanked him properly. Tomorrow, after breakfast, I will be giving the three of you your school books and assignments. Every night after dinner, you will have two hours to work. You can work together or separately. That's a decision I leave up to you for now."

She nodded at the buddies, who then stepped forward to inspect our pottery, M'Lady One inspecting mine, M'Lady Two inspecting Robin's, and M'Lady Three looking at Teal's. They ran their fingers over the plates and around the bowls and then looked at each other and shook their heads.

"Bumps and crevices," M'Lady One said.

"Inferior work," M'Lady Two agreed.

M'Lady Three dropped Teal's bowl and plate and they shattered on the floor. The same was done to Robin's and mine.

"Eat off the table tonight and try again tomorrow," M'Lady Three told us.

"Before you leave, you will wash their bowls and dishes carefully and then clean up these broken inferior bowls and dishes," M'Lady Two said.

"There was nothing wrong with my bowl. That wasn't fair," Teal protested.

I looked up at Dr. Foreman.

She smiled at me.

Soon, she was surely thinking, soon you will be my girls and whatever I ask you to do, you will do.

The four of them left the dining room and Teal lowered her head to the table and started to sob.

"Don't do that," Gia said sharply.

Teal raised her head slowly and looked across the table at her. "Why not?"

"There's no point in trying to get them to feel sorry for you or any of us for that matter. We can't do much, if anything, to help you. And it doesn't do you any good here to feel sorry for yourself."

"Oh, you're so damn smart," Teal said, flicking the tears from her cheeks.

"No, not smart. Desperate," Gia replied with no emotion.

"Why are you here?" I asked her.

Mindy began to serve herself food.

"Lots of reasons, I suppose." Gia began to serve herself as she spoke. "They called me an arsonist."

"Arsonist? What did you set fire to?" Robin asked.

Gia paused. "My own house." Then, in the coldest, most matter-of-fact tone I could imagine, she added, "Almost killing my baby brother."

The three of us sat staring across at her.

"You'd better eat," Mindy urged. "They'll be back very soon and whatever you've eaten will be it."

Robin dipped the serving spoon into the mashed potatoes and dropped a glob on the table. Then she took some vegetables and some chicken and did the same.

My stomach churned both with disgust and with hunger. I quickly copied her. Reluctantly, Teal followed and the three of us ate like dogs over a table, gobbling the food, drinking some water, and staring blankly ahead. All the food tasted bland. The chicken had been boiled until it fell apart when touched, and there was no salt or pepper or any seasoning on anything.

"The chef has to be a reject from some fast-food joint," Teal said.

Sooner than we expected, the buddies entered and announced dinner was over. Mindy and Gia rose immediately and left the table.

"The kitchen sink is right through that door," M'Lady One told me, and pointed.

I gathered Gia's dishes and Robin picked up the silverware and Mindy's bowl and dish. Teal stood there watching us.

"That table better be gleaming when we return," M'Lady Three told her.

Teal followed us into the kitchen and found the sponges and cleaning liquids. "I never cleaned anything," she moaned.

"Oh, give me that already," Robin snapped, and took everything out of her hands. "You just dry the dishes Phoebe washes. I'm tired and I want to get out of here."

She returned to the dining room and Teal stood beside me while I washed off the pottery.

"Don't you want to try to run away with me? You can't want to stay here a moment longer than you have to," Teal urged.

"I do, but I'm afraid. I've lived in the city all my life. I wouldn't know a poisonous anything and I'm so tired, I don't think I'd get far anyway."

"Maybe we just have to follow the dirt road out. Maybe they're lying to us and we're not that far from a town?"

"You see any lights out there at night? And what if they're not lying? You have any doubt that they wouldn't bother to come rescue us? I don't."

"I won't make it through another day like this," she moaned.

"You'll make it."

"I don't deserve this. My parents were just very upset. My father and mother will take me back if they know I'm sorry. I've just got to be able to call them and tell them," she said, nodding at her plan. "Maybe, maybe I can sneak in here during the night and use the phone in Dr. Foreman's office."

I raised my eyebrows and looked at her. "And if you get caught? That's the Ice Room for sure, I bet."

"And I bet there isn't even such a thing. It's just something they say to keep us terrified."

I tilted my head and looked at her. "Do you want to be the first one to find out if there is or isn't?"

She started to shake her head and raised her hand too quickly, knocking Gia's dish out of mine. I was just about to give it to her to dry. It flew up and away, shattering on impact with the floor, the pieces exploding in every direction. For a moment we both stared in disbelief. I felt the blood draining from my face. Teal's eyes bulged and her mouth dropped open. She looked at me.

"Why didn't you wait until I saw you were handing it to me?" she cried.

"Wait until you saw? Why didn't you watch how you were swinging your hands wildly?"

"I wasn't. I . . ."

We both turned to the doorway. M'Lady Three was standing there, her arms folded under her small bosom, her shoulders back.

"Who did that?" she asked, nodding at the pieces of ceramic dish splattered over the floor. "Who threw that plate?"

"Nobody threw the plate," I said. "It was an accident."

"There are no accidents at Dr. Foreman's School. You did that deliberately."

"We didn't," I insisted. "You weren't here to see it."

She smiled coldly. "I was here as a student just like you two, remember? I know what you're thinking, feeling. You're angry because you had to eat off the table. This is just your way of showing it."

"That's not true," Teal wailed.

M'Lady Two came up beside M'Lady Three and looked at the shattered dish. "I remember doing that."

They both nodded.

"We didn't do it on purpose," I shouted. "Just because it's something you two might have done doesn't mean we did. Stop saying we did."

"You won't make any progress here until you admit to your guilt, to your meanness and selfishness, and you hog-tie that anger," M'Lady Two said. "Now, finish up here, clean every piece off the floor, and come outside immediately."

They left.

"Nice work," I told Teal.

I turned back to the sink and washed the remaining silverware and pottery. Teal dried everything carefully and placed the remaining pottery so softly on the counter, I could barely hear it touching. We both picked up the pieces and put them into the garbage bin.

"What are they going to do to us now?" Teal muttered. "Put us in a scaffold?"

It sounded silly, but my eyes widened. Anything was possible in this place.

Robin was already outside, her shoes on when we walked to the front door.

"What did y'all do?" she whispered. "I heard them talking about y'all. Your buddy"—she nodded at me—"sounded as though you let her down. I get the feeling they'll be punished if we don't do exactly as they expect and rewarded if we do. Maybe they're still under obligations of some sort to Dr. Foreman."

"I don't believe it. I think they're just sadists," Teal said. "They enjoy doing this."

"Well, what did y'all do in there?" Robin asked.

"We broke Gia's dish, but it wasn't our fault," Teal moaned. "It was just an accident."

"Okay," M'Lady Three said, coming out of the house. "Robin, you return to the barracks and go to bed. You two, follow me."

Robin looked at us with sympathy, but also with relief that she wasn't being included in whatever new punishment we were to suffer. We were led around to the rear of the cow barn where we saw M'Ladies One and Two waiting, each holding a blanket. Behind them were what looked like coffins.

"What is this?" Teal asked, stopping.

"This is the death of evil. Dr. Foreman wrote an interesting paper on the concept," M'Lady One said. She approached me and started to wrap the blanket around me.

I pushed it away and stepped to the side. "What are you doing?"

"You will want this blanket, believe me. It gets very cold in the desert before it gets warm again."

I shook my head. Teal turned to run, but her buddy was right there to seize her and hold her, screaming and kicking.

"If you cooperate, it will be so much easier," my buddy told me. She smiled. "We're doing it for your own good. You'll thank us someday, just the way we thanked our buddies and Dr. Foreman."

"You're all sick, crazy," I cried, and continued to back up. But M'Lady Two was behind me and wrapped her pincerlike arms around mine, also practically lifting me off the ground. M'Lady One wrapped the blanket around me quickly, then ran wide tape around that while I kicked and struggled. It was as good as a straitjacket.

All the while Teal was screaming at the top of her voice. When they were finished with me, they let me stumble and topple to the ground while they went to M'Lady Three and assisted her in doing the same thing to Teal. After both of us were snugly wrapped in the blankets, they took the lids off the coffins.

Teal's voice was so shrill, it seemed far off to me. I was shaking my head, my eyes closed, and mumbling my pleas. They can't be doing this to us, I thought. This can't be happening.

"It was an accident," I said. "Really, it was just an accident."

I felt myself being lifted and opened my eyes to see myself being lowered into the coffin.

"Please don't do this," I begged. "I'll do anything. Please. Let me talk to Dr. Foreman. Please."

"Dr. Foreman knows all about it," M'Lady One said.

The lid was put over me. I could see a number of holes drilled in it to permit air, but it was still a coffin and a lid and I couldn't move.

I could hear Teal's hysterical screams go hoarse and finally muffled, so I assumed she was in her coffin and the lid put over her as well.

"There are no accidents at this school," we heard the m'ladies chant.

I closed my eyes. Teal was struggling madly, twisting and turning her body in the coffin. It went on and on, and finally she grew quiet.

"Teal?" I called. "Teal, can you hear me? Are you all right?"

There was just silence and then the cry of a coyote. It grew closer, then there was another and another. It sounded as if they were right near us. My heart was thumping and I was sweating now. I managed to get some more space inside the blanket. The tape stretched a bit, but I could do little more.

Suddenly, I heard the distinct sound of Natani's drum. The slow, rhythmic beating was accompanied by a soft, melodic chant. It was truly like a lullaby. Thankfully my eyes grew heavier and I either fell asleep out of exhaustion and fear or simply passed out.

The next thing I knew the lid was being removed and the sunlight was blaring down on me. I felt myself being lifted out of the coffin and stood. I was confused and groggy, barely aware of what was happening. The tape was removed and the blanket unwrapped. The air, not yet heated to the temperatures of midday, felt soothing. I opened my eyes and focused on Dr. Foreman, who stood there smiling at me.

"Good morning, Phoebe," she said. "You have come through this well. I'm proud of you. Something rotten in you was buried forever last night, I'm sure. I want you to shower and come directly to breakfast. Then we'll talk before you start your daily chores today, okay?"

"I'm thirsty," I muttered. "Very thirsty."

"You'll feel better soon, a lot better. We always feel better when we peel off a miserable part of ourselves."

I looked at the other coffin. The buddies were removing the lid and reaching in to lift Teal out. Her head drooped. She did not regain consciousness.

"What have you done to her?" I asked under my breath. The buddies were holding her upright and her head still dangled loosely.

Dr. Foreman approached her, took something out of her pocket, and put it under Teal's nose. Teal's head snapped up and she shook it sharply before opening her eyes.

"Good morning, Teal," Dr. Foreman sang. "You look like you've buried something rotten and miserable, too. I just know the both of you will be so much better for it."

The buddies unwrapped Teal, but she was so wobbly, they had to hold on to her. They looked to Dr. Foreman, who seemed unhappy about that.

"Walk her about for a while. She'll get her legs back. I want them both showered and then brought to me," she said.

"Will do, Doctor," M'Lady Three said.

While she and M'Lady Two walked Teal about, my buddy directed me to the shower. Slowly, my arms and legs aching, I got undressed and went under the freezing water. I lifted my head to drink and swallow as much as I could. It did revive me. M'Lady One had a towel ready for me. While I was drying myself, I saw Robin, Gia, and Mindy leaving the house and heading for the fields where Natani was waiting for them. Robin looked like she was afraid to look my way. Just like the other two, she kept her head down, her eyes to the ground with only a passing glance my way when she walked by.

We are becoming like them, I thought. Robin is first. I'll surely be next.

"Let's go. We don't have all day to pamper you," M'Lady One told me.

Pamper?

I saw Teal walking on her own now, but her face was so empty of any feeling, any awareness, she truly looked like someone in a hypnotic state. Mechanically, she began to undress and then stumbled under the showerhead and stood there stupidly. M'Lady Three turned it on, and she jumped and screamed.

"Wash!" they all shouted at her.

She looked my way and began to scrub. Because of her sunburn, it hurt far more. I felt sorry for her, but as Gia had so coldly pointed out at dinner the night before, there was little we could really do to help each other. It was everyone for herself here in the end.

Afterward we were brought to the house and left in Dr. Foreman's office to wait for her. Neither of us had said one word to the other.

"Are you all right, Teal?" I asked her.

She lifted her head slowly and turned her droopy eyes toward me. "My throat aches."

"You were screaming so much."

"I dreamed I heard a drum all night."

"There was a drum and chanting. Natani must have been there. It helped me."

"Yes." She turned her head slowly to look forward again, her eyelids barely open.

Dr. Foreman entered with two glasses of orange juice in her hands.

"Here you two are," she said as if she had really been looking everywhere for us. "Drink some juice first."

We both took a glass and drank.

"Slowly, girls, slowly. You don't want to give yourselves bellyaches."

She sat in her chair and watched us for a moment, that same happy smile on her face. She was the crazy one, I decided, but I dared not say it.

"Now where were we? Oh, yes, you were both about to apologize for your misbehavior last night, I believe."

"It's not fair," I was about to say. I was going to describe just how the plate had come to be broken, but Teal lifted her head quickly.

"I'm sorry," she said. "I'm really sorry. I won't do anything like that again. I swear."

"Oh, that's so good to hear, Teal, dear. You don't know how words like that please me. They fill my heart with so much joy and make every ounce of effort I spend on you girls worthwhile whenever I hear a sincere apology."

She turned to me expectantly.

I glanced at Teal and nodded. "Yes. I'm sorry, too. It was wrong and we won't let it happen again."

"That is just wonderful. Something terrible did die last night. We buried it together. We have so much more to bury before we're through, but I know we're going to succeed. Now, Teal, what do you think we should bury next?"

Teal looked up, terrified.

Dr. Foreman laughed. "Oh, I don't mean in the coffin. Hopefully, neither of you will sleep there again." Teal's face immediately softened with relief. "But we have other ways to bury bad things. I'm hoping now that the two of you, the three of you, all of you, in fact, will be doing it yourselves. So, let's get back to where we left off the first time we all met here. What is one thing you did that you know contributed to your being brought here? Teal? Why don't you be first."

Teal tilted her head, her eyes full of defeat. "I vandalized the girl's bathroom in my public school. I broke the mirrors and clogged up the toilets and turned on all the faucets to flood the place. My father had to pay for the damages."

"And how do you feel about that now?"

"I wish I hadn't done it," she said readily.

"Why?"

"It upset my parents."

"Is that the only reason?" Dr. Foreman pursued.

Teal looked at me frantically. I could see it in her eyes: What was the right answer? What was the answer Dr. Foreman wanted, the answer that would free her, get her out of the limelight and danger?

"No," Teal said. "It was wrong. It made it impossible for anyone to use the bathroom for a while and it was a juvenile thing to do."

"Yes, that's true. Why did you do it?"

"I was angry."

"At whom, Teal? At whom were you angry?" Dr. Foreman leaned toward her with excitement in her face. "Well?"

"I don't know. Everyone, I guess."

"No, not everyone. Someone. Who, Teal? Whom were you trying to hurt the most? Tell me."

"My father," Teal cried back at her, the tears streaming from her eyes. "My father!" she shouted.

Dr. Foreman smiled and sat back. "That's good, Teal. That's a wonderful start. I know you're hungry and you need something in your stomach before you go to your chores, so I'm excusing you now. Go to the dining room and have some breakfast and then report to Natani in the field. Go on."

Teal looked at me and lowered her eyes with some

shame before leaving the office. I watched her and then turned back to Dr. Foreman.

She had her fingers pressed together at the tips and sat there staring at me.

"We're gong to become good friends, you and I," she said. "You're going to help me with the others, and someday, I believe, you will serve a tour of duty as a buddy here." She smiled. "I know you will," she said with cold confidence, so cold it put a chill in my heart and washed ice water over my resistance. I tried to swallow, but couldn't. Her eyes were burning into me. "I am good at predicting that sort of thing, Phoebe. You'll see."

"What do you want from me?" I asked, barely holding on to my dwindling pride.

"I want your loyalty, Phoebe. I want your complete and utter loyalty." She leaned forward. I thought she was going to reach out to touch my hand, but she didn't. She just continued to stare a moment, then said, "And I'm sure you will give it to me eventually. The faster you realize that, the better it will be for everyone."

She sat back again. My heart wasn't racing now. It was more like it had actually stopped. I couldn't feel my pulse. My blood seemed to have frozen in place.

"Now tell me," she said, "which one of you, all of you, has spoken about running away?"

I raised my eyebrows.

She smiled. "I know it wasn't you, Phoebe. I know my girls. You're too realistic to contemplate such a thing. You're street savvy. You know what it means to survive out there. There are all sorts of jungles and deserts in the world. You don't have to come here to know that, not you. So who was it? Someone is trying to get the rest of you, or the three of you, to try it. I know. It's typical. Is it Robin or is it Teal, or has one of my other two been clever enough to lie to me? Did Mindy or Gia propose the idea?"

"It's not right to tell on someone," I said.

"Of course it is if telling on them will help them. What if this person actually attempts to run away? She'll die, Phoebe, and you"—she stabbed the air between us with her long, thin right forefinger—"will be very, very responsible for that death. I will hold you fully accountable and that will mean a very long, long time here as a student. Maybe you'd never leave."

Student? I thought. How could she get away with calling any of us that? Teal was right, of course. We were victims, prisoners.

"Well? Am I wrong about you? Will you be loyal to me and become one of my girls or not?" Her voice was full of dark threats.

"She just said it because she's frustrated and afraid and tired," I said.

"Who?"

"She didn't mean it. You can't punish her any more."

"Who?"

I took a deep breath. I was tired and hungry and afraid. I felt lower than the low.

Any one of them would turn me in, I told myself. Any one of them would make a deal with the devil to avoid any more punishment, and maybe Dr. Foreman was right about it: I would be helping her, saving her. Maybe she would try to run away now. I would be responsible in a sense, wouldn't I?

"Teal," I muttered.

"Who?" She wanted me to say it loudly and clearly and firmly. She wasn't going to accept a little bit of victory. She wanted a full, complete, and unquestionable victory.

"Teal," I said louder.

She nodded. "I knew it was Teal, Phoebe. You did the right thing in being honest with me. I'm proud of you. You're going to succeed here. You're going to become something. I want you to come to me or to one of the buddies if she continues to talk about this. If she does and you don't, I won't appreciate it and you will be hurting her more. Do you understand? Do you?"

I nodded.

"Good. Now go have yourself some breakfast. We'll talk again soon," she said, standing.

I rose. My head lowered itself with shame as I walked to the door.

"It's always hard to do the right things after doing the wrong things for so long," Dr. Foreman called after me as I left her office.

You're the one who doesn't know the difference, I thought.

But that was a sentence I would not utter aloud, even to the others.

I had something worse to keep locked in my heart now. Rationalize all that I might, make any excuse that I could think of, it was still the same thing, a betrayal. That was what I had committed in there, under Dr. Foreman's threatening eyes. I was afraid, more afraid than I had ever remembered being. Even the rats hadn't frightened me as much. Now nothing was clearer to me than this secret pain I had to carry and not show—none of us could be trusted. Not if I was the one who betrayed one of us so easily. I had thought I was stronger than the others. What a laugh, I thought. I might be the weakest of us all.

The cloud of depression darkened and fell over me as I walked on. We were all running down a street that would eventually become a dead end. The result of all this was never clearer to me.

She will win, I thought. Eventually, Dr. Foreman will get everything from us that she wants, and the most horrible thing of all will be that we will willingly give it to her.

5

Catfight

Even though I knew no one, especially not Robin or Teal, would suspect I was a snitch, I had difficulty looking either of them in the eye. Robin was intrigued about everything that had happened to us. It frustrated her that while we worked in the field this time, the buddies hung around seemingly just to make sure we didn't speak to each other. Finally, they grew bored and left. Robin nearly leaped out of her clodhoppers to get at us.

"What happened to you guys? Why didn't you come back to the barn to sleep?"

"We had to bury our evil," Teal said dryly.

"Huh?" Robin looked to me for a more sensible reply. Was there one? I wondered.

"They put us in these coffins they keep for a little extra persuasion," I told her, then described it. She paled, even through her darkening tan, as I spoke. Even her lips turned pale white. While I spoke, Teal kept her head down and leaned on her shovel.

"They can't do these terrible things to us," Robin exclaimed.

Mindy, who had been working on the other side and had been listening, laughed.

"They can't! It's illegal for sure," Robin insisted.

"So call the cops," Mindy taunted.

"I can't stand her," Robin muttered, glaring at Mindy. Her eyes suddenly grew smaller with a new suspicion. "You want to know something? I don't think she did anything wrong."

"What are you talking about?" Teal asked, looking up quickly.

"I think Mindy is here just to aggravate and annoy us to death. She's like one of these plants. She works for Dr. Foreman. She's a spy or something. I'm going to make her admit it," Robin said, throwing her shovel to the ground.

"Don't do anything stupid," I warned, and looked around. "They hear everything we say, I think. Even when they're not around."

"What do you mean they hear everything we say?" Robin asked. Teal looked at me with new fears in her face.

"Just that. I don't know. Maybe this place is bugged with microphones or something. I get the feeling sometimes that when Dr. Foreman asks us a question, she already knows the answer," I said.

The two of them looked at me. Out of the corner of my eye, I saw Mindy cross the field toward us. Gia finished what she was doing and sat back on the ground, embracing her legs and lowering her head.

"What did she ask you?" Mindy fired at me, still crossing.

"What?"

"What was the question that she already knew the answer to?"

"Who's talking to you?" Robin snapped at her.

"What was the question?" Mindy repeated, ignoring her.

"I didn't say there was any specific question. It's just a feeling I have about her, that's all," I said quickly, maybe too quickly.

"Yeah, well, it's a good feeling, a true feeling, so watch your mouth," Mindy advised. "And watch what you say about any of us."

"Who are you to tell any of us what to do and not to do?" Robin demanded. "Maybe you should be the one who should watch her mouth."

"What? What's that mean?"

"How come you know so damn much about this place?" Robin stepped toward her. "What did you do to be brought here anyway?"

"I don't think it's any of your business," Mindy said, and turned to walk back.

Robin shot forward and grabbed her arm, spinning her around. "That's a lot of bull. You seem to know about everyone else and everything else. We should know something about you. Unless there isn't anything to know. Is that it? Well?"

"Leave me alone." Mindy turned to walk away again, but Robin seized her arm again, this time more firmly.

Mindy tried to break free, grimaced with pain, and screamed. They both struggled in the middle of the new field of tomatoes. Natani came hurrying out from behind the barn and the buddies were crossing the yard, M'Lady Three leading the charge. Neither Mindy nor

Robin appeared to notice. Robin wouldn't let go of her. She was turning and twisting her as if she were a big rag doll. They continued to wrestle until Robin threw Mindy to the ground. She fell over a few newly planted tomato plants. Robin reached down to pull her up again.

"Stop it!" M'Lady Three shouted. The three buddies ran forward and M'Lady Two wrapped her arms around Robin and lifted her up and away from the sprawling Mindy.

"It's her fault!" Robin screamed, kicking and squirming. "She's been taunting and teasing us ever since we got here."

Mindy stood up and brushed herself off. Three of the new plants were smashed. Natani knelt beside them and handled them gently.

"Nice work, stupid," M'Lady Two told Robin. "That's a capital crime at Dr. Foreman's School for Girls, destroying food, food we all need."

Robin relaxed with fear and M'Lady Two released her.

"I didn't destroy food. I . . . she . . ."

"Blaming someone else for things you do is worthy of five demerits," M'Lady Two said.

"All right, both of you, march back to the house," M'Lady Three ordered. "The rest of you keep working."

We watched Robin and Mindy walk ahead of the buddies. M'Lady One looked back at Teal and me so we started to dig again. Gia returned to work and finished placing another plant. All the while I noticed how little interest she had taken in what had occurred. She hadn't come to Mindy's aid when Mindy and Robin were struggling and she offered no help afterward, didn't try to defend her. They really had no friendship.

The realization that the two of them could be here so long together and not become significant to each other depressed me further. Was that how it would soon be for the three of us? We would just slide down this tunnel of anger and fear until we hit bottom and sank into some swamp of disgust?

Two of the smashed plants were too damaged to remain in the ground. Natani dug them up and carried them away. He returned with new ones and planted them himself. About a half hour later, Mindy came back to the field. She glanced at us and returned to work. Gia didn't speak to her at all.

"Where's Robin?" Teal asked nervously, looking back.

The ranch house was ominously quiet. We could hear bees buzzing at the corner of the cow barn and the pigs slushing about their pen, grunting. About midday, M'Ladies One and Three came out to tell us to report to the pottery barn.

"You're not only going to try to make your own bowl and dish again, you're going to make a new dish for Gia and you're going to stay there and do it until you do it right, even if you have to stay there all day and all night. And Dr. Foreman, remember, is giving you all your schoolwork to start today," M'Lady Three told us. "So you better not waste a second moaning and groaning about how hard your life is."

"Permission to speak?" I asked.

"What do you want?"

"Where's Robin?"

"She's where you go if you do something Dr. Foreman considers way over the line."

"Where's that?" Teal asked. M'Lady Three glared at her. "Permission to speak?"

"That, Teal, is the Ice Room."

"Where is the Ice Room?" she asked.

"Wherever you keep your worst nightmares," M'Lady Three replied. "Now get moving. You're wasting precious time."

"I can't imagine anything worse than what was done to us last night," Teal muttered. "She is stupid. After what we told her, she goes and loses her temper. She could have gotten me into trouble again, somehow."

"I'm sure she's sorry now," I said.

Teal looked hatefully at Mindy. "I don't trust her either. I don't trust anyone." She glanced at me and I shifted my eyes away guiltily. "Anyone."

We marched back to the pottery room. Natani wasn't there, but we knew how to proceed. It took us the remainder of the day to produce five pieces of pottery our buddies approved. Just before they returned to inspect, Natani came in and without speaking helped us. Actually, he was the one who produced the finished products. He left before the inspection.

"All right," M'Lady One told us. "Return to the barracks. You have your schoolwork waiting. You have an hour to make use of before dinner. Every minute of time here is to be productive. Laziness is just as bad as anything else and is rewarded with demerits."

We found textbooks on our cots and sheets of assignments alongside them. There was work to be done in literature, science, math, and social studies. Everything had a specific deadline, the first being tomorrow.

"When do they expect we'll be able to do all this?" I moaned.

Teal shook her head. "This is crazy. She's giving us impossible things to do just so she can punish us with these sadistic things for not doing them. I don't care if I die out there. Tonight, I'm going to sneak some food away from the dinner, even if it's just a piece of chicken or something, and I'll find something to put water in. I'm leaving this place," she vowed. "I'll get someplace where there is a phone and I'll call home. Once my parents find out how gruesome this is, they'll come get me. You can come with me or not," she concluded with a heavy note of definiteness.

"You can't sneak enough food out of there, Teal. And you'll need more than a can of water. You don't know what direction to go in. At night you won't see anything. You could get terribly lost. It won't work."

She didn't reply. She sat on her cot with her back to me and then lowered herself to her side. I looked at her and thought, Was there any hope to an attempted escape? Could she be right? Should I go with her?

Mindy and Gia came in, glanced our way, then went to work on their academic assignments. I opened my math book and looked at the explanations and the problems. It might as well have been written in Greek, I thought. Maybe it was. I closed the book and walked to the doorway. Mindy glanced at me, then looked at her books. Gia never looked my way. Teal was still lying still. She had probably fallen asleep, exhausted. I didn't know what was keeping me awake and moving me.

I saw Natani come out of the cow barn carrying a pail of water that he dumped. Then he went back inside. None of the buddies were in sight. We knew that they lived in the hacienda, probably in the very rooms I had first thought would be ours. What a wishful dream that was, I thought now, and laughed at my naive optimism and innocence. We hadn't been here long, but to me at the moment, it seemed like months.

I gazed back at Teal once more, then left the barracks

and crossed to the cow barn. Natani was adjusting the flow of water into the troughs. He looked up as I approached, then looked at the faucet again.

"I'm sorry my friend broke your plants," I told him.

"They are not my plants," he said. "They are yours. It is from these plants, from everything we do here, that you have what to eat and drink. Very little comes from anyplace else."

I jumped on what he said. "How far away is anyplace else, Natani? Really. How far away are we from anywhere?"

He stood up and wiped his hands on a cloth. "Many days, walking."

"But doesn't Dr. Foreman leave occasionally? There's a van, of course. The van they used to bring us here. There has to be a road that leads to places, a place to get gas, whatever. Where is this place?"

"The van comes once a month with food and other supplies. We have a big gas tank here for the van and the tractor. A truck comes and fills it once a month, and we run our electric generators on natural gas. That comes regularly, too.

"When the doctor leaves, she goes to a place where a small plane waits for her and takes her quickly to where she wants to be and brings her back. She doesn't go very often."

I looked around. Perhaps microphones really were secretly placed everywhere. Would Natani tell them whatever I asked him or said? Was he someone to trust? Did he fool us by helping us? I had to know as much as I could. I had to risk asking him questions. Teal sounded so determined. What if I did decide to go with her? Would it be madness?

"Do you like working for Dr. Foreman?"

"I don't work for Dr. Foreman," he replied.

"What do you mean you don't?"

"I work for what grows. I work for the animals. I work for the sun and the moon and the stars. My people were here long before Dr. Foreman or anyone else. Signs, houses, papers, don't change the way things grow, the sun's rising and falling. I do what I have always done."

"She doesn't pay you?"

"The earth pays me."

Maybe he's just crazy, I thought. Maybe the sun fried his brain.

"What if someone ran off, Natani? Just left one night and walked away in the right direction? People can walk for days and days, right?"

He smiled. "Once, a vulture picked up a squirrel at the edge of the desert and flew off with him. The squirrel awoke and screamed, 'I am not dead. How dare you take me?' The vulture, shocked himself that the squirrel wasn't dead, opened his mouth and the squirrel fell to the desert floor. The squirrel brushed himself off. He was insulted. Imagine, he thought, being thought to be dead. He started to strut in one direction and then stopped, scratched his head, and started in the opposite direction. Once again, he stopped and scratched his head. Where were the trees, the rivers he knew? What sort of place was this with ground so dry even rocks looked unhappy?

"Nervous and worried now, he walked faster, again stopped, and turned to go in another direction. Each time, he walked faster. He grew very tired, very thirsty. Nothing made any sense to him. He could not understand the way and he saw no creatures who could give him any information. The lizards and the snakes were afraid of him. He didn't belong there so they did not trust him enough to wait to hear his questions.

"Night came and he didn't like where he had to sleep. Something crawled over him and made him jump and he was awake so long, he barely had any rest before the sun came up. He scurried up a small hill and looked around. As far as he could see, there were no trees, no streams, no place to gather food and no one he knew.

"He walked on, desperate now. He tried to keep himself in one direction, but every once in a while he leaned too far to one side or another, and soon he realized he had been walking in a great circle. Everything looked the same. Very thirsty, very weak, he finally stopped and fell to the dry earth. His eyes closed and opened, closed and opened, and then closed.

"And lo and behold, the same vulture appeared and strutted up to him. He opened his eyes and looked at the vulture, who seemed to be smiling.

" 'I thought you said you weren't dead,' the vulture said.

"The squirrel tried to move, but couldn't and did die. The vulture picked him up and carried him off again.

"The vulture knows. He or she who doesn't belong out there will soon belong to him. Patience rewards him. He will wait, and to those who scream back at him, 'I am not dead,' he will say, 'You are dead. You just don't know it yet.' "

Natani turned back to pour some feed in the trough.

"But people cross the desert. You do, I bet, or did, didn't you?" I insisted.

"People who know how to speak with the desert can live with it, but there is little forgiveness there. A mistake, a misunderstanding, and soon, the patient vulture, the desert's undertaker, appears."

"If we had food and water . . ."

"You cannot carry enough. You must know how to get the desert to give it to you."

"You could show someone how to do that, couldn't you, Natani?"

He didn't reply.

"You could show someone enough to help her get across the desert to where people live, couldn't you?"

"When it comes time, I will teach you what I know."

"When is that?"

"When it comes time. It's not for me to decide. It's the doctor who decides."

"What do you mean? She lets us try to escape?"

"It's her way. I do not understand all her ways, but it's her way. She is a very wise woman."

What was he talking about? How did he know how wise she was and wasn't? Where did she find him? Was he just here when she arrived as he said? He couldn't like what he saw happening to the girls. He must despise the buddies. I saw the way he just looked at them when they spoke to us or even to him. It was as if he could look through them or put himself in a different place when he wanted to, but why did he bother? Why did he stay here? Surely there was another farm, another place unlike this where he could be happy.

None of it made any sense to me. I felt like I was spinning in a nightmare.

"Why are you here? Why don't you work on a happier place without all this?" I asked, waving my arms. "Are you really part owner or something?"

He smiled and shook his head. "No, nothing but what I have made myself belongs to me."

"Then why are you here? Of all places, Natani, why Dr. Foreman's School?"

He looked like he wasn't going to answer anymore, and I thought I was probably wasting my breath, but suddenly, he looked at the hacienda and then at me.

"The doctor helped my daughter's daughter, and I have made her promises that are as strong as the sun. I do not understand all her ways, but she does not understand mine. The birds do not understand the lizards but they live side by side. Each has its own way. This is how it is," he added, and returned to his work.

I left the barn and returned to the barracks. Teal still had her back to Gia and Mindy and me.

Gia looked up. "You shouldn't have let her sleep."

"She's exhausted. We're both exhausted."

"You've got to start your work, show Dr. Foreman you're making an effort."

"I don't understand that math. I couldn't even begin to do it."

"You can do it," Gia insisted. "Let me see what she gave you as your first math assignment."

I brought the book and the assignment sheet to her and she nodded. "It's the same one we had to do. Okay, sit." She patted her cot.

I sat and she started to read and explain it to me. Mindy glanced at us every once in a while, but said nothing. Before we were summoned to dinner, I did understand the first lesson.

"Thanks," I said.

"You can show Teal how to do it now," Gia told me.

I woke Teal up but she was too groggy and cranky to listen to anything. She still mumbled about running off as soon as it was dark enough to escape. Dr. Foreman's words returned to me. I'd be responsible if Teal went off and died out there, and Dr. Foreman would be displeased with me. Who knew what that meant?

M'Lady Two came to our door and summoned us to dinner. I was hoping we would find Robin at the house when we got there, but she was nowhere in sight. We took off our shoes, washed our hands, and went in to have our dinner. Just a simple thing like having our own bowl and plate had now become a wonderful thing. We went through our ritual of thanking each other and begging each other for forgiveness, then ate what seemed to be a more tasty food that Mindy described as polenta, a mush of cornmeal, black beans, and a beef in some sort of sweet sauce.

Dr. Foreman arrived and declared she was rewarding all of us for putting in a decent day's work. We were given a plate of cookies for dessert. Mindy, Gia, and Teal were assigned to washing dishes and silverware, and I was told to clean the dining room afterward. While I worked, Dr. Foreman reappeared. She watched me for a few moments. I had the sense she was waiting for me to say something.

I stopped working, thought about Natani's tale of the squirrel, and then turned to her.

"What is it, Phoebe?"

"I'm afraid for Teal."

"Tonight?"

"Maybe."

"You've done a very good thing, Phoebe." Dr. Foreman stepped up to me and took my hands, turning them to look at my palms.

"Follow me." She led me out of the dining room, down the corridor, to a bedroom. It was surprisingly bland and unfeminine. There were no pictures on the walls, no pretty curtains or rugs, nor any photographs of family or friends. What kind of a family did she have? I wondered. Had she ever been married? Did she have a boyfriend, children of her own, parents still alive?

The king-size, four-poster bed looked so comfortable and luscious with its oversize cream-colored, fluffy pillows and comforter, I longed to crawl into it and sleep for a week.

She smiled at the covetous expression on my face. "All good things will come to those who earn them, Phoebe. Reality checks, remember?"

I nodded and she took me into her bathroom, opened a medicine cabinet, and plucked out a jar of some skin cream. She rubbed it into my hands.

"Natani isn't the only one with miracle medicines here," she said, smiling. "You don't want your skin to get too soft when you work a ranch, but you don't want to irritate anything and get infections either."

"Thank you."

She put her hands on my shoulders and looked into my face. "You're going to be one of my girls. I'm confident of that. Now return to your barracks and do your schoolwork."

I thought I heard what sounded like someone sobbing and thought about Robin. Where could she be? Was she sent away? Wherever she was sent, it would be a blessing, I thought.

"Where's Robin?" I asked, and Dr. Foreman's smile faded.

"Robin is defeating a very bad part of herself. She will be better tomorrow. Go on."

I left, went out, put on my shoes, and crossed the yard to the barracks, wondering if I had heard someone crying and if it was Robin. What horrible thing was being done to her? Could it be worse than being in one of the coffins?

As soon as I entered the barn, I stopped with surprise.

On my cot was a mattress, a pillow, and a blanket,
and on the blanket was a pair of blue coveralls, the
same white, short-sleeve shirt Mindy and Gia wore, and
a pair of panties. I was being rewarded. I was pleased,
of course, but at the same time I felt a dark sense of
foreboding and guilt as I took off the coarse sack dress
and the oversize diaper.

When Teal, Mindy, and Gia returned, they stopped
and looked at me sitting on my cot and reading.

"Why did you get all that?" Teal asked.

I shrugged. "It was just here when I returned."

Mindy smiled coolly, her eyes small. "Sure it was. It
just grew there."

"Leave her alone," Gia snapped. Mindy turned with
surprise. "You're no angel. You have no right to judge
her or any of us."

"I didn't say that I did."

"What does all that mean?" Teal asked. "Why are
you arguing?"

"Around here, the fewer questions you ask, the better
off you are," Gia told her. "Get your work done or
you'll soon be where your friend Robin is."

"Where is she?" I asked quickly. "I think I heard her
crying when I was with Dr. Foreman before. Is that
where the Ice Room is? In that house."

"You didn't hear her crying," Gia insisted.

"I did."

She was quiet.

"If I didn't hear her crying, who did I hear crying?"

"Forget about it. You don't want to know," Gia told me.

"Is she in the Ice Room?"

Gia didn't reply. Instead, she turned to Teal and said,

"If you want to do your friend some good, just keep your mouth shut."

"She's not my friend. We only met when we were brought here. We hardly know each other. I probably know just as much about you as I do her, or you," Teal said, nodding at Mindy, "or Phoebe."

"You're better off," Mindy said dryly, and went to her books. Gia did the same.

Teal walked slowly to her hard cot, her eyes on me. We were all like a bunch of alley cats, scratching and hissing at each other, I thought. It made me feel sick inside. If I followed Gia's advice, I would walk around with a head full of air. Teal looked like she was going to burst into tears again and have another tantrum. It wouldn't do anyone any good, least of all her.

"I can show you how to do the math assignment," I said. "Gia showed it to me earlier."

"I don't care. I'm not doing any of this," Teal said, and kicked her books.

Mindy and Gia looked up and then went back to their work.

A deep sense of dread passed through me.

Where was Robin? I wondered, looking at the doorway. Why wouldn't Gia talk about her? What was happening to her?

What would happen to Teal?

And then to me?

I worked until lights out. Teal went to sleep before, her back to me.

When I crawled under my blanket, I luxuriated in the softness of my mattress and pillow. My fatigue seemed to seep down through my legs and into the bed. I drifted into my first comfortable night's sleep in a long time, and I was so deeply asleep, I didn't hear anything around me. When I opened my eyes, I didn't resent the morning light as much as I had the day before. Mindy and Gia were just rising, too. I sat up and turned to Teal.

Cold shock began at the base of my stomach and shot up to my heart.

Her cot was empty. She was gone!

I turned to the others. "Where's Teal?"

They both looked as if first noticing she wasn't there themselves.

"Maybe she's so eager to get to work and start on the new vegetables, she got up and left before dawn," Mindy said.

I looked at Robin's empty bunk. "Why isn't Robin back?" I muttered. "What have they done to her?"

"Didn't you hear what Gia told Teal last night? You're better off not asking questions." Mindy smirked at me. "But you've already learned how to be better off."

"What's that supposed to mean?" I shouted at her. She turned her back on me, pulled on her shoes, and started for the door. "If you hadn't opened your big mouth, Robin wouldn't have gotten into trouble," I screamed.

Mindy turned slowly. "How did she get sent here if she wasn't in trouble?" she retorted, and walked out.

Gia looked at me. "Just get to work. It's the only way to get out of this place."

She left. I sat there fuming, but I wasn't sure if I was fuming at Mindy for being right about me or just fuming at myself for doing what I had done.

Had Teal run off? Was she out there in the desert, dying like Natani's squirrel? Surely, since I had told Dr. Foreman what Teal was thinking about doing, she wouldn't have let her do it.

I hurried out, hoping to find her beside Natani, planting cucumbers and carrots in the section of land he had irrigated. I saw Mindy and Gia joining him, but no sign of Teal or Robin. M'Lady One, looking like she was dragging herself out and about herself, came strolling toward me. She smiled when she drew closer. "Don't you look and feel better in those clothes?"

I didn't say anything.

She stopped in front of me. "You're a quick learner, Phoebe. That's good, and since you're my assignment, it helps me, too. Don't screw up and we'll both be happier people." Then she nodded at the planting. "Get to work."

"Where's Teal? Don't start with that permission to speak. Just tell me what happened to her," I demanded.

Her smile faded. "Maybe you're not so smart after all." She started to turn away and I reached out and touched her arm.

"Did she run off? Does Dr. Foreman know? Is she sending someone out there to bring her back?"

She spun on me and poked me hard with her thick, right forefinger in the chest between my breasts. It threw me off-balance and I fell back, sitting on my rear and looking up at her. My chest smarted. She might as well have poked me with a pipe, I thought.

"Don't you ever touch me again, understand? Don't you put your paws on me, girl," she fired down at me. "No one touches me. The last one who touched me was a sorry rat."

She looked insane, beyond rage, like someone who had slipped into a second personality and was capable of great violence. It occurred to me that all the buddies were former Foreman wards, which meant each of them had done terrible enough things to cause them to be sent here. What were my buddy's crimes and sins? Was she really cured or was she still quite capable of whatever acts of savagery had brought her to Dr. Foreman's School for Girls?

I rose quickly and turned away from her, heading out to the field.

"Don't you dare touch me again, understand?" she screamed after me.

I kept walking, my shoulders hunched up. In my neighborhood in Atlanta, I had seen people under the influence of drugs and alcohol. I had seen hard kids practically brought up in the streets, but something in my buddy's eyes I had not seen. It was as dark as death.

I stopped next to Mindy and Gia and listened to Natani's instructions about how to plant the different vegetables, trying hard to keep my attention and concentrate. Every once in a while, I looked back at the house, but I didn't see my buddy or anyone else. Instead, I started to work and desperately worked at keeping myself from thinking about any of it.

Just after we finished our morning chores and were heading toward the house for breakfast, we saw a lot of dust down the dirt road and heard the van approaching. All three of us hesitated at the fountain and watched as the van pulled up. M'Lady Three stepped out of the van. A dark-skinned man was driving. He looked like an Indian, too. He stepped out and went to the rear. They opened the door and pulled out a stretcher. Teal was lying on it, her face looking swollen and red. I saw what looked like a large circle of red on her right calf, which also looked swollen. She was grimacing with pain and looked like she had screamed herself hoarse. She didn't open her eyes.

"What happened to her?" I cried, hurrying toward them.

"Get back," M'Lady Three ordered. They carried her toward a corner of the hacienda. The three of us watched until they disappeared. Then we heard the door open and looked up to see Dr. Foreman.

For a long moment, she and I fixed our gazes on each other like two combatants locked in an unrelenting grasp. Then she smiled.

"Breakfast, girls," she sang, turned, and went inside.

Mindy and Gia were looking at me. They knew what I had done. They knew why I was so shocked.

"Don't ask about Teal," Gia warned.

"Just keep giving Dr. Foreman what she wants and get out," Mindy added.

They both walked into the house. I stood there for a moment. If I could cry, I would, I thought.

But shock, fear, and exhaustion had stolen all my tears.

It made sense I was in the desert. Even my well of sorrow was dry.

My second shock came when I entered the dining room and found Robin sitting at the table. She was hunched over her plate eating and drinking ravenously. Her body trembled and she looked like she had been rolling around in a coal bin. Her hands, however, were clean. She looked up at me and quickly looked down at her food.

"Robin. What happened to you? How are you?" I asked.

Mindy and Gia paused in dishing themselves some scrambled eggs and looked at me, their eyes full of warning. I didn't care. I had to know.

Before I could say another word, however, M'Lady Two was at the door.

"Girls, Dr. Foreman wanted me to tell you that she wants you all to devote this afternoon to academic studies. This is actually a reward. We're easing the restriction on talking. You're free to speak to each other at all times in the barracks and on the grounds, but don't forget to excuse yourselves and thank each other."

My first thought was this confirmed for me that the barracks was bugged. Dr. Foreman wanted us talking now. She wanted to hear what we said and thought.

"You're to spend the day in your barracks doing your lessons and homework," M'Lady Two continued. "If you do all your work properly and you have a satisfying session, you will have free time after dinner."

"Free time? What can we do with free time here?" I asked.

"Breathe," she replied, and laughed.

After she left, I turned back to Robin, hoping she would tell me something about what had been done to her.

"Stop looking at me," she snapped. It took me by such surprise, I turned to Mindy and Gia.

They both looked at me with I-told-you-so expressions. I served myself some breakfast and ate with my eyes straight ahead. I couldn't remember ever feeling more alone and lost, more helpless than I felt at that moment.

Afterward, on our way back to the barracks, Gia stepped up beside me.

"Even though they're easing up on the no-talking restrictions, don't keep asking Robin about the Ice Room," she said. "She's been told it's forbidden to talk about it, and if she does, she can end up back there. Basically, she's ashamed of herself."

"Why would she be ashamed of herself?" What did Gia know?

"Because of what happened there and what she promised or said to get out."

"How do you know?"

Gia stopped. She didn't look at me. She just gazed ahead, her eyes growing small, dark. "Because I was there, too." Then she walked on, leaving me behind, staring after her.

I looked back at the house and thought about Teal. I really couldn't blame her for running off, but what was the point of Dr. Foreman forcing me to tell on her if she let her go off like that? Nothing made any sense to me. Nothing I did seemed to help. Whenever I thought things might be getting better, they were actually getting worse. I was afraid to make any more decisions. We could talk, but I was afraid to talk. What if I said the wrong things? What were the right things?

Standing there under the glaring sun, I felt suddenly like I couldn't move. Any direction I took, anything I said or did, would not help me. I was filled with a sense of dread and terror of any decision I might make. Even walking to the barracks seemed like it might be wrong.

Suddenly a cold wave of panic nailed my feet to the desert floor. I couldn't even swallow. My heart was pounding as if I had been running for miles, though. It was getting harder and harder to breathe. I was caught in some sort of invisible web. My arms and legs were stuck. I could almost see the spider approaching. I've got to do something, something . . .

I didn't realize I was being watched, and not by any of the buddies or Dr. Foreman. Natani stood so still and so quiet, I could have walked past him and not realized it. Finally, after looking at me for some time, I guess, he came forward, materializing out of thin air.

"The rabbit," he said, "grows so afraid, he cannot move. He trembles in place and the fox has a pleasing time of it. Your eyes are clouded with fear, daughter of the sun. Open them wider, look beyond. Go where the sun goes." He pointed to the western horizon. "See yourself outside and you will not tremble in your footsteps."

I looked where he pointed. See yourself outside? Yes, think about anyplace else but here. I thought of Atlanta, of being with my old friends, of laughter and freedom and the neon lights, the music, the noise. Envisioning it seemed to wash a cool relief over my body.

"See yourself outside," I muttered, driving the lesson home to my heart.

"Yes," he said, and put a turquoise stone in my hand. "Keep this close. It is a piece of the sky that fell many, many years ago and it will remind you to look up and see yourself outside." Then he walked off.

I turned the stone in my fingers, then looked up at the sky. Who knows, I thought, maybe it was a piece of the sky. I put it in my pocket and felt myself regain my strength. My breathing eased and I started across the yard again. When I stepped into the barn, I saw Robin was sitting with Mindy on her cot and working with her on the math assignment. Gia was nearby, her books opened.

"It's better for each of us if we work together," Gia said. "We can break up the assignments and each take something we're each good at."

"I'm not a great reader," I admitted.

"Well, we already know you're not great at math either. What are you good at?"

"Making excuses for not being good at anything," I replied, and Gia actually laughed. It was as if a thin wall of ice had shattered between us.

"Okay," she said. "I'll partner up with you. Come on, we'll start on the social studies assignment."

I picked up my book to join her, then noticed Robin's cot. It had a mattress on it, a pillow, and a blanket, and Robin was wearing the same coveralls and shirt.

"You were rewarded," I said excitedly. "How come?"

She looked at me with joyless eyes and then looked down at the math text.

"Let's just get this done," Gia said, urging me to drop the subject.

She didn't need to. Robin's quick, subdued looks were enough. I understood. Whatever she was being rewarded for was not something she was happy to describe. What terrible things had been done to Robin and what had she given Dr. Foreman as a result? Was it something about me, something I had said? I ran back whatever I could remember saying, drawing in my thoughts and words like a fisherman reeling in fish. Many things would have angered Dr. Foreman, I thought, but from the way Robin looked, she wouldn't tell me even if she wanted to tell me. She looked the way I had felt right after I had given up Teal. I felt sure I was not the only one who betrayed.

And more important, perhaps, was what Dr. Foreman had been after right from the beginning. She would find ways to turn us against each other until all each of us had was herself and Dr. Foreman. She was the spider I had envisioned out there. I and the others were trapped in her web now.

I quickly put my hand into my pocket to feel the stone.

Natani's words returned.

Think of the sky. See myself outside.

Yes, that would be my chant.

That was what would get me home, I thought, wherever home might be.

6

Group Therapy

Teal didn't return to the barracks for nearly four days. Every time I started to talk about her and wonder aloud what was happening to her, Gia came at me, telling me to stop asking and to mind my own business. I wanted to suggest that Teal was my business and should be hers, too. We should all be each other's business. Whom else did any of us have here? But neither Robin nor Mindy spoke up in support of me. They avoided my eyes, looked away, went about their work. Teal could be gone for good and none of them would have asked after her. It would be as if she had never existed, the same if I had never existed.

I began to wonder if Teal hadn't been sent away, maybe placed in a formal detention center or even a prison. I told myself she would be better off. We all would.

I mumbled this idea loud enough for Gia to hear, and

finally she fixed her dark, steely eyes on me and said, "Don't ever believe Dr. Foreman when she threatens to send us back. No one gets sent back. Dr. Foreman does not fail, does not give up. If one way doesn't work for her, she tries another and another. You either change to her liking or . . ."

"Or what?" I quickly countered.

"Or you don't, but you don't leave unless it's on her terms."

"The buddies left."

"Did they?" Gia tossed back at me. "They're still here, aren't they?"

"Because they want to be."

She smiled at me as though I were a child.

"Well? Why else would they stay? What's here for them? Even if they enjoy torturing us, it's not enough. Don't they have boyfriends or want them?"

Gia was thoughtful for a moment. I could see that was something she had thought about, too.

"She has ways we don't even know exist," she said. "She has ways of changing your head. Don't try to understand the buddies, why they are like they are. I don't want to even think about it. I just think about . . ."

"About what, Gia?"

"Nothing," she said quickly. "I don't think about anything anymore."

"Why not?"

"Why not? It's like being in a prison cell with a window that looks out on the most beautiful place, a place you can't go to, but only see from behind bars. That's why. Do you understand me? Do you?" she shouted.

I just stared at her.

"You and your damn questions. Making us think," she said, making it sound as if I were responsible for all her pain. Before I could protest, she walked away quickly.

Finally, one night after dinner, we returned and Teal was there, lying on her cot, which now, like the rest of ours, had a mattress, a pillow, and a blanket. She was in what I called our school uniform, too, only her hair, her hair had been cut down to where she was nearly bald, her beautiful hair was gone. She lay there with her eyes wide open, staring up at the ceiling and looking even more drained and in shock than Robin had when she had been released from the Ice Room.

"Teal!" I cried, and hurried to her side. "How are you? What did she do to you?"

The others watched and listened but remained behind me.

"Are you okay? What happened to you? Where have you been all this time? What happened to your hair?"

She didn't answer for so long, I thought she wasn't going to say anything, but then she turned her head slowly and looked at me with eyes so cold and empty, they put a chill in my heart.

"My hair," she said, "escaped."

"What?"

"That's how we do it." She propped herself up on her elbows so she could look past me at the others. She looked like the idea was exciting to her. "We escape in pieces. Maybe my teeth will be next or my ears. Right, Gia? Mindy? That's how it's done, isn't it?"

Neither replied. They ignored her and went to their own bunks.

"What are you talking about? You're not making any sense. Did you get far? What did you do?"

She stared at them a moment longer, then turned to me, her eyes as angry and dark as Gia's. "I would have made it. I know I would have made it. I saw light in the distance, but I got stung by a scorpion."

"A scorpion!" I stepped back as if it were still there and could sting me as well.

"That's what they said. It made me pretty sick and it hurt so much, I thought I would die. My leg swelled up. All I did was stop to rest awhile and I guess I stopped right beside one, but you don't have to go out there to find them. They're here, too, you know." She looked around the barn as if that information made her happy. "You could get stung just as easily sleeping in this filthy barn."

I looked at Gia and Mindy. They continued to undress and get themselves ready for bed.

"That's not true, is it?" I asked.

"Of course it's true," Mindy replied.

"Gia?" I asked.

She paused and thought a moment before turning to me. "You know what a minefield is? How they put bombs in the ground to blow up enemy soldiers who might step on the wrong spot?"

"Yes, so?"

"Well, that's what it's like being here. You're always walking through a minefield. If it's not one thing, it's another, and Dr. Foreman doesn't do much to make it any safer for us either. In fact, she plants the mines."

"You don't mean she puts things in here, do you?"

"What do you think?"

"That's crazy. That's . . . we could be killed or something."

"Hello. Welcome to your nightmare," Gia said, smiling.

She seemed to take such pleasure in telling me all these horrible things.

"Yeah, well, if it can happen to me, it can happen to you," I threw back at her.

She shrugged. "It's already happened to me."

"What? What's that supposed to mean? What are you saying, Gia?"

She ignored me. Robin got into bed without speaking and Teal continued to stare up at the ceiling.

"Well, it hasn't happened to me!" I screamed.

The door opened. M'Lady Three was standing there.

"What's going on in here?"

My heart was pounding. I half expected either Mindy or Gia would point a finger at me to earn more of those precious positive merit points, but this time no one spoke.

"You had better get some rest, my little princesses," M'Lady Three said. "You'll need it. Tomorrow, we're whitewashing the cow barn and it will take all day."

She closed the door and the lights went out. All I could think of now was something creepy crawling over me. I felt as if I were back in my Atlanta apartment, waiting to feel a rat scurry over my feet.

"They can't do this to us," I muttered. I was thinking aloud. "If we die, they'll be responsible. They'll get into trouble."

"No, they won't. They'll just make up a good story," I heard Mindy mumble. "I'm sure she's done it before. I'm sure she's made up a whopper about Posy."

"Who? What did you say?"

"Shut up and go to sleep," Gia commanded sharply. "Keep your mouth shut, Mindy."

"What did she say? Who's Posy? Gia?"

"If you don't shut up, we'll all get into trouble and it's going to be hard enough tomorrow. You heard her.

Believe me, we know what it's like when they pile it on," Gia said.

"I won't let her cut my hair like that," I vowed.

"Of course not," Mindy said, laughter in her voice. "Teal didn't let her either. You heard her. Her hair ran off."

"Maybe that's what happens when you get bitten by a scorpion. Your hair falls off," Robin offered, and the two of them laughed.

"I'll give you a maybe," Mindy said, propping herself up on her elbows. "Maybe Teal wasn't stung by accident."

"What?"

"Maybe someone followed Teal and when she lay down to rest . . ."

"I'm warning you, Mindy," Gia said.

"Okay, okay. Good night, ladies," Mindy sang.

That couldn't be true, I thought, could it? Dr. Foreman had her stung by a scorpion to teach her a lesson?

I lay there with my eyes open, listening. Was it possible to hear something crawling over the straw-covered floor? After a few moments, I could hear Teal's breathing get low and regular. Robin whimpered and then went silent. Maybe it was my imagination, but I thought I heard someone crying just as I had when I was with Dr. Foreman in the house.

This time I knew it wasn't my imagination. I did hear someone crying.

It was me.

I cried myself to sleep just as I used to when I was a little girl and no one came to my bedside when I had nightmares or fears. It made me think I was going backward, getting younger and younger. One morning I would wake up in here and I would be an infant.

I had no idea how or when I fell asleep, but I did. The morning light was like an alarm bell. Everyone groaned and rose before M'Lady Two opened the door to announce we were to line up outside like troops. When we dressed and stepped into the unrelenting sunshine, we were made to recite our prayer as usual, then told to march over to the barn for our individual assignments for whitewashing the cow barn. Each of us would be responsible for a specific section. Cans of paint were open and ready with the rollers. Ladders had been set up as well.

"Try not to make a mess of things," M'Lady Three said. "Breakfast in two hours. Get started."

We began our halfhearted attack on the sides of the barn. Teal was the first to wail complaints. She splattered herself with some paint and moaned about its getting into what was left of her hair. The mess wasn't what made it terrible, however. I think they deliberately chose to have us begin on the east side of the barn. That way the rising sun would be sending its hot darts into us the whole time. In a matter of minutes, everyone looked drained and defeated; even Mindy and Gia were feeling it more than usual. Mindy trembled so badly on her ladder, it rattled.

At one point she turned and looked at Robin, Teal, and me angrily. The fury in her face made me uneasy. I couldn't stand being stared at so hatefully.

"What is your problem, Mindy?" I asked.

"I'll tell you my problem. They're only making us do this because of you three and the stupid things you do. Robin starts a fight with me and Teal tries to run off. You break plates, talk back. I know Dr. Foreman believes we should all share the punishment. I know how she thinks. It applies to everyone, anyone, no matter who she is and what she has or has not done. So thanks."

"Stop it," Gia told her. "You know you're not going to make it any better for any of us by bitching. No one here knows it better than you, Mindy."

Mindy was quiet again, but she didn't like it. Her strokes were harder, her anger pouring down through her arm.

"I don't care how you think," Teal told Mindy. "Or you, Gia. I'm not sorry I ran off. I almost made it."

"Oh, really. You almost made it, Teal? Made it to what?" Gia asked.

"To a phone. My father would have come for me."

"Your father?" Mindy said, laughing. "I heard your story. Your father put you here, just like mine put me here."

Teal looked at me and Robin and then turned back to Mindy. "Your father did this to you also?"

"Just work and shut up," Mindy said. "You've made enough trouble for us."

"What did you do? What's the big secret, Mindy? You know everything we did, why we're here." Teal turned to Gia. "What did she do that's so much worse than what you did or what I did?"

Gia paused and looked at Mindy as if she had never considered it from that viewpoint before.

"Yes, Mindy, what did you do?" she teased.

"Shut up, Gia. Just keep your mouth shut."

"She did a lot of things with a lot of boys."

"Shut up, I said." Mindy's anger made her wobble again on her ladder.

"And a baby."

"Shut up!" she screamed so hard and so loudly, her face turned crimson.

We heard a door slam and M'Lady Two came out of the house. Gia turned quickly and began working again. We all did the same. Mindy, still fuming, stared needles and pins at Gia and then shot them at us.

"What's going on here? More talk than work? Well? You should have had more done by now, Teal."

"I'm still weak and tired from being sick. I shouldn't have to do this."

"You'll be sicker yet if you don't do your fair share," M'Lady Two warned. "I want to see you all double what you've done by the time I return, understand? Otherwise, plans for the day might be changed, radically changed, and you won't like it, believe me."

She stood there watching us for a moment, then walked back to the house.

"Thanks, Gia," Mindy muttered.

Gia said nothing. None of us did. Her words had left our imaginations to run loose and I could see it on the faces of Teal and Robin; they weren't just running loose, they were galloping through every possible horrifying scenario involving a baby.

Finally, we were told to put everything aside to go to breakfast. No one even attempted to speak to anyone else. Mindy was sullen and Gia avoided her bee-stinging eyes. Robin, Teal, and I said nothing to each other or either of them. The air about us felt as if it were laced with TNT. Someone rubbing her hands together too vigorously could set off an explosion.

We washed up and entered the house. At the table everyone mumbled the forced thank-yous to everyone else, then we ate like five mutes. Silverware clanked against bowls and dishes. I could hear everyone chewing, swallowing, drinking, each of us keeping her eyes forward, looking into her own dark and troubled thoughts.

"Good morning, girls," Dr. Foreman cried from the dining room doorway. She practically sang it. "What a glorious day and I see you've all gotten off to a productive start. How wonderful. This afternoon, around noon, I want you all showered, cleaned up, and brought back here for some refreshment, after which we will hold one of my famous group sessions. Mindy and Gia are well acquainted with them, aren't you, girls?"

"Yes, Doctor," Gia said quickly. Mindy nodded. Both of them looked so frightened, it frightened me.

"Good. Well eat up, girls, waste not, want not." Then Dr. Foreman was gone as quickly as she had appeared.

Mindy and Gia looked after her and then looked at each other, the air between them still heavy and flammable. Gia began to eat again.

"Why is she making us part of their group session, Gia?"

"How would I know?"

"We're not going to get through this," Mindy muttered. "We're never going home."

"Shut up," Gia told her.

"She's going to stop us."

"Quiet, Mindy."

"She doesn't want anyone to be free. Not since Posy. You know I'm right, Gia. You've said it yourself many times."

"Stop it!" Gia snapped.

M'Lady One appeared in the doorway. Both girls quickly returned to eating.

My buddy glared at them for a long moment. "Something wrong?" she asked, her eyes small with suspicion. "Someone planning something nasty?"

No one responded.

"All right, let's get moving, girls. You have a lot to

accomplish by noon. Robin and Teal, you clear the dishes and wash down the table. The rest of you, start back to the barn and your work."

Gia gulped the rest of her juice and stuffed another piece of bread into her mouth as she stood up. I followed her and Mindy out to put on our shoes and start for the barn. When M'Lady One was far enough away, I stepped up beside Mindy and whispered, "Who was Posy?"

She looked at me as if she was going to reply but then glanced at Gia and walked faster, pulling away from me and closer to M'Lady One. Gia dropped back.

"Stop asking questions or you will be sorrier than you could ever think possible, and it might not be only because of what they do to you," she threatened sharply.

We returned to work. From time to time, I saw Natani pause in his own work and look our way. I thought I saw him smile at me, but it was hard to tell as the sun rose higher in the sky and made even the dirt gleam. At noon we were told to stop, clean up in the shower, and return to the house. We had just about completed the east wall of the barn. Everyone had spots of paint on her face, hands, and arms, as well as in her hair. Teal was the most depressed about it.

"I used to go to a beauty parlor once a week," she said, running her fingers through her stubs.

"Lucky you," Gia said.

"At least I had a reason to go."

"Keep your mouths shut," M'Lady Two called. "Just walk to the showers."

We were given soap, brushes, and towels and made to scrub until every spot of paint was off our bodies. Then we dressed and started for the house.

At the house we were treated to wonderful ice-cold

lemonade. No one was ashamed to show how much she enjoyed it and coveted every drop. After the cold shower and this refreshment, I did feel better.

"Is it going to get easier?" I asked Mindy.

She tilted her head. "What?" She batted her eyelashes. "What was your question?"

"Are things going to get better now?" It seemed like a fair question to ask. We had all been through fire, punished, beaten down to where we were all obedient.

"Better?" She smiled. "Things are only going to get worse," she predicted with a smile that was so cold, I thought her teeth had turned to stone.

We were marched into Dr. Foreman's office and told to sit. Gia and Mindy kept looking at each other as if they knew exactly what was coming and it wasn't good. Teal had her head back, her eyes closed, and Robin sat staring forward, her eyes like sockets without bulbs.

Dr. Foreman entered smiling warmly and sat in her chair with a notebook in her hand. For a long beat of silence, she just sat there looking at all of us like a proud parent might contemplate her children. Was I right in thinking that we had reached a point where she was pleased?

"Okay, girls," she began, "we can finally get down to why you've all been sent here. We can finally go after your recuperation and get you all set on the right road. Everyone here has done something to lead me to believe she can change, she can improve, but you all have a ways to go yet, and now that you have spent quality time together and gotten to know each other better . . ."

I was expecting her to compliment us about it, but she surprised me when she continued, "You all know who among you has the least chance of achieving immediate success. Unfortunately, whoever that is will only hold the rest of you back." She panned us slowly, her eyes pausing on each of our faces, then moving on to the next and the next, spending a little more time on mine. "You've all got to think of what's best for everyone and not for yourself. That's the only way to help yourself.

"Now, the most important thing to achieve is honesty. I'm sure you'll all agree. Honesty requires trust, and you girls are the best to decide who among you can and cannot be trusted. Am I right?"

There was a deep thump in my chest. In the back of my mind I wondered if she would tell everyone how I had betrayed Teal, use me as an example.

"I want you all here to hear each other because I do not like it when one girl goes behind someone else's back. That's deceit. We've all got to face the blunt truth about ourselves. I know how hard this is to do. For most of you, if not all of you, deception, dishonesty, conniving, have been the order of the day. How refreshing it will finally be for you to throw all that off and be truthful." She smiled as if she were offering us a party.

She rose, scooped up five pencils from the top of her desk, and handed each of us one. Then she gave each of us a piece of paper.

"Let's begin, however, with a secret vote. That's the best way to break the ice."

I glanced at Mindy. She looked absolutely terrified.

Gia looked angry. "We've done this before, Dr. Foreman. Can't we be excused?"

Dr. Foreman's face hardened even though she kept the smile on her lips. "Yes, Gia, you have done something similar before, but not satisfactorily. Not yet. And besides"—Dr. Foreman's eyes gleamed as she nodded at Robin, Teal, and me—"you have new companions now. Things can't be the same. Every situation is different and you've got to be able to adjust to new situations all the time, adjust to different personalities. That's what it's going to be like out there, right?"

Gia looked like she was going to say something more, but then stopped and looked down.

"Right?" Dr. Foreman insisted.

Gia looked up. "Yes."

"Good. All right. Now let's begin. I want you each to write the name of the girl you think will take the longest to improve and leave the school."

I was stunned. Vote on who among us was the worst?

"What if we don't know enough yet about everyone else?" I asked.

"Oh, I think you do by now."

"We weren't permitted to speak to each other much and . . ."

"You've seen and spoken to each other enough to make the decision I expect," Dr. Foreman said sharply. Then she smiled. "If you can't choose, then write your own name down, and of course write your own name if you believe you are the weakest one."

Was this really some kind of a serious vote? What would happen to the girl who won this vote? Would she be treated more harshly? Isolated from the rest of us? I looked at everyone else. No one was going to write her own name. Why should I write mine?

"But . . ."

"Quickly. We have a lot to do and you're all going to be sent back to the barracks afterward to complete your schoolwork. There are due dates for all your assignments, remember, tomorrow being one."

I looked at the others. Robin was writing and so was

Teal. Mindy stared down at the floor like she was giving it all real thought, but Gia wrote a name quickly on her paper. Whom was I to choose? There was no doubt in my mind. It would be Teal because she was the one who whined the most and she had tried to run away. I felt so guilty about having betrayed her, but from the way Dr. Foreman was looking at me, those eyes of hers so full of awareness, I was afraid if I didn't write Teal's name, she would know I wasn't being honest.

"Fold your papers and hand them to me."

We did so and Dr. Foreman sat with them all in her lap.

"Okay, let's begin." She opened the first paper. "Teal," she read. She looked at Teal, who glanced at all of us and then looked away with fear.

Dr. Foreman unfolded another. "Teal."

The third was the same.

Opening the fourth, she said, "Teal."

Then she opened the fifth and smiled. "Robin? I guess we can safely conclude you wrote Robin, Teal."

Teal looked terrified and shook her head.

"I don't imagine Robin would have written her own name, and you wouldn't have written yours, dear. There's no point in denying it now. Instead, we'll ask you to tell us why you think Robin is the weakest in the group. You seem to be the only one who thinks so." She still made it all sound so harmless and friendly.

Teal looked at Robin, who was glaring at her hatefully now. She glanced toward me as well, and I thought from the way she looked at me that she had expected I would have written Robin's name and not hers.

"She . . ."

"Yes? We're all ears. Go on, Teal."

"She hates her own mother. She couldn't care less if she goes home or not," Teal offered weakly.

"Oh, and you just love your parents, especially your father, who you said doesn't love you. She stole money from her own father," Robin reminded us. "That's why he sent her here. They can't stand each other."

"That's not the whole reason why and you know it," Teal countered. "Anyway, you're always going to get into trouble because you're stupid. You let a boy talk you into being part of an armed robbery. That's a serious crime."

"Oh, I'm stupid? You're the one who runs off into the desert not knowing where she's going or anything, and I'm stupid. Besides, everyone else voted for you, didn't they? I'm not the only one who doesn't trust you."

"That's true, Teal," Dr. Foreman said. "Everyone else did vote you as the weakest in the group. Why do you think that is?" she asked as if she really didn't know the answer.

Teal opened and closed her mouth. She looked like a deer caught in the headlights of a car.

"Well? Think, my dear. I need to know what you think," Dr. Foreman said.

"I don't know. They're all jealous of me, maybe," Teal muttered.

"Jealous of you?" Robin said, and laughed. She looked at me, her eyes asking me why I wasn't speaking up. Gia and Mindy were both looking straight ahead, clearly showing that they wanted to be somewhere else, anywhere but here.

"Well, let's get some opinions about that," Dr. Foreman said. "Mindy, are you jealous of Teal? Is that why you voted for her?"

"You know that's not true, Dr. Foreman."

"I know it's not true, but how would anyone else, Mindy? Go on, tell them why you're not jealous of Teal."

"I'm not." She looked at Gia.

"Gia's not going to speak for you, Mindy. You speak for yourself," Dr. Foreman ordered.

"My family is probably as wealthy as hers, but I'm not a selfish brat, and I don't think she's prettier than I am. She's weak and complains and moans all the time. She's spoiled silly and can't stand any discomfort. I've seen her tantrums. That's why I picked her," Mindy exclaimed, the words rushing out of her like someone finally giving up a secret.

Dr. Foreman nodded, satisfied, and then looked at me.

"Why did you choose Teal, Phoebe?"

"She tried to run away," I replied quickly, hoping she wouldn't make me say anything else or ask me anything else.

"I would have thought that showed strength, determination, courage," Dr. Foreman said. Robin's eyebrows lifted with surprise. "Wouldn't you, Phoebe?"

"Well, no, not if you're doing something impossible. I mean, I told her what Natani had said. I told her how easy it is to die out there and she still went."

"At least I tried to do something for myself. I didn't just whine and complain like they do," Teal said.

"Is that what they do?"

"Yes. And don't say you don't, Robin. She was the one who got into a fight, wasn't she?" Teal accused. "She thinks Mindy is your spy," she revealed, snapping her lips shut as soon as she had.

A heavy silence fell over us for a moment.

"Oh?" Dr. Foreman asked.

Robin seemed to wilt in her chair when Dr. Foreman turned toward her. She shook her head.

"Is that what you thought, Robin? Mindy here was my spy, someone I planted in the barracks?"

"No, I mean . . ." She looked toward me for some help, but I looked away.

With a look of great patience, Dr. Foreman turned to Mindy, who was smiling gleefully at Robin's discomfort.

"Why would Robin think you were my spy, Mindy?"

Mindy's smile wilted. "I don't know," she muttered.

"Well, you said something that gave them this ridiculous idea, didn't you? What sort of things were you telling them?"

"I didn't tell them anything," she cried defensively. Then she pointed at me. "Phoebe was telling them that you had microphones secretly placed all over the place."

"Microphones?" Dr. Foreman smiled. "You really believe that, Phoebe?"

"Sometimes it seems like it. Gia's always saying I shouldn't be asking questions."

"Oh. You didn't tell them I have microphones all over the place, did you, Gia?"

"No. She's exaggerating. She's just a big mouth and I was trying to tell her she would get herself and someone else, maybe all of us, into trouble if she didn't keep that mouth shut." Gia fixed her eyes angrily on me.

"So why didn't you write her name on the paper?" Dr. Foreman shot back at her like a prosecutor in a courtroom.

"I should have," Gia replied without hesitation, glaring at me. "I'd like to change my vote in fact, from Teal to Phoebe."

"Phoebe, what do you say to all this?"

"Gia's just being vicious and spiteful. I know she thinks Teal is the weakest."

"Maybe she's not. Maybe it was courageous to try to escape like that," Robin muttered like someone thinking aloud.

I spun on her. "You don't believe that. You're just trying to kiss up."

"Don't tell me what I believe and what I don't believe, and I don't kiss up." Robin smiled at me, her lips twisting toward the right corner of her mouth. "I'll tell you what I don't believe. I don't believe you when you say you only hurt that boy with a statue. I bet you weren't really just defending yourself. I even think you killed him."

"What?"

"What are you saying, Robin?" Dr. Foreman asked.

"She told us she's here because she hit someone and supposedly put him in the hospital, but I'm beginning to wonder if that was all that really happened and if it really happened the way she said it did. She makes herself seem like such a goody-goody while the rest of us admit to doing bad things. That's not honest, is it, Dr. Foreman?"

All of them were looking at me.

"Is that true, girls? Does Phoebe make herself out to be a victim?"

"Yes," Teal said. "She does."

"What do you think, Mindy? Could Phoebe have been the right choice?"

"Maybe."

"Is that right? You're the one who's always warning everyone. You're the one who might be the most afraid and weak here," I practically shouted at her. "You're the one who talks about this Posy."

I immediately felt the heat rise up in the room. Mindy sank in her chair and looked quickly at Dr. Foreman. Gia, who never looked afraid, suddenly had eyes filled with terror.

"Is that so, Mindy? You talk about Posy?" Dr. Foreman looked more at Gia, who quickly shifted her eyes away guiltily.

"No," Mindy said. "I don't."

"How would she know her name if you hadn't talked about her?" Dr. Foreman leaned toward her, grasping the pencil the way I have seen boys grasp switchblades.

"It . . . I didn't say anything. I just mentioned her."

"How did you mention her, Mindy? What did you say about her?"

"Nothing. Really," she wailed.

"I thought you weren't going to talk about Posy anymore," Dr. Foreman said to Gia.

"I don't!" she exclaimed. "She does!"

Dr. Foreman sat back. Mindy looked down. Gia was biting down hard on her lower lip, so hard I could feel the pain in my own. Silence seemed to fall like an iron curtain between us.

"Okay, girls," Dr. Foreman finally said. "These sessions are what I call purges. We get some of the hateful, spiteful, evil things out of our system. We don't have to be deceitful about any of it anymore. You all have much to do to repair yourselves, and this has been a beginning."

She held up the slips of paper. "We'll take this vote again sometime soon, perhaps, and it will be interesting to compare the results. For now, I want you all to return to the barracks and do your schoolwork." She stood and opened her office door.

We rose and filed out. The m'ladies were waiting for us in the hallway.

"Be sure they go directly to the barracks and get to their schoolwork," Dr. Foreman told them. Then she reached out and touched Mindy's shoulder. "I'm not angry at you, Mindy. I have great faith in you. I know you're going to continue to do well for me, for yourself, right?"

Mindy nodded, and Dr. Foreman lifted her hand from Mindy's shoulder.

No one said anything. We put on our shoes and in a silent parade marched across the yard. I heard Natani on his drum in his hogan. No one else seemed to notice or care. After we entered the barracks, the door was closed and we all went to our respective bunks.

The silence and heaviness in the air was so thick, I could have molded it into a dark plate to put into the kiln.

"Are we going to work together or what?" I asked.

No one said anything.

We might as well all have been in separate buildings, I thought. I started to read the chapter in science, but my eyes drifted off the page.

Mindy was staring at the floor. Suddenly, she started to tremble.

"Stop it," Gia told her.

She didn't. She grew worse, shaking harder.

"What's wrong with her?" Robin asked.

Teal stood up. Drool was running down the sides of Mindy's mouth and she was making a small but deep moan.

"Maybe you should call for someone," Teal said.

"No, leave her alone." Gia got up and seized Mindy's shoulders, shaking her. "Stop it, Mindy. Stop it. You know what will happen if you don't."

She shook her head. "It . . . doesn't . . . matter. She's

mad at me, really mad at me this time," Mindy gasped. Her eyes were wide with such terror, it took my own breath away.

I turned to Gia, pleading with my eyes for her to do something.

She smirked and took a deep breath. "She's not mad at you, Mindy." Then Gia shouted at me, "Damn you. Did you have to tell about Posy?"

"I didn't tell anything. I don't even know who Posy is!" I cried. "She's the one who mentioned her. How were we supposed to know we shouldn't say the name?"

"Who is she?" Robin asked. "What's all the damn mystery about that y'all know and we don't?"

"Yes," Teal followed. "Who is she?"

"Why can't we mention her name?" I demanded more firmly.

Gia rose and looked at us while she kept a hand on Mindy's shoulder. Mindy continued to tremble and held on to her.

"Well?" I said. "Who was Posy?"

"She was Dr. Foreman's daughter," Gia said.

7

Posy's Story

"What do you mean, her daughter?" I asked. "Dr. Foreman is married? Where is her husband?"

"I don't know if she's married or not," Gia said.

"You don't know?"

"We don't know. Is there something wrong with your hearing?" she shouted at me.

"Well, how do you know she has a daughter?" I came right back at her.

"We know." Gia paused and looked at Mindy before turning back to us. "Whether she was married or not isn't the point. Posy wasn't her actual daughter. She was adopted and you don't necessarily have to be married to adopt someone."

"Adopted?"

"Adopted?" Mindy turned to mimic me. "Yes, adopted. You ever hear of it?"

"Mindy was adopted, too," Gia revealed.

"Oh. Well, I still don't understand it all. What was Dr. Foreman's daughter doing here?"

"What's good for the goose is good for the gander," Mindy sang.

"What?" Teal asked, stepping forward. "What are you saying?"

"It's what Posy used to say after Gia found out she was Dr. Foreman's daughter. Right, Gia? It means whatever was good to do to anyone else here was good to do to her. Right, Gia?"

I looked at Gia, who wasn't answering.

"So she was here as a . . . a student or whatever we are?" I asked.

"Yes, one of us lost souls," Gia said. "Posy was, shall we say, a bit of a disappointment to her brilliant mother."

"Sort of what all of us are to our respective mothers, real or otherwise," Mindy added, her words dripping out of the corners of her mouth.

"This is still very confusing," Robin said. "Why would Dr. Foreman have her own daughter, adopted or otherwise, in this place?"

"You are thick," Gia said sharply.

I saw Robin's face show crimson, even through her now deep tan. "I'm thick?" She started toward Gia, her hands clenched into fists. "You want to see how thick I am?"

"Stop it!" I cried at Robin. "Look, I'm not as smart as you are, Gia, but I can see that ripping us apart is what Dr. Foreman wants."

Gia relaxed her shoulders and looked at me and then at Mindy. Then she sat on her cot.

"Probably," she admitted.

"Why?" Teal asked. The three of us were around Gia and Mindy now.

"I don't know everything either, but I know she doesn't want us to be strong, and if we all got along and protected each other, it would be us against her."

"Exactly," I said. Gia looked up at me. "She had us tearing each other apart pretty good in there. It's exactly what policemen like to do when they arrest you and start to question you. They get you fighting among yourselves and pretty soon someone gives someone else away and it all falls apart."

"How come you know so much about all that? How often have you been arrested?" Mindy asked me, her face scrunched up with both disgust and curiosity.

"Enough," I said.

"Where is this Posy now?" Teal asked, still thinking about her. "And what kind of a name is Posy? I can't see Dr. Foreman naming a daughter Posy, can you?" she asked me. "I would have expected something more like Hortense."

"Posy named herself Posy, I think," Mindy said. "Isn't that what you said, Gia?"

"Yes. I can't remember Dr. Foreman calling her anything but 'young lady.' "

"You never met this Posy, Mindy?" I asked.

"No. She was already gone by the time I arrived. Gia told me all about her."

"Well, what happened to her? Where is she? Did she graduate or something?" Teal asked Gia.

Gia's laugh was thin and maddening. "Graduate? Yes, I guess it is a sort of graduation when someone gets out of here, if she gets out of here." She was silent a moment; then, after glancing at Mindy, she turned back to Teal and said, "I don't know."

"Why not?" Robin asked.

"We can't be sure, right, Gia?" Mindy said.

"What does that mean? Did Posy tell you something?" I asked Gia.

"It wouldn't have mattered if she had. When she was first brought here, she told Gia so many different things, it was obvious she was a habitual liar."

"Really?"

Gia nodded. "For the longest time, I didn't know she had any relationship to Dr. Foreman at all, much less being her daughter. She never called her or referred to her as anything but 'Dr. Foreman,' and I never saw anything warm between them, anything even to suggest they had once lived in the same house."

"Tell them what she did say, Gia," Mindy urged.

Gia looked at her and then turned to us. "Posy would talk about her parents as if they were the most wonderful people. They had everything imaginable and they loved her and were just heartbroken over the fact that she was here. In the beginning I didn't know she was lying. She made it all sound believable. I mean, she had it down to the smallest details, the colors of her bedspread, the dolls her father had bought her, her secret magical place in their beautiful big home that she shared with an adorable little sister, I think she called Tamatha."

"Amazing," Teal muttered.

"All of it was her fantasy," Gia said. "Nothing more than her long wish list."

"Gia says she was a habitual liar or something. We're not even sure about the bad things she had done, exactly why she was here, right, Gia?"

Gia nodded. "Sometimes it seemed to me she was here only because she couldn't tell the truth."

"Well, then how do you know she was telling the truth when she told you she was Dr. Foreman's adopted daughter?" Teal questioned.

"She never actually told me she was," Gia said. "I told her and she finally admitted it."

"Tell them what she said then, Gia," Mindy urged. It was weird to me how she enjoyed hearing about it all so much, as if she really enjoyed reliving Gia's experience.

Gia laughed. "She said she didn't tell me because she didn't want me to think she was getting any special treatment. That was a good laugh. If anything, I was getting special treatment, not her, but she always had to have a rosy excuse for everything," Gia said bitterly. "Rosy lies, I should say."

"I don't get it," Robin said. "If she didn't tell you herself first and neither of them showed how they were related, how would you know?" She looked poised to hear Gia insult her again, but instead, Gia looked at Mindy, who shook her head.

"What difference will it make now if they know," Gia asked her.

"One of them is sure to betray you. You know that."

"I always thought she knew anyway, Mindy. Was I wrong?" Gia asked, her eyes small and fixed on Mindy.

"What's that supposed to mean?"

"You know what it means."

"No, I don't," Mindy said, looking around as if searching for a way out.

"Sure you don't," Gia said, twisting her lips.

"What's going on?" Teal asked me. "What are they talking about now?"

I shook my head. "What is going on, Gia?"

She thought for a long moment, then shrugged. "Oh, what difference does it make anymore?" she muttered. "It was my idea to do it. I'll admit to that. I was bored," she offered as a defense. "I wasn't here all that

long, but it was obvious to me it was going to be a
drag. The early nights, lights out, no television or
radios or anything, just work and studies and those
damn therapy sessions, those questions, prodding,
making me think of things I didn't want to ever
remember. On and on until . . ."

"Until what?"

"I was curious and, like I said, bored."

"So?" Teal asked, impatient. "You were bored. Big
deal. A news flash. She was bored. What did you do
about it?"

"I decided to spy on Posy and Dr. Foreman when
Posy was in there alone."

"How could you do that?" I asked.

"I found a way. There's a basement to the house. The
door is on the other side and it was opened late one
afternoon when I had some free time. I just wandered
down the steps and in, almost as a way to escape the sun
and heat as anything else. I heard voices and followed
the sounds down to my right. There's a floor grate in
Dr. Foreman's office. As soon as I knew what it was and
where I was, I ran out. I was terrified of being discovered listening in. I didn't even know who was in there
with her."

"It couldn't have been me," Mindy said quickly.

"No, it wasn't Mindy because she wasn't here yet. I
didn't tell her anything about Posy for a while after she
had arrived."

"Almost a month after," Mindy moaned.

"I'm not exactly used to trusting people," Gia said.

"Wow," Robin said. "Imagine, putting your own
daughter through all this."

"Your mother is putting you through it, isn't she?"
Gia fired at her. She could be so mean and angry some-

times. It made me feel that if I brushed against her, she might explode and blow me up with her.

Robin was about to snap back at her, but hesitated, thought a moment, then relaxed her shoulders. "Yes, she is. Mother darling is doing exactly that."

"Well, then it shouldn't surprise you. It shouldn't surprise any of us. Dr. Foreman believes in everything she does to us. She has this grand plan, this collection of theories. Every one of us is another case study for her. I once glimpsed at some papers on her desk and saw it."

"Saw what?" I asked.

"She's writing about each of us all the time. We'll be collected in some book and she'll probably win some prize. And all at our expense!"

"Tell us more about Posy," I said, folding my legs and squatting on the floor like a little girl who had asked to be told a story.

"I didn't get to know her all that well. Like Mindy says, she was always lying to me anyway. She was here a little over a month or so. One day she arrived with Dr. Foreman when she returned from one of her periodic trips away from the ranch. I came in from work and found her sitting right there." Gia nodded at my bunk.

"She smiled at me and said, 'Hi, my name's Posy. Don't call me anything else, please.' You would never know she was sent here as any sort of punishment. Nothing bothered her. Everything was interesting to her. I got so I hated hearing the word. *Interesting.* 'Isn't this interesting?' 'Isn't that interesting?' "

"What did she look like?" Teal asked, sitting beside me.

"She wasn't much bigger than I am," Gia said. "I thought she was about twelve, but she swore she was sixteen, dark haired, pretty with soft brown eyes and a dimple in her right cheek. She liked to walk on her toes and said she was once taking ballet lessons."

"Another lie, no doubt," Mindy muttered.

"She swore it was true of course, like her swearing to anything meant anything," Gia said, "but I had no other way to determine anything about her, not even her age."

"Didn't you ask her why she was here? What she had done?" Robin asked.

"No."

"No?"

"I didn't have to ask. She told me right away. She said she was here because she had trouble following rules. She claimed she just forgot all the time. She made it sound so innocent."

"What rules?" I asked.

"Any rules. She said she just forgot and didn't mean to hurt anyone's feelings. She proved that by ignoring the rules here. She talked without permission when she first arrived and it did them no good to scream at her or punish her.

"She just looked at them with that same sweet smile on her face, making the buddies feel like they were the ones who were to be pitied.

"She never blamed anyone for anything no matter how cruel they were to her, including her monster of a mother."

"Did you try to get her to stop thinking like that?" Teal asked.

"Of course. I tried to get her to see how stupid she was being by forgiving them or understanding them or calling them interesting. She would just say, 'They can't help it. They just like me so much they can't help trying to help me.' For three days they wouldn't let her

eat anything, and all she could say about that was she
was a little too heavy anyway."

"It doesn't sound like she belonged here," I said.
"Sounds like she belonged in some mental institution."

"Don't we all," Mindy muttered.

Everyone was silent, contemplating what she had
said.

"Dr. Foreman believes she can change anyone.
That's the point," Gia finally piped up. "Don't you get it
yet? No behavior, not even mental illness, can't be
changed or cured. She thinks we're all Skinner
pigeons."

"Skinner pigeons? What's that?" Robin asked.

I looked at Teal to see if she knew. She shook her
head and shrugged. "I wasn't exactly a good student,"
she said. "What is it, Gia?"

"Didn't anyone tell you guys anything about this
place and Dr. Foreman before you were sent here?" she
asked.

"Not much more than this is your last chance," Teal
said, smirking.

"Same for me," I said.

"Me, too," Robin chimed.

"Dr. Foreman is a behavioral modification scientist.
They believe they can change the way people act and
think by using certain techniques like carrot and stick,
positive and negative reinforcers. Do this and there's a
reward; do that and there's a punishment. If it's
repeated and repeated, it gets so carved into you, you
behave accordingly."

"But why did you call us all Skinner pigeons?" I
asked.

"This scientist, Skinner, is famous for getting people
to believe in these things. He did it with pigeons in a

box. If they pressed a lever, they got fed. They soon understood that if they did this, they were rewarded. If they didn't, they weren't. That's what Dr. Foreman means by her stupid reality checks. We get rewarded for doing what she wants us to do, and when we do something she doesn't . . . we suffer. That's reality. That's the way it is out there," Gia said, waving toward the door.

"Dr. Foreman," she concluded, "believes those theories apply to everything. She can change anyone. We're not here just to be good little girls. Just like she said the first day, we're here to be changed, completely and utterly remade."

"Posy had to be very frustrating for her," Robin said. "Here she was a so-called expert on all this and her own daughter was a problem."

"Exactly," Gia said. "She has success with strangers, like our buddies and like us. Her methods do work most of the time. You're not going to get into any fights so quickly now, are you, Robin? You don't want to go back to the Ice Room."

Robin looked at me and then looked down.

"And you, Teal. You going to run away again?" Gia taunted.

"Maybe."

"You won't. Anyway, the difference with Posy was no matter what they did to her, what negative reinforcement they applied, she smiled at them. And then she would go and make up a story about it like she had to clean the pigpen all by herself because we were too busy or she was good at it. They would just get angrier and angrier at her. She never let them make her face reality. You know she never had a mattress, pillow, and blanket the whole time she was here."

"How could she stand that so long?" Teal asked.

Gia shrugged. I began to wonder if she didn't admire Posy as much as she pitied her.

"She told me she was used to sleeping on hard surfaces. She liked to go camping, and mattresses and sheets and pillows made her itch and sneeze. I actually believed her for a while. She was really good at it, at telling tales. I can just imagine the stories she had people believing. It must have driven our Dr. Foreman bonkers.

"But . . . Natani liked her," Gia said wistfully. "He favored her, talked to her all the time, taught her stuff, like how to meditate and step out of pain. That's the way she put it. I know the good doctor wasn't happy about that and eventually told him to stay away from her."

"Why does he obey her, work for her?" Teal asked.

"His granddaughter was a drug addict. She managed to get her on the straight and narrow. At least, that's what I think," Gia said.

"It's true. He told me something similar," I said, "just not in as much detail."

"Whatever. He must owe her big time to put up with all this," Robin said.

"He doesn't see it that way," I told her.

"Then he really is a crazy Indian," Teal quipped.

"Well, how did Posy end up? I mean, why don't you know what happened to her?" I asked Gia.

"No one would talk about her. I quickly saw it was forbidden to mention her name. One morning she was just gone, and when she didn't return for days, I knew she was gone for good. At first I assumed she was sent home or somewhere else."

"So, then that's what happened," I said, shrugging. "What's the big mystery?" From the way Mindy and

Gia glanced at each other, I saw they had other ideas. "What?"

"I'm sure I saw her from time to time, but only at night," Gia said.

"And then you stopped seeing her altogether, right, Gia?" Mindy said.

"You never saw her at night or otherwise?" Robin asked Mindy.

"Never."

"So, then she is gone," I concluded. They didn't look convinced. "Is there something else?"

"The one thing I think Posy needed more than anything was company, friends. She tried so hard to get us to be her friends. I could tell she was making up story after story about all the best friends she had. She often contradicted herself or forgot a name or a story," Gia explained.

"So?"

"So Gia thinks Dr. Foreman decided her best way to change her was to isolate her from people. She hated being alone most of all," Mindy said.

"So much so that she invented people to talk to, just like a little girl or little boy might."

"I often heard her talking to someone, and then if I asked her who she was talking to, she would say no one, but she would smile at the air as if someone invisible to me was standing there. It was weird, eerie. Sometimes, I got so I thought I saw someone standing there myself," Gia explained.

"Maybe you're just as crazy as she is," Robin told her.

Gia shrugged. "Maybe I am."

"So if Dr. Foreman wanted to keep her away from people, what did she do?" I asked.

"It's just a guess. We have no real proof of anything and we would never say it loud enough for anyone to hear it," Gia offered.

No one spoke for fear she would stop.

"That door I told you about? The one going down to the basement?"

"Yes?" I said.

"It has a lock on it now."

"Maybe she just didn't want you sneaking down there anymore," I said quickly.

"I thought that was it, too." Gia eyed Mindy. "Especially after she seemed to know I had been there."

"I never said anything!" Mindy exclaimed. Gia shot her a skeptical look. "I didn't. I swear!"

"Well, what changed your mind?" Teal asked her, ignoring Mindy.

"Occasionally, I've heard crying, coming from the basement," Gia said. "Mindy thinks she has as well, right, Mindy?"

"Well, I wasn't exactly sure about that," Mindy said cautiously.

"What are y'all saying?" Robin asked, looking like her heart had stopped. "Dr. Foreman is keeping her daughter in the basement, like a prisoner in solitary confinement?"

"Maybe," Gia said.

"To this day?" I asked.

"What are we if not prisoners? But don't ever say it or suggest it in front of one of the buddies. Actually, never mention this again ever."

"How long has it been since you stopped seeing her, even at night?" I questioned.

"About a week or so before Mindy arrived," Gia said. "That's about four months, right?"

Mindy nodded.

I turned to Robin. "Locked in a basement to be kept away from people for more than four months? That would be worse than the Ice Room, wouldn't it?"

"No," Robin said.

"Why not?"

She stared at me.

"Because you're not put into the Ice Room," Gia answered for her. "The Ice Room is put into you."

"Put into you?" I looked at Robin. She was nodding. "I don't understand."

"Leave it that way, Phoebe. Sometimes, it's good here to not understand. You're better off," Robin said.

But I was a moth drawn to fire. I couldn't stop thinking about it.

Like some fatalist who knew she was headed for disaster no matter what road she took, I had no doubt in my mind that I would understand what they meant someday.

"Since Natani favored her, maybe he knows something. Have you ever asked him?" I inquired.

Gia raised her eyebrows. "Have you ever asked Natani a question about anything yet?"

"Yes."

"So you know how he answers. He doesn't give straight answers. Instead, he tells you some Indian folk tale about animals and you're supposed to get the point."

"Maybe that's his way to avoid reality," Mindy suggested.

"Or maybe it's his way not to," I said.

No one spoke again for a long moment.

"Let's do our homework. At least it's something to do and it keeps her from blaming us for something else," Gia said in a tired voice.

Everyone returned to the books and we were soon working together, each of us every once in a while pausing to think about that locked basement door. I know that's what was on their minds. It was on mine and I could see the fear, like some sheet of thin ice sliding over their eyes.

Of all the things they told us about Posy, the story about her inventing friends and speaking to invisible people lingered in my mind more than anything else for some reason. In the working silence, our subdued voices, the turning of pages, I could imagine a sweet, petite girl like Posy sitting beside us, cheering us up with her unyielding smile, her vision of everything through rose-colored glasses, and her stories, her fantasies. Who cared if they were true or not? They gave us all hope and made us feel better about ourselves.

Then she was plucked from our midst, stolen away because she helped us resist. Even though we had never met her, hearing about her like this put her into all our minds. I could sense it, and despite Gia's and Mindy's attempts to forget her, she was still here with them as well. In the end, hearing about her, listening to Gia's obvious affection for her and fear about what might have happened or be happening to her, appeared to mend the rift among us. Just a little while ago, we were at each other's throat in that room with Dr. Foreman. Now we sensed that we really didn't have anyone else but each other. Posy, even without Robin, Teal, and me ever having met her, gave us that, I thought. It was truly as if an invisible person stood with us, comforted us.

After we completed our work, we were permitted some free time before dinner. M'Lady Two took our homework and test papers and in a threatening tone told us she was taking it all to Dr. Foreman, who would grade everything herself. Failure, we were to remember, meant demerits. No one said anything, but I could hear the same thoughts in a chorus. Piling threat after threat on us, waving fingers and sentencing us repeatedly to hard labor, lost its impact when it was done so often and so much. What's new? I thought, and so did the others. M'Lady Two must have remembered herself at our stage. I could see it in the disappointment she expressed in her smirk when we didn't look like we were shaking in our shoes.

"Don't go anywhere you're not supposed to go," she warned, and left.

Where could we go? I thought. There were some shady places, and the breeze this late afternoon didn't feel as if it had been born in a furnace. Mindy, Gia, and Teal sat on what little grass there was under a tree. Robin and I went to look at the horses. We were told that it wouldn't be long before we would be brushing them down, cleaning their stalls, and feeding them, too. One of them, which Robin identified as a dark brown stallion, looked like he was dreaming of jumping the corral and galloping off toward those mountains in the distance.

"We had two horses on my grandfather's farm," Robin said. "He called them Buck and Babe. They weren't really riding horses, but when I was little, he would put me on either one and, holding the reins, lead me about. It was practically the only fun I had on that farm and one of the few times he acted like a real grandfather instead of a soldier in the army of God or something. I remember that sometimes I would catch him looking at me as if he expected to see Satan's face emerging out of mine. He expected me to do bad things. After all, I was mother darling's daughter. I guess he's happy now that he was right. It probably has made him even more of a fanatic. I pity my grandmother."

"What would happen if we got on the backs of some horses and rode out of here? You think we could ride to somewhere?"

"Horses aren't camels," Robin said. "They need water, too, and we wouldn't know which way to go."

"We're so damn trapped," I muttered. "Maybe no better off than Posy if she is in that basement." I glanced at the hacienda. The very thought of being a prisoner in the darkness below for so long put a chill through me, even in this heat.

Natani emerged from the barn, saw us, but kept walking toward a water trough. Using a hose, he filled it. I glanced at Robin and then approached him.

"Hello, Natani," I said. He nodded. "I bet you have seen many girls like us come and go."

He nodded again, turned off the water, and began to wrap the hose neatly around its holder.

"Are there any other girls here now?" I asked, eyeing Robin. "Besides the five of us, I mean?"

He didn't answer. He tightened the faucet, then stood and looked out at the horses, who had lifted their heads and started toward the water trough.

"I see only what I see. You must see only what you see, too," he finally replied, and went back into the barn.

"What's that mean? I see only what I see?" Robin asked.

"I think he's afraid to say anything," I said, nodding. I looked back at the house. "I don't know about you, but I'd like to find out if she's locked up down there."

"What for?" Robin folded her arms under her breasts. "What could we do about it anyway? We can't do anything for ourselves, much less for someone else. Forget about it. That's what he meant when he said see only what you see. Don't go looking for things you can't see. He didn't live as long as he's lived poking his nose into someone else's business." She started away to join the other girls.

I watched the horses drinking a moment, then followed Robin. Gia looked up when I sat. I could see Robin had told her I had spoken to Natani.

"You're not playing with fire," Gia said. "You're playing with TNT and I'm telling you now, we're not going to get blown up with you."

"Oh, let's stop talking about her. Let's just relax," Teal said.

It was difficult to let ourselves relax. I could see everyone had nerves as taut as tight guitar strings. The breeze, playing through us, sounded the same high-pitched note. Gia lay with her eyes closed. Teal stared at the horizon, dreaming of floating out there, I'm sure. Robin had her head down, and Mindy played with blades of grass like a little girl, forming shapes. No one spoke. A door slammed and we all looked toward the house. The three buddies laughed at something, then got into the van and started away.

"Where are they going?" I asked.

"Wherever it is," Teal said with some excitement seeping into her voice, "it's close enough for them to get there and back quickly enough. I knew there was someplace. I knew I wasn't imagining those lights."

"Forget it," Gia said.

"Why?" Teal asked.

"It's nothing. It's an Indian trading post off the reservation. They can get magazines, candy, cigarettes, but not much else. There's nothing to do there and it's miles and miles this side of nowhere. This is the Mojave Desert."

"They have more than cigarettes," Mindy said, her lips twisting.

"How do you know?" I asked.

She didn't reply.

"Gia?"

"We know. We heard them talking about it."

I stared at her and she looked away. "How did you hear them talking about it, Gia? Was that something you heard when you were in the basement?"

"No."

"Then how?"

"We just heard."

Mindy laughed and Gia threw her an angry look. She smiled and shook her head.

"What else haven't you told us?" Robin asked.

"Nothing."

"Oh, tell them," Mindy said.

"So now you want me to talk, is that it, Mindy? You're no longer worried about being betrayed?"

"It doesn't matter anymore, Gia. What else can they do to us that they haven't already done?"

"They'll think of something." After a moment Gia turned back to me. "One night, we went spying on them. We went around the rear of the hacienda and climbed up on the lower roof. We could look into their windows. We just wanted to see how well they lived, how nice their bedrooms were compared to our barn."

"And?"

"We saw them partying."

Mindy laughed. "Partying?"

"That's what it was," Gia snapped. "They had some

weed. Probably got it from some Indian or something. They were laughing and enjoying themselves."

"And they had a magazine with pictures of naked men."

"You're kidding!" Teal said, coming to life.

"Does Dr. Foreman know?" Robin asked.

"What do you think?" Gia replied.

"You could tell on them," Teal said quickly. "Or threaten to tell on them."

"Oh, that would be terrific. Get them in trouble and that way they won't be as hard on us," Gia mocked.

"Well, I just thought . . . what do you think, Phoebe?"

"I think I'd like to make friends with them and be invited to their bedrooms," I quipped, and held my serious expression just long enough for them all to think I wasn't kidding. Then Gia laughed and the rest of them joined her.

We were all quiet again.

Teal stared down the gravel road. "I don't care if it only goes to an Indian store. It goes somewhere," she said in a loud whisper.

None of us disagreed. The shadows grew longer as the sun slid down toward the mountain. Everything that lived and spent its time in the daylight here surely gave thanks for the mountains, I thought. Funny, I realized, how I had never once thought to be grateful for anything in nature.

Maybe I was not grateful for anything at all.

Maybe that was why I was here.

8

Confession

In the days that followed, we were given new chores, which included learning how to milk cows. We were then made to do that first thing in the morning instead of working in the garden, after we recited our morning chant, of course. Added to the milking of cows came the caring and feeding of the horses. Once again it was Teal who moaned and groaned the most, complaining about her callused hands, the odors, and the hard work. We were truly exhausted when the sun set, but we knew that didn't mean the end of our responsibilities.

Dr. Foreman had given us all passing grades on our schoolwork, but then she added more and more to our assignments as if she was trying to see how much we could accomplish before crying "Uncle!" A new and more efficient and effective spirit of cooperation had been born among us, however, and Gia was smart. Robin commented that she was actually learning faster under Gia's tutoring and better than she had in regular school and I couldn't disagree. To our buddies' chagrin, we actually enjoyed working together. M'Lady One couldn't resist commenting, "Aren't you all turning into nerdy little goody-goodies."

No one responded. We just kept working. I was afraid this new spirit of cooperation would be torn apart at the next group therapy session, but we didn't have another like that. Instead, Dr. Foreman began what she described as a new and more personal round of analysis and healing. She called us in one at a time, me being the last. When one of the previous four returned, I looked at her and waited in anticipation, hoping to hear something that might help me when I was summoned to see Dr. Foreman.

However, whoever talked with Dr. Foreman returned in a cocoon built out of painful memories or fears and didn't want to speak. Gia was like that for days afterward, as was Mindy. Teal seemed sadder, more defeated, and Robin angrier. It was as if the invisible bonds that had grown among us were cut again. When it came my turn, I was truly frightened. What powers did she have? What would she do to me?

The afternoon of my appointment, Natani was showing me how to groom a horse he called Wind Song. A quarter horse, he had a short back, muscular chest, and muscular hindquarters. The other girls weren't as interested as I was in horses, and I could see Natani liked that I was. The only time I had ever been close to a real horse before was when I had watched a parade in Atlanta.

Natani was demonstrating how to use the hoof pick and telling me why it was important to remove the buildup of dirt and debris. Longtime exposure to bacteria could cause infections, he said, and stones could eventually cause bruising.

Wind Song was patient and cooperative as though the horse understood what Natani was telling me and doing. When I commented about that, he nodded and said, "He does understand. Not words, but actions. That's how animals speak to each other and how we speak to them, by what we do, not by what we say."

"There can be no lies between us then," I muttered.

He smiled at me. "Yes, daughter of the sun, yes."

I was afraid when he handed me the pick, but soon I was doing it and Wind Song was just as calm as he was when Natani worked on him. Before I could finish, M'Lady One was at the door of the horse barn.

"Dr. Foreman wants you," she said. "Now!"

"Can't I finish this first?"

"No. It's time for your therapy."

Wind Song turned toward her as if he could feel my nervousness. He bared his teeth, snorted, and shook his head. Natani looked at me hard, but I'm sure it wasn't difficult to see the anxiety in my eyes.

"In here," he said, holding his hand over his heart, "is your hogan. No one can come in there unless you say yes."

"Move it, girl," M'Lady One shouted.

I handed the pick back to Natani and started out.

"He's a crazy old loon," M'Lady One muttered as we walked toward the house. "All that peyote has gone to his head and turned his brain into mashed potatoes. I don't know why Dr. Foreman keeps him here."

"Why are you here? Why do you want to do this rather than be out there with people, having fun, getting on with your life?" I dared ask her.

"Why am I here? It's the least I can do for Dr. Fore-

man. She's done so much for me. If you don't appreciate her yet, it's because you haven't improved enough.
But don't worry," she said, smiling, "you will. She has
never failed yet with one of her wards."

"Never?"

"Never. It's just a matter of time. Longer for some
than others maybe, but just a matter of time, so don't
think you're anything special."

"You're improved?" I fired back at her. The smile
flew off her face like a frightened bird lifting off a
branch.

"Yes, I am." Her eyes were small and cold. "If you
think I'm mean now, just imagine what I was and what
I can be again if I have to be."

"If that's true," I said, pausing to take off my shoes,
"then you've really not changed, have you?"

"Oh, you're so arrogant and smug. You're lucky
you're going in there to therapy or I'd have you digging
in the cesspool for that remark."

"Is that what you had to do?"

I thought she would get angrier, maybe even come at
me, but instead, she smiled. "Worse. Which is what you
can look forward to, Phoebe bird. Now get in there, and
if you're smart, which you're probably not, you'll keep
your wisecracks to yourself and be very, very cooperative."

Holding that cold smile on her lips, she watched me
go into the house.

"Go into the office, Phoebe," Dr. Foreman called
from the dining room. She was speaking with the cook.

I entered the office, but I didn't sit. Curious about
what Gia had told us Dr. Foreman was doing with our
case studies, I looked at some of the papers on her desk.
That was a mistake, but not because she came in behind

me and caught me doing it. It was a mistake because of what I saw.

It was a letter faxed to my uncle Buster and aunt Mae Louise. The letter was from the doctor at the clinic where Mama was being treated.

It began with the words, *I'm sorry to inform you . . .*

I should have stopped reading. I should have backed away from the desk and pretended I had not seen the fax, but I didn't. I drew closer and picked it up and read . . . *that Mrs. Elder passed away last night. We believe her last visitor brought her some bad crack cocaine, not that there is any good crack cocaine, and it had a dramatic and fatal effect on her heart. We have turned the information over to the police. Please accept our condolences and contact us concerning Mrs. Elder's remains as soon as possible.*

The letter seemed to float out of my fingers. It struck the edge of the desk and fell to the floor.

"Pick that up immediately," I heard Dr. Foreman say. She was standing behind me in the doorway.

I looked at her, then did what she said.

"Who do you think you are searching through papers on my desk?" she asked as she entered.

"I didn't search through papers. I just saw . . ." I glanced at the paper again. I had a right to look at this anyway, I thought. This is about my mother, I told myself, and then it hit me harder, sharper, like a slap across my face. My father is gone and my mother is dead now, too. Even though Dr. Foreman hovered just behind me, I had to read it again to be sure I hadn't imagined it. Remains? It made it sound like leftovers. Send a doggie bag for what was left of Mrs. Elder.

"Put that down and sit," she commanded. I didn't move. "Sit!" she shouted, pointing at the chair. "Right now."

I put the letter on the desk, went to the hardwood chair she had facing her desk, and sat. She sat behind her desk and looked down at the letter from the clinic. She seemed to be reading it for the first time.

"I was going to tell you about this myself, break it to you in a far more charitable and considerate fashion when I thought you were ready," she said, her voice a little softer.

I wondered if she was telling the truth. The paper had been at the center of her desk and turned so that anyone approaching from the doorway would see it immediately. According to the date on the letter, it had been sent out almost a week ago. How long had she had it? Did she get it the same day my aunt and uncle had? Why hadn't she told me immediately? Was she worried about what the news would do to me? Was she worried it would interfere with her efforts to change me? At the moment I was more curious about that than I was angry.

"How does this information make you feel?" she asked, and sat forward as if any syllable I uttered would be earth-shattering in importance.

I shrugged and looked away. Why did she always keep the window curtains closed in this office? Was she afraid we would find something far more interesting to look at out there? My eyes drifted to the floor. Where was that grate Gia had described? Was anyone listening in on this conversation? Was Posy down there? I heard nothing, not a peep.

"When you've been apart from someone like you have been apart from your mother, news like this"—she held the paper up—"doesn't seem real. Long-distance death loses its impact. You have to be close up, right there sometimes, to believe it at all.

"But despite the face you're trying to put on, I can

see you believe it, Phoebe. Holding it all bottled up inside you won't help and it doesn't make you stronger. It eats at you from within. If anything, it makes you weaker. I'm always telling my clients that, because it's one of the truest things about human nature, you know. Shutting your emotions up, never expressing your feelings, just causes it all to fester and sour, and that ugly degeneration comes out in how they look, how they think, and what they do. It's poison. It's truly as if you were poisoning your own blood."

She sat back, relaxed. "What was the nicest thing, the happiest thing, you remember about your mother?"

"I don't remember anything nice or happy."

"Sure you do. You're just afraid to recall it now, afraid to mention it because that will make you feel sad, and believe me, Phoebe, you're afraid of being sad, afraid of it more than any of the other girls here," she assured me with a wave of her hand toward the door. I said nothing, just stared at the floor. My head felt as if it were full of angry bees.

She rose and walked slowly to the front of her desk, then leaned back against it.

"Think back," she coaxed. "Surely you have good memories of when you were just a little girl. Think, remember. I want you to try, Phoebe."

"Why? Why do you want me to do that?"

"I want you to feel, to see and understand the most basic human needs in you."

"You're right. I don't want to be afraid and I don't want to be sad. Okay? You're right." Hot tears bubbled under my lower eyelids. "Satisfied?"

"I'm not worried about being right, Phoebe," she said slowly, and smiled. "I have nothing to prove."

I raised my eyebrows skeptically at that and I could

see she didn't like it. She stopped smiling, stepped away from the desk, and stood as firmly as a steel pole, her eyes sharp, angry, bearing down on me.

"I'm already a success at what I do. I have the respect of my peers. I have been awarded many honors, and courts, judges, counselors, and other psychiatrists have given me the trust and the responsibility to reshape and save girls like you, so this is not about ego."

"What's it about then?"

"Right now? It's about you. Do you realize"—she reached back for the letter from the clinic—"that you are really all alone in the world now?"

I tightened the embrace of myself and looked at the closed window curtains.

"Oh, I know you have an uncle and aunt, but I also know you're not fond of them and you do not believe they are very fond of you. You believe they would rather you disappeared. Am I right?"

I didn't answer.

"I said, am I right? Wasn't that in the autobiography you wrote for me on orientation day? Well?"

"Yes."

She nodded, satisfied. "You were correct in your analysis of them. They haven't even called to see how you reacted to the news. I've heard nothing," she said with such vehemence, I thought she was enjoying the pain her words imposed on me. They were like whiplashes, slicing and stinging my weakened wall of protection.

"In this world," she continued, returning to that teacher voice of hers, "someone without any family, without any friends, loses any sense of herself and any reason to go on and do anything with her life. Like it or not, this is your new home, Phoebe," she said, holding her arms out widely apart.

"We are your new family. I want you to believe that and I want you to trust me, trust that I have your best interests at heart, no matter how hard and severe I might seem to be. We have demons to drive out of you, important changes to make. Just like a surgeon has to cut out a cancer, I have to cut all that out of you. Oh, not with a knife, a scalpel, of course, but with every available technique at my disposal. All I ask is you cooperate and try to help yourself.

"Is that asking for too much?" she followed in a tone so reasonable, all I could do was shake my head.

"Good. I think you're different from the others, Phoebe, and I don't mean the color of your skin or your background or anything like that. I think you have potential. There's more to you and a lot more to save."

She stood there looking at me. I kept my eyes directed at the floor, then I sniffed back my tears and closed my eyes and took a deep breath.

Of course she was right about what I was feeling and what I was desperate to avoid. Good memories, happy memories, of Mama were trying to rush in and I was holding the door closed, but I could hear Mama's laughter, catch a glimpse of her in the mirror as she fixed my hair or talked to me about how to make up my eyes like hers. The images were leaking in under the door. These memories weren't memories of the woman I had seen at the clinic after I had run away from my uncle and aunt. These were memories of my mama of long ago when I was still young enough to forgive her for her weaknesses and her failures, when I was still young enough to believe things would be better for us all.

"You want to cry, Phoebe. I can see it. Go on. Have a good cry. There's no shame in that."

I wiped away a fugitive tear quickly and shook my head. She approached me and touched my shoulder. I looked up at her. Should I trust her with my tears? I wondered. Was she sincere? So many cruel things were done to us here. Was she right in doing them? Did we need that? Was it the only thing that would change a girl like Robin or like Teal, Mindy, and Gia? Or me? What terrible thing had Mindy done with a baby? And Gia, I was sure, setting fire to her own home, among other things, surely made her a lost cause out there. Suddenly, I began to wonder if Dr. Foreman wasn't the last and best hope for girls like us after all.

"Poor Phoebe. You didn't deserve the life you had. You don't have evil in your heart. You never really intended to hurt anyone, did you?"

"No."

"Of course not. All sorts of events, social and psychological experiences, have put you in a place you don't want to be in."

"What's going to happen to me?" I asked, flicking off another errant tear.

She smiled. "You're going to get out of that terribly dark place. You're going to grow and improve and become one of my girls, a Foreman girl, proud and strong and capable."

She returned to her chair behind her desk, folded the letter, and inserted it into an envelope. I watched her put it into a drawer.

"The funeral was yesterday," she said.

"Yesterday?"

"Yes, I wish I could have sent you back for that, but it wasn't possible. Your uncle and aunt understood. I finally decided to call them. Actually, they weren't at all disappointed about your not attending the services," she added dryly, sounding like she was on my side against them. "That's why I said what I said before, but none of that is important now. Forget about them. Someday when you're more confident of yourself, when you're better, you'll visit the cemetery and you'll be strong enough to bury all the ugly and nasty feelings right there alongside your mother's coffin."

She smiled as though that was a wonderful dream, a dream I should pursue.

"Now, let's make good use of this session and talk about other things, okay?"

I nodded and sucked back the remaining tears.

"Good." She folded her hands and leaned forward. "When you were all here in group therapy, I was somewhat amused to hear Mindy being accused of being my spy. The truth is I don't find Mindy making much progress. I would never solicit her help for anything just yet. Actually, Phoebe, I expect her to be here long after you leave."

"Really?"

"I'm afraid so. She's a very, very troubled girl. She tries to convince me she's better. She even tries to be my little spy and tells me about the others, about you. I know she's simply attempting to ingratiate herself with me, win my favor. She's very transparent, albeit a very sneaky person, our Mindy. I bet you have no idea that she told me about Teal's intention to run off before you told me, do you?"

I shook my head.

"She heard her talking about it and she told me. When I asked you about Teal, I wanted to see if you were capable of being honest. You were and you are

and you're going to do well here. So," she said, sitting
back, "I've decided to make you my confidant."

"What do you mean?"

"I mean you're going to be special to me, Phoebe.
Would you like that?"

I was afraid to say no, so I nodded.

"I thought you might, but if I am to trust you more
and more, you have to trust me more and more. That's
understandable and fair, isn't it?"

"I guess so."

How unexpected all this was, I thought. I had come
trembling into this office, expecting her to do something
more to me, something that would send me out of here all
bottled up and wounded inside just like the others. I half
expected to end up in one of those Skinner boxes Gia had
described, but here she was making me feel special.

"What did Mindy do before? I mean, why is she
here?" I dared ask. I was anticipating the usual sort of
response to this. It was none of my business. I should be
concerned only with my own problems, but again, she
surprised me.

"She gave birth to a baby and left it in the rear seat of
a broken-down vehicle. A passerby luckily heard the
infant's wail and brought the police. Someone had seen
her go into the vehicle and she was arrested. It wasn't
her first experience with police and courts."

"What about her parents? Didn't they know she was
pregnant and wonder about the baby?"

"I am always amazed at how much parents do not
know about their own children, Phoebe. What about
your mother? Did she know much about you, what you
were doing?"

"No. She wasn't around enough to ask or care, and
my daddy was on the road too much."

"And even if they were there more, would they know everything?" she asked, tilting her head a bit.

"No."

"Exactly."

Her small smile grew softer. Then she stopped smiling and sat firmly again.

"What do you think of Gia?" she asked in a sharper tone. "She troubles me. She's very smart, I know, but I'm afraid I'm not really making enough progress with her."

"I don't know." I didn't. I had no idea how to look for progress here or even what she meant by it.

"She's still very volatile," Dr. Foreman continued as if she and I were two psychiatrists conferring about one of our patients. "Without warning, she can become a very violent person. I bet you've sensed that, haven't you, Phoebe? You come from a world full of violence. It's not a stranger to you."

"No. It isn't."

She nodded, happy at my answers, I could see.

"Gia's parents are better off financially than yours were, but they were just as much into themselves. Besides, Gia has always been good at fooling people, lying. She's one of the best I've seen, actually. And very clever. She did something no one else I've treated for similar problems ever did."

"What?" I could see she wanted me to ask, and for some reason, that set off alarm bells inside me.

"She made up a person and blamed everything she could on her. She was so good about it that many people believed the person actually existed. At one point," she said, almost laughing, "the police were looking for Gia's imaginary person, sent out one of those all-points bulletins."

She paused and looked even more serious and concerned. "I have come to the conclusion she herself now believes this person exists. I'm working very hard at curing that, and I am going to need your help with it from time to time."

"Made up a person?"

"Yes," she said, smiling. "With amazing details, too. Clever in a way, isn't it? But she is very smart, our Gia. I know from our last talk here with everyone that Mindy has mentioned Gia's imaginary person to you and the others, and I'm sure Gia's spoken about her as well since. I just don't know how much she has said and if she continues to talk about her since the group therapy session."

"About who?" I asked, my heart now pounding and reverberating through my bones like the beat of a steel drum.

Dr. Foreman smiled. "You know, Phoebe. Posy."

I tried to swallow, but a lump in my throat felt like a small rock.

"Well?" she asked.

"Well, what?"

"Is she talking about her? What did she tell you about her?" she demanded.

I shook my head. "Nothing. I mean, nothing much."

She held me in her eyes so firmly, I thought I couldn't turn my head to the right or to the left. I couldn't even lower my gaze to the floor again.

"Haven't you heard anything I've said here today, Phoebe? Didn't you hear about all the responsibility and trust I have decided to place in you? Are you going to disappoint me now, now that I have determined you are worth all my effort and energy? Are you going to have me throw you back into the water as if you were some sick fish? Well?" she said, raising her voice and widening her eyes with fury.

I was frightened. I was very frightened, but I was more terrified of telling her that Gia claimed Posy was her daughter, and not only that, that her daughter might be locked up in the basement right below us. What would she do to Gia and then to the others and what would they think of me?

In the back of my mind a little voice whispered, "What if Gia was the one telling the truth?"

I gathered all my ability to slip away, an ability I had employed many times before to escape from the chains and shackles adults in authority could throw over me. Too often in my life, I'd found myself having to avoid punishments and blame. The trick was never showing I was afraid and guilty. I would go on the offense and usually that worked.

But Dr. Foreman was the expert in all this. I had no doubt she had dealt with girls as good at it as I was, if not better. Still, I chose that route.

"I don't listen to their garbage talk," I said with as much anger as I could muster. "Sure, I heard her mention someone named Posy, but it wasn't anything I cared to hear about. I have my own troubles."

She didn't change expression. She continued to hold that gaze, fix those eyes on me. I tried not to blink, not to look shifty, but she didn't nod or smile or in any way look satisfied.

"You're making a big mistake here today, Phoebe. It will bring you even more pain than this," she said, opening the drawer, taking out the envelope that contained the letter about Mama and snapping it in the air. "You'll be out there alone. The other girls won't help you. You should hear the bad things they say about you,

Gia, especially. I know she's lying, they're all lying about you, but it doesn't matter. None of them would be friends with you on the outside anyway, would they? You'll go back to your world and they'll return to theirs, right? Why protect anyone but yourself now?

"Besides, if you care about them, if you have some sensitivity and conscience about it, then assure yourself this is the best way to help them. Just like you tried to help Teal."

"But you let her run off anyway," I said as sharply as I could.

"Of course, I did. So she would learn something, but thanks to you, she was under surveillance the entire time and luckily, too. After she was stung, she might have wandered into worse places because she can't tolerate pain. She has a very low boiling point, being spoiled so much. No, you did a good thing then. You did save her life. Do a good thing now.

"Tell me exactly, in as much detail as you can, what Gia said about Posy."

She leaned forward expectantly.

"She didn't tell me anything specifically. She was talking to everyone."

"That's what I mean, Phoebe," she snapped, her eyes flickering with heat and ill temper. "Don't play with words with me. We're not in court. Well?"

"I just heard her say something about a girl who was here before."

"Are you going to have me pull every word out of you? What did she say about the girl?"

"That she was a liar," I said. "Made up stories."

"And?"

"That was it. Now she's gone. I didn't think it was anything to talk about."

She snapped back as if her body were wrapped in rubber bands attached to the chair.

"I was mistaken about you, Phoebe. You're not ready for what I want to do for you. You need more time." She put on that cold smile again. "That's all right. Time is something we have at our disposal here. I'm going to give you time to think about today. Perhaps you'll come back to me on your own, perhaps not. It doesn't matter. In the end, Phoebe, you will return.

"You're free to resume your chores." She waved her hand at the door.

I rose quickly.

"Wait," she said when I reached the door.

I turned and saw her open the desk drawer.

"Take this with you. It's all she left you, apparently, the news of her unnecessary death."

"I don't want it."

It was as if I had refused a valuable gift, insulted her, and disrespected her ancestors all at once. She whipped her head back, tore the envelope in two and threw it in the black metal wastebasket beside her desk.

"Consider that your attendance at your mother's funeral," she said, and turned her back on me.

It was as if my feet were turning to balloons. I walked out, but it seemed more like I floated along. M'Lady One wasn't there waiting. No one was there. My heart was still thumping as I sat and put on my clodhopper shoes. Almost the second I put on my left shoe, I felt it, and it was like no pain I had ever felt before. I screamed and threw off the shoe.

The pink insect with its back end curled up fell out, partly crushed. I looked up in a panic. My foot seemed to be swelling up right before my eyes.

"Help!" I screamed. Where was everyone?

M'Lady One appeared in the doorway. She had to have been standing right there all the while, I thought.

"What seems to be the trouble?" she asked sweetly and calmly despite my cry.

"I've been bitten by that!" I cried, pointing to the dying insect.

M'Lady One came down the steps casually and looked at the insect. "What'dya know about that, you've been stung by a scorpion, too."

"A scorpion?"

"Big deal. Put your shoe on and get back to work."

"But shouldn't I be given some medicine?"

"No. Now get moving or I'll assign you that cesspool digging instead of permitting you to return to the horses."

I looked in the shoe and shook it out and did the same with the other. The pain started to increase in my foot. It was traveling up my ankle. I felt it rising in wave after wave, the tide of it already reaching into my stomach.

"It hurts a lot!" I moaned when I stood up.

"You'll get over it. You're tough, a girl of the streets with a big mouth. What's a mere scorpion sting to you?"

"I want to see Dr. Foreman."

"I'm warning you to get moving and get moving now."

"She should know what happened to me."

I started for the stairway and she blocked me. M'Lady Three appeared in the doorway, a bottle of Coke in her hands. She sipped from it, her cheeks going in and out as she sucked on the bottle. Then she stepped down.

"What's going on?"

"She's refusing to return to her work detail," M'Lady One said.

"I was stung by a scorpion. There it is." I pointed to the ground.

M'Lady Three continued down the steps, picked up the dead scorpion, put it in her pocket, and turned back to me. "Refusing to return to her work detail after you told her to do it?"

"Yes."

"That's insubordination."

"I'm not trying to be insubordinate. I want to see Dr. Foreman. I've been stung I tell you! My foot is on fire."

M'Lady Three put the bottle of Coke down on the ground and stepped beside M'Lady One. They were like a wall now between me and the steps to the house.

"Start walking," M'Lady One said, pointing to my right.

"I can't walk. It hurts too much," I cried.

"Stop your whining. No one cares about your little pain. You're insubordinate. That's a ten-point demerit. You're not going back to your soft chores. You're going to the Ice Room."

"*No!*" I screamed.

Dr. Foreman finally appeared in the doorway. "What's going on, girls?"

"Phoebe refuses to return to her work detail," M'Lady One said.

"I was stung by a scorpion. It was in my shoe." I looked at M'Lady One. "I bet she put it there."

Dr. Foreman didn't move. "Where is it?"

"She put it in her pocket." I pointed to M'Lady Three.

"Is that true?"

"Of course not, Dr. Foreman."

"Make her empty her pocket," I cried.

"We don't lie to each other here," Dr. Foreman said. "My girls and I have an unbreakable chain of trust among us. If she says it's not in her pocket, it's not."

"But . . . it is. Wait, look at my foot." I took off the shoe and my stocking. Then I lifted my foot so she could clearly see the swelling.

"I don't see anything unusual," she said dryly.

"What?"

"I'm like you, Phoebe. I see and I hear what I want. Insubordination means a session in the Ice Room. M'ladies, do your duty."

"Yes, Dr. Foreman," M'Lady One said.

Dr. Foreman glared at me a moment. I was frozen, my foot still dangling before her. She turned and went back into the house.

"Get the shoe back on and move," M'Lady Three ordered.

I shook my head.

M'Lady Two came walking across the yard. "Trouble?"

"Not much. Phoebe here was insubordinate and is to be spending a session in the Ice Room. She's continuing to be insubordinate, which means that session will be longer," M'Lady One explained calmly. She could have been reporting the weather.

I turned away. I couldn't run from them, not with the pain in my foot. I was unable to put any weight on it, and where would I run to?

"You know what one of these is?" M'Lady Two asked, bringing a small, black metal thing out of her pocket. It looked like a man's electric razor. "It's called a stun gun. Ever see one used?"

I had. Willie Sturges had bought one and as a joke

used it on Dennis Hampton, a fat boy in our tenth-grade class who was always the butt of jokes. I couldn't believe how fast he went down and how he writhed in pain. The sight made me sick and I ran. I really thought Willie had killed him. Afterward, I saw Dennis, still looking stunned, his pants showing where he peed on himself, stumbling along home. Everyone but me thought it was pretty funny.

"Please," I said. "I really did get stung."

"And you're about to be stung again, only this will be far worse," M'Lady Two warned.

"Move," M'Lady Three said, pointing.

"I can't walk," I cried.

"Hop," M'Lady One said. "Now."

They closed in on me. I started to my walk, but merely putting my toe to the ground increased the pain. The tears were streaming down my cheeks. I could feel my shortened breath straining my lungs. My stomach churned.

"I'm getting sick," I moaned.

"Poor little Phoebe bird," M'Lady One chimed, and they all laughed. "What's happening to the tough girl we all knew and loved?"

"Where are we going?" I screamed, or at least I thought I had.

When we rounded the corner, M'Lady Two rushed ahead and opened a door. I hesitated and looked back. Where were the other girls? Where was Natani?

The room inside looked dark. All I could think about was the way Robin had been after she had been put in the Ice Room and the things Gia had said about it, too.

"Listen to me," I pleaded. "I just found out that my mother died. I don't mean to be insubordinate. I'm upset."

M'Lady One pretended she was playing a violin.

"I'm sorry. I'll go back to my work. I promise I won't say anything nasty to any of you."

"It's too late for promises, Phoebe," M'Lady Three said. "Weren't you told that? When you came here, you left all your promises and excuses behind you. You're naked here. It's reality. You are rewarded for good and punished for bad. It's simple and it never changes."

I looked through the door. All I saw from where I was standing was the foot of a bunk. What was the room, just a solitary confinement? I'll get through it, I thought. I'll show them.

The sting was singing louder, however, and the churning that had begun in my stomach turned into nausea. I faltered and M'Lady One came to my side and kept me from falling.

"This is going to be good," she said. "The Ice Room on top of it all. I tell you, Phoebe, I couldn't do it."

"Me neither," M'Lady Two said. "Glad it's you and not me."

"You're all a bunch of wimps," M'Lady Three said. "Phoebe's going to show you up. Aren't you, Phoebe? Girl of the streets, tough."

"I think I'm going to throw up," I said.

"Get her in there before she does. I hate the smell," M'Lady Two said stepping back.

M'Lady One twisted my arm and pushed me through the doorway. There was a bunk, but at the head of it, there was what looked like a helmet with wires attached.

"What is this?"

"We've told you before. It's your worst nightmare," M'Lady One said.

I tried to resist, but her hold was so firm, I thought

her fingers would break through my skin and flesh. She turned me into the room, and together she and M'Lady Three forced me to lie down.

"I'm sick!" I screamed. "I need a doctor, medicine!"

They put the helmet over my head and strapped it on tightly. I resisted but I couldn't keep my arms from being straightened and then a strap was fixed over my chest, just under my breasts. It was just as it had been when I'd woken up in the plane that had brought me to this hell.

A visorlike part of the helmet was lowered over my face. It was dark and their voices grew more muffled because of the earphones over my ears.

"Enjoy," I heard, and heard them leave the room, closing the door behind them. Their voices drifted away and there was only silence.

What was this? A helmet over my head with a visor to keep me in the dark and in the quiet? It was stupid. The coffin was worse, I thought. This isn't so bad except I felt so sick and the pain was still as sharp as ever in my foot. I was getting hot, too, and it wasn't just from the stuffiness in the room. I knew I was developing a fever. The nausea built up until I started to vomit, but I could only turn my head a little to spit to the side. Finally, that stopped, but it left me feeling so tired, so weak.

I'll just sleep, I thought.

I'll beat them. I'll sleep and get better and beat them. This wasn't so terrible.

Ice Room?

There was nothing icy about the Ice Room. It was just as I had suspected, a lot of intimidation, a lot of scary talk and nothing else. Robin just couldn't take being locked up and strapped down and forced to be in darkness. I'm stronger than she is. I can wait it out. I'm stronger than the whole lot of them, even the buddies, I told myself. I am special. Dr. Foreman was right about that.

I'll sleep, I assured myself. I'll sleep and I'll get better. Keep telling yourself that, Phoebe, I chanted. You'll get better. You'll beat them. Think about something good. Think about Wind Song and Natani and the beautiful desert sky and the horizon and tomorrow. Tomorrow, yes, getting out of here, getting away from here. Remember what he said about the hogan. Don't let them into your house. I wouldn't.

I can do this. I can win, I thought.

And then.

It began.

9

Dr. Foreman's Spy

At some point your screaming becomes so high-pitched it seems to be coming from someplace else. It's like someone else is screaming in the distance and you can barely hear it, but that sensation doesn't happen immediately. First, you practically blow out your lungs with the effort and your vocal cords strain and you grow hoarse.

It all began with the sound I heard through the earphones in the strange helmet, an all too familiar squeaky sound that quickly built into a horrific chorus. First, I could hear only one, then another and another until I knew there was a pack of them.

Rats.

I don't know what the helmet and the visor were, but what I saw and heard was truly lifelike. I soon realized it was something I understood to be called virtual reality, but to me no virtual was involved. They were all over me, crawling, sniffing, nibbling. It was reality. I could actually feel their cold noses, their tiny teeth, their slimy tails, and their little claw feet.

They didn't just run over my body. They gathered and began to explore every part of me, going up the leggings of the coveralls and over my thighs, between my legs, under my panties, then under my shirt, pushing themselves under my breasts, sniveling around my nipples and climbing up my throat to my mouth, pushing between my lips, shoving their heads into my mouth. They were at my ears as well, worming their way into my head. Their fur was wet, their tails long and slimy, the tiny nails in their claws painful.

I could even smell them, smell this putrid, stale odor that they picked up from wallowing through piles of garbage and dead animals. Waves of revulsion traveled up and down my entire body to add to the nausea I was experiencing from the scorpion sting.

And I could do nothing to drive them off. Because of how tightly I was strapped onto the cot, I could barely wiggle, not that it would have helped, of course, since they weren't actually on me.

It was no good closing my eyes. The images were projected through my lids, and in these images, the rats were at the lids, forcing them open. I screamed and screamed.

And then suddenly, as quickly as they had come, they were gone. I don't know how long they were there, but they were gone and there was just darkness, the relief of total darkness.

Moments later Dr. Foreman's voice began softly.

"Phoebe, my poor Phoebe. I'm here to help you. You believe that now, don't you?"

All I could do now was whisper and I was afraid she wouldn't hear me.

"Yes," I said, my throat straining with the effort. "I do. I believe it."

"That's good, Phoebe. We need trust between us. It's what I have been telling you ever since you were brought here. You can trust me and I can trust you now, can't I?"

"Yes, Doctor, yes."

"That's good, Phoebe, so good."

Her voice was so soothing. I was actually afraid she would stop talking.

"I was so worried about you, worried about your bad behavior."

"I'm sorry, Dr. Foreman. I'm sorry."

"Sure you are, Phoebe. You never mean to hurt anyone. You're a good girl. Let's get back to our little talk, okay? You were going to tell me about Gia and Posy. Remember?"

"Yes, yes."

"What exactly did Gia say about Posy, Phoebe?"

"She said she was your daughter and that you couldn't stop her from lying and breaking rules and inventing imaginary people, and she was an embarrassment to you so you locked her up in the basement," I rattled off.

"I see. Anything else?"

"That she was adopted."

"Adopted. Yes, that makes sense. This is very good, Phoebe. This is a real breakthrough. You and I are going to depend upon each other a great deal more now. Would you like that?"

"Oh, yes, Dr. Foreman, yes."

"We can't have you ever being insubordinate again, Phoebe."

"I won't be. I promise. I know promises are not considered important anymore, but I do. I really do."

"I believe you, Phoebe, but as you've seen already, only action means anything."

"I feel so sick, Dr. Foreman. I'm so sick. I'm nauseous and I threw up. I was really stung by that scorpion. I'm not lying."

"I know. You'll be fine, Phoebe. Don't be concerned. I want you to sleep now."

"I'm nauseous again."

"I said I want you to sleep."

"Okay, I'll sleep."

It was quiet enough for me to hear the rhythm of my beating heart thumping in my ears. I held my breath. Was that the sound of squeaking again? Were they returning?

Despite my terror, I did fall asleep, but right before I did, I told myself I had been so stupid. I had put my fear in that biography I wrote in the orientation room. I had given myself up before I had even arrived here. She's too smart, I thought. She will get what she wants. M'Lady One was right. Dr. Foreman doesn't fail. There was no Posy. There couldn't be anyone she didn't change or mold into the person Dr. Foreman wanted her to be.

I didn't realize it until much later, but before the door was opened again, I had slept all day and through the night, waking and then becoming nearly comatose repeatedly. The helmet was unfastened and light burned through the shadows. It was so painful. I grimaced and closed my eyes, but the light was too strong.

"What a mess she is," I heard M'Lady Two say.

"Let's get her to the showers."

"You're disgusting, Phoebe bird. You've spoiled your coveralls and you stink so badly, I don't think the buzzards would even bother with your remains," M'Lady One said.

I was weak. I couldn't lift my head, but they pulled

me up. My legs gave out immediately. They scooped
their arms under mine and dragged me out of the Ice
Room. M'Lady Three was there with a wheelbarrow.

"I thought we would need it," she said triumphantly.
They all laughed.

They lifted me and dropped me in the wheelbarrow,
my legs twisted, my head hitting the metal sharply. I
moaned and tried to get more comfortable, but they
were rolling me along and bouncing me over the dirt
and gravel so hard, I did all I could to keep my head
from repeatedly smacking the inside of the wheelbarrow. When we reached the showers, they began to tear
off my clothes. Then they put me under the shower and
ran the cold water. I screamed, but I had lost my voice
the night before, and all I actually did was open my
mouth. I welcomed the water in my throat.

They stood by watching me squirm.

When they decided I had had enough, they shut off
the water and tossed me a towel. I was given new
panties and a new pair of coveralls and a new shirt.
They barked their displeasure at me. It was taking me
too long to dress, but I had no energy. My foot still
looked quite swollen. I put my clodhopper shoe on as
carefully as I could and they scooped me up again.

"You'll walk on your own now," M'Lady One charged.
"Dr. Foreman wants you fed, so head for the house."

I limped forward. I didn't see any of the others, but I
thought I caught a glimpse of Natani watching from a
corner of the barn. The buddies kept chiding me for
moving too slowly, poking me in the ribs and back. I
shuddered but kept moving, accepting the pain every
time I put my foot down, swallowing it back and moving ahead, driven now by my need for something more
to drink. My mouth still felt as if it had been turned into

sand and my tongue into one long razor blade. I
touched my lips to see if there was any blood, but they
were so dry, it was like touching wood.

They had to help me up the stairs and then direct me
to the table where I was given juice, some soft-boiled
eggs, toast, and jam. I was still too nauseated to eat
much, but I knew I would need something to build
my strength, so I made as much of an effort as I could.
Only M'Lady One remained behind to watch. When
Dr. Foreman appeared, I felt myself flinch. Every cell
in my body, every part of me, was afraid of her now.

She smiled. "How's my girl? Those spider bites can
be so devastating."

I wanted to ask why she didn't believe me when I
told her then, but I didn't even move my lips.

"You're going to need a little TLC now. Just like Teal
did, only Teal thinks the world owes her TLC." Dr.
Foreman told M'Lady One, "Take her to the guest bedroom. Give her two Tylenol and the ice pack for her
foot." She turned back to me. "You'll be a lot better by
this evening. I need you to be strong for me, Phoebe. We
have a lot of work to do together now, you and I, right?"

I nodded.

"Good." She looked at M'Lady One. "Send me Gia
after you see to Phoebe," she ordered sharply.

"Okay, Doctor."

I was too tired and too numb to think about anything,
but I felt vaguely sorry for Gia and wondered how she
and the others were going to treat me now.

M'Lady One helped me to a bedroom. The mere
sight of a real bed made me relax. I couldn't believe
how wonderful it felt to lie down on a thick mattress.
She gave me the pills and some water and brought me
the ice pack.

"Keep it on your foot," she said, pulling me up so I could hold it there myself.

"You put that scorpion into my shoe, didn't you?" I managed to ask her in a hoarse voice.

She smiled. "Now how could I do a terrible thing like that? Remember? I'm a different person now. I don't do mean things to people anymore," she replied, and left.

I kept the ice pack on my foot, but the pain there was receding anyway. I was so tired, I couldn't stay upright and eventually just gave up on the ice pack and fell asleep. It was probably the best sleep I'd had since I'd arrived at this ranch. I didn't wake up feeling energetic, but I felt a great deal stronger. The nausea was gone and I didn't think I had a fever any longer either. I saw that the sun was low, falling behind the mountains in the west. I had slept through the day.

"Well," I heard from the doorway, and looked up at Dr. Foreman. "You've woken just in time for dinner. That's good. I want you to eat well tonight, Phoebe. You have to get stronger, okay?"

"Yes, Dr. Foreman."

"Good. Go on to the dining room then."

I slipped my feet into my shoes cautiously. I couldn't help it. Memory of that sting was still so vivid, I thought my foot would rebel and refuse to go into the shoe. Dr. Foreman watched me and then stepped back as I started out of the room.

"It's a comfortable room, isn't it, Phoebe?"

"Yes."

I hadn't looked at anything but the bed, but now I saw a dresser and a mirror, a small desk and chair, and a vanity table with another mirror. The floor was done in a blue-and-white tile with an oval, cream area rug next to the bed. Beside the bed was a pole lamp with a shade that looked to be made of seashells. There was even a radio on the nightstand.

"This could be your room, Phoebe." I glanced at her a little too hopefully. "We'll see." She indicated I should walk ahead of her to the dining room.

The others were already there eating. They all looked up when I appeared, all except Gia. She kept her eyes on her food.

"As you all heard, Phoebe hasn't been well. She is therefore excused from any kitchen chores tonight," Dr. Foreman announced.

Mindy smirked. Robin and Teal stared at me enviously.

Dr. Foreman put her hand on my shoulder. "Get something to eat and then return to your bunk and get some rest, Phoebe. You don't have to work on any school assignments either."

The more favors and privileges she placed upon me, the more embarrassed and ashamed I felt. The others sensed it and were now all looking down at the food. I went to my place and began to fill my plate with food. I was hungry and thirsty. Dr. Foreman stood there watching for a few moments, then left.

No one spoke for a while.

Finally, Teal broke the silence. "You were in the Ice Room, weren't you?"

I nodded.

"What was it like? What happened? What did they do?" she asked, her eyes wide with expectation. "Robin won't tell me anything about her experience," she added, glaring at her.

I just shook my head.

"Talking about something like that causes you to relive it," Gia mumbled. "So shut up."

"Don't keep giving me orders," Teal shot back at her.

She looked at me again. "What did she mean you weren't well?" she asked, refusing to be quiet even though Robin and Mindy and not just Gia were now glaring at her so hard, anyone else would have been intimidated.

"I was stung like you, by a scorpion, and this was right after Dr. Foreman gave me the news that my mother died last week."

"What?" Robin asked. "Your mother died?"

"Some drug she took affected her heart and she died in the clinic she was in."

"Why did she wait so long to tell you?" Teal asked.

"I don't know." I know I sounded like it, but I couldn't help it: I was searching for sympathy, and understanding.

"Oh. This is all so terrible," Teal said. "And then to be stung by a scorpion. Where were you stung?"

"It was in my shoe."

"How could it be in your shoe?" Robin asked, grimacing.

"Spiders can get into shoes when they're left outside. It's not a big deal," Gia said dryly.

"Well, it got under my overalls, so I guess it could get into a shoe," Teal added.

Robin smirked and stared at her. "You know, now that I think about it, Teal, how come you didn't get put in the Ice Room for trying to run off?"

"I don't know," Teal said quickly. "I was too sick, I guess. They put me in one of the bedrooms here. Maybe she was afraid I would die and she would get investigated and then go to jail."

"Phoebe's sitting here after one day. How come it took you so long to get well enough to be returned to the barracks?" Mindy questioned, her eyes now also full of suspicion.

"I had a worse reaction obviously. Maybe it was a bigger spider or a more poisonous one or something, and don't forget I had been out in the desert a long, long time walking. I was two miles past total exhaustion and my feet were sore and I was very dehydrated. I should have been sent to a hospital, not kept here," Teal whined loud enough for someone outside the dining room to hear.

"The way we're being treated, we'll all end up in a hospital soon," Robin offered.

"Exactly." Teal nodded and turned to Gia. "Maybe that's where Posy is. In a hospital."

Gia looked up sharply and glanced at me. Then she dropped her fork so hard, she almost cracked her dish. "Why don't you all shut up? All this whining and moaning, day in and day out. That's what she wants you to do. I'll tell you who's going to end up in a hospital here, me. I'm going to get sick as hell listening to all this groaning and crying."

"Is that right?" Teal retorted, her eyes filling with indignation. "You never cry? You never moan or complain? You're little Miss Perfection."

"Stop it!" I cried, slapping my hand on the table. "Gia's right. Just stop it. Everyone just shut up."

Teal folded her arms under her breasts and turned to me.

"Please," I added.

The rage drained out of her face. She looked at Mindy, Robin, and Gia and went back to her food.

We ate in funereal silence, all of us staring out as if our eyes had been turned around and we were looking in at our own dark thoughts. I was sure we resembled inmates on death row contemplating their end.

Afterward, I returned to barracks alone and went to bed. The others marched in slowly when they were finished with the kitchen chores. Teal announced that thanks to having to pick up my load, she was too tired to do any schoolwork. No one said anything different, even though the expectation was they would all receive a demerit for turning in the work late. Someone turned off the light before the buddies could.

The door opened and M'Lady Two looked in. "Tired girls?" She laughed. "I'll let everyone know you went to bed early. Maybe we'll get you up earlier."

I heard the door close and then I heard Robin say, "And let them know you should drop dead, too."

Teal laughed and Mindy giggled. Gia was quiet. Dr. Foreman's warnings about how volatile she could be returned. Was she planning some sort of revenge? Was it safe to fall asleep with her only a few feet away? I wanted to apologize, to explain, and to get her to see I had no choice, but I was afraid to do it. Instead, I lay awake for as long as I could. Finally, my eyelids refused to be open and sleep came sweeping over me like a cool breeze.

The way the morning began, I thought the silence that had fallen among us would continue all day. No one spoke. With little more than a grunt, everyone rose, dressed, washed, and went to the bathroom. Reciting the morning chant was the most words any of us uttered for hours, even at breakfast. While the others milked the cows, picked chicken eggs, fed the pigs, and did some weeding in the garden, I was assigned to feed and brush down all four horses, as well as clean out the stalls. I worked almost mindlessly, moving as if I were a robot or someone in a drugged stupor.

Once in a while, I would pause and think about Mama. Had she died in her sleep or did she get an attack and panic and die while they were trying to help her? Was she sorry in the end? Did she think at all of me? Think of my daddy? I couldn't imagine anything more lonely than to die among strangers, to have no one around you who would shed tears over your passing, no one who was more than just professionally interested in what was happening to you. You would know that when it was over, they would shake their heads and most likely within the same hour, maybe the same minute, return to their normal daily lives. Some who witnessed your passing might not even remember to mention it to anyone afterward. You were, after all, just a statistic.

What did the doctor ask in that letter? What she should do with Mama's remains? How do you write such a question? Surely the doctor was thinking, we've got to get her out of here. She's one of our screwups. Come get her, sweep up this mess, remove it from our sight.

Did Mama deserve it? Was she so wicked that she was being punished?

Is that what was happening to all of us now? We were bad; we had all done illegal things, some of us worse than the others. Both Mindy and Gia were nearly responsible for killing another human being, and Teal and Robin were thieves. Should anyone feel sorry for us? Should we be upset at the cruelty of the buddies? Was Dr. Foreman right? Could she cure us of evil, turn us into good people? Should we resist? Should I blame myself for surrendering completely?

These questions circled in my brain like mayflies. The more I tried to swipe them away, the more they came. They were relentless. I had to stop working and hold on to something to keep myself from spinning and fainting. I caught my breath and started to brush down one of the horses; then I saw Gia in the doorway. She had a small garden spade in her hand. With the sunlight behind her, her face was in total darkness. She looked more like a ghost or a shadow coming to life as she slowly walked into the horse barn toward me.

I stepped to my right and took hold of the handle of the shovel we used to clean out the horse stalls. I wasn't going to let her hurt me. She stopped about halfway.

"You think you told her something about me that she didn't already know?" Gia began.

"She made me. She put me in the Ice Room and you know what she can do to you. You were the one who said you're not in the Ice Room. The Ice Room is in you. Now I know what you meant. That helmet thing . . . there were rats all over me and she knew how much I hated them."

"She didn't have to do that to you to get information. She just wanted to break you, Phoebe. She already had Mindy tell her everything I said about Posy. Mindy denies it, but I know she did. She pretends to believe me, but she doesn't. Dr. Foreman has her thinking otherwise."

"Is it true, Gia? Are you making up Posy?"

"What do you think?"

"I think you are," I said, my eyes on the hand that held that spade like a switchblade.

She smiled coldly, her small mouth stretching and curling in the corners with disgust. "You're going to be a Foreman girl then, are you? You're going to stay here or come back here and become a buddy someday so you can torment and torture someone like you?"

"No."

She crossed over to a bale of hay and sat, digging her spade into it.

"She told me what Mindy did with her baby," I said.

"Did she?" Gia smiled and shook her head. "Dr. Foreman used the same technique on me, telling me what Posy had done. This was afterward, of course."

"After what?"

"After the imaginary Posy disappeared, but that's what imaginary people do, don't they? They disappear."

"What did she tell you Posy had done?" I asked.

"Why do you want to know if you don't believe there ever was a Posy?"

I didn't say anything and she looked at the horse behind her. "Posy liked the horses, too. She would have slept with them if they had let her. I told you Natani took a liking to her just as he has taken to you. He taught her many things, but the most valuable was how to escape."

"Are you saying she escaped? I thought you believed she was put into the basement and might even still be there."

"From time to time, Posy escaped, and maybe in the end, forever."

"I don't understand, Gia."

"Do you know anything about meditation?"

"No. I mean, it's a religion or something, isn't it?"

"It's not a religion, but it's part of some religions. It's part of what Natani believes."

"What does that have to do with Posy?"

"He taught her how to meditate, to leave this world and enter some spiritual place, and when she was there, no one could touch her, hurt her. It got so she would rather be there than here all the time, and it wasn't long after that when she disappeared." Gia looked like she was crying now. I thought I saw a tear glistening on her cheek.

I stepped closer to her. "It doesn't make any sense to me. I don't know what any of that means."

"Maybe you can get Natani to show you."

"I want to believe you, Gia. I really do, and I don't want to hurt you. I'm sorry I betrayed you in there."

"You didn't betray me in there, but you are betraying me out here," she said, standing. She took her spade out of the hay.

"What does that mean?"

"You don't believe me. That's more important to me."

"I said I want to believe you."

"Do you?"

"Yes."

"Okay, we'll see. I'll give you the chance to prove that." She started out.

"When?" I called after her.

She turned back. "Maybe tonight."

"How?"

"We'll get into the basement."

"I thought you said the door had a lock on it. How can we get in?"

"Leave it to me. We'll get in and then we'll see if Posy is there or if she was," she said, and walked out of the horse barn.

Wind Song reached over the stall door and poked me in the back of my head.

I looked at him.

Was that meant to be a warning? Did he see something in Gia's actions?

Was I as crazy as Gia? Now I believed what Natani had told me . . . horses and people could talk to each other.

Meditation? Escape? What was she talking about? How was I supposed to understand any of this? More important, how had I fallen into this whirlpool of pain and confusion?

Every time Gia saw me the remainder of the day, she looked at me weirdly. She said nothing else to me about the basement and Posy, so I thought it was just something that had flown in and out of her mind as quickly as a hummingbird. However, just before we started to the house for dinner, she stepped up beside me and whispered, "Don't tell the others anything about this. It will just be you and me, understand?"

I nodded, but it all made me nervous. The one thing I didn't want to do was get into any more trouble here, but I didn't want to anger Gia any more than I already had either. I was so anxious about it all that I didn't eat well, and sure enough, before the dinner ended, Dr. Foreman came into the dining room.

"How are my girls doing tonight?" she asked, her eyes fixed mainly on me.

We all muttered all right and thank you.

"You should make sure you eat well, Phoebe. You have to keep up your strength for the challenges that lie ahead, and believe me," she said, looking at everyone now, "there are challenges. I would like to speak with you before you return to the barracks to do your homework, Phoebe. Come to the office when you're finished with your kitchen duties."

I nodded and returned to eating, but the other girls, especially Gia, looked at me and then each other.

"What's that about, I wonder?" Mindy asked.

"I don't know," I said.

"What I don't know is why she is so worried about you eating and you getting stronger," Teal said. "She didn't watch over me like that after my horrendous episode."

"Well, then," Mindy said, "maybe your episode wasn't as horrendous as you make it out to be."

"What are you talking about? You were there when they brought me back. You saw."

Mindy shrugged. "I know how to put it on, too."

"Put it on? Listen to that. Phoebe, tell her what it's like to be stung by one of those . . . things."

I looked up. "It's painful, makes you nauseous. I think I even had a fever."

"See?" Teal jumped on the end of my words.

"That's Phoebe, not you," Mindy said, barely looking at her.

"I wish it happens to you, that's all. Then we'll see how horrendous it is and isn't."

"And I wish you get bitten by a rattlesnake in the bathroom in your you know what," Mindy countered.

Teal flung a glob of her mashed potatoes at her, hitting her in the cheek.

"Bitch!" Mindy screamed. She was about to toss her glass of cranberry juice at her when M'Lady Three appeared in the doorway.

"Problem?" she asked.

"No," Mindy said quickly.

"You're a bit of a messy eater, aren't you, Mindy? Why don't you do all the dishes, silverware, and clean off the table yourself tonight? Maybe that will make you neater. You have any problem with that?" she asked quickly.

"No," Mindy said, shaking her head. Some of the mashed potato fell to her plate. She wiped her chin and looked away quickly.

"Good. The rest of you, except for Phoebe bird, return to the barracks. Let's go."

Teal, Robin, and Gia rose. Mindy lowered her head, but I could see the tips of her ears were so red, they looked like tiny candle flames. She didn't lift her head until they were gone.

"She'll be sorry," she muttered. "Just wait and see."

"Don't get into a fight again, Mindy. They're just hoping you will," I advised her. "And then you'll know what it's like in the Ice Room."

She looked at me with surprise, not expecting anything nice or kind from anyone, I think, especially one of us.

"Right," she said. "Thanks." She began to gather the dirty plates and bowls. I thought about helping her, but something told me Dr. Foreman watched us in this room. Maybe there really were microphones or secret cameras all over this place.

"See you later," I said, and went out and down to Dr. Foreman's office.

To my surprise she wasn't sitting behind her desk, but on the sofa instead. She was reading a magazine and looked up and smiled.

"Hi. Come on in."

I did and she indicated I should sit on the sofa.

"I can't believe some of the fashions young people your age are wearing these days. Look at this, for example." She turned the magazine to show me an actress wearing what looked like nothing more than two large Band-Aids over her breasts and a flimsy skirt. She had what resembled a dog collar around her neck. "And she's about to enter some award show. Would you wear that?"

I shook my head.

"I didn't think so. Mindy might. She probably wore things like this. She was a classic nymphomaniac, you know. You know what that is, of course."

"A nympho? Someone who has a lot of sex."

"Yes. Only she had those tendencies ever since junior high school, even sixth grade. To me a girl who is so wild and loose with her body has no respect for herself. I know your mother was very loose, right?"

I nodded. What could I do, deny it? She obviously knew a lot about all of us, and I did write about some of Mama's sexual escapades when I wrote my autobiography for Dr. Foreman.

"I'm impressed that you don't have those tendencies, Phoebe, but you did get yourself into trouble because of sex in your new school, didn't you?"

"I guess so." I had met a boy in the nurse's office as he had preplanned and the nurse caught us. It wasn't something I had done often before. In fact, I had never done anything that serious in school. I wanted to explain it, of course, describe how I had been desperate and angry and didn't care. However, she didn't need my explanation.

"You were most likely getting at your aunt. You wanted to embarrass her and your uncle, didn't you? You didn't want to be there and you were hoping you would be sent home, back to Atlanta, where you could be with your father, right?"

"Yes."

"Only he wasn't home very much. You would have ended up even worse than you did, Phoebe. In a way you were lucky to get into so much trouble so quickly and be sent here. I can't imagine what would have become of you had you not been picked up at the clinic. Strike that. I can imagine. I've seen girls who had to live in the streets. It's not a pretty sight, and their life expectancy isn't any better than the life expectancy of young women in some third world countries.

"Sometimes"—she sighed and looked toward the window, which had the curtains drawn open for a change—"I feel as if I have been chosen for my work, given all this responsibility by a higher power." She looked pensive for a moment, then shook her head and smiled. "Here." She handed me the magazine. "I'm sure you're interested in all this nonsense anyway."

I looked at the magazine. I did want it, but if I took that and brought it back to the barracks, I would have some explaining to do.

On the other hand, I saw that if I didn't take it, she would be angry, suspicious, and I was more afraid of that than anything.

"Thank you," I said.

"You're welcome, Phoebe. So, tell me, how did Gia treat you today?" she asked, holding her soft, friendly smile.

There was little question in my mind that she already knew.

"She was angry because I told you what she had said about Posy."

"Her Posy," Dr. Foreman muttered. "Yes. You told her you had no choice, of course."

I nodded.

"You're free to tell the other girls about it. If Gia sees no one believes her, it will help. Should Gia get violent or physical, I want to know immediately, understand?"

"Yes, Dr. Foreman."

"Good. How did she defend herself? Did she tell you anything else about her Posy? Claim she did anything?"

"She said she worked on the horses like I am." The more I told her that was true, the less I might have to tell her what I feared to tell her, I hoped.

"Yes, well, of course it was Gia who worked on the horses. You believe that, don't you?" she said quickly.

"Yes, I do."

"Good. As I mentioned before, Mindy troubles me more and more these days," she suddenly said, changing the subject. "She's really regressing."

"Regressing?"

"She's becoming more and more like she was when she first arrived here. She's too aloof, too distant most of the time. I think she's actually getting worse in some ways. I'm getting bad vibes these last few days. I want you to keep an eye on her, too, for me. Keep track of what she says, does, whenever you're around her."

"Everything she says?"

"You'll know what I want. Enjoy the magazine, but be sure to get your homework done first, understand?"

"Yes, Dr. Foreman."

"And no one else is permitted to read it, not even over your shoulder."

"But . . ."

"I don't want to hear that they have," she added, her eyes full of threat.

I nodded.

"You're excused."

I rose and started for the door.

"Phoebe."

"Yes, Dr. Foreman?"

"I think you could look a lot prettier than that so-called actress, even in those ridiculous clothes. I can see you in a modeling career someday. Would you like that?"

I nodded.

"Good. I'll see what I can do about finding you a good modeling school when the time comes."

Every time she offered to do something good for me or said something nice to me, I felt worse.

Why was that?

Why should I care about anyone else anymore? She

was right after all. They would all forget me and have nothing to do with me once we all left this place, especially if I returned to my neighborhood in Atlanta or someplace like it. I was tempted to reveal the rest of it, describe exactly what Gia was planning to do tonight.

"Was there something else you wanted to tell me, Phoebe?"

Did she know already? Was she expecting me to tell? Was this another test and was I failing it?

What kept me from telling her, I do not know, but I couldn't do it.

"Yes," I said. "Thank you."

She smiled. "You're welcome, Phoebe. Most welcome," she said, nodding slowly.

I turned and left the house.

On the way back to the barracks, I was tempted to throw away the magazine, but I worried that she might ask me to return it. I know I was becoming what Gia called paranoid, too. I couldn't help looking around, searching for hidden cameras, microphones, or perhaps one of the buddies watching me from a hidden place.

Robin, Teal, and Gia looked up when I entered. They were already working on math problems. I noticed Mindy was still not back.

"Where did you get that?" Teal asked quickly, eyeing the magazine.

There was no point in lying about it. "Dr. Foreman gave it to me, but she warned me not to let anyone else look at it."

Teal immediately recoiled, pulling her head down and her arms back. "Oh, we can't look at it. Only the special Phoebe can look at it. Big deal. Who cares about some stupid magazine anyway?" She returned to her homework.

Robin stared at me with an expression of disappointment.

"I didn't ask for it. She gave it to me."

"Of course she did," Gia said. "She did the same
thing with Mindy soon after I arrived. It's another one
of her little ways to set us against each other and
depend on her."

I wanted to warn her not to say so many terrible
things about Dr. Foreman aloud. Surely a hidden micro-
phone or two were in the barracks, but if I warned her,
Dr. Foreman could hear the warning as well.

I said nothing and they returned to the homework.
Gia asked me to join them and helped me with my
assignments. I put the magazine under my cot and got
my books and notebook. After a while, we all wondered
what was keeping Mindy. Even alone, she should have
finished by now, we thought. Of course we had no way
to tell how much time actually went by since none of us
had a watch and there were no clocks, but Robin esti-
mated it was nearly a good two hours.

M'Lady Two appeared in the doorway and told us to
prepare for bed.

"Where's Mindy?" Teal asked.

"It's none of your business where Mindy is. Your
business is where you are."

I thought Teal was going to say something else, but
she looked at me and then turned to her cot. Before we
were all actually ready to go to bed, M'Lady Two shut
off the lights.

"My business," Teal muttered. "My business is getting out of here."

No one said anything more. The air felt so heavy,
even the starlight streaming through the windows
looked droopy. I closed my eyes and hoped I would fall

asleep quickly, but I didn't. I saw from the way Teal was lying that she had, and Robin had turned her back to me and looked very still as well.

When Gia poked me, I nearly jumped and screamed. She had moved so quietly to my bedside.

"I don't like it," she whispered. "If Mindy's not back by now, Dr. Foreman has her, and there's no telling what will happen to her. Did she indicate she was unhappy with her in any way?"

I hesitated. Should I report what Dr. Foreman had said to me?

"Yes," I whispered. "You should be careful about what you say, Gia. I really do believe there are microphones hidden around us."

"It doesn't matter. She knows what we think. Okay, let's go."

"Go?"

"To the basement, like I said we would."

"But, with Mindy gone and all, don't you think it would be more dangerous?"

"That makes no difference. Don't worry. The buddies are already into their own thing by now. They're not going to stand guard over this place. Get up, put on your clothes quietly."

"But . . ."

"Either you want to know the truth or you don't, Phoebe, but you better not call me a liar and let the others believe it. Make up your mind." Gia's face was so close to mine, I could feel her breath. "Okay. I'll go with you."

In the back of my mind I thought that if we were caught, I would tell Dr. Foreman I was going to tell her what Gia wanted to do and went along because she was going to do it with or without me. It was a weak excuse that she would probably see right through, but it was all I could come up with quickly.

Hopefully, we would find an empty basement and that would end it.

Maybe Dr. Foreman would even congratulate me. Was I terrible in hoping for that, hoping for another reward, perhaps less work, sleeping in that comfortable bed in her house, and going to a school for modeling? Was it terrible to want things for yourself, even at the expense of the others?

Natani knew how to survive out there in the raw desert world, but I had to learn how to survive here and in the world I would eventually return to, for as Dr. Foreman had made clear, I had no one but myself now. I almost never did. That was true, but at least I had had a place to call home.

That was gone forever. I guess I really did have nowhere to run to.

Did any of us? Really?

I saw Gia was already dressed and waiting.

Everyone has her own way to survive, I thought.

Maybe this was just hers and maybe I had no right to ruin that for her.

But one thing I had learned and learned painfully, choice was a privilege. Here we did what we were told or what was expected of us.

Now I was Dr. Foreman's little spy.

And I had almost nothing to do with the decision to be so.

10

Good-bye, Posy

When you grow up in a city where there are always some lights on and almost always noise and traffic, your nervous system has a hard time adjusting to a world of pitch darkness and silence. For one thing, you suddenly realize the majestic starlight. Almost always, even during the short time I lived with Uncle Buster and Aunt Mae Louise in the suburban community of Stone Mountain, there were streetlights or other lights that washed out the stars and there was some traffic, people walking, music from cars.

Out here in the desert, especially late at night, the uninterrupted sky was peppered with pinholes of light, some of them so big and bright, I waited to see if they were planes. They weren't. They were simply unblocked, crystal-clear, dazzling beads of illumination. I thought to myself that if I ever wondered how God could see so much, this could be the answer. The stars are His eyes and He has so many of them.

Here on the ranch, the darkness was so different from the darkness I had known in Atlanta. This darkness was like the darkness in a dream. All of the structures, even the hacienda, were now inky silhouettes. The stillness made me conscious of my heavier, anxious breathing and the crunch of our footsteps over the gravel as we walked toward the back of the big house. There wasn't a light on anywhere inside, which meant the buddies were asleep, too.

I looked toward Natani's hogan. He wasn't anywhere in sight. He could be outside, cloaked in a shadow. Most of the time, he was just there, appearing as if he formed out of thin air, walking so softly on those moccasins that even birds didn't realize he was atop them. However, this late I imagined he was within his little house, asleep on his blanket. Even the farm animals were deathly quiet. If they weren't asleep, they were like me, listening. I did think I heard a horse snort. It was probably Wind Song, I thought. He could sense that I was out here and he wanted to know why.

"Move it," Gia whispered, and beckoned for me to catch up with her.

Suddenly she turned and headed quickly toward the tool shack.

"Where are we going?"

"I need something," she said. "You'll see."

When we reached the shack, she opened the door an inch at a time, moving the hinges as softly and as quietly as she could. Apparently, she knew exactly where what she wanted was located, because it was so dark inside, I couldn't tell a rake from a hoe. I was always thinking about snakes, although Natani had told me that snakes would look for a rock warmed by the day's sunshine and curl up on it at night. Gia didn't seem to have an ounce of fear about them. She was in and out quickly, a screwdriver in her hand.

She nodded toward the house again and we walked around the corner to the metal doors that opened on steps leading down to the door of the basement. When we were there, she indicated we should be as quiet as could be. My eyes were used to the darkness now, as were hers. Nevertheless, she surprised me by digging into her coverall pocket to produce a cigarette lighter.

"Where did you get that?" I whispered.

I could see her smiling. "I stole it from the buddies. When I was in there with Dr. Foreman one day, she left me alone and I wandered through, popped into the buddies' quarters, and found it on a desk. I got back to her office before she knew I had been about the house. I thought it would come in handy one of these days. It has.

"Here." She handed me the lighter. "Flick it on when I say. I just need to see where the hinges are screwed in. Go on, flick."

I did so and the small flame threw a lot more light on the doors than I thought it might. She started the screwdriver and had me turn off the light. I crouched and watched as she worked, moving with such care, I barely heard anything. She put each screw she took out into her pocket.

"We'll fix it when we leave," she whispered. "That way no one but you and me will know we were down there."

I nodded.

When all the screws were out, she lifted the hinge carefully and folded it over with great care, barely making a sound.

Then she stepped back. "Ready?"

I wasn't, of course. I could never be ready for this, but then, I thought, we'll go down there and look around. There'll be nothing there and she'll change on the spot, maybe even admit she had made up Posy. The whole thing would finally be over and done. It will be better for both of us. Dr. Foreman will stop questioning me about it and surely congratulate me on helping her cure Gia.

She lifted the door ever so gently and held it open just enough for me to slip in and under.

"Go ahead," she said. "Flick the lighter so you can watch your step. When you're down far enough to make room for me, I'll come in and close the door softly after us."

I hesitated and looked up at the dark windows. They were more like mirrors now, reflecting starlight. On the stucco walls, shadows danced almost like savages glee-fully watching me do something stupid.

"Go on before someone hears us," Gia urged. "Go."

I took a deep breath and snapped the lighter on again. In the glow I could see that the stone steps were chipped and cracked. I saw spiderwebs in every corner, but fortunately, no sign of any snakes. Gia put her hand on my shoulder, pressing me downward. I lowered my head and stepped onto the first step, then turned and slipped under the opened metal door, backing down carefully. I held the lighter up in front of me. My arm was trembling so much that the little flame wavered, but stayed lit.

"Okay," I said.

"Wait."

"What?" My heart seemed to thump and come to a stop in anticipation. "Gia? What is it?"

"I think I hear something. Just keep still."

To my surprise and shock, she lowered the metal door. I didn't move a muscle. The light went out so I had to flick it on again. Then I heard a strange new sound, like a tiny grinding. What was that?

"Gia?"

I stepped up until my head was an inch or so from the metal door.

"Gia, what's happening?"

The grinding continued and then stopped.

"Gia?"

I heard nothing. I waited and listened.

"Gia?" I called more frantically. I pressed on the metal door, but it didn't lift. "What's happening?"

At last I heard her whisper through the crack, "I can't face her. Go on inside yourself and talk to her."

"What?"

I listened and heard nothing.

"What did you say, Gia? Gia!"

I pushed on the metal door. It moved, but this time the hasp and the lock stopped it from going any farther.

That grinding.

She had put the hinge back, screwed it in. I was locked within. My heart pounded until the blood filled my face and the pounding echoed in my ears. I pushed and pushed, but the metal door didn't budge. It was heavy, too.

I thought about screaming for help, then stopped before I started and thought, how would I explain this to Dr. Foreman now? I hadn't done anything but violated rules. The buddies were sure to pounce on me.

"Gia, please. Let me out. Please," I begged. "We'll both get into so much trouble if you don't. Please. Hurry."

I thought I felt something on my ankle and spun

around, losing my balance. Fortunately I caught myself on the side of the concrete before I fell down the remaining steps, but in doing that, I dropped the lighter. I heard it bounce down the steps. Now, in the pitch darkness, I was sweating more from panic than heat. I heard myself whimper.

Slowly, using my foot, I searched each step until I felt something move. I hesitated, waiting to see if it would move again, but under its own power. I touched it, and then, confident it was the lighter, I knelt down in careful increments and felt for it. When I had my hands around it, I permitted myself to breathe again.

I flicked it on.

I had the lighter, but what was I going to do?

I looked at the door at the bottom of the stairs. Maybe it was unlocked and maybe I could make my way through the basement and then upstairs and out the front door of the hacienda without anyone hearing or knowing. It was worth a try. Certainly, I couldn't stay here all night and I didn't want to shout for help if I didn't have to.

I continued down the stairs and turned the door handle, pushing gently on it. The door groaned so I stopped and waited, listening to see if anyone moved about above. There was no sound so I pushed again and the door opened enough for me to slip through. I thought about it again, looked back up the stairs, realized I had no choice, and went into the basement.

It wasn't much of a basement, just a single, long room. I lifted the lighter as if I were imitating the Statue of Liberty or something and turned slowly. There was furniture, a small bed and a dresser. The bed had a light blue pillow and a blanket. Someone had obviously slept there. The pillow was still indented with the shape of her head.

Over to the right of the bed was a small desk, resembling the desks we had sat at when first brought to the orientation room. Instead of a stool, there was a wooden chair. I saw a small lamp on the desk and approached slowly, gazing into the dark depth of the basement. What frightened me the most, of course, was the possibility of rats.

But the basement floor was bone dry and actually looked as if it had recently been swept and vacuumed. I didn't see any spiderwebs either. I lifted the lighter a little higher and the darkness retreated a bit more. I could make out a short stairway at the far end. I didn't see into every dark corner yet, but I didn't think anyone was there.

I walked down a bit farther and held the light high enough so I could find the floor grate Gia had spoken about. I didn't, but I thought I did hear voices, so I turned quickly and retreated.

I approached the desk and found the switch for the lamp. To my joy, it lit, and with that illumination I could clearly see the whole room. Except for this little bit of furniture, there was nothing and, I concluded, releasing the hot breath I had bottled up in my lungs, no one in the basement.

I gazed at the desk and saw an envelope. The envelope wasn't addressed, but when I picked it up, I realized something was in it. I took out the paper and unfolded it. This was a letter and it began with *Dear Mom and Dad . . .*

I sat on the chair and began to read the letter.

First, I want to tell you I'm all right. It was very, very hard at first. Dr. Foreman made it seem as if this was going to be a fun place with strict rules, but nevertheless, not an unpleasant experience. She and I had a wonderful talk when I first arrived. She explained how her first concern would always be my well-being, but she wanted me to understand that sometimes, she would appear very cruel and unreasonable to me. She compared herself to a dentist.

"I've got to drill away the rot in you," she said, "the decay that's poisoning the healthy part of you."

I thought that was very reasonable and I promised her I would always try to see things from her point of view. We got started on a good note.

Here at her school, she has older girls to assist her. She told me those girls were former students. At first, I couldn't believe it. She had given them so much responsibility. How could they have been in enough trouble to be sent here and then become trusted assistants?

Dr. Foreman said that when I improved, I would probably make for a great assistant, who she calls buddies because they help the new students. They acted tough and hard, but I knew they were only trying to help me.

Anyway, I have another reason for writing this letter. Dr. Foreman has gotten me to understand that I can't improve until I admit to my problems and weaknesses. She says girls like me have to go through a process not unlike the process alcoholics experience. We have to stand up and confess first. We have to say, "I am an alcoholic."

Of course, I'm not an alcoholic. I have to say I'm a liar and a deceitful person. So, first, let me say that. I have lied and deceived you both many times. I'm sorry about it, but I'm most sorry for what I did right before I was sent here. I know it was a horrible thing to do to make Tamatha sick by putting that insect poison in her food. I was so angry, but that didn't justify it. As

Dr. Foreman says, I have got to learn how to channel my anger into other, more productive activities and learn how to talk about the things that bother me. I can tell you I worked hard at hiding everything and it wasn't your fault that you never knew half the terrible things I had done. You didn't deserve to have a daughter like me.

Thanks to Dr. Foreman and her treatments, I can now do all that she suggested I should do. I'm ashamed, of course, and I'm sorry, too. We don't promise things here. Promises are like soap bubbles. They look really beautiful, but when you touch them, they pop and fall to earth and are gone. Dr. Foreman says, "They're not worth the air they're written on." She has a wonderful way of putting things sometimes.

So I won't make promises about the future and how I will behave. I'll just do the right thing.

I don't want you to believe that all this has happened overnight. It took a long time and I had to do many, many things that I know would be unpleasant to anyone else, especially some of my so-called friends. Dr. Foreman has shown me how none of them were really my friends.

There is only one other girl here at the moment. Dr. Foreman says the new girl and I are sort of between scheduling periods, and new girls will be arriving soon. Dr. Foreman just doesn't take anyone that people want to send here. She spends a lot of time analyzing and thinking about the girl and her problems first.

This other girl who is here is a lot like me in so many ways, but she is very unhappy and still very angry at the world and everyone in it. She hates me for being happy about anything. She calls me Pollyannaish and says my eyes are blinded by stars. She's very intelligent, but very bitter.

Dr. Foreman decided recently that she was not a good influence on me and we, therefore, had to be separated. She gave me a new place to stay. At first, it was a very lonely place and then, one day, a man, an Indian man who is in charge of the ranch animals and farming, told me that the world is really inside you and not outside you. His name is Natani and I did not understand what he meant, of course.

But he showed me how to look inside myself and find the world I needed. That's really where I go now. In the beginning, I was there for very short periods. Those periods grew longer and longer until I realized I could go there forever, if I wanted. I told Natani and he didn't say I should or shouldn't. He said I would know myself how long I should be away.

This is probably confusing you. I know it's hard for anyone who hasn't done it to understand.

But, I can't explain it any more than to say, I'm happy, happy enough to want to stay here forever.

So, Mom and Dad, I wanted to write this last letter to you and tell you good-bye, but not a sad good-bye. Oh, no. This is a happy good-bye for I am not leaving you. In my world we are always together and, Mom, you are as beautiful as you were when you were a young woman, and, Daddy, you are as handsome as you were when you were a young man, and do you know what else? You don't get old in this world. You are young forever and ever, and you are always laughing and smiling. We're together the way we should be, the way we once were, and you always have time for me.

So be happy for me, Mom.

Be happy for me, Dad.
I love you more now.
Forever,
Posy

I stared at the name and then I reread the letter.

Something creaked behind me and I spun around, half expecting now to see a fragile, diminutive, young girl smiling. There was no one and it was deadly silent.

I folded the letter and put it back into the envelope and left it on the desk. I wanted to get out of here as quickly as I could. I switched off the small lamp and flicked my lighter. Moving slowly to keep the flame from going out, I headed toward the short stairway.

When I reached the foot of it, another light went on and every breath in my body flew out of my body like a flock of sparrows abruptly frightened. Every bone turned to marshmallow. I felt as if I had stepped into a pool of ice water, the cold racing up my legs into my stomach and over my breasts, pushing my blood into my head.

There, in a tiny circle of illumination created by a large flashlight pointing up just under her chin, was Dr. Foreman. Her face absorbed the light and emerged from the darkness as if it were made of some luminescent substance, her eyes dark and gaunt, her teeth incandescent. Actually, she looked more like a skeleton resurrected.

"Careful, Phoebe," she said. "Watch your step, dear."

I didn't know what to say, what to do. I was still too frozen to move.

"Don't be afraid. First, I want you to return to the desk and get that letter. Go on." She pointed the flashlight to create a lighted pathway for me. "Go!"

I moved quickly, snapped up the envelope, and returned to the stairway.

"Come up now." She directed the beam of light to the wooden steps. "The lighting down here doesn't work. It hasn't for as long as I've had the place, but it never mattered. I don't use the basement that often. We clean it from time to time and check our plumbing, but that's about it," she explained, as if it were important for me to know the most insignificant details about the house.

I started up the stairs and she turned and opened the door that led into the downstairs hallway.

"Come along."

I followed her down the hall to her office. The house was as quiet and as dark as the basement had been. She flipped the light switch and entered, turning to encourage me to follow. I know I was moving, but I was so frightened, I didn't think about it. I floated in behind her and sat on the sofa.

She pulled a chair up and sat right in front of me, smiling at me. I still held on to the letter, expecting she would take it, but she didn't ask for it or pluck it from my fingers.

"Look at you. You look like you've actually seen a ghost."

"I'm sorry, Dr. Foreman. I thought that if I did what Gia wanted, she would change. I would tell her there was no Posy and then she would stop talking about her, but she tricked me and locked me in and . . ."

Dr. Foreman actually laughed. "Cure Gia? That's what you hoped to do in one evening? I only wish it had been that easy, Phoebe. Gia has been here almost a year."

"A year? But Mindy told us she was here four months and Gia was here seven."

"That's what Gia told her, I'm sure. Actually, that makes sense. It was about five months ago that Posy left. In her bizarre counting, that's how she sees it."

"What do you mean since Posy left? I thought there wasn't any Posy? That letter downstairs? Was that written by the real Posy?"

"No," she said, still laughing. "That was Gia, but that was when Posy left. It's all as I told you."

"I don't understand," I said, shaking my head.

"You will." She looked very pleased.

"You're not mad at me for going down there?"

"No, Phoebe. It was my idea. When I spoke with Gia after you told me what she was saying, I convinced her to do exactly what she has done."

"What?"

"I told Gia she had to do it, she had to get you into the basement so you could see for yourself that Posy was gone. Actually, she went about it cleverly. I didn't think about the details, unscrewing the hinge, screwing it back on, all that. I expected to find her down there with you. She how bright she can be? If some of the girls sent to me would put their energy and ingenuity into worthwhile and good things . . ."

She shook her head and contemplated me again. "I knew you didn't believe me completely. I thought that this would be the best way for you to see for yourself and understand. You do now, don't you?"

"No, not really." I didn't know whom to feel sorrier for, myself or Gia.

Dr. Foreman looked impatient and annoyed for a moment, then softened.

"All right. I'll spell it all out for you. Gia was the one in the basement. I put her there as part of a therapy program I designed. She had cleverly invented this fictional character so as to avoid any hardship, any pain inflicted on her. As long as she had Posy, she could deny her own problems. They were Posy's problems, understand?

"Making Posy my daughter was her way of getting back at me."

"Why didn't you just send her away to a clinic or something?" I asked.

"She wasn't crazy. She was clever and still is. I knew I would eventually help her if I kept trying and utilizing some of my own methods. They worked. She wrote that letter as a way of saying good-bye, which was also quite clever I thought."

"What is all that about Natani?"

"Natani." She shook her head. "He's delightful with his Indian ways. He has no idea how often he has helped me with my girls. That's why I keep him on, actually. He's a calming factor. Sort of a release valve. This place is a pressure cooker at times."

"But, Gia told me I'd find Posy down there so she still believes in her. She's still not cured, right?"

"Well, it doesn't matter that she still believes there was a Posy. The most important thing now is after you tell her and show her everything, she won't be using Posy ever again as a scapegoat. That's my first goal in treating her. Anything she does now, she knows is her own fault. Unless, of course, she creates someone else, but I don't think she will. I think she's finally past all that and on her way."

"What do you want me to do?"

"Specifically, you will return to the barracks and you will tell her there was no one there, and you'll give her that letter. You'll tell her you read it. You know it was a letter to Posy's parents and you know she's gone for good. And you know Posy lied when she said she was my daughter.

"So," she continued, leaning over to pat my knees, "you see, you really will have helped me. Unwittingly, perhaps, but nevertheless, you will have."

I shook my head. It was all still so confusing, so off-the-wall for me, the way she had used me and was still using me. If anything, it made me want to get out of here even more. I think she saw that in my face.

"For now, I don't want any of the other girls to know about any of this. It's our little secret, our problem to solve. I expect you to carry out this order, Phoebe," she said sternly. "You understand what I want?"

"Yes."

"You've made some nice strides these past few days, Phoebe. I can see you growing and changing and becoming someone who can be trusted with responsibilities. You're going to be fine, despite the unfortunate hand you've been dealt in your life."

She stared at me with that soft smile on her face again, the smile that deceives, that gives girls like me so much hope. I remember seeing a mean boy tormenting a stray dog once in Atlanta. He spoke to it softly, kindly, and the dog wagged its tail and filled its heart with trust as it drew closer, and when it was close enough, the boy swung the stick he had behind his back and struck the animal so hard, it lost its balance, scraping its paws over the road to get its bearing and get away, but it wasn't fast enough to avoid a second cruel blow. It managed to run off then, the boy's evil cackle following it like some flame of hate and rage. The boy turned and looked at me. He had a face full of anger, but also satisfaction. He had hurt something and taken revenge on a world that rained pain on him, I thought.

And then I thought what great pain was showered down on Dr. Foreman to make her the way she was?

If she knew I even thought such a thing, she would lose that smile so quickly, my head would spin.

"Okay, Phoebe. Go on back to the barracks. Take the letter and do as I said."

I rose and walked out of her office, down the dark hallway and out the front door. The grounds that had been dreamy with a ceiling filled with stars now just looked dark. I felt as if I were walking through a tunnel at the end of which was only a deep hole.

When I reached the barn, I paused and looked back. I thought I could make out a tall, darker shadow on the steps of the hacienda.

Doesn't she sleep? I wondered, and entered the barn.

Gia was in her cot and looked to be asleep. Everyone else was.

I approached her quietly and knelt at her side, poking her gently.

Her eyes opened and she looked at me, but she didn't sit up.

"I'm sorry," she said. "I had to do it that way."

"I know."

"Did you see her?"

"No, but I found this letter she wrote. She's gone. It's a letter to her parents telling them good-bye. I read it and I know she's gone, and I also know she was lying about being Dr. Foreman's daughter. Whatever you heard her say to Dr. Foreman wasn't true. Dr. Foreman probably just humored her until she could help her. Read it all and you'll see."

She glanced at the letter, but she didn't move.

"Take it and read it in the morning," I said, offering it. She started to shake her head.

"You have to take it." I shoved it under her pillow.

I stood up and only then realized that Mindy was back and in her cot. She was lying there, her eyes wide-open, staring at me.

"Where were you?" I asked.

"I had a special session with Dr. Foreman. Where were you?" The silvery starlight through the windows put an evil glow on her smile.

I didn't reply. I went to my cot and fell asleep almost a second after I closed my eyes. I was so deeply asleep so quickly, I thought the poke in my ribs was part of my dream. Finally, I realized it wasn't and awoke.

Gia was at my bedside, her face close to mine. "At least now you know I wasn't lying. There was a Posy."

She returned to her cot. Mindy watched her and looked at me.

I don't think I had ever really prayed properly in my life. Daddy did his best to teach me religion and took me to church whenever he had an opportunity, but I always had trouble talking to an entity that never spoke back. I used to sit in the church and wait anxiously to hear some great, booming voice come down from the ceiling or out of the altar. When it didn't, I just thought everyone was pretending.

I asked Mama about it once and she told me I was a fool, but my daddy was a bigger fool.

"God talks only to the rich," she said. "Why you think they're so damn lucky?"

I didn't know what that meant either.

I still didn't really know what it all meant.

But what I did know as I lay there was I was going to

find a way to ask God to help me and get me out of this place.

I wasn't rich, but I had confidence that He would find a way.

But what it would take me a long time to understand was why He chose the way out for me He chose.

11

Inward Journey

Gia was certainly different after my basement experience. She seemed less angry, but more depressed. The
defiance we had sensed within her when we three had
first arrived was gone. She no longer snapped at Teal or
Robin, and especially not at me. In fact, I saw her
avoiding me. All I had to do was turn her way and she
would quickly shift her eyes or look down to avoid
mine. It was almost as if she were ashamed of what I
knew.

She had less energy, too, worked slower, ate slower,
and ate less. Mindy could babble in her ear and she
wouldn't turn on her and whip her with any words, any
warnings, as she had usually done since the day we had
arrived. It was almost as if she were truly shrinking
inside herself, disappearing the way her precious Posy
had disappeared.

Dr. Foreman looked pleased about all this. I saw the

smile of satisfaction on her lips when she looked at Gia
now. It soaked me in a new downpour of rage to know I
had been manipulated and used to help bring this about.
I was the one who felt guilty now. I felt responsible for
the changes in Gia, even though Gia had trapped me in
that basement.

No one does anything she really wants to do here, I
concluded. It might take some time, more time for one
of us than another, but eventually, Dr. Foreman pulls
our strings. We move like puppets on a stage she
creates.

I think she caught these thoughts in my eyes when
she glanced at me and saw how hatefully I was glaring
back at her. She didn't cut her face with the sharp, cold
smile I expected. Instead, she fixed her gaze on me
thoughtfully for a few moments, then turned away
slowly and walked off. I can't say I wasn't frightened
by that, but my anger disguised it well.

These dark realizations should have left me as
depressed and defeated as Gia now was, but instead, it
restored my inner fury and strengthened my defiance.
Certainly I was afraid of being returned to the Ice
Room and having the rats, real or not, running all over
me. So, I worked at my chores. I obeyed all the rules. I
recited the morning prayer in which we gave thanks to
Dr. Foreman. I recited the apologies we were supposed
to make to the buddies and to ourselves. I did all I was
told to do obediently, but a fire was building inside me.
I could feel the heat around my heart. It made me toss
and turn at night. It put a little more strength in my walk
and it made those mountains in the distance look closer.

Like the cornered rats that filled me with terror, I
bared my teeth. I raised my back and I looked for an
opportunity to strike out.

Despite what I was sure Dr. Foreman saw in me, she continued to be pleasant, to offer me new privileges, to drive a wedge between me and the others. I knew I couldn't refuse anything, but I believed in my heart that she knew she hadn't defeated me yet. Of course, that frightened me more than anything. She was not going to give up. She had so many other techniques and plans yet to employ. Something new could come from any direction at any time. The expression *you're walking on thin ice* never had more meaning for mc than it did here. I knew I would in time fall through and she would have me wrapped in something so terrible I would lose my name. I would be erased and re-created in her image. It gave new meaning to the word *clones* that Gia had used when she used to talk more angrily about our buddies.

As Dr. Foreman had warned us that first day in the orientation room, she did have godlike powers in her world and we were surely in her world. Her voice cracked like a whip above our heads, even, I noticed, when she spoke to the buddies. They were her girls, but they were almost as afraid of her as we were when they were in her presence.

Only Natani seemed to have a sense of well-being and peacefulness here. He moved through all this as if he were truly in his own world, isolated from the loud shouting, the biting sarcasm, the punishments inflicted on us, and the clouds of depression that hovered above our heads. How could he do that? I wondered. It was like a man walking through a raging fire, never singed, not even sweating.

I studied him with more interest, especially now that I had read the letter written by the imaginary Posy. Was that all part of Gia's madness or was there really such a thing as escaping into yourself? Was there a way to fortify yourself, to do something that would protect you from Dr. Foreman's bullets and arrows? And if there was, would Natani, who supposedly owed her so much, be willing to show it to me? Was that what he was trying to do when he had told me to keep my hogan closed inside me?

I was still the one he favored to work with the horses. Gia had said that Posy had loved working with the horses, and Gia said Natani had taken a special liking to her. Of course, now I knew that she meant herself. She just couldn't believe anyone would or could like her, and if they did, they had to be liking her imaginary second self.

A little over a week after my experience in the basement, I was brushing Wind Song when Natani came into the barn and began to repair a stall door.

I took a deep breath and turned to him. "Natani, can you show me how to escape from unhappiness, to travel to another world, a world inside you?"

He paused and looked at me without saying no or saying yes.

"I'm afraid that if they put me back in that place, the Ice Room, or do something equally terrible, I'll crack up completely. I need someplace else to go."

He nodded and sat back on the barn floor.

"There is a story," he began, "about a desert rat pacing back and forth in front of a tortoise and pausing once in a while to look at the tortoise, who had a smile of contentment on his face.

" 'What do you have to be contented about?' the rat asked him. 'It's one hundred and twenty degrees. Ravens and buzzards are circling around us all day. Who knows when it rained last?'

" 'I am contented,' the tortoise replied, 'because

when something unpleasant happens, I just return to my shell. In here I can cross over to a world where it is cool, where there are no ravens and buzzards, and where there is always a cool and refreshing stream.'

" 'How can you have all that in there?' the rat asked, amazed. 'Your shell is far too small.'

" 'No,' the tortoise said, 'this world in which you pace and worry is too small. In here, there are no horizons, no bottoms to streams, and no roof to the sky, because in here, I make my dreams.'

" 'How do you make dreams?' the rat asked.

" 'Ah,' the tortoise said, 'if you knew that, you would be a tortoise, too.'

"And with that, he pulled into his shell and the rat went on pacing and worrying until he wore himself out and a buzzard had him for breakfast."

Natani turned to go back to fixing the stall door.

"I don't understand your story, Natani," I said. "What does that have to do with me and my problem?"

He paused again. "First, you must become the tortoise, daughter of the sun. First, you must make yourself a shell."

"But how?"

"You must find a place where you can make your dreams safely. But, there is another story I must tell you. It is the story of a tortoise who grew so contented and so satisfied with his dreams, he never came out of his shell. He starved to death."

"Yeah, well, I might be better off," I muttered.

He thought for a moment and then nodded. "Tonight, when the clouds are asleep, too, you come to my hogan and I will help you find your shell."

A part of me was afraid, not of what Natani might do and say, but afraid that he might be doing something

Dr. Foreman wanted him to do. She had told me she tolerated him and that he served a purpose. She seemed so
powerful. It was hard to imagine any place or anyone
on this ranch of hers that wasn't in some way under her
control.

What if she had expected I would ask Natani for
some sort of help now? What if she assumed I would
because of what I had read in Posy's letter? She might
even have told Natani to expect me to ask. How much
in debt to her was he? Were the animals the only ones to
trust on this ranch? The only ones who didn't lie?

I didn't say anything about all this to either Teal or
Robin, and certainly I wouldn't have said anything to
Mindy or Gia. It saddened me to realize that no one
could be trusted even after all this time together, that we
were all so beaten down and defeated that they might
betray me as quickly as I might betray them. In the end
we will have no place to go and no one else to turn to
but Dr. Foreman, I thought. It was almost as if I could
feel two large hands molding us into forms the way we
had molded our ceramic dishes and bowls.

There was truly no other escape but Natani's tortoise
shell, whatever that was. I would either get up the
courage to sneak out of the barn tonight and go to his
hogan, or I would continue to be the desert rat and pace
and worry until Dr. Foreman, like the buzzard, plucked
the soul out of me and turned me into one of her famous
Foreman girls. That had been Gia's prediction for me,
but ironically, it was turning out to be a prediction she
should have made for herself. We were all closing up,
but not in the sort of shell Natani had described. We had
met as strangers and we were returning to being
strangers.

These days the buddies didn't have to enforce the

no-talking rule when they wanted it to be enforced. We all ate quietly at dinner after mumbling thank-yous to each other, chewing mindlessly, staring at nothing. Mindy was the occasional exception. She had the most nervous energy, I thought. The silence appeared to heighten it. Her eyes darted about as if she was expecting something terrible to occur or someone to yell at her. She nearly dropped a plate during cleanup and turned white with fear for a moment. Was Dr. Foreman right about her? Was she regressing, becoming worse instead of better each day?

After we ate dinner, we did at least help each other with the school assignments, but that was still for selfish reasons. No one wanted to earn any more demerits. Our grades were all passing and even the buddies had to admit we were doing well on that score. This was still Gia's doing. She seemed alive actually only when it came to schoolwork, and I began to feel sorry for her, sorry that she wasn't at a real school because she seemed to enjoy studying, reading. It was the only time now that we heard any excitement in her voice, saw any brightness in her eyes. She might even make a good teacher someday, I thought, a real teacher with students who were interested and cared.

Funny how memories of school suddenly became desirable. I had hated it so much when I was there, or at least, I thought I had. Now when I recalled the chatter, the excitement, even the classes, I felt a longing I hadn't thought I would ever feel. This was in no way like the school I had known and abused.

This particular evening, after dinner, we had only a little schoolwork in comparison to what we had been given beforehand nightly. It left us with some free time, and to the surprise of us all, M'Lady Two showed up with a half dozen relatively recent magazines popular with teenagers.

"Dr. Foreman says you all deserve some foolish and wasteful reading. You can share these among you." She dropped the magazines at her feet.

Teal started eagerly for the pile, moving like a starving person toward food, but Gia stopped her with "Don't touch them!" She said it with such hysteria, Teal practically jumped back.

"What? Why not?" She looked at the pile. "What's on them?"

"In them," Gia whispered. "It's what's in them." She stared at them, then looked up at all of us. "Subliminal messages," she muttered.

"Huh?" Robin said, scrunching her nose. "What's that?"

"It's a secret way to get you to think what she wants you to think," Gia said.

Robin pulled her head back and looked at Teal, who shook hers and shrugged. Mindy didn't move, didn't speak.

"We don't understand, Gia," I said. "How can she put something in a magazine secretly?"

"She can! It's like you go to the movies and they stick a few frames of popcorn in the movie. It flashes by too fast for you to realize it, but you suddenly want to get up and get popcorn."

"You're crazy," Robin said.

"It's a proven thing. I read about it," Gia said.

"So she gets me to eat popcorn. Big deal," Robin told her, moving to the magazines.

"That's just an example. She'll get you to do something else. She never does anything, gives you anything, unless it helps her control you, change you."

"You're a paranoid." Robin picked up the magazine she wanted and looked at Gia. "When are you going to learn? Adults always get us to do what they want one way or another. You're the one who taught me that." Robin looked at Teal, who moved to the magazines next. Mindy shrugged and did the same. Gia looked at me and shook her head in pity. Her warning got me thinking.

Dr. Foreman had given me a magazine and told me I wasn't permitted to let any of them read it. Was there something in it specifically for me, something that made me do what she wanted? Maybe there was. Maybe Gia wasn't as crazy as they thought, at least when it came to this.

I turned away from the pile without taking any magazine.

"You're not taking a magazine? You believe her nonsense?" Robin cried, amazed.

"I'm just not interested in any of the magazines."

"That's bull. You took one from her already. Now, because of what Gia's saying, you're afraid," Robin said, smiling. "Gia has you afraid."

"So, I'm afraid. Think what you like. I stopped caring about what any of you think about me," I said. "Just like you stopped caring about what any of us think about you."

I went to my cot to lie down. Robin and Teal thumbed through the magazines excitedly, talking about the clothing styles, the new television shows, the movies they were missing. They moaned over this dreamy young male actor or that. They did it all with exaggeration to make me jealous.

Teal began to describe some of the wonderful things she had at home and Robin talked about her music, admitting she even wished she could listen to her mother darling's singing and playing. Both wondered aloud what was the latest hit record, and suddenly, I realized what Gia was saying.

I sat up and exclaimed, "That's it!" They all looked at me.

"What's it?" Teal said, smiling.

"Gia's right."

"She's right?"

"Only it's not sub whatever she called it. It's right there in front of you, in front of us. Just listen to you talking. She wants you to see what you're missing, to moan and cry about it all."

"Why?"

"So you'll be sorrier about what you're missing, and more obedient and hope more that you'll go home," I said.

"Yes," Gia said, nodding and whispering. "Yes. You understand, Phoebe. Good. These magazines, anything like that, are a form of subtle torture, torment." She turned to the others. "Don't you understand what we're saying? Look at yourselves, what you're wearing, your hands, your hair, and then look at the girls in the magazines. What would you do, would you give, to be like they are?"

The three of them looked at the magazines and then at me.

Robin was the first to understand. I could see it spread through her face, brighten her eyes. She flung her magazine across the barn as if it were poison. Teal stared sadly for a moment, then dropped hers where M'Lady Two had put the pile. Mindy looked wistfully at her magazine and then flipped it.

"I hate her," she said in a loud, hoarse whisper. She

slammed her folded arms against herself so hard, I thought she might have cracked a rib. Then she went to her cot.

Moments later, they were all on their cots and back to being enveloped in a coat of depression. Gia and I exchanged looks of satisfaction, but also sadness. Who wanted to be right about such a thing?

The girls said nothing more. They were all asleep before the lights were out in fact, but I couldn't fall asleep.

I could think only of Natani's shell.

When I felt it was safe, I crawled out of bed, quietly put on my shoes, and tiptoed out of the barn. I stood for a few moments outside and studied the yard. Lights were on in the hacienda, especially upstairs where the buddies stayed, but everywhere else was in darkness and thick shadows because the sky was partly overcast with a thin, long sheet of clouds sliding over the stars.

As I started across, I heard a coyote howl, then a bird that seemed to be on fire flew from the roof of the horse barn into some high brush. I tried to keep within the shadows until I turned the corner and headed directly for Natani's hogan. There was no way to tell if he was awake. There was no light. I knocked softly on the frame of the doorway, and when I heard his voice, I slipped into his home. He was sitting in a lotus position and in front of him was what looked like a pile of ordinary rocks.

"Sit, daughter of the sun," he said, indicating I should take the place before him.

I hesitated for a moment, then did it, folding my legs like his. He reached back and cupped a jug.

"Drink this first," he said, offering it to me.

I wasn't particularly crazy about the smell, and again

I thought, what if this was all arranged by the good Dr. Foreman?

"What is it?" I asked.

"It is something that will start you on the path, help you find your way. Just this once. You won't need it after this. I promise."

"How can this drink do that?" I looked at the tea.

"You will see things as they really are, and when you do, you will be in your shell."

Skeptical and still afraid, I nevertheless began to drink the tea. While I did, Natani began a soft, low chant and tapped on a small drum. As I continued to drink the tea, I couldn't help but think about some of my friends back in Atlanta and how they would laugh and ridicule me for being with this old Indian man. But of course, they were there and I was here.

I wasn't put off by the taste, and I think that even if I were, I would have forced myself to drink it all. I was that desperate. I waited for more instructions, but Natani just continued to chant and play his drum. I was beginning to feel more disappointment than anything else. Here I was sitting in an old Indian man's shack, listening to him play a drum and sing some song I couldn't understand. I couldn't help feeling ridiculous. Maybe that was Dr. Foreman's intention. I was a fool after all.

Natani knew some things, but he was still an old, nutty man. Everything in Posy's letter was part of an imagination gone wild. It all started to make more sense to me. Dr. Foreman didn't care if we talked to Natani or asked him for his mystical help. He was a big joke, a dead-end road that didn't lead out of here after all.

Suddenly though, I became aware of a slow dance of golden lights rising out of the pile of stones between us.

They turned red and moved in rhythm to Natani's drum. I rubbed my eyes, but they were still there so I closed my eyes, but the shapes continued. They went from yellow to red to gray and then blue. They looked like jellyfish, but became small balls that elongated and turned to ribbons of light. Finally, they all became bubbles and rose quickly, popping and disappearing.

Natani's drum seemed to be beating inside me now. When I looked at him, I focused on a crease in his shirt, and for some reason it looked beautiful. The shape of it, the way it flowed along and softened, was all fantastic to me. It made me feel good to make such a discovery.

I gazed around the hogan and stared for a while at a feather he had on the wall. My eyes were like magnifying glasses because every part of the feather stood out, its shape, its color, its texture. Again I thought, how beautiful it is and how wonderful that I have made the discovery.

I felt myself smiling, and although I couldn't explain why it should be, I was content, happy. For a moment I thought of Natani's story and the rat's question to the tortoise: Why are you so content?

The drum stopped and Natani reached for my hand and guided me to my feet. "Go look at the world you have come to hate."

I turned and stepped out of the hogan.

The darkness was lifting like a curtain. I looked at the hacienda, the horse barn, the pigpen, the barn in which we slept, and it all just seemed to come together, but in a lovely way. Each shape was unique and yet I could feel the way everything flowed into everything else and flowed into me.

Suddenly, I wanted to embrace all of it, the weeds that grew at the sides of the buildings, the railings on the hacienda, which were so amazing in the way they were the same and yet different, each with something unique about it that I had not seen before, the garden with plants that were like ocean waves in the breeze. I loved everything.

"What do you see?" Natani asked me.

"Everything." I held out my arm and I felt myself touch the railing, touch the weeds, touch the plants. I could reach the very stars that pulsated, each resembling a tiny heart beating. It made me spin around and laugh. "It's all beautiful!" I cried. Even the ground looked beautiful, spreading before me like a soft carpet, the grains of sand dazzling.

"If you see the world as it is, you will see you are a part of it and none of it will make you unhappy," he said. "The world itself is a great shell. There is no other to seek.

"First, be at peace with your surroundings. See how you are a part of all that there is and how all that there is becomes you. All else will follow, daughter of the sun. I have given you only a small window. You must understand how you should not hate the wind for being the wind or the sun for being the sun. Soon, you will not hate yourself for being who you are either. If you do this, you will need nothing more. You will find your way in and out of your shell and nothing will harm you."

A moment later he was gone. He had stepped back into his hogan.

I don't know how long I remained there looking at everything as if for the first time. I don't remember returning to the barn and getting back to my cot, but then I was there, and for a long moment I wondered if I had ever left the barn. Had it all been a dream?

I fell asleep and did dream. I saw my daddy beckoning to me. He wanted me to come with him, to go somewhere with him. I was very little. My hand was lost in his. He lifted me into his arms. I could feel him carrying me along. Where was he taking me? What did he want to show me?

Outside our window on a ledge, a sparrow had built a nest and the eggs had cracked open. Tiny baby birds were crying and their mother was rushing to and fro with insects for them to eat.

"They're like you," Daddy said. "This is your nest."

I was fascinated.

I had forgotten that time, those birds. The way Daddy had held my hand and watched them with me. How could I have forgotten all that?

My daddy closed the window softly and carried me back to bed, where I fell asleep with a smile of contentment on my face that would make the desert rat and even the tortoise envious.

In the days following my visit to Natani's hogan, I wasn't able to tell anyone what he had taught me. I wasn't sure what it was myself exactly. All I knew was, whenever I felt overwhelmed, annoyed, or angry, I would stop, take a deep breath, and concentrate on something beautiful around me. The bad feeling would lose its grip on me, and after a while whatever it was that had caused it no longer seemed important.

The buddies, especially M'Lady One, took my behavior to mean I had lost all resistance and defiance. They had me where they wanted me. At least, that was what they believed. I could see it in their satisfied faces and even heard them say things like "I knew it was just a matter of time with her. They think they're all so tough until they get here."

Even hearing that sort of thing didn't bother me. If it was so important to them to win, let them win, I thought. What was it they actually won anyway? I guess it was the satisfaction in knowing no one was better than they were, no one could resist and fight what they couldn't resist and fight. That made them comfortable with who and what they were now. Whether they were uncomfortable wasn't important. It was a waste of energy to hate them. Someday, they would be gone forever from my life.

None of the other girls seemed to have what I now had, especially Teal. Of all of us, even after what we had each experienced in one way or another, Teal was still the most impatient, upset, and annoyed. Being terrified of any new punishment kept her from being too loud or ever openly refusing to do anything. She never muttered anything within the hearing of any of the buddies and was always subdued and as submissive as a puppy in Dr. Foreman's presence, but when she could, when it was safe, she moaned and groaned.

She hated the wind for what it was doing to her skin and she hated the sun for the same reasons. This was a filthy, dirty place. We were all going to die of some disease. We might as well just run off and die in the desert as she had almost died. What was the point of waiting for a release that would never come?

I was tempted to send her to Natani. I even started to talk to her about it, but she shook her head and said, "He's as crazy as the rest of them here. Why would he stay here? Why would anyone choose this place?"

It did no good to tell her that this was his world and he was happy in it. She could never understand how anyone would be happy in a world without television, movies, cars, parties, clothes, and jewelry.

Perhaps it was the rhythm of our lives here, the sameness of our chores, our schedule, the ordinary meals, the continuous schoolwork, and the dreaded therapy sessions with Dr. Foreman that tore at Teal more, but I could see she was growing worse with every passing day. Like Gia, she ate less and less. She was soon almost as thin as Mindy.

And she returned to her chant: "I'm going crazy here. I can't stand it much longer. I've got to get out of here. I've got to try to escape again. Why would those damn buddies enjoy this? Why did they come back? If I ever got the opportunity to get away, you wouldn't see me within a hundred miles of this place."

She recited it all one morning when it was just she, Robin, and me out there working in the garden. Mindy and Gia had been given orders to straighten up and clean out the shed.

"It could be they're having more fun than we think," Robin offered. "And I don't mean just tormenting and lording it over us. Remember what Gia and Mindy told us about spying on their partying."

Teal nodded. "Yes, at least they have that, don't they? Why don't we spy on them one night, too, and see just what it is they do have?"

Neither Robin nor I replied. Stepping out of the prescribed order of things had become frightening.

"Well, what's wrong with that idea? At least it will be something fun to do. Robin?" Teal continued, her voice building with enthusiasm.

"I'd be afraid of getting caught," Robin simply admitted.

"We won't get caught. Phoebe?"

"I'm not interested in them."

"Me neither. There couldn't be more uninteresting

people on the face of the earth. It's just something to do, something that we weren't told we have to do," Teal moaned. When neither Robin nor I replied, she said, "Oh, forget it. I'll do it myself. I don't need you."

Robin and I still said nothing. Sometimes, I thought, it was better not to talk, to be like the animals, to listen and see and react only to actions.

Teal realized her threat wasn't getting her anywhere with us and she returned to whining. "Come on, Robin, don't be such a wimp. It's something to do and who knows what we'll see. Maybe we'll learn something. Come on. Do it with me. Please. What's the big deal? We'll peep in a window, that's all, but I'd like to see them with their panties down. I'd like to have something on them. It will make us feel better. You'll see. Please."

Robin looked at me and shrugged. "I guess it might be worth a smile, and if we were very careful about it . . ."

I shook my head. "It's not worth anything to me."

"We'll sneak out tonight," Teal said excitedly, building on Robin's weak moment. "Okay?"

"Yeah, maybe," Robin told her.

"Good. Come on, Phoebe. One for all and all for one. We came here together," Teal reminded me as if that solidified us for life and we owed each other.

I had to laugh. It seemed years ago when we'd first met in that concrete room. "Yeah, we're about as loyal to each other as people in the same chain gang." I laughed again. They laughed, too.

The sound was so rare, it was alien to me for a few moments. Laughter, fun, excitement. How far back had I left them? Was it possible to regain any part of myself or was it all being buried for good out here?

How long had it been since I had done anything that was in the slightest way fun? Parties, boys, pizza, my desire for it all seemed to have gone into hibernation, and that really bothered me. The only thing that made my heart pound now was fear.

"All right," I said. "Maybe."

"Should we tell Mindy and Gia?" Teal asked.

"I don't think so," I said.

Subtly, I had begun to feel the division that had existed when we had first arrived. It had all returned.

"Phoebe's right. They've already done it anyway," Robin reminded us. "It won't be as interesting to them. We'll just have to be very quiet about sneaking out."

"Okay," Teal said. Nothing could discourage her now. She was on a roll.

In fact, she was so cheered by the idea of such an adventure she worked harder, and that night she ate better than she had all week. I thought one of the buddies or Gia would be suspicious and realize something was up, but no one seemed to notice, especially not Mindy, who was spinning someplace deep in her own thoughts. She was doing it more and more now, sometimes actually talking aloud to herself.

What was happening to her? Was it something Dr. Foreman actually saw or actually caused?

Against this cloud that both Gia and Mindy kept around them was the light of Teal's brightened eyes. It was infectious. Robin looked excited and happier, too.

Perhaps something good had already come of the idea, I thought.

I just hoped nothing bad would.

12

Pajama Party

Just above the metal doors that opened on the stairway down to the basement, there was a slanted roof that looked like it was part of a recent addition to the main section of the hacienda. The roof was different, even though the walls were the same shade of stucco. We didn't go back there much, but I had seen it when I was with Gia and could see it from the cornfield when we worked there. Above the roof was the line of windows that we assumed, from what Gia and Mindy had described, were in the rooms occupied by the buddies, rooms we had once hoped would be ours.

Teal, now emboldened by her excitement, went behind the hacienda right before showering for the night and returned to report what she had seen. We had decided not to ask Gia or Mindy about how they had spied on the buddies. That would tip them off that we were going to do it now, too.

Teal said a metal drum was rolled over in the yard right behind the hacienda. She said we could stand the drum up, then stand on it to boost ourselves onto the short roof.

"It was probably the way Gia and Mindy did it," Teal said. "It's easy."

Pretending to go sleep was hard. Now that I had committed to the spying, I was filled with anxiety that made me feel as if I had swallowed a dozen live butterflies. They were flapping their silky wings against the inside of my stomach. I couldn't stay in the same position on my cot for more than a minute or so, and I was afraid my tossing and turning would stir Mindy's or Gia's curiosity.

Neither she nor Mindy said anything to indicate they heard or were still awake, but I still thought Teal was getting up too early. She squatted and tapped Robin on her shoulder. I watched them, and for a moment I seriously considered not going along. They hesitated and beckoned. I took a deep breath, glanced at Mindy and Gia, who looked dead to the world, and then I rose, picked up my shoes, and carried them as I walked as softly as I could over the straw. We said nothing to each other. At the door, Teal smiled. She looked as excited as a young girl on her birthday.

Maybe she had gone nuts, I thought. Maybe I was letting a crazy person lead me into disaster. If I had any real weakness, it was not thinking things out carefully and long enough before doing them. Look how easily I had been led to the slaughter back at Stone Mountain when I lived with my uncle and aunt. If I had been more cautious and skeptical, I wouldn't be here now.

Or would I?

Was this my inevitable fate, a destiny I could prevent

as much as I could prevent the sun from coming up every morning?

Teal opened the door softly and slipped out. Robin and I looked at each other to see who would go out next. It was on the tip of my tongue to say, "Let's just go back to bed, Robin," but I didn't and I feared that I would later regret it.

She went out and I followed.

For a long moment, the three of us just stood there in the darkness listening and waiting to see if anyone was outside watching us. It was quiet. Not even a coyote was howling tonight. Teal nodded at the house and we made our way through a tunnel of shadows, winding from the barn toward the rear of the hacienda. Once there, we looked up and saw the lights were on in one of the buddies' rooms. We could hear music leaking out from under an opened window. Silhouetted behind a sheer curtain, figures moved like in a puppet show and there were short rolls of laughter, happy thunder.

For a while we stood looking up at the window, none of us speaking. Maybe they, like me, were trying to remember when they had had as good a time.

"What could they possibly be doing that's so much fun here in this disgusting place?" Teal asked, now gazing up with both jealousy and anger.

"Pajama party?" Robin offered, her voice dripping with sarcasm.

"I'm sure whatever it is, it's not going to be worth our coming out here and risking getting in trouble for," I said, hoping Robin would agree at last.

"Let's find out," Teal insisted, and led us to the overturned barrel.

We rolled it close to the house, then stood it up.

Because of the slant of the roof, only another three feet or so remained to the edge of it.

"See? This will work," Teal said, and climbed up on it.

She began by getting most of her arms over the roof and then jumping up and pushing. I was surprised she had the strength to lift herself and swing her leg over the edge of the roof so easily. She looked so thin and fragile to me these days, but she was determined and hoisted herself completely onto the roof. She sat in a pool of self-satisfaction and smiled down at us.

"See? Piece of cake. If I can do it, you two can do it," she challenged.

Robin was next. Teal helped pull her along and they were both up there. I hesitated and looked around, half expecting Dr. Foreman herself to step out of a shadow from which she had been observing.

"C'mon already," Teal whispered.

I got up on the barrel. For me it shook, probably because of my nervousness and hesitation, and that panicked me. I caught hold of the edge of the roof and the two of them grabbed my arms, but when I lifted my feet, the barrel toppled and I dangled there.

"Great!" Teal moaned. She and Robin then struggled to pull me up.

Finally, scraping my left forearm, I got most of my body up and over the edge. I swung my feet around and lay there, panting.

"How are we going to get off now?" Robin moaned, looking at the barrel on its side.

"We'll just lower ourselves slowly and jump. We're not that high up," Teal said, refusing to be discouraged. "Ready?"

Robin nodded and the three of us, kneeling to stay

low and out of the light that poured from the window of the hacienda, walked slowly over the roof toward the illuminated window. As we drew closer, we heard both the music and the laughter get louder.

We hesitated.

Teal indicated we should lower our bodies to keep out of sight. Practically on our stomachs, we inched toward the window. A loud peal of laughter from all three buddies stopped us for a moment. My heart was thumping. My forearm burned where I had scraped it, and I felt so weak in my stomach, I thought I might lose my balance and go rolling down and over the edge of the roof.

Teal wiggled like a snake under the window to the other side. She beckoned to Robin, who rose a bit and pressed her back to the wall. Moving on only her heels, she drew closer to the window, then they both waited for me. Another loud roar of laughter came from the buddies and the sound of someone clapping.

Robin reached down for my hand. I clasped hers and crawled closer to the window. Then Robin leaned in small increments until she was looking into the room. What she saw made her jaw drop. She looked at Teal, who peered in and then pulled back quickly, her head against the wall.

Stepping back to make room for me, Robin tugged at my hand and I rose to look through the window.

M'Lady Three wore a pair of jeans and a bra. She had her thick arms around M'Lady Two, who was in her uniform, and they were dancing. M'Lady One was on the bed to the right, dressed only in her bra and panties, smoking what looked like a joint and laughing as the two danced.

M'Lady Three had no rhythm. She was like a tree

trunk, unmoving. M'Lady Two turned out and moved well to the beat. Then M'Lady Three let go of her hand and reached for the joint M'Lady One was smoking. She lay beside M'Lady One. M'Lady Two kept dancing while the other two shared their joint, watched, and laughed.

How could they do this without Dr. Foreman knowing and approving? Was it some way of rewarding them? Or were they just confident she wouldn't hear them or bother with them?

Suddenly, M'Lady One clapped her hands and cried, "Take it off, take it off," at M'Lady Two, who was still dancing. She laughed and turned to them and began a striptease.

Robin leaned in to look over my shoulder, and Teal lowered herself and peered in now through the opening in the window. We watched in awe as they cheered on M'Lady Two. She dropped her jacket and undid her blouse, turning and swaying to the music as she disrobed. When she stepped out of her skirt, the other two stopped cheering and watched with fascination.

"This is stupid and disgusting," Teal whispered.

Robin shook her head and put her finger to her lips.

The striptease continued. M'Lady Two unfastened her bra and held it up and then flung it at them. They laughed and sat up watching as M'Lady Two slowly took off her panties. Then she bent over and wagged her rear end at them and they laughed. When she turned and straightened up, she looked toward the window and we didn't get our faces back fast enough. That was clear from the expression on hers.

Teal scampered on all fours under the window and we rushed to return to the place where we had boosted ourselves up on the roof. We could hear the window being opened wider.

"Who's out there?" M'Lady Three cried.

The three of us stopped and dropped on our stomachs, hoping we weren't seen. We held our breath, but our hearts were pounding like three jungle drums.

"I see them," I heard.

"Let's get them!"

Teal rushed to get to the edge of the roof, lost her grip, and rolled over with a short scream. I heard her hit the barrel below.

Robin and I swung our legs over the roof and, as gracefully and carefully as we could, lowered ourselves and dropped. We fell on our rumps, but neither of us got hurt. Teal was squirming on the ground, holding her ankle and crying.

"I smashed it against the barrel," she moaned. "It feels like it's bleeding!"

"No time to look," Robin said.

Without delay, we got her up and had her put her arms around our shoulders. Then we moved as quickly as we could, staying within the darkest shadows, Teal limping along. We were practically carrying her most of the way. When we heard a door close behind us, we tried to go faster. Teal moaned and nearly fell, even with us doing most of the work. Neither Robin nor I looked back.

When we reached the barn, we opened the door and hurried in, setting Teal on her cot.

"My ankle feels like it's on fire."

"You'll have to put up with it and keep quiet, Teal," I said. I helped her get her shoes off and then we got her under her blanket and made it to our cots and under our blankets just as the door was opened. Incredibly,

neither Gia nor Mindy had awoken, or if they had, they
pretended to be asleep.

I thought the buddies would put on the lights and
start screaming at us, but it was quiet. I had my back to
the door and looked at Robin, who had hers to the door
as well. Finally, I did hear footsteps over the straw and,
moments later, jumped when a stiff forefinger was
poked sharply into my side.

I spun around.

M'Lady One was kneeling at my cot. In the moonlight that poured through the barn windows, I could see
her dropping her cold smile over me. "Been flying
about, Phoebe bird? You and your new friends?"

I started to shake my head, but M'Lady Two pulled
the blanket off Teal, who screamed. M'Lady Three
approached her. Mindy and Gia finally turned and sat up.

"What's going on?" Mindy asked.

"We're doing a bed check. Shut up and go to sleep,"
M'Lady Three ordered.

Mindy lay back and practically pulled her blanket
over her head. Gia remained sitting up and stared
silently.

"Get up," M'Lady Three ordered Teal. She looked at
me helplessly and struggled to her feet, swallowing as
much of her pain as she could.

M'Lady Three saw the blood leaking through Teal's
white sock. "Hurt yourself running about, did you?"
she asked in a mock sweet voice.

Teal nodded. "I need to go to a doctor. I need an
X ray. I might have broken my ankle."

"Oh, sure. We'll just bring the limousine right up
and get you into it. Move!" M'Lady Three ordered,
pushing her toward the door.

Teal started to cry. "I can't walk on it!" she moaned.

"Move," M'Lady Three repeated, poking her sharply in the ribs.

Teal limped toward the door. "What do you want? Why do I have to go outside? It's late," she pleaded.

"I want you to enjoy the cool evening air."

I started to get up to protest, but M'Lady One put her forefinger between my breasts and pushed so hard, I lay back down.

She hovered over me. "Just relax, girl. You're not going anywhere."

"Leave her alone. She's really hurt," I pleaded.

She smiled. "Suddenly, you care about each other? How sweet."

I looked at Robin who was back on her side, shivering in fear that she would be next, I was sure.

"If you don't bring Teal back in here . . . ," I started to threaten.

"You'll do what, Phoebe bird? Huh?"

"I want to see Dr. Foreman," I said, starting to sit up again.

"Oh, you'll be seeing her. Don't worry about that. You want to spend some time in the Ice Room first?"

"You're disgusting. You're all disgusting."

M'Lady Two drew closer. "You better shut your mouth, or we'll shut it for you for good."

She had as mad and as wild a look on her face as I had ever seen on anyone. I swallowed hard and looked at Gia, who was staring at me without any feeling, any expression, not even slight interest.

I folded my arms under my breasts and lay back again.

The two buddies turned and followed Teal and M'Lady Three out of the barn, closing the door behind her.

"What are they going to do to her?" Robin wailed.

"What did you do, spy on them?" Gia asked us, speaking as if she were in a dream.

"Yes," Robin said. "Teal remembered your telling us about it, about their partying."

"You went up on the roof and looked in their windows?"

"We did and we saw worse than you saw. They weren't just listening to music and smoking pot. They were dancing and striping for each other. They're sick and disgusting. Wait until we tell Dr. Foreman what we saw. Right, Phoebe?"

I didn't respond.

Her words died like hollow threats in the dark. Gia went back to sleep and Robin turned on her side, but I sat up for awhile and listened for Teal. I heard nothing, not a cry, not a loud voice, nothing. Finally, I couldn't keep my eyes open any longer and lay back.

Teal wasn't there in the morning. The first thing I did after my eyes opened was sit up and look for her, but her cot was empty. Gia and Mindy were dressing silently. Robin was still asleep. I woke her.

"They never brought Teal back," I said. I wondered why they had chosen her out of the three of us. Why hadn't they taken Robin and me, too?

Robin looked worried, but said nothing. We dressed and stepped outside and the buddies were there as usual, waiting to hear us recite our prayer.

"Where's Teal?" I demanded.

"The prayer," M'Lady One said, stepping up to me.

We did it and then I asked after Teal again.

"That girl," M'Lady Two said, shaking her head, "keeps getting hurt. She shouldn't have walked so much on that injured ankle, but we couldn't stop her from going around and around. Now she's in the infirmary again, but she'll pay for it. As you know, there are no excuses for not doing your work. Dr. Foreman will give her five demerits for this."

"What will she give you when she finds out what you did?" I muttered.

"What did you say?" She stepped up to me again, her nose touching mine. I stepped back. "Well? Did you say something? Did you threaten something, Phoebe bird?"

"No."

"Very wise reply for a stupid girl. Get to work, all of you."

I looked at Robin, whose head was down the whole time. Mindy was muttering to herself and Gia was staring ahead, her eyes so dark.

I took a deep breath and turned to go into my shell, chanting to myself.

From the confident way they acted, I was sure that the buddies had told Dr. Foreman what we had done, but they had given her selected information, of course, leaving out what they had been doing. To my surprise Dr. Foreman didn't ask Robin or me anything specific about it. Teal was kept in the infirmary and apparently not questioned either. Dr. Foreman didn't come charging out of the house, her eyes blazing with anger.

However, the silence made me more nervous. It was like the moments before a bomb would explode. Our days weren't any different, except Teal wasn't with us. One afternoon we saw Dr. Foreman leave in the van and I didn't see her return that day. She wasn't there at dinner either. What does all this mean? I wondered.

The next morning, I did see the van out front again,

and later in the day Dr. Foreman sent M'Lady One to call Robin and me in from the garden work.

"This is it," Robin said.

We hurried to her office, expecting now to hear her anger over our spying on the buddies. She was sitting at her desk, filling out some papers. When we entered, she looked up.

"Oh, Phoebe, Robin," she said in a friendly voice, "I want you girls to take some lessons from Natani."

"Lessons?" I asked. Was she going to make fun of his idea of the shell?

"Yes. I usually start the girls on these lessons earlier, but we've had so much orientation and setting up to do, it's just all taken a second seat. I find it more effective for Natani to work with no more than one or two at a time. He's expecting the two of you in his hogan after dinner tonight. You're excused from any other schoolwork for now. I'll ask you to be polite and give him your full attention. We'll talk about it all afterward. That's all. You can return to the gardening." She returned to her paperwork. "Oh," she added as we were leaving. "Don't discuss it with the others. I hate these petty jealousies that develop. They'll have their turn when it is their turn."

We left in a daze.

"I thought for sure we had bought it," Robin said as we walked down the steps. "What is this about, lessons from Natani? He gives us lessons in farming as it is. What else could he possibly teach us?"

"I'm not sure," I said. "The way she talked, it sounded like some sort of reward or privilege, but yet, I can't help being very suspicious."

"Oh, well. No homework. I'll take whatever little gifts I get here. That's for sure."

We returned to work and, as Dr. Foreman had

ordered, said nothing about Natani and the lessons. All day I waited to see if Teal was being released. I listened when the buddies talked to each other, too, to see if they would mention her and anything that had been done to her, but it was as if she had never been here. Not a word about her was spoken.

Once again, she wasn't at dinner, and once again, neither Gia nor Mindy seemed to care or be interested. What did interest and surprise them was our not returning to the barn to do our schoolwork.

"How come you're excused from that?" Mindy asked irritably.

"We have some other chore to attend to," I said.

"Ah," Mindy said, nodding. "You're finally being punished, aren't you?"

"We'll let you know," I said.

Gia made her eyes small, studied me for a moment, then walked off silently.

Robin and I headed for Natani's hogan. When we got there, he had us sit on the floor. The rocks were gone but he had animal skins in a small pile. Both of us eyed them timidly as we sat, especially the snakeskin.

"What are we here to learn?" Robin asked him.

"The desert."

He said he wanted to begin first with the desert's poisonous creatures. He reached into his pile and plucked out the snakeskin, which was so long and real the two of us gasped and sat back when he held it up.

"Sidewinder," he announced as if he were introducing us to one of his pets, and moved his body to show us how it moved and from what it got its name. "In the sand, it makes this shape." With a stick he drew parallel J-shaped marks. "Tells you it's been here. If the mark is very fresh, you take another path."

"I would take another path if it was months old,"
Robin muttered.

"Snakes come out at night. Sleep in burrows or
under brush. They don't try to hurt you if you leave
them be," he said. "That's a good lesson about most
things in nature."

"I would have no trouble leaving it be," I said. Robin
nodded in vivid agreement.

"Sometimes, foolish person blindly invades its safe
place and it will strike." He held up his healing pouch.
"Inside is rattlesnake weed." He dipped his hand in to
take it out and show it to us. "If someone is bitten, cut
the wound immediately, suck out poison, and squeeze
juice of the plant into cut. Chew plant and swallow
juice. Make you vomit."

"Ugh," Robin said. "Do you have to tell it all in such
detail?"

"Person who has been bitten is very sick, sweating.
Bind the wound with plant after it is boiled. It will save
the person's life maybe or keep him from being very,
very sick."

"Why is he telling us all this now?" Robin muttered,
squinting. "We should have learned it all the first day
we arrived at this hellhole."

He put the pouch down and reached into the pile of
skins to show us a lizard with brightly colored, beadlike
scales on its back.

"Gila monster," he said, holding it up. "Poisonous
bite." He shook his head. "Let it be and it let you be."

"It will have no problems from me ever," I said,
inching back when he brought it closer.

He then showed us four other lizards, the chuckwalla, the desert night lizard, the thorny devil, and the
armadillo lizard, just so we would know them and not

be afraid of them. He held up another skin he called a blind snake and told us it was harmless.

"It doesn't look harmless to me," Robin muttered. "A snake's a snake."

Natani stared at her a moment. "Once the night lizard asked the rattlesnake why he ran from men and got so angry if they came too close. The rattlesnake replied, 'A man's a man.' "

"Very funny," Robin said. I smiled and she looked like she saw the point, too.

"Scorpions you know," Natani continued, but showed us dried scorpions anyway so we could tell the difference between the poisonous and nonpoisonous, and then he held out a dead poisonous black widow. One creature I didn't anticipate was a centipede he said had venomous pincers and could give a painful bite.

"Always shake out clothes and blankets good when in the desert," he warned. "You can have a bad surprise putting on shirt with one of these inside."

One final creature was the velvet ant. Natani said the wingless females could inflict a painful sting and he called them "cow killers."

I could see Robin was getting paler and paler. "All of these creatures are around us, some right under our noses?"

Natani nodded and she looked like she might heave any moment or maybe faint. She was swallowing hard and shaking her head. "If I knew all that was here, I would have chosen a maximum security prison."

Why had Dr. Foreman decided to have Natani do this now? I wondered. Was this our punishment? To be confronted by all these frightening creatures and insects so we would dream about them at night or tiptoe about this place? Was it meant to keep us confined and discourage us from wandering about the ranch? If so, it was working. Robin looked like she would roll herself up into a ball and stay that way, and my stomach was so tight and twisted inside, I thought I would donate my dinner soon to the ants and spiders and snakes.

Natani pushed all the skins and creatures aside and sat across from us.

"Traveling in the desert is harder during the day, but the poisonous creatures I show you come out only at night. Animals in desert know to burrow and sleep during day."

"Sounds like a peachy keen life," Robin said dryly. "What is all this?" She turned to me. "Are we going for a hike or something?"

"Maybe," I said.

"Not me," Robin said. "They'd have to drag me screaming and clawing. That can't be on the agenda, can it?" She looked from Natani to me for some assurances, but all I could do was shake my head.

"Let's wait and see," I said.

"Always cover your head in desert," Natani continued, ignoring our conversation. "Shorts, less clothes, are not good. Sun can be like a knife. You already know," he said, looking at Robin. "But I will teach you now how to make fire in the desert."

"Fire in the desert? That's like bringing ice cubes to Eskimos," Robin said, grimacing. "Why would anyone need a fire in the desert?"

"Fire is a way to signal, cook food, make water good. You know it can be very cold at night, too."

Natani showed us how to use a stick with a piece of dried wood or the thick branch of a bush to generate enough friction. Once the smoke started, he bore down harder, then fed the area with some dried twigs, constantly blowing on the tiny embers. They flamed up and he sat back.

"You try." He gave both of us the means to work a friction fire. Robin and I got the smoke started, but both of us failed to get the flame going until Natani demonstrated again. Finally, we both got a flame. It felt like a major accomplishment.

"Isn't it easier to just carry a pack of matches?" Robin muttered.

Natani's eyes darkened, then brightened again when he looked at me. "Natani can't teach in one day what it takes a lifetime to learn, and what you learn here is good forever. Everywhere there are deserts, even in the middle of your cities."

"What is that supposed to mean? Don't worry about it, Natani," Robin said, nodding, "I'm not exactly going to need to know all this when I get out of here. I promise you, I won't even look at a desert on television."

M'Lady Three poked her head into the doorway of Natani's hogan and we all turned when she asked, "Are you finished in here?"

"No," he said.

"Well, that's too bad. Dr. Foreman wants to see them now."

I looked at Natani. Something in his otherwise impossible to read face frightened me. He wasn't happy for us.

"Now," M'Lady Three snapped.

We rose and emerged from the hogan to walk to the house.

"How was your lesson from the chief, girls? Think you could survive a day in the desert without your makeup?"

"You survived, didn't you?" I fired back at her.

"Are you saying if I did it, you could do it?"

"Maybe."

She laughed.

"And then again, maybe you didn't survive," I said.

She stopped smiling and reached out to grab my shoulder and turn me around to face her. "What's that supposed to mean?"

I didn't reply. She kept her eyes fixed on me, the fury so hot between us, Natani could make a fire with a stick he held up in front of our faces.

"Get moving. You haven't changed," M'Lady Three muttered as we walked. "You haven't improved one bit despite your act. You might have fooled some people around here, Phoebe bird, but not me. Remember that."

I wanted to turn around and just charge at her and scratch those hateful eyes out, but I kept walking.

To our surprise, Teal was alone in Dr. Foreman's office. She had a crutch and was seated on the sofa. She didn't look up at us but, instead, kept her eyes fixed on the floor. I thought she looked a little thinner and paler, but other than that, not much different.

"Teal!" Robin cried. "How are you? Where have you been?"

"Here," she said quickly. "Where else?"

"Well, what happened?" Robin asked, sitting beside her.

"Nothing. Dr. Foreman determined that I had a sprained ankle and kept me in one of the rooms."

"The room with the big bed and canopy?" I asked, slowly lowering myself to the sofa.

She looked at me with small eyes and nodded.

"Didn't she ask you how you sprained it?" Robin questioned.

"She already knew all about it," Teal said.

"But . . ." Robin looked at me. "She never said anything about it to us. Things haven't changed much, right, Phoebe?"

"I don't know. Have things changed, Teal?" I asked, my eyes drilling into her. She shifted hers away quickly and shrugged.

"What . . ." Robin buttoned her lip as Dr. Foreman marched into the office and sat behind her desk. Suddenly, she looked more like a judge in a courtroom to me.

"Periodically," she began, "I review the progress my newest girls are making and I send this report to the courts, to the families, so everyone will know what to expect and when to expect it.

"In some ways, many ways," she continued, looking mainly at me, "you have made great strides in a positive direction. You have learned how to obey rules and you have become somewhat less self-centered.

"Now we are at what I like to call the first of many crossroads. How much faster and further you go in a positive direction will soon be understood, and after that, I will be able to evaluate you and make my report.

"To get right to the point today, the three of you know that I have been very disappointed in your behavior lately. I have waited to see which of you would come forward to tell me about it, which of you has grown in moral capacity to know enough to come to me and confess, to relieve yourself of the guilt you must be carrying.

"I can't tell you how disappointed I am, especially in one of you." She again looked more at me than she looked at Robin or Teal. "I waited and waited and hoped, but, alas, I realize we have a way yet to go.

"So," she said, leaning against the desk and folding her arms under her breasts, "let's begin.

"Teal has told me that it was Robin's idea to commit this stupid night foray to spy on your buddies, to climb on a roof and endanger yourselves."

"What?" Robin cried, practically leaping up.

I looked at Teal, who kept her face turned away from us.

"She's a big liar. She's the one who came up with the idea," Robin shouted. She poked Teal in the shoulder. "How could you tell her that?"

"None of that," Dr. Foreman said sharply.

"Well, she's lying, Dr. Foreman."

"Phoebe," Dr. Foreman said, "is she lying? Was it her idea?"

Teal turned sharply and looked at me, her face so full of fear, I couldn't help but feel sorry for her. I also thought of myself and how I had betrayed her. I wasn't any better than she was, and neither was Robin.

"As a rule I don't like any behind-the-back tattle-tales," Dr. Foreman said, now firmly fixing her gaze on me. "That's sneaky and it doesn't show me any real growth. You have probably all done something like that in the past, and you know very well that you can put on one face with the authorities and another for your friends. It's deceitful and not the sign of someone who has truly found herself and her moral way.

"Either I hear a confession and an agreement about that from the other two, or one of you or two of you reveal to me this instant whose idea it was.

"Well?" she snapped, rising to her full height and glaring down at us. "Whose idea was it?"

"It wasn't Teal," I said.

"What?" Robin screamed, spinning on me now.

"It was Gia's idea," I said quickly. Why it came to me to do that, I couldn't say for sure. I think it was a combination of things. First, it was truly Gia who had put the idea into our heads, and second, assigning blame to someone who was already condemned in Dr. Foreman's mind didn't seem such a terrible thing to do. It was like blaming a murderer on death row for another murder. What difference could it possibly make to him?

Dr. Foreman's eyes grew smaller, darker. "Gia?"

"Yes," I said without hesitation.

"Then why did Teal assign blame to Robin?"

I looked at Teal. "She's more afraid of Gia than she is of Robin. We all are."

Dr. Foreman held those scrutinizing eyes on me for a long moment. She walked to the front of the desk, folding her arms under her breasts and nodding slightly. I thought she was just going to start screaming at me for being a liar, but something kept her from it.

"Are you saying Gia accompanied the three of you as well that night?"

"Oh, no."

"Then what are you saying, Phoebe? Gia did this before or she just came up with the idea?"

Robin and Teal were looking at me with faces of hope, both counting on me to come up with the right answers to get us out from under the hot lights of Dr. Foreman's eyes.

"I don't know, Dr. Foreman."

"You don't know?"

"I can't be sure of anything Gia tells me." This time I held my gaze and met her perceptive eyes. She knew what I meant.

"Don't make me sound like a prosecutor, Phoebe."

"I'm not," I whined.

"Did Gia tell you that she spied on my girls? Yes or no?"

"Not exactly."

"What?"

"She said Posy had done it," I told her.

Teal and Robin looked even more shocked at my mention of Posy's name. They turned quickly to see what Dr. Foreman's reaction would be. She looked thoughtful, but not enraged. She turned to Teal and Robin.

"She told you two this as well?"

"Yes, Dr. Foreman," Teal said quickly. "I'm sorry I didn't tell you. Phoebe's right. We were all together when she spoke about it and what she said Posy saw. We were just bored and we were told how much fun the buddies were having at their so-called parties, so—"

"I'm not interested in that," Dr. Foreman snapped, thought again, and walked back to her desk chair. "I'm disappointed." Then, after a beat of silence during which she looked as troubled as I had ever seen her look, she added, "In all of you."

After another quiet moment, she looked up sharply at us, wearing a face of utter disgust, and said, "You're dismissed. Return to your quarters until I call for you."

"You mean, stay in the barn?" Robin asked.

"Are you deaf? Yes. Now go." Dr. Foreman waved at the door.

The three of us got up slowly and walked out, each of us holding her breath.

Had we escaped a terrible punishment? Dr. Foreman had so wanted to divide the three of us again. I could almost see her tasting the new victory. Surely that was what had disappointed her, but when she was disappointed, she was so depressed and angry, it made Mama's tantrums look like child's play, I thought.

None of us spoke until we were far enough away from the front of the hacienda not to be overheard.

"How could you do that?" Robin began, grabbing Teal so hard, she almost pulled the crutch out from under her. "How could you say I was the one?"

"I didn't know what to say. She had me trapped in that room and it was terrifying. First she was so nice, so thoughtful and concerned, and then she was so angry, I thought she was going to boil me in a big pot, and I was very frightened whenever the buddies came around. I was stuck in that bed and the door was always locked and—"

"Forget about it, Robin," I said. "You would have given up your mother."

"Big deal. I'd give her up for a piece of apple pie right now," she said, still fuming. Then she relaxed and looked at me and smiled. "That was good thinking in there, Phoebe. I didn't remember Gia saying it was Posy who did it, but that was a good idea. It stopped her cold. I could see that."

"Yeah, thanks for getting me off the hook," Teal said, limping along. "I'm surprised she let us go so easily. I guess Gia might be right after all. I guess Posy was her daughter."

I stopped walking. "There was no Posy. She has no daughter. Posy was just someone Gia made up."

They both stared at me.

"How do you know that for sure?"

"Gia wanted to prove to me that there was a Posy and that she was in the basement."

"How?"

"I went there with her one night and she tricked me and trapped me below. But it wasn't her fault. Dr. Foreman had her do it."

"Why?" Teal asked.

I told them about my experience in the basement and the letter.

"You've kept that all to yourself?" Teal complained.

"It wasn't anyone else's business," I said, "and those were Dr. Foreman's orders."

"You could have told us anyway."

"Oh, suddenly you're my new best friends? C'mon, if she told you to keep quiet about something that involved me, you would become a total mute. Don't put on any airs or try to make me feel bad, Teal."

"She's right," Robin said, still unforgiving. "You gave me up and I don't care what they did to you."

"And she's right about what you would have done, too."

"Okay, so we're not exactly loving friends. What's the difference whether or not Phoebe told us about Gia and the imaginary Posy?" Robin said. "She's right. It had nothing to do with us."

"Oh, how I hate this place," Teal moaned.

Robin turned back to me and smiled. "You were even more clever than I first thought, Phoebe. Blaming an imaginary person that Dr. Foreman wanted you to keep secret. What was she going to do? Call you a liar? And in front of us?"

I looked back at the hacienda. "I don't know. Maybe it was smart. Maybe it was the dumbest thing I've done since I was brought here. Whichever it was," I said, starting along again, "I have the feeling I'm gonna find out soon.

"Maybe sooner than I imagine."

We continued along, silence like a big black sheet falling over us with just the sound of Teal's crutch poking the dried earth accompanying us back to our barracks.

None of us looked forward to sleeping tonight.

We'd all see those eyes.

Dr. Foreman's eyes at the end of our session, full of the most utter disgust and contempt I had ever seen in the eyes of an adult who was looking at me.

What would cause such rage? I wondered.

And then I thought, perhaps we . . . or maybe just I was the first candidate she had ever had that she thought she might fail to make into a Foreman girl after all.

Something told me she would never permit a failure to leave this place.

Even Posy, imagined and unreal, had to be made to disappear.

13

Marooned

To our surprise, not only didn't we hear a second shoe drop, but in the morning we were greeted with unexpected gifts. M'Lady One entered with her arms full of clothing. She distributed prettier white blouses and khaki walking shorts as well as new socks and pairs of light brown sneakers. Teal was depressed because we were also provided with new hairbrushes and she had no hair to brush.

"Is this some sort of a reward for work or something?" I asked M'Lady One.

"No, stupid," she said. "It's a punishment."

"I almost feel like a human being again," Robin cried after she put on a blouse and brushed her hair. "These shorts aren't too bad either."

Teal checked for a label and saw where they were made in China. "Probably fall apart in a day or two," she muttered, still pining over her shortened hair. "The sneakers aren't bad though."

I was cautiously happy. Only Gia looked upset about it. She stared at everything as if one of those centipedes Natani had shown us might be lodged in something. All of us were changed and dressed and she hadn't changed into anything yet.

"What's wrong, Gia?" I asked.

"I don't know. This is not like her. I don't know."

"She probably had the clothes lying around or maybe it's like those prisoner of war camps where someone comes to inspect and she's just getting us ready for it," Robin suggested. "What do you think, Phoebe?"

I stared at Gia. "I don't know what to think. Maybe it's like the magazines, huh, Gia?"

"Maybe," she said finally, putting on a blouse. "Maybe it's something more."

"Maybe it's something more, maybe it's not like her, maybe it's maybe. You can drive someone nuts," Teal shouted at her. "Why don't you just take it and be grateful and get yourself out of here already? Or don't you want to go home?"

Gia looked at her as if it were a good question. "Maybe I don't." She turned her back and put on the shorts.

Mindy watched her and then gazed at me with concern.

"Well, I know I do. I'd crawl out on my hands and knees if I had to. Almost did," Teal reminded us.

"It's not over yet," Gia said, looking up as she buttoned her shorts. "You may be on your hands and knees yet."

Teal smirked, shook her head, and sat to put on her new sneakers. "I have about fifty pairs at home, every color you can imagine, every new style." She sat quietly, remembering.

"Let's go, ladies," M'Lady Three said from the door. "This morning you're going directly to breakfast. No morning work detail."

Again, we looked at each other. I began to really wonder if Robin wasn't right. We were going to be inspected by some agency and Dr. Foreman was putting on a shiny new look.

"Was this place ever inspected since you've been here, Gia?" I asked.

"No. Or at least not that I know of."

"Then, I'm right," Robin decided. "It's obviously time for an inspection."

"Well, I can tell you this," Teal said, "if someone pulls me aside to ask me how things are going, he or she is going to get an ear so full, his head will tilt to one side."

"Just remember," Mindy cautioned, "if you're not shipped out soon after you spill your guts, one of the buddies might spill them for you."

"I don't care! I'm sick of all this and I want the world to know it!" Teal screamed at her.

Mindy just smiled at her, which irritated Teal even more.

"You're sick," she said. "You're all sick," she continued, looking mostly at Gia.

"Shut up, Teal," I said.

"I want to go home. I'll do anything to go home," she moaned, and hobbled along.

We did have a more elaborate breakfast, even some Danish pastries, which reinforced our theory that we were about to be observed and evaluated by some government agency. Gia ate tentatively, looking everything over twice to be sure rat poison wasn't over it or something. She made me nervous, but Robin and Teal weren't in any way intimidated. They ate as much as they could, as did Mindy, who reminded me of a starving dog, gazing around her after almost every bite to be sure no one was nearby to take it away.

Toward the end of breakfast, M'Lady Three came into the dining room to announce the day's chores and assignments.

"Mindy and Gia are to report to the garden as usual. Teal, Robin, and Phoebe are going on an off-grounds work detail and, after they clean up in here and put everything neatly away, are to report outside to get into the van."

"Off-grounds?" Teal asked first. "What's that?"

"That is off-grounds, an outside area. You still speak English, don't you?" M'Lady Three quipped.

Teal looked at me, but I was staring at Gia, who was staring back at me, and what I saw in her eyes, I did not like.

"Move it!" M'Lady Three ordered, and Gia and Mindy left the room quickly, neither looking back at us. "Clean up. Ten minutes to departure," she shouted at us.

"What's this mean, working off-grounds?" Teal asked me as soon as M'Lady Three was gone.

"I don't know, but I don't like it."

"I guess we really are like prisoners on a chain gang," Robin said. "We're probably volunteered by Dr. Foreman to work on a road or something just like inmates."

"How can I work on a road? I'm injured," Teal protested.

"I'm sure they'll find something you can do," Robin said, taking dishes off the table.

I helped her and Teal was left to clean the table off. Robin and I washed and dried the dishes and silverware, neither of us talking much at all.

"Stop looking so worried, Phoebe," she finally told

me. "At least we're getting out of here and can see some new scenery."

"I hope you're right," I said without confidence.

When we were finished, we joined Teal and all walked out front to where the van was parked. M'Lady One was there with three small bags, the kind of backpacks you could wear over your shoulders.

"These are your off-grounds kits," she explained, and opened one up to take out its contents. "First, a canteen full of cold water. Drink it sparingly. Second, bars of nutritional food. Each of you has three. A towel to wipe your ugly faces, some tampons just in case, a vial of cyanide just in case you're captured." She laughed. "Just kidding, of course. Who would want to capture you?

"All right," she said, opening the van doors, "get in. There's work to be done."

"How far away are we going?" Teal asked.

"We were thinking of your sweeping streets in New York. How far are you going? Just get in and shut up."

Robin got in first and I followed, then we helped Teal in with her crutch. M'Lady One shut the door immediately.

"This brings back fond memories," Robin said.

"If there is even the slightest chance of getting away once we get to wherever we get," Teal said, "I'm going for it."

"On a crutch?" I asked.

"I said I'd crawl if I had to and I will."

"Maybe I would, too," Robin added.

A tiny bit of light came through the crack in the door so at least we weren't in total darkness as we had been the first time we were in this van. I sat back and tried to relax when I heard the engine start and felt us pulling away. Then I glanced to my right.

Something was there.

"What's this?" I muttered, reaching for it. It looked familiar.

I held it up.

"What is it?" Teal asked.

"Phoebe?" Robin followed.

I looked at the two of them. "It's from Natani. It's his healing bag."

"What's that for? I mean, what does it mean that he left it in here?" Teal asked, whining.

"It means, we're in bigger trouble than we imagined. Dr. Foreman is finally punishing us."

"I don't understand," Teal said.

"I think I do," Robin said.

"Well, tell me, big shot."

"Maybe we should just wait to see," I said. "Let's not panic until we have to panic."

"Oh, great. And here I thought we were going on a picnic," Teal moaned.

We were all quiet, listening to see if we could hear anything that would give us even a slight hint as to where we were going and what we would be doing. The roughness of the ride, however, began to reinforce my worries. I couldn't see Robin's face clearly, but I was sure the same was occurring to her as well.

"How far away are they taking us?" Teal cried after what was surely a good hour. "I'm so nauseous, I'm sorry I ate anything this morning."

Finally, the van stopped. We heard a door slam and then the back doors were opened. The brightness made us all squint for a few moments.

"Ladies," M'Lady Two said, standing there and looking in at us. She wore a wide-brimmed hat.

Robin crawled out first and I followed with Natani's

medicine bag around my shoulder. I reached back to get Teal's crutch, then Robin and I helped her down. We stood there looking around. We were, as I had feared, in the middle of the desert. The mountains, in fact, looked farther away than they did when we were at the ranch.

"Where are we?" Teal asked first.

"That's top-secret information," M'Lady One said.

"We're going for a long walk in the desert, aren't we?" I asked. "This isn't a work detail."

"Believe me, Phoebe girl, a walk in the desert is a work detail," M'Lady Two replied, smiling.

"How can I walk in the desert? I can't walk back at the ranch that well," Teal complained.

"You can walk just like the rest of us. You've been using that sprain as an excuse from work long enough," M'Lady Two said. "Ready?"

"I'm not going," Teal declared, and folded her legs to sit on the ground.

M'Lady One looked at M'Lady Two.

"I'll meet you at the designated spot," M'Lady One said, and got into the van. We watched her start the engine and drive away.

"This way, girls," M'Lady Two said, and began to trek forward.

No one moved. She stopped and looked at us. Teal tried to keep her mask of defiance over her face of fear.

"I'm walking and meeting that van," M'Lady Two said, pointing at the van, which was disappearing over a hill. "If you girls want to remain here, you can," she said, shading her eyes to gaze up at the noonday sun burning down on us. "However, I wouldn't advise it."

She started away. I looked at Robin.

"We've got no choice," I said, and began to follow.

"No," Teal moaned.

"Come on," Robin said, helping her to her feet.

We started behind M'Lady Two, who moved at a steady, quick pace over the sand and rolling small hills. I quickly envied her wide-brimmed hat and remembered Natani's advice to always have our heads covered in the desert. He had also advised against us wearing shorts, and suddenly I realized these sneakers were not proper shoes for this as well. So Dr. Foreman's apparent gifts were not gifts after all. We would have been better off dressed in the outfits we had. She had set us up to suffer out here. M'Lady One's sarcastic reply to my question wasn't sarcastic after all. Punishment had a new meaning and certainly a capital *P*.

I looked back and saw how Robin and Teal were already struggling. The crutch looked to be more trouble than it was worth, especially over this kind of terrain.

"I can't walk this fast!" Teal screamed.

M'Lady Two didn't turn around. She kept her pace and kept her direction.

Robin caught up with me. "What's going on? Why are they doing this to us?"

"It's the punishment. Remember what Natani said about clothing, covering our heads, all that? She gave us all this before putting us out here, and these are exactly the wrong things to be wearing."

"Damn her."

"Yeah, well, it's too late for that." I was breathing heavily already. How could M'Lady Two walk so fast and so steadily? I wondered. She was probably the best at this and that was why she had been chosen to lead us.

"I'm burning up," Teal moaned, catching up to us and wiping her forehead.

I thought a moment, then reached into my bag and took out the towel. "Wrap it around your head. At least you'll get some protection from the sun this way."

"I need sunglasses. My eyes ache!" Teal complained.

"Mine, too," Robin said.

"Walk with them closed half the time," I advised. M'Lady Two was pulling farther and farther away. "Come on, we can't lose her out here." I quickened my steps.

Teal kept complaining and struggling. Finally, out of disgust, she threw her crutch down and hobbled. Before long, she was putting weight on the ankle and enduring the pain just so she wouldn't be left too far behind. From the way the sun moved in the sky, I was sure we had already walked a good hour.

"Can't we rest for a while?" I called to M'Lady Two. She kept walking, not even turning her head.

"Why isn't she tired, too?" Robin asked. "I was going to drink some water, but I didn't want to do it until she stopped and did it."

"That's a good idea," I said.

"I've already drunk some of mine," Teal admitted.

"Don't drink any more," I warned.

"Why not? We can't be going too much longer before we reach the van, can we?"

"Look out there," I said. "Any sign of a van for miles and miles?"

Teal paused and panned the scene before us. The cacti stood like sentinels over the sand, rocks, and bushes. There wasn't a house or a road, or any sign of civilization, for as far as we could see in any direction. Heat seemed to be steaming up from the earth. Nothing moved that we could see. It was as if the whole world had come to a complete stop.

"Where are we?" Robin asked.

"What is this? Stop!" Teal screamed, the panic settling in her throat like a lump of coal and turning her scream into more of a desperate screech, but I was sure her voice didn't even reach M'Lady Two.

"Just keep going," I advised.

At one point M'Lady Two was so far ahead, she disappeared over the top of a knoll. We all walked faster. I even broke into a run because I saw how we had lost too much distance and how long it would otherwise take to catch up to her. When I reached the top, I stopped and the other two caught up with me.

"What is it?" Teal asked. "Why are you stopping?"

Robin and I turned our heads and put our hands on our foreheads to shade our eyes. Sweat was running down my forehead, under the towel. I had to wipe it away to keep my eyes open.

"I don't understand," Robin said.

"What?" Teal moaned. "What is it now?"

"I don't see her," I said angrily. "Do you?"

"Huh?" Teal shaded her eyes and looked as well. "Where could she be?"

The knoll slanted down on our left. I thought she might have gone that way and then back around to the other side to lose us and frighten us a bit, so I walked quickly and than ran to the end and went around it. Robin followed.

We both stood there looking for her.

"Do you see her?"

"No," I said.

"Maybe the other side or maybe . . ." Robin looked ahead. "Maybe she reached that hill before you had gotten to the top."

"That's pretty far away, but I hope so," I said. "She's

not heading back from what I can see, although I'm not sure if that's back or not anymore," I added, pointing.

"Well, the sun is going west and it was . . ."

"Directly overhead. I can't remember. Let's get going. She must be over that far hill just as you say."

We started in that direction and Teal met us in the middle.

"Did you see her? Is that where she went?" she asked, nodding in front of us.

"We think so, but we're not sure."

"This is crazy."

"No. It's part of a plan, I'm sure," I said. "They want us to be frightened, to suffer, to cry and to panic."

"Well, I have news for them," Teal said. "We are doing all that so they can stop it. Stop it!" she screamed.

"Keep walking," Robin said. "You're just acting like an idiot."

"I'm acting like an idiot? My feet are burning. These sneakers are too thin and the sand is so hot it's like walking over the top of a stove."

"Maybe we can catch a bus over the next hill," Robin told her.

"Funny. Boy, are you funny."

"You're wasting your energy, both of you," I chastised, and I walked harder and faster, leaving them a good twenty or thirty yards behind me, their bickering sounding like a dozen chipmunks. When I reached the far hill, I stood and looked around again, and again I saw no sign of M'Lady Two. Where could she possibly be? The cacti were too narrow for her to be hiding behind one and the bushes were too low, I thought. I would see her.

While I waited for Robin and Teal to catch up, I took my first drink of water. Then I sat on the sand, near

some brush. One of Natani's thorny devil lizards peered
out at me curiously. I watched it and was amazed at
how still it could be. As soon as the other two came up,
it pulled itself back into the darker areas of the brush.

"What?" Robin asked.

"She's gone," I said.

"Gone?" Teal said.

"How can she be gone?" Robin wondered, and lowered herself to the ground. She saw I had taken a drink
from my canteen and took out her own.

"It's like she just disappeared into thin air," I said.

I stared at the vast stretch of desert sand and brush in
all directions. Still, nothing large enough to be M'Lady
Two moved. The heat wavered over the ground, making
it all look unreal. Above us, there wasn't a cloud in the
sky. It seemed all sun, one gigantic ball of fire bearing
down and over us.

I watched another lizard, a chuckwalla, burrow itself
deeper into the sand and I nodded.

"What?" Robin asked, seeing a smile on my face.
"What's so funny? We're lost in hell."

"I think I know what she did. She had time to bury
herself in the sand before we reached the top of that
first big hill back there. In our panic and excitement, we
might have walked right past her."

"You're crazy," Teal said. "She couldn't do that."

"It wouldn't take all that long to do, and who would
have expected it? We were looking out there, searching
for the sight of someone walking."

"I can't believe it," Teal insisted.

"I can," Robin said. "I think Phoebe's right."

"Well . . . well, why would she?" Teal asked, the
dread and the fear slipping into her voice.

"She waited until we were far enough away and then

she came out of the sand and probably walked back to where the van dropped us off," I said, imagining what their plan might have been.

"You mean, they've left us out here?"

"See that, Teal," Robin said, "when you're left to your own, you can think and reach conclusions."

"Very funny. They wouldn't, couldn't do that. Why, look at this?" Teal said, waving her arms at the desert around us. "This is the desert."

"You ran off into it before, didn't you?" Robin said.

"I didn't get half as far as we've already walked. I followed a road that just disappeared on me, but it wasn't like this. There was . . ."

"What?"

"That road. I thought about going back to it. I just got too tired. This is different. This is really the desert."

"You sure made it sound like you almost got away," Robin reminded her. "What are you saying now, you went only a little ways from the ranch before you had to take a rest?"

Teal was silent.

"You probably didn't get half a mile away. How pathetic."

"At least I tried," she whined.

"Can't you two shut up?" I said.

"What do you really think is happening, Phoebe?" Robin asked.

"It all makes sense now . . . Dr. Foreman ordering Natani to give us desert lessons, giving us these clothes . . . we're in another one of her tests, I suppose. If we survive, we'll be better for it. Something stupid like that."

"Then she knows where we are?" Teal asked hopefully.

"In a very general way, maybe."

"A general way? What if we die out here?"

"So, we tried to run away and we died," Robin said. "Right?"

I nodded.

"Well, what should we do?" Teal practically screamed.

I stood up and brushed off my legs.

They both looked up at me.

"Yeah," Robin said, "what should we do?"

"Survive." I started to walk again.

"Wait," Robin said, rising.

I paused and looked back. "What?"

"Why are we going in that direction? Shouldn't we try to get back to where we were?"

I thought a moment and shrugged. "Can you remember the way back?"

"Yes," Robin said. "Or we could just follow our steps or look for something familiar."

"You have to be kidding. Familiar?" Teal said. "It all looks the same."

"We'll look for our steps. We'll get back there to that place, I'm sure," Robin insisted. "And then we could follow whatever road they took, or hopefully whatever is left of the tire tracks."

"Okay," I said. "Let's try."

We began to walk back. For a while we did see signs of our steps, but the wind had come up and the sand was beginning to flow like waves in the sea. Soon, it was as if we had dropped a tablespoon of water in the ocean and then tried to find it again. Teal was screaming and complaining constantly, but the wind took her voice off as well.

At a particularly large clump of bushes and near

some cacti, I paused to give us a rest, then took a second swig of my canteen. We hovered around each other.

"Are you sure we're not going too far on the right?" Robin asked mc.

"No, I'm not sure. I'm not sure of anything anymore."

"What does that mean?" Teal cried. "You don't know where you're going now?"

"I'm not your desert guide, you know. I'm no better at finding my way around here than you are."

"But you're leading us and we're following."

"So you lead," I said.

"I'm so tired," Teal replied instead of arguing. "Can we take a longer rest?"

"We're going to burn up out here," Robin reminded her. "Look at your legs. Look at mine."

I nodded and reached into Natani's healing bag to come out with the ointment he had once used on them. They recognized it immediately and began to smear it on their legs and arms and each other's neck, neither complaining about how it made them look now.

"Do your faces, too," I advised. I took some and put it on my own.

"Why are you doing that? Natani calls you daughter of the sun because you're black, doesn't he?" Teal asked, sounding jealous.

It made me smile. "Yes. I have an advantage out here, but black people do get sunburn and do get skin cancers. My daddy told me that and I never forgot it."

Teal looked skeptical.

"You know . . ." Robin said, looking around and watching the wind roll dried brush over the sand. It bounced and flew with such ease. "Maybe we should follow Natani's advice about traveling in the desert and wait until the sun goes down."

"What are you talking about?" Teal said sharply. "If we don't get back to the van, they might think we're lost and leave without us or something and then we'll really be lost."

"If they were really worrying about that, Teal, they wouldn't have left us out here like this," I said. "I doubt very much that they're sitting in some hot van waiting to see if we'll make it back. Robin's right. It's harder to travel in the desert now."

"Well, what are we going to do?"

"Have lunch," I said, "and then burrow under the sand and take a nap."

"What? I'm not burrowing under any sand. That's disgusting, and who knows what sort of things will be crawling all over us."

"Suit yourself." I opened one of the nutritional bars.

Robin did the same. Petulantly, Teal followed. She reached for her canteen again, and I held out my hand.

"You're drinking too much too fast."

"So?"

"Look around. I don't see any restaurants. If you run out of water way ahead of us, we'll have to give you some of our own and then we'll all suffer more."

Teal looked at Robin, then tightened the cap on her canteen and stuffed it back into her bag.

Using the bag, I began to dig myself a ditch in the sand. Robin did the same, and soon we were low enough to cover ourselves with sand and keep the sun off our exposed legs and arms especially. Teal watched, still stubborn. I put the bag over my face and closed my eyes. The wind continued to blow around us.

"This is insane!" Teal screamed.

However, it wasn't long before we heard her start to dig, mumbling and complaining all the while.

"You're listening to a crazy old Indian. Maybe this is wrong," she said.

Neither Robin nor I answered.

We heard her scream in frustration and then she was quiet. Soon, I did feel cooler, not cool, but cooler, and it was enough to permit me to close my eyes and seek some rest. Soon I surprised myself and actually fell asleep.

I woke first and not because I was fully rested before Robin and Teal. I felt something on my stomach and then on my chest. When I opened my eyes, the sun was almost completely down behind the mountains in the distance, but it was light enough for me to realize I was looking at the side of the head of a Gila monster, the poisonous lizard. I did not move a muscle. Eyeing me, it didn't move. My heart began to pound so hard, I was sure that would frighten it.

But it was Teal's scream that did that. She had woken and sat up and saw it on me. The creature scurried off and disappeared quickly.

"What was that?" she asked. Robin sat up and wiped her face.

"Gila monster," I said, amazed at how casual I sounded about it. "Okay, we each take another drink of water and then we continue."

As we started walking again, the sun continued to descend. Soon night began to slide over the desert sky and stars popped out brightly. There was no moonlight, but the sky was so clear that the starlight was enough to illuminate the desert. The sand glistened and the silhouetted cacti seemed to look even more like soldiers at attention.

302 V. C. ANDREWS

Robin was the first to hear the coyotes. I was too deep in thought and Teal's ears were full of her own stream of constant moans and complaints, curses and cries.

"Look," Robin shouted, pointing to her right.

We stopped. A pack of coyotes was moving rapidly parallel to us, but not coming at us.

"Oh, my God," Teal said. "Do you think they want to eat us?"

"Probably, but as I understand from what Natani told me, they are cowards," I said.

"Cowards in a pack create their own courage," Robin said wisely, "but as long as we look strong, they'll keep their distance, I'm sure."

"I'm glad you're sure. How do we show them we're strong and unafraid of them?" Teal asked.

We all thought a moment.

"Let's start singing," I said. "What do we all know?"

"Singing? Are you crazy?"

"No, she's right," Robin said. "How about the national anthem? We all know that. We've heard it enough at school."

"The anthem? You're kidding," Teal said.

"No, no, look. See how the cacti are already standing at attention."

"Huh?"

"Good idea," I said.

We started walking again and Robin began to sing as loudly as she could.

"Oh, say can you see by the dawn's early light . . ."

Teal reluctantly joined in and soon our voices carried over the desert. None of us could reach the high notes and our sad attempts brought some laughter.

"Let's play ball," Robin shouted when we finished.

We walked on and soon lost sight of the coyotes.

"See, it worked," I told Teal.

"They weren't afraid of us. They just couldn't stand our singing," she said.

We laughed again, and then, when we reached the top of a knoll, I decided we should rest and eat another nutritional bar.

"It's time for dinner," I declared, and folded my legs. They did the same.

"Wait, wait," Teal cried, holding her hand out. "No one eats without thanking everyone else and saying I'm sorry."

"Exactly," Robin said, and did it. I did the same and then Teal did and we laughed again.

"Do you think Mindy and Gia are sick with worry over us by now?" Teal asked.

"No. I think they're sick about having to do all the dishes and clean the table and whatever else we did together," Robin told her.

"I didn't mind the work so much. I just mind someone telling me I have to do it or I don't get to eat," Teal said.

"Come on," I said. "You minded the work. When did you ever really work? You told us about your maids and your servants."

"Well . . . okay, I hated the work."

"I can't understand you," Robin said. "You had so much. Why did you get yourself into so much trouble all the time?"

"I had a big house and my family has lots of money, but I just didn't feel like I belonged. It's hard to describe."

"No, it's not," I said. "Blood doesn't make family."

"What does?" Teal asked me.

I shook my head. "I don't know."

"Love," Robin said. "As corny as it sounds, real love, someone who cares about you as much as, if not more than, he or she cares about himself. That's what a mother's supposed to be," she said bitterly.

"But," she added after chewing some of her bar, "I guess she was brought up without love so she didn't know how to give it to me. Anyway, I'm tired of hating her. Hate is exhausting."

We were all quiet. Her words seemed to settle the same way in us all.

"I don't think there was anything I wanted more than my mother and father and my brother to love me," Teal said.

"Why is it that the one thing we all need more than anything, we all have a hard time giving to each other?" Robin asked.

I had no answer.

I finished my bar and lay back with my head on my hands and looked up at the sky blazing with stars.

"If you lie back like this," I said, "and concentrate on the stars, you can feel like you're falling into them and not looking up. Try it."

They did and agreed.

I told them about Natani and the shell. I had told Teal but she had mocked it back on the ranch. Now she listened as attentively as Robin did.

"I guess you have to be out here to understand what he meant," Teal admitted.

"It gives you some power, some control over yourself, something they can't take from you," I told them.

"I'd like to learn more about that," Robin said.

"Maybe we are, right now," Teal commented, and again we were all silent.

It was funny, I thought, but out here, with our lives really still in some great danger, we had suddenly grown closer to each other than we had back at the ranch where we suffered so many of the same fears and punishments. Here, at least for a little while, we were unable to be too selfish. What happened to one of us happened to all of us.

"We're going to make it out of here," I suddenly declared.

"Yes," Robin agreed. "We will."

"We will," Teal repeated.

"Everyone ready?"

"Aye, aye, Captain," Robin said, saluting. Teal started to struggle with her surely painful ankle, and Robin reached out to help her.

"Thanks," she said.

We stood up, fixed our packs, and started to walk again.

"We need a new song," Robin declared. "I've got one. It's one of my mother's, one she wrote herself. She'd never believe I remember it and would sing it, because I used to make so much fun of it, but here I go.

My heart is a prison and you've got the key,
But darlin' there's no prisoner I'd rather be.
So build up those walls and chain me to your
    heart,
For darlin', oh darlin', we can never be apart.

"That's corny," Teal screamed. "But I like it. Keep singing. It'll keep the vultures away."

I laughed.

Robin continued to sing. She had a good voice and she put real feeling into the words, too, I thought, and then suddenly I was jealous.

She was reaching back, thinking of her mother, connecting with her, even this far away.

That was something at least.

I wished I had a song in my heart. I wished for it more than I even wished to get out of this desert trap.

For I knew, if I had a song like that, there wasn't a desert hot enough or long enough to defeat me.

We walked on.

The stars following us.

The night circling with all the creatures that had fled the heat emerging and I'm sure wondering who we were.

It was a question on our own lips.

Who are we?

Would we ever really know?

Perhaps if we do get out of here, I thought, perhaps then, we would.

With every step I took, with the heat fleeing and the cold descending, I longed for the comfort of Natani's drum, for I knew in my heart dangers were lurking in the patches of new darkness around and in front of us.

However, I really wasn't a stranger to all this.

I had known poisonous creatures all my life. Just like here, they lurked in the shadows, waiting to strike.

The shadows that hid them on the street were cut from the same blood-hungry darkness.

And just like in my city, we couldn't get home without walking through them.

14

Natani's Lesson

The later it became out in the desert night, the brighter it grew because more and more stars seemed to appear, and those that had appeared were bigger and seemed closer. At one point when we reached the top of a hill, I looked up and felt as if something, some power, could lift me at any moment and send me flying into space as if I had become a rocket.

I was tired, and my throat was dry. My legs ached, especially in the calf muscles, but at that moment, I had a wonderful sense of pleasure. I was truly in Natani's shell. I felt part of all that was around me. There was still no sign of anyone, no lights in the distance, no sounds, no reason to be hopeful, but I had gone beyond panic and anger and found some other place to rest my emotions. It was truly as if I was rising above the hardship and misery.

"Why in hell are you standing there and smiling?" Teal asked as Robin helped her up and beside me.

I turned to her.

I had become the desert tortoise and she had become the desert rat. It was truly as though Natani were standing there beside me.

"I know we're in trouble, but look at how beautiful it is out here," I said.

"Oh, brother. I'll take you to Disneyland as soon as we get home," Teal said. "All expenses paid. You'll stay at the best hotel they have."

"Somehow, I don't think it will be the same thing."

"No. It won't because we'll have the biggest, softest king-size beds, a plush bathroom, and lobster and steak and big fat rich desserts for dinner, and we'll swim in a magnificent large pool and in our skimpy bikinis drive boys mad with lust and desire."

"Is that what you like to do?" Robin asked

"So do you, so don't put on any goody-goody acts," Teal told her.

I thought they would begin another one of their chatty arguments, but instead, Robin smiled and shrugged.

"Sometimes," she admitted. "Phoebe?"

"I don't even own a bathing suit," I said. "Where would I have used it?"

"As soon as we're out of here, I'm buying you one," Teal vowed.

"And where are you getting all this money for five-star vacations and clothes and travel?" Robin asked.

"I'll blackmail my brother or something, but I'll get it."

"You know if you keep talking like that, Dr. Foreman is going to think you're not cured," Robin said.

We all laughed, but then, as we continued to look out

into the desert darkness where pockets of thick shadows disguised what lay ahead, our laughter wound down into smiles that faded.

"I don't think we're heading in the right direction," Robin said. "From this perspective, we should be able to see something out there, don't you think?"

"I don't know. Maybe in the morning."

"Are we going to stop and sleep now?" Teal asked. I heard the hope in her voice.

"The more we walk now, the less we'll have to do in the heat," I said. "We'll stop midday tomorrow and take another long rest. Maybe we'll find some real shade."

"Or water."

"Yeah," Robin said. "I'm sure there's a fountain out there somewhere just waiting for us."

I started down the hill. Teal groaned with disappointment, but followed Robin. For a while we trekked in silence. I wasn't watching Teal and didn't realize she was not only falling behind, but because she was closing her eyes too often, she was wandering too far to the right, practically walking in her sleep. Robin, like me, was plodding along, lost in thought and not paying attention to Teal either.

Suddenly, we heard a frightening rattle sound and then Teal's scream. When we turned around to look, she was five yards or so off our trail and she had walked right into a low bush under which a sidewinder rattlesnake was concealed. It had given a warning, but she had either snapped to attention too late or lost her bearing and stepped too closely to it.

Robin and I saw it whipping from side to side in its flight, its body gleaming until it disappeared under a rock almost as if it was ashamed of the damage it had caused. For a moment neither of us could move. A cold wave of panic turned our feet into fifty-pound dead weights. Teal had fallen to her side and was screaming in such a high-pitched voice, it seemed to be coming from inside my own ears. She had her hands around her leg and was rocking.

Both Robin and I got hold of ourselves and charged at her.

"What happened?" Robin screamed.

"It just bit me. I'm going to die! A rattlesnake bit me. I'm dying, I'm dying!"

I fought back the panic that was trying to climb up my legs as if I had stepped into a pool of ice water. Then, Natani's instructions came back to me. I turned in a new panic. What could I use to lance a wound? We had no knives.

Teal's screams were vibrating my very bones.

"Calm her down!" I screamed at Robin, and reached into the bush under which the snake had been resting. I broke off the thickest branch I could, then took it to a rock and worked on sharpening the edge.

"I'm going to die."

"If you don't settle down, you will," I screamed back at her as I worked. "You're making your heart race and that's sending the poison out over your body faster. Stop it!"

She paused and looked at me and then at Robin.

"She's right, Teal. Calm yourself."

"What are we going to do? We'll never get me to a hospital in time," she moaned, tears streaming down her cheeks.

"Natani taught us how to handle a snake bite. He put something in his bag," I said, bringing the sharpened branch back to her. "Straighten her leg out and let's see the bite."

I saw the holes made by the snake's teeth clearly.

"I've got to lance it, Teal. It's going to hurt. Just bite your teeth together and try not to think about it."

"How am I not going to think about it?" she screamed back at me.

"Think about the boys you're going to tease at the pool," Robin told her.

I held her leg with one hand, then brought the sharpened edge to the teeth marks and pressed. She screamed and I hesitated, my own heart probably pounding as hard and as fast as her heart was pounding.

"Can you do it?" Robin asked me.

I swallowed, or thought I had, and nodded.

I brought the branch back and pressed harder and faster until the skin broke and I could tear down through the wound. Blood seeped out around the incision.

"Do you remember his instructions?" Robin asked.

"I think so."

"You think so?" Teal asked through her cries.

I placed the bag on the ground and carefully looked at the contents until I located the rattlesnake weed. Then I looked at Robin.

"Got to suck it out now," I said.

"I've already had dinner. Okay, I'll do it," Robin said, which surprised me. She looked at Teal. "This doesn't mean we're in love," she told her, and brought her mouth to the wound. She sucked and spit, sucked and spit. When I thought it was enough, I tapped her on the shoulder and she sat back. Then, again following Natani's instructions, I squeezed the juice of the weed into the wound.

"What is that? It looks like some weed," Teal said.

"It is, but it has medical powers," I said. "Natani told us."

"Maybe it's just in his imagination."

"We'll know soon," Robin said.

"Thanks a lot."

"You're going to have to chew this now, Teal, and swallow the juice. Swallow as much as you can."

I gave it to her and she grimaced. "It tastes horrible."

"Chew it!" Robin and I screamed at her simultaneously.

She closed her eyes and chewed.

"We have to make a fire, Robin, and boil the leaves in water."

"What water?" she asked.

I smirked and lifted my canteen. "What choice do we have?"

We broke another thick branch, and I sifted through the sand and rocks under the brush until I found the thickest dead twig I could. I beat it open with a rock and brought the first branch to it. Robin gathered some dry moss and we took turns rubbing and rubbing, spinning the branch just the way Natani had shown us. It seemed to take forever, but finally there was some smoke. Encouraged, we both worked harder and harder, bearing down as he had instructed until, finally, a tiny flame was born.

Cheered, we fed it the dry moss carefully until we had a good flame.

"I can't believe you two did that," Teal said, watching calmly, her eyes opening and closing. Suddenly, as if the sight of the fire was too much, she began to heave. She vomited hard and fast, moaning and groaning.

"He said whoever was bitten would be very sick," I reminded Robin.

"Oh, I'm going to die," Teal moaned, embracing herself.

Using more branches and thin vines, I devised a way to hold the canteen over the flame. Into it, I stuffed the remaining snake weed. When I thought the water was boiling, I fished out the leaves, and then, using the thin vines of the bush, we wrapped them around Teal's wound, again as Natani had instructed. Teal vomited again, but now she was just dry heaving and really suffering.

"What do we do now?" Robin asked.

"Looks like we take our rest earlier than I had hoped," I said.

Using the backpack to fix a pillow for Teal, we urged her to try to sleep. She was shivering now. The desert night had dropped the temperature to where it was actually cold. Robin fed the fire, building it until we had some decent flames.

"Make it gigantic," Teal muttered. "Maybe someone will see it and come help us."

"Maybe," Robin said, and started to forage for more wood.

"Be careful, Robin. I used all the snake weed in the bag on Teal."

She walked on tiptoe, gently moving brush, avoiding big rocks, and gathering twigs and branches as quickly as she could. Teal watched with a dazed look on her face.

"Will I be all right?" she asked me.

"Sure," I said.

Of course, I had no idea if she would be all right. How poisonous was the snake? How much poison was in her body? How effective was Natani's weed medicine? Was it crazy to believe in him? The treatments he had given Robin and Teal for their sunburn seemed to help, and the ointment he had given them for their hands helped. The Indians lived side by side with all this danger, these creatures. What they had to help themselves must work or they wouldn't use it, I thought.

Teal's eyes closed and opened. She shivered and moaned. If she died out here, it would be so horrible, I thought. It made me rage against Dr. Foreman, but I did so silently, for I didn't want to stir Teal up and worry her any more.

Robin returned again and we fed the fire. It did provide warmth. The embers rose with the smoke and traveled out and away with the wind.

"Anyone looking for us would see this," Robin said.

I nodded.

We both looked at Teal. She seemed to have fallen asleep, but every now and then she would shudder and moan and cry.

"Maybe we didn't get the poison out fast enough or all of it," Robin said.

I shook my head. Her guess was as good as mine. We continued to sit on both sides of Teal, our knees up, looking at the fire. Coyotes howled around us, the wood crackled.

"Once, when I was very little, I went on a picnic with my mother," Robin said. "She had some boyfriend with us, but I can't remember his name. I remember we made a fire and they roasted marshmallows for me, and then we had hot dogs and my mother sang and played her guitar. I fell asleep on the blanket, and when I woke up, there was no one there. They were off in the bushes or something."

"Weren't you afraid?"

"I was for a while and then I watched some birds and got intrigued with how hard they worked at feeding themselves. It was a particularly beautiful day, too. I remember that, and I remember really enjoying myself. Finally, my mother and her boyfriend came from wherever they were and her boyfriend carried me on his shoulders all the way back to our farm. I can't remember his name, but I remember his hair. It was a reddish yellow and I had clumps of it in my small fists, holding it like the reins of a horse. Sometimes, he cried out because I was pulling on his hair too hard, but I remember feeling as if I was on the top of the world, seeing everything from an adult's height.

"I never went on another picnic, and I never saw that boyfriend again. Sometimes, I used to think of it as a dream I had when I was very young. If I mentioned it to my mother, she would look as if she didn't remember it at all. I don't think it was a special or important day for her.

"After a while, it slipped out of my memory, but just now, as we were staring at the fire, it returned and I recalled my fists full of reddish yellow hair. That's silly, isn't it? The only thing I really remember vividly, that hair."

"No. Maybe you remember it so well because it made you feel safe to hold on to it."

She turned and looked at me. "Maybe." She smiled. "Maybe that's what I was looking for through the fire, a way to feel safe again."

We were quiet.

Teal moaned.

I lay back and Robin did the same. Before we fell asleep, we each had our arms around Teal, and that was how we were when the sun woke us with its stinging good morning.

Teal looked groggy, her cheeks stained with lines her tears had made zigzagging their way off her face. Robin and I sat up and watched her wipe her eyes. She looked at us and blinked as if she had forgotten everything. Then she spoke and sent new chills of fear down my back and Robin's, even in this desert heat.

"Where's my mother?" she asked.

"What?"

She sat up and looked at us and then around us, shaking her head. "I've got to get home."

"What is she talking about?" Robin asked.

I shook my head and reached out to feel her forehead. It was so hot, I had to take my hand away.

"She's burning up."

"If I don't get home quickly, my father will be very angry and he'll ground me again," Teal said. "Who's driving me home?"

"We have to walk first," I told her.

"Walk? To where? Can't you call a cab?"

"Can't you see where you are?" Robin asked.

Teal turned to her, her eyes blinking. "Who are you?"

"Great," Robin said. "What do we do now?"

"It'll pass," I said. I stood up and looked out to my right and to my left. Had we gone too far off the trail back? Nothing suggested we were heading in the right direction. It all looked so similar, the same hills, the same cacti and bushes. I glanced at the sun.

"We should probably go more to our left," I said.

"You don't understand," Teal muttered. "I can't stay any longer. I'm already well past my curfew."

"Me, too," Robin told her.

Teal touched her lips and looked at her fingers and then at us.

"I'm very thirsty. I'd like a Coke or something, please."

"I'll call the butler," Robin told her, and looked at me.

I checked Teal's canteen. It was bone-dry.

"We better get some water in her," I said, and gave her my canteen. I didn't see how the boiling would have harmed the water. It was just very warm.

The moment it touched her lips, she complained, "Isn't there any ice?"

"Gee, we're all out. Here, try this." Robin gave Teal her canteen. The water was cooler. Teal gulped at it.

"Easy," I said, and lowered the canteen. "You can get yourself sick drinking that too fast now."

"I am sick. I want to go home this instant. Where's the phone?"

"Gee, we forgot to pay the bill so they turned off our service," Robin said.

"You're not very funny." Teal's eyes grew small as she scrutinized Robin's face. "Are you Jeff's cousin?"

"No. Jeff's my cousin," Robin said. For a moment that did confuse Teal and I actually smiled, although I couldn't see what we had to laugh about now.

"Let's get her up," I told Robin, and we helped Teal to her feet.

"Ow!" she screamed, and looked down at her leg wrapped with the leaves. "What happened to me?"

"You hurt yourself dancing last night," Robin said. "It's the best we can do for now. We've got to walk on."

"I can't walk."

Robin tried to pull her forward but she resisted.

"Oh, great. What do we do?"

"Come on, Teal. You have to try or you won't get home," I said. I took her other arm, and together Robin and I forced her to take some steps. She cried with every one taken, putting as little weight on the bitten leg as she could. Finally, Robin put Teal's arm over her shoulder and that way we were able to get her to move forward a little faster, but I knew Robin couldn't carry her for long.

We took turns, resting every hundred yards or so.

"We're not going to get very far this way," I said.

Teal's eyes were closed and she was rocking softly from side to side.

"You better put the top up. It's too hot," she muttered. "And stop to get me a drink. Anything. Even a beer."

"Yes, it is too hot," Robin said. "Phoebe, can you raise the top on the convertible, please?"

"She's delirious."

"I wish I were. Who wants to realize what's really happening and where we really are," Robin said. "What are we going to do, Phoebe? We can't carry her all the way out of here. We don't even know if we're heading in the right direction, and we've just about run out of water."

I shook my head. I was out of ideas. Gazing around, I spotted something on a branch.

"What's that?" I asked Robin.

She shaded her eyes and squinted. "What?"

"Looks like . . . something tied to that bush." I rose and walked ahead to my left. It was a ribbon. Something was wrapped on the end of it, tied so it wouldn't fall out. I undid the knot and a small turquoise stone fell into my palm. An electric surge of hope shot through my body.

"Natani!" I screamed.

"What?" Robin shouted back, standing.

"I think this was left here by Natani." I looked farther ahead and saw what was definitely another ribbon.

"C'mon," I said, hurrying back. "He's showing us the way."

"Why didn't he just show himself and help us?" Robin asked.

"Maybe he's afraid of what Dr. Foreman would do or say. I don't know. Let's go."

We got Teal standing again and again took turns helping her walk. She mumbled gibberish, phrases and sentences from memories, about people she knew, things she had done, words she had exchanged with her mother, her father, and her brother. Most of the time, her eyes were closed.

On the ground under the third ribbon, we found a basket. I uncovered it and pulled out leather canteens filled with water, packs of dried food, and a pot with matches in it.

"What's that for?" Robin asked.

I unwrapped another packet and found some more snake weed. "He wants us to boil this and change her bandage, I'm sure."

"It would help if he would just send for a helicopter."

"Somehow, I don't think he can do that, Robin. Come on, let's not waste time now. Gather some wood."

She did and we built a fire quickly. Once again, we boiled the leaves, then I changed Teal's bandage, this time using some tape Natani had left as well. We were able to give Teal a good drink of water, then wipe her down. She seemed to become more comfortable.

It was becoming scorching again. We had a hard time making it to the next hill, but when we got there, following another set of ribbons, we looked out and saw what was clearly the ranch.

"I never thought I'd be glad to see that place again," Robin said.

"Me neither."

"I'd like my breakfast now," Teal declared.

"Oh, sure, miss. What would you like this morning?"

"Just some scrambled eggs, orange juice, cinnamon toast, and coffee."

"Is that all? We'll have it for you in a jiffy," Robin told her.

Teal nodded, her eyes still closed.

"Let's take a good rest before this last piece." It looked like a good mile or so to me. We sat and ate what Natani had left.

"I have no idea what I'm eating," Robin said, feeding Teal as well. Teal ate as if she were really having what she had ordered.

"Me neither, but it feels good in my stomach."

Whatever it was, it seemed to renew our energy. After some more water, we fixed our towels on our heads, smeared some more of the sun protection on our skin, and started toward the ranch.

When we were about four or five hundred yards from the corral in which the horses were kept, Wind Song trotted to the railing and whinnied, raising his head. The other horses gathered beside him and looked out at us.

"At least someone is happy to see us," Robin muttered.

Like three soldiers home from battle, we limped along, Teal still relying on our shoulders and keeping most of her weight off her right leg. As we drew closer, the buddies began to appear, coming around the corner of the horse barn. None of them rushed forward to give us any assistance. They stood watching us limp home until we were close enough to hear them.

Then, they began a silly cheer.

"Come on, girls. You can make it. Keep coming. Two, four, six, eight, who do we appreciate? Phoebe bird, Phoebe bird."

They laughed and clapped.

"She was bitten by a rattlesnake," I said when we were standing right in front of them.

"Did it die?" M'Lady Two asked, and the three of them laughed.

"If she does or gets sicker, you'll be sorry as hell," Robin said, her eyes blazing at them.

"Whoa," M'Lady Three cried. "Listen to her. A couple of days in the desert and she thinks she's tough or something. I'll tell you, girls, I'm really impressed. How did you manage to find your way back?"

"How could you leave us out there like that?" I countered.

"It broke our hearts to do it," M'Lady One said. "But we have to do what we have to do. Go shower up and wait in the bunkhouse for Dr. Foreman," she followed curtly.

"What about Teal?" Robin asked.

"She'll live, although I can't say the same for the snake."

"She can't walk on her own," I said.

"We'll take care of her. Move it."

Slowly, we lowered Teal to a sitting position.

"I'm sorry, Mother," Teal said. "It couldn't be helped. Our car broke down."

"Oh, did it?" M'Lady Two asked. They all laughed again.

"She still has a high fever. She's delirious. She needs medical help," Robin said.

"She was always delirious," M'Lady Two said. "Will you two get moving or do we move you?"

"We're not leaving her," I declared, reaching a firm, quick decision. I reached down to help Teal up. Robin did the same.

"I told you we would take care of her," M'Lady Two said.

"Like you've been taking care of us?"

She stepped forward threateningly, but I didn't flinch.

"Go on," I said. "I have just enough strength to fight one more battle."

"Me, too," Robin said.

Maybe it was the ordeal in the desert. Maybe it was the wild, determined look on both our faces, or maybe it was just the sight of us, standing fast despite all that we had endured, Teal wavering between us, whatever, but M'Lady Two hesitated, then relaxed and backed up.

"Take her to the house yourselves then," she ordered, and stepped aside.

We walked on, struggling because Teal was doing less and less to move herself now. Despite the effort, both Robin and I reached down into some reservoir of energy, fueled by our anger, our hate, our indignation, by years and years of our pain and suffering. We stumbled and nearly fell. The buddies roared with laughter, then, suddenly, I could hear Natani's drum. Robin heard it, too. We looked at each other and found the strength to cross that yard to the front of the hacienda.

As we continued, I kept my eyes forward, never wavering, so I didn't see or know if Gia and Mindy were watching us. When we stood at the steps, the front door opened, and Dr. Foreman, dressed in a cool, mint green skirt suit, her face freshly made up with a brighter lipstick and even some eye shadow, looked down at us and smiled.

"Oh, I just knew you would do well. I just knew you had it in you to be cooperative, unselfish, and resilient. My girls, my Foreman girls, always come through for me, for themselves. What a wonderful day," she cried.

Was she blind? Could she not see that Teal was practically comatose and we were standing on legs held up only by sheer determination?

"Teal was bitten by a sidewinder," I said. "She's delirious."

"And you knew what to do, I see," Dr. Foreman replied, still not moving to help us. "Natani's lessons. How fortunate that you paid attention. Imagine if you paid attention in regular school as well. Maybe now you will. See?" she asked as if in that simple question she justified this whole experience, her techniques and theories and all that was done to us in the name of recovery.

"Teal is very sick," I replied in a dry, stiff voice.

She blinked rapidly, but held that cold, egotistical smile I had come to hate, to have dreams about shattering.

"She'll recover," she said, "and she'll be better for it."

"Have you been bitten by a sidewinder?" I fired back at her.

"Don't be insubordinate." She nodded at the buddies. "Take Teal to the infirmary immediately."

M'Ladies One and Two moved forward and lifted Teal from our shoulders. Then they scooped her under her legs and carried her up the stairway. Dr. Foreman stepped aside and opened the door for them.

"Are we home?" I heard Teal ask.

"Yes," M'Lady One said, and laughed.

The door closed behind them and Dr. Foreman turned back to us. "I want the two of you to shower and change back into your coveralls and wait for further instructions in your bunkhouse. You may rest while you wait." She turned and walked into the house before either Robin or I could say another thing to her.

"Let's go, girls," M'Lady Three said.

We turned and crossed the yard to the showers. Both of us were actually looking forward to the cold shower. We couldn't swallow enough water and it felt wonderful on our bodies. Soaping up, scrubbing our hair, revived us both.

"Enough, girls. Move it," M'Lady Three shouted.

I looked for Mindy and Gia and didn't see either of them in the gardens or the pigpen. We slipped on our shorts and blouses and battered sneakers before going to the barn bunkhouse. Both of us stopped dead on entering.

Our three cots had been stripped of their mattresses, blankets, and pillows. Our coveralls and old blouses were on them and our clodhopper shoes beside them.

"Why?" I asked, turning to M'Lady Three.

She shrugged. "You had demerits. You have to earn what you get, remember?"

"This stinks. It's unfair!" Robin cried.

"Welcome to the real world. You have to learn how to deal with unfairness. Not that this was unfair. Rest up, girls. You'll need it, believe me," she said, and left.

"Look," Robin said, nodding at Gia's and Mindy's bunks. Mindy's was stripped down as well. "I wonder what she did to deserve her unfairness."

"I don't care anymore," I said. "I'm too tired to care about anything, even this."

I went to my bunk and swept the coveralls and blouse off. Then I thought again and rolled them up to use as a pillow. Robin nodded and did the same.

In minutes, we were both dead to the world, asleep. Soon after, however, we were poked and prodded until we woke up. M'Ladies Two and One were there with notebooks in their hands, the same sort we had been given at orientation.

"You've slept enough, girls. Dr. Foreman wants you both to start on your journals. She wants you both to write about your experience out there and what you have learned from it. She expects details and honesty," M'Lady One said, and handed me a notebook with a pen.

Robin was handed hers as well. We both just stared blankly at the notebooks.

The buddies smiled, then left.

"She must be kidding," Robin said.

"I strongly doubt it," I said.

"I can't keep my eyes open, much less write something."

We looked at each other and came up with the same cry: "What more can she do to us?"

I put the notebook down and sprawled out again. Robin did the same and we were asleep almost as quickly as we were the first time. We slept well into the late afternoon and woke this time when we heard the door open.

Gia stood there looking at us. I sat up quickly.

"Gia. Where's Mindy?" I asked, seeing she was alone.

"Mindy's gone."

"Gone?" Robin asked, sitting up. "You mean she was sent home?"

"No, I mean gone." Gia walked to her cot. She sat, staring down at the floor. I looked at Robin and then rose and walked over to Gia.

"What happened to her, Gia?"

She looked up at me. "I couldn't stop her. She used the scythe Natani had us use to cut the high grass. I was working and suddenly realized she was no longer in the field. She had been strange all morning after a session with Dr. Foreman. She wouldn't tell me anything about it, but I could see she was very upset, more upset than ever. I kept asking her about it, trying to find out something, some reason for her deep depression.

"Finally, she muttered something about never going home and how it was her fault.

"I tried to get more information to help her, but she clammed up and just went to work with me in the field. As I said, I was working and thinking and not paying attention to anything and then suddenly realized she was no longer there.

"So, I went looking for her and found her in the barn, sitting on the floor. She had taken the sharpest scythe and she had cut both her wrists very deeply. There was so much blood already, but she was smiling at me. I shouted for help, of course. No one was around, so I ran to find Natani, but he wasn't there either."

"That's because he was out there helping us," I said, looking at Robin. She nodded. "What happened then?"

"I tried to stop the bleeding, but that was impossible. She said, 'Leave me be. I was wrong. I'm going home.'

"So I ran out again and went to the house where I found Dr. Foreman lecturing our buddies in her office. She demanded to know why I had entered the house without permission. She stood there screaming at me. Finally, I managed to tell them about Mindy and they ran out to the barn.

"I saw them carry her off, but I knew it was too late. Later, the van took her away. I saw them carrying her out of the house. This afternoon," she continued after a long beat of silence, "I think Dr. Foreman was to meet with the police. Did you see how nice she looked?" she asked as if that really mattered to any of us. "She'll make it look like an accident."

"How horrible," Robin said.

"You know what was done to us, how we were left out there in the desert?" I asked.

"I know." She looked up at us. "I didn't expect you would make it back."

"Natani helped us. That's why he wasn't here when you needed him," I said.

"She's going to get away with it," Gia said. "She got away with Posy. She'll get away with all this, too."

"Maybe the police are still here or someone from the social service agency. Maybe we can talk to them," Robin suggested excitedly.

"No," Gia said. "They're gone. She did her good job on them, I'm sure. We're high-risk girls, you see. Anything can happen and it's not going to be her fault. Look at all the girls she's helped, the ones she's released back into society to be productive citizens. Once in a while, she loses one. It can't be helped. The girl was beyond redemption. I know her whole speech. I've heard it before. I've heard it all my life, that speech. How terrible I am. How beyond help. How self-ish. How downright no good.

"Sound familiar?" she asked us.

"Not as much maybe, but I've heard it, yes," Robin admitted.

I thought about my uncle and aunt and how they saw me. "Me, too."

"Won't Mindy's family be upset, angry, demand answers?" Robin wondered.

"The family that failed, that gave up? Please," Gia

said. "They'll feel sorrier for Dr. Foreman. They'll even apologize for giving her a girl she couldn't cure."

"She's more dangerous than we'll ever be," I said, "because she gets them to believe she does it all out of some desire to be good."

"Exactly." Gia looked past me at the cot. "I see you were given the notebook to fill. I have one, too." She reached under her pillow to show it to us. "I'm to write about what I learned from Mindy's failure."

Gia put it aside and looked at us again, finally realizing Teal wasn't there.

"Where is Teal?"

I told her what had happened and where she was.

"She'll take good care of her," Gia said. "She might even have her transported to a real hospital or something. She can't afford to lose another girl so quickly."

"She almost lost all three of us out there."

"That's different. You ran off. You were beyond her help, her ability to do anything. If you didn't show up, she would have called the police and covered her rear end. Don't worry about Dr. Foreman. She's invincible," Gia said.

She lay back and looked up at the ceiling, her hands folded on her stomach.

"What do we do?" I asked. Robin shook her head.

"Nothing," Gia said. "Go write in your notebooks. I have mine half-filled."

"I'll write something. What I write will make her ears burn," Robin threatened.

Gia smiled. "Good idea. That's what I'm doing."

We had no idea what she meant.

But we would.

Soon.

We would.

15

Posy Returns

Teal wasn't sent to any real hospital. Natani's Indian medicine worked well. After another two days, she appeared at the barracks, weakened, but essentially well enough to be on her own again with just a little limp in her walk. The snake bite and the events afterward appeared to have erased most of her memories of our desert ordeal. Robin and I had to describe it all to her, and as we did, she kept shaking her head and saying, "I did that? We did that?"

Apparently she had been in more of a daze and in more confusion than we'd realized after she had been bitten by the sidewinder.

Apparently because of her condition, Dr. Foreman did not give her a notebook to fill with thoughts and lessons learned. Neither Robin nor I had really done much in ours, but we were told we would not be given back our mattresses, blankets, and pillows until we had completed the notebooks.

I was afraid of writing anything truthful, afraid that somehow Dr. Foreman would find a way to use it against me, use it as a weapon to tear me down, just as she had done with my revelation about my fear of rats. Gia was writing in hers, but we had no idea what she wrote. She wouldn't reveal it. She just kept mumbling, "I'll remind her. I'll remind her."

One of the first things I did when I had free time was to thank Natani. He said nothing, admitting to nothing until I described how I had found my shell and used it to help get me through the ordeal.

"So now I shall no longer call you daughter of the sun. You are daughter of the tortoise," he said, and came the closest to laughing with me.

"You shouldn't stay here, Natani. This is a mean and ugly place. You don't belong here."

"I must stay with my plants, my animals, my trees. We look after each other. Someday, daughter of the tortoise, you will learn that the Earth Mother is your true friend and the only home you will have."

"I think I learned that already, Natani. Thanks again for what you did for us."

He nodded and smiled. "You did well with what you learned."

Because of our near exhaustion and what we had endured, we weren't given heavy, long labor during the first few days after our return. Most of my day was spent helping Natani with the horses, work I had come to love. One afternoon, Natani asked me if I would like to learn how to ride Wind Song. I was terrified of the idea, but he told me I was ready and Wind Song approved. I had little doubt that he could speak to horses.

Natani showed me how to ride bareback. His first instruction was to mount Wind Song from the left side. Even at his age, he was nimble enough to leap and swing his leg over Wind Song's back. I tried it and failed miserably, probably because I was too frightened. Finally, he boosted me up and I swung my leg over. It was not exactly the most comfortable place to be, but Natani said I needed to relax and believe in myself, and if I did, it would be like riding on a cloud.

"Be one with Wind Song. He will know if you feel like a stranger. He will not expect it or like it if you don't join with him," Natani advised.

I put my hand on Wind Song's powerful neck and he shook his head and then tapped the ground with his right hoof.

"He says hello," Natani told me.

"Hello, Wind Song," I replied.

Natani handed me the reins, which he wanted me to take in my left hand first.

"Never let go of the reins," he said. "It is how you talk to Wind Song, to tell him which way to turn and when to stop. He is rein trained." Natani showed me how to lay the reins on Wind Song's left side to turn him right and vice versa.

"Do not pull back when you are standing still. He will think you want to go back. Hold the reins like a bird: too tight and you will choke it, too loose and it will fly away, daughter of the tortoise.

"Wind Song likes you, but he will want to ride you and not you ride him. It is natural to him. He is a proud animal, full of spirit, so be firm with your movements. You must feel his moves, and when he starts to turn where you don't want him to turn, stop him, because once he is into it, it will be hard to make him change his mind."

"Do I say giddap?" I asked.

Natani smiled and shook his head. "You watch too many cowboy-and-Indian movies. You press firmly with your heels into his sides when you want him to go forward. Don't worry about hurting him. You won't, but he will know you are serious if you press firmly. Bounce with him, daughter of the tortoise." Natani then slapped Wind Song on the rump and he started around the corral.

Bounce I did and I came down too hard and fast. Natani told me I was being too stiff. I knew I had to hide my fear, but it was hard. Finally, I discovered that Natani was right: If I relaxed, it was less difficult and I didn't bounce as hard. I softened and I could feel I was riding better and better. After a few more trots, Wind Song stopped as if he was testing me, and Natani urged me to move him ahead. I did so, firmly kicking with my heels. He began to trot again and Natani shouted for me to practice turning him.

"Firmly, firmly," Natani called to me. "Do everything to show him you mean it."

It was easier than I had expected, and soon I began to enjoy it. I even turned him sharply, then started around again just to see if I could make him do that. My courage was building with every minute I rode.

Look at me, I thought. Look at me. Who on the street in Atlanta would believe Phoebe Elder would be riding a horse bareback?

On my next turn, I saw M'Lady One standing next to the fence. She was smiling, but it wasn't a friendly, happy-for-me smile. It was impish. I looked to Natani, but he didn't see her.

As we drew closer, she leaned over the fence. "Having a good time, Phoebe bird?"

I was about to say yes when she flicked a cigarette lighter, one of those that had a knob permitting you to increase the flame. Wind Song caught sight of it and reared sharply to his left, whipping into a gallop. I tried holding him back, but he was excited and afraid. I thought he was actually going to try to leap over the fence, but he stopped short and raised his forelegs. I lost my grip and slid off his back, splashing down into the horse manure.

M'Lady One, now joined by the other two buddies, roared with laughter. Wind Song trotted away and stared at me, snorting, brushing the ground with his right hoof like a bull about to charge. Then Natani entered the corral and walked toward him. He held out his hand and placed it on the horse's head. For a moment Wind Song looked like he would throw it off, but he didn't. He calmed down and stood still, his tail slapping at flies again.

"I guess she's a born rider, huh, Natani?" M'Lady One called.

Natani said nothing. He helped me up and I started to brush off.

"It's lonesome in the saddle since my horse died," M'Lady Two sang, and the three of them walked away laughing.

Natani stared after them, his eyes dark. Then he tilted his head as if he heard something and looked off to the right where some clouds slid beside each other, the bellies of them all dark.

"She flicked a lighter, Natani. She frightened Wind Song."

He nodded. "I saw." He continued to stare out at the

clouds. "The wind is angry. There will be thunder inside us. That will be enough for today."

What does that mean? I wondered. I stood there and watched as he led Wind Song back to the stables. I was so angry and frustrated. Maybe that was what he meant by the thunder inside us. There was enough inside me to cause a flood, but all I did was mumble curses under my breath as I went to the showers to clean off the manure as best I could.

Afterward, I told Robin and Teal what I had done and what had happened. I also told them what Natani had said as he looked off at some dark clouds in the distance. Gia was nearby and listened, but these days she was more introverted than ever. She kept her distance, kept to herself as if she was afraid we would do or say something that interfered with her thoughts. Sometimes, I would catch her pausing in her work, staring at the hacienda, her lips moving, but no sounds coming from her. After a while she would realize I was watching her and she would return to work.

At dinner she was no less quiet and to herself. She ate, did her chores, spoke only when she had to speak, then returned to the barn barracks where she read over what she had written in her notebook, did some homework, and went to sleep. She was going to sleep earlier and earlier each night. Robin asked me about her. She and Teal had noticed the dramatic changes, too, but whenever I asked Gia if she wanted us to do anything, she shook her head and said nothing. Once she did say, "Not now."

Did she mean she wanted nothing now or nothing was wrong now?

I assumed her behavior might have a lot to do with Mindy and how much she missed her. Despite the way she used to snap at her and criticize her, Mindy was still closer to her than we were. It made sense. She had spent more time with her. Occasionally, I would see her staring at Mindy's cot, but even her staring was different now. She seemed to be seeing things. Her eyes would grow larger and smaller, her lips would move, and sometimes she would shake her head or nod slightly. She was so intense about it, she was lost in it. The barn could fall down around us, and she would still be standing there, looking at that empty cot, I thought. She heard nothing, would respond to no one, and then, when she was finished, just turn and curl up on her cot.

Didn't Dr. Foreman see these changes in her? I wondered.

Every day after we had returned from our desert ordeal, I anticipated some sort of therapy session with Dr. Foreman, either with the three of us or one at a time, but she wasn't around as much. We didn't see her at dinner for three nights in a row, but we did see the van coming and going with her.

"She's probably working on replacements, not that I have any high hopes about us being released any too soon," Robin said.

I imagined she was right. There did seem to be a new stirring about the ranch. The buddies were on our backs less and more to themselves, one day going off on a so-called R-and-R trip and returning laden with lots of goodies, I was sure. They were too happy and light-hearted. We didn't dare go to the back of the house to spy on them, but we had little doubt they were partying.

And then, a little more than two weeks after our return, it happened.

We would spend many hours reviewing the details, trying to make some sense of it. We would also spend a lot of our energy trying to forget it. It would be the stuff from which nightmares were made. Every scream I heard thereafter would nudge the memories and fill me with cold shudders. The same would be true for Robin and Teal, maybe even more so, especially for Teal. There was never a question about her being the weakest of the three of us, the most thin-skinned, although by the time this was over, she was probably as hard as a turtle shell compared to the friends she had and the friends she would make.

Natani once told me that life, time, experiences, spin more and more of the cocoon around you, insulating you against more of the same in the future or anything that can hurt you.

"We are truly like trees," he said. "As their bark thickens and they grow taller, wider, so do we."

I suppose it was his way of telling me not to be afraid of life, but to profit from it, to always be a student, to never turn my back on anything. One of the first things he had told us when we had first arrived was "I know you are not happy. But you must remember that life's sorrows often bring great joys." With that attitude, he would never be depressed, never be sad very long. It made him as strong as the tree trunk he sometimes resembled.

It's no exaggeration to say that sometimes a series of events or even a single event would make you feel as if you had passed through a lifetime. That night was one of those times. It seemed to last forever, and for a while it was as if nothing had come before and nothing could come after.

I woke with a start. My cheek felt like a cold hand had been on it, a very cold hand, the hand of death itself. I listened and thought I was still sleeping, dreaming, because what I heard seemed so far off, seemed like something coming from deep down inside me, a voice echoing up from a well or out of a tunnel, a long, thin cry.

I sat up.

The stars were blazing, but there was more light than usual and it wasn't from what Natani called "the pregnant moon." I scrubbed my cheeks with my palms and swung myself around. Gia's cot was empty.

Curious and also confused now, I slipped on my coveralls, shoved my arms through my shirt, and put on my clodhoppers. I stood up and looked at Robin and Teal, who were both asleep, their backs to me.

The scream I had heard in my dream grew louder and became a chorus.

"Robin!" I cried. "Robin, Teal."

Robin turned and groaned. Teal did not wake up.

"Whaaa?" Robin groaned.

"Listen. What is that? Listen."

She ground her eyes with her fists as if she heard through them and then sat up slowly.

"What do you think that is?"

"I don't know," she said.

I went to Teal's cot and poked her in the shoulder. She spun around angrily and looked up at me.

"What do you want? It's not morning already, is it?"

"Listen," I said.

"What?"

Robin was getting dressed, too. "Shut up and listen," she ordered.

Teal sat up, groaning. Then her eyes widened. "What is it?"

"We don't know. Come on," I said. "Get dressed."

Reluctantly, she did and the three of us went to the

door. I hesitated. The screaming was louder now, much louder. I opened the door and it looked as if the whole world was on fire. The blaze that came from our right had flames that seemed to be scorching the very stars. The three of us stepped out, astounded, our faces caught in a ghoulish yellow glow.

Natani and his nephew were rushing about.

The hacienda was consumed in flames. The screaming we heard came from the rear.

"Someone's trapped," I said, and we hurried across the yard and toward the rear of the house. When we got there, we stared up in shock.

The slanted roof upon which we had climbed to spy on the buddies was streaked with flames. Part of the center of it had fallen in. In the windows we could see the buddies, all three of them looking out at us, their faces so illuminated by the flames that licked and traveled along the edges of the main house that they looked as if the fire was already burning within them, making them glow like lightbulbs.

The front of the hacienda was consumed in even bigger flames so that the fire had sandwiched them inside the house. M'Lady Three tried to step out of the window, but the roof in front of her became a bed of fire almost the same instant. The fire seemed truly to counter every move they made, every idea they had for escaping.

Behind us, Natani and his nephew were struggling to get a ladder up against one yet-to-be-consumed section of the roof. We watched as Natani's nephew climbed up the ladder as quickly as he could, smacking at the flames with a wet sack to see if he could make a pathway for the buddies.

We could see the fire inside the house eating away

the walls behind them. M'Lady Two, stepped out of the window and turned toward Natani's nephew, who was now at the top of the ladder, beating at the flames. She lifted her left arm protectively and edged forward in his direction, but the roof, weakening all around that window, gave way and in the same instant we saw her fall into the belly of the fire. She went down without a sound. It was a sight so unreal, I had to convince myself I wasn't still asleep on my cot in the barn.

The flames as if in a march of victory rose to heights above the windows. Through them, I could see M'Ladies One and Three. They were screaming, but we couldn't hear them. It was a silent movie in vivid color. The roof above them caved in and the house seemed to crumble and fall into itself. Natani's nephew leaped from the ladder as it, too, fell forward. He hit the ground nimbly and Natani helped him up.

All of us stepped back farther and farther. The waves of heat were burning our faces.

"Get back," Natani shouted at us. "Back, back."

We retreated to the center of the yard, where we stood and watched the house burning. Off in the distance, like lanterns in the night, two revolving lights appeared. Someone was coming, but far too late, I thought.

Behind us, the horses were neighing in fear and kicking at their stall doors. Natani rushed back, his arm extended upward, his hand tracing the embers that were being carried in the smoke. I realized his concern immediately. They were moving toward the barn and the barn was dry, especially the roof.

I joined his nephew and him and we got the horses out of the barn and into the corral.

"They'll still be very frightened," Natani said.

He ordered his nephew to open the corral so the horses could go as far as they needed. Then he turned his attention to the other animals. I worked at his side for what I later realized was hours. Robin and Teal began to help as well. Natani's foresight proved correct. A section of the horse barn caught fire. His nephew tried to contain it with their water hoses, but it was too little and had limited reach. It wasn't long before the horse barn was too far gone to save.

The lights I had seen belonged to a fire truck and an ambulance with two paramedics. There wasn't much for them to do but stand by like us and watch the hacienda burn to the ground. Soon after they had arrived, a sheriff's patrol car drove up and then another.

Exhausted from our efforts to save all the animals, Robin, Teal, and I sat in front of our barn barracks, which had escaped the embers because of the wind's direction. We watched the police, firemen, and paramedics conferring with Natani. It all remained unreal to me. Their faces glowing, the flames, the crackle of the fire, the tower of smoke that the wind carried into the desert. Through it, the stars twinkled as if the heavens approved of it all.

"Where's Gia?" Teal asked, and Robin and I looked at each other.

During all the excitement, our frantic activity and terror, none of us had thought about her.

"I haven't seen Dr. Foreman either," Robin said.

We turned back to the dwindling conflagration and stared at the flames like three hypnotized people, no one speaking, no one moving. Finally, Teal leaned against me. I put my arm around her and Robin put her arm around me. It was the way the police and the woman from the social service agency found us. We were like three girls frozen, discovered at the top of some very, very high mountain. I'm sure we looked as if it would take a crowbar to pry us apart.

We had sat there together throughout the night and into the first morning light. The fire had burned the house to its foundation. It still smoldered enough to send up a significant tower of smoke I was sure could be seen for miles and miles.

Strangely, other Indians appeared out of the desert as though they had always been out there. I couldn't imagine from where they had all come, but at least a few dozen men and women and some children were on the property. I saw from the way they circled Natani and spoke to him that they respected him greatly. Later, I would learn that he was actually a descendant of a famous Navajo medicine man, and the Indians had high regard for inherited powers.

The woman from the social service agency introduced herself as Mrs. Alexia Patterson, but insisted we call her Alex. All three of us had been through enough layers of the juvenile system to understand it was her way to get us to see her as a friend and not a bureaucrat. A sheriff's officer was with her when she first approached us. I could see that he knew exactly what the ranch was used for and who we were. He wore a hard look of accusation and suspicion and wanted to talk to us first.

"Let them clean themselves up," Alex told him. "They've worked hard helping with the animals and everything, Lieutenant."

He grunted a reluctant okay and we walked in a daze to an outside sink where we washed our faces and hands, our necks and arms. The stench of smoke and burned wood was so thick it was deeply embedded in our very skin. It would take more than a rinsing to get it off our bodies. It would never wash off our souls and hearts.

While we cleaned up, Alex and the sheriff's deputy stood off to the side talking and watching us. The terror and shock we had experienced leveled off, but rushing in to replace it were waves of anxiety. What would happen to us? What had happened to Gia? What did the authorities think about us?

"How are you doing, girls?" Alex asked, walking over to us.

"Ginger peachy," Teal told her.

Alex didn't blink. She smiled and nodded. "That, um, barn or building over there?" She pointed to our barracks. "That's where you girls slept?"

"Yes," Robin said. "It's the first-class accommodations here."

"I think," the sheriff's deputy said, stepping up beside Alex, "that the time for smart talk is well over." He glared at us and no one spoke.

"This is Lieutenant Rowling, girls. He and I have to ask you questions. Why don't we all go into that building then and have a talk," Alex said in as sweet a voice as she could muster. Lieutenant Rowling nodded his approval, but kept his eyes fixed on us with the accuracy of a pair of well-aimed pistols.

We all walked to the barracks.

After we entered, Alex stopped and looked around the Spartan quarters. She was truly surprised that the floor was covered in straw and all the cots but one were without mattresses, pillows, or blankets.

"I don't understand," she muttered, and looked at the sheriff's deputy, who just shrugged. "Let's sit here," she said, nodding at my cot, which was the closest.

We sat on it and Lieutenant Rowling pulled another one closer. Alex sat on that, but he stood glaring down at us.

"How many of you are there at present?" she asked.

"There were five of us when we three came. There were four of us last night. Mindy's dead. She committed suicide," I told her.

Alex looked at Lieutenant Rowling, who smirked. "Who committed suicide?" he asked.

"Mindy."

"Mindy Levine," Robin said.

"You saw her commit suicide?" he asked.

"No, Gia told us that happened. We were out in the desert," I said.

"Who's this Gia?" he asked, looking from me to Robin and Teal.

"She was the other girl, the fourth girl," Robin told him.

"You said you were out in the desert. What does that mean?" Alex asked.

"We were being punished. We were taken out there and left to find our way back," I explained. "Teal got bitten by a rattlesnake. Natani saved our lives." I felt like I was repeating a recording, speaking with little or no emotion, just reporting facts.

Again Alex's eyebrows hoisted and she looked at Lieutenant Rowling.

He shrugged again. "You guys should know more about this place than we do," he said defensively.

Alex nodded. "We should. But, we obviously don't."

"Yeah, well, that's for later. Right now," he continued, bearing down on me especially, "what do you know about this fire?"

I shook my head and the other two did the same.

"We woke up and saw the whole place illuminated, so we dressed and stepped out and saw the house was in flames. We ran around back and watched Natani and his nephew, the cook, try to save the buddies."

"Buddies?"

"Assistants, I suppose you would call them," Teal said dryly. "We had better names for them."

"Do you know anything about Gia?" I asked.

"What about Dr. Foreman? Was she in the house or what?" Teal followed, her arrogant, demanding tone making her sound more like the Teal I knew.

"We're asking the questions here," Lieutenant Rowling said so sharply it was as if his tongue were made of razor blades.

"Okay, girls," Alex said, giving him a stern look and then turning back to us. "For now, I want you to rest. We'll get you something to drink and eat. I'll return soon."

She and the lieutenant left the barracks.

"How come they didn't know about Mindy?" Teal asked. "If someone dies, especially like that, wouldn't the police know?"

"It's all very weird," Robin said.

I agreed and then my eyes went to Gia's cot. The edge of her notebook could be seen just under her pillow. I went to it and pulled it out. I opened the cover and sat on her cot to read.

"What?" Robin asked when I shook my head.

"I guess she returned to being Posy. She starts this off with a 'Dear Mother.' "

I started to read on. "No, wait. Maybe not."

"Read it aloud," Teal said.

I looked up at them, then did what she asked.

"Dear Mother,

"Did I ever tell you about the first day I saw you, when I was ten and they brought me to you? How does a girl get over the fact that her real mother and her real father gave up on her completely and agreed to give her away, give her to you, let you adopt her and make her your daughter?"

"What an imagination she had," Teal said, shaking her head. Robin nodded.

I continued reading.

"I never understood it all, of course. I always expected I would go home someday, no matter how you explained it. You told me you wanted to be my mother now. I would be a shining example of your powers, your abilities. You would be sitting out there on my high school graduation day and my college graduation day and you would be so proud of me.

"I'm very smart, you said. You said you could tell that and you were sure I was going to be an excellent student once I was cured.

"I must tell you I never thought of myself as sick so I never understood why you called it being cured. Sick to me was sneezing and coughing, bellyaches and headaches, but not being angry and afraid and alone. How is that being sick? From what I have seen of other kids my age, and especially the ones who were brought to you, being angry, afraid, and alone is more normal these days than being sick.

"There you go, I'm sure, shaking your head and pursing your lips. More proof that I'm sick, more proof that I'm sick. That's what you're saying and what you've been saying since the day I was brought to your home.

"I understand my parents being afraid of having me

in the house after the fire, but I never stopped believing they would come back for me someday. Not until now. Now I know they won't. You wouldn't want them to. You wouldn't want to give up your prize patient, would you?

"You made fun of my Posy. You did everything you could to kill her, to crush her like some insect, but she got away, just like Mindy. We can get away from you, but not all of us. Not all of us can stand up to you and your little army of so-called buddies.

"You know what frightens me the most today, Mother? That I'm finally calling you Mother. That you got your way with that, but now I'm terrified that you will win, that you really will be sitting out there on my graduation days and I will be your little protégé, your shining example, and you will use me to get rid of every Posy who is out there and every Mindy.

"I was thinking I would give you this to read, but then I thought, if I do, you will find a way to overcome. You always do. You're the best at what you do, Mother. You will always win. You will always have your way with us.

"Guess who has come back tonight?" I read, and looked up at Robin and Teal, who were sitting there mesmerized. I looked back at the notebook. *"That's right, Posy. And guess why? She has a plan. I don't know why I didn't think of it on my own. You've had me spinning in circles, I guess. Anyway, she's here to help. She hasn't forgotten me. She couldn't leave me behind after all.*

"We're on our way to activate our plan, Mother. You'll know it all very soon.

"I wonder if my real mother and father ever really asked after me. You said they didn't, but maybe, maybe you were lying to me. Maybe they haven't forgotten me

completely. Maybe they'll think about me now. Posy
says they will.
"*And Posy knows.*
"*Posy always knew.*"
I closed the notebook.
"I feel so sick inside," Teal said. "So sick and tired."
"What's new about that?" Robin muttered, then
quickly added, "So do I."
We all looked up when the door opened and a female
sheriff's deputy entered carrying some sodas and a bag
of sandwiches and candy bars.
"Hi, girls," she said. "Brought you something to eat
and drink."
She set it all down.
"Chocolate bars?" Teal said, opening the bag. "And
subs. They look like they have everything on them!"
"They do," the deputy said. "I didn't know what you
liked, of course, so I got the works. Enjoy. Mrs.
Patterson and Lieutenant Rowling will be back to speak
with you all soon."
She left and Robin dug into the bag. "Roast beef.
And a Coke. I think I forgot what that tastes like.
Look." She held up a bag. "Potato chips!"
Teal was already eating and closing her eyes with
pleasure. I was the most surprised of us all that I had
an appetite after what we had just been through, but
nervousness burned calories, I guess. I ate as fast as
they did and enjoyed what I was eating just as much.
When we were finished, we went to the doorway
because we heard a loud roaring sound. We saw a helicopter landing. Two men in suits and a uniformed
policeman who looked like a general emerged, bent
over to avoid the propellers, and ran toward the ruins of
the house. Many more patrol cars, another ambulance,

firemen and police were moving about the grounds and around the smoldering hacienda. Off to the left, I saw Natani and his nephew surrounded by policemen, who were listening to them answer questions.

"Who's that in the helicopter, the president?" Teal wondered aloud.

"What's going to happen to us now?" Robin asked.

Both Teal and I turned and looked at her. Funny, I thought, how I had never even considered it until she had just mentioned it. What would be done with us?

"Whatever it is, it'll be a vacation compared to this," Teal replied.

Somehow, I didn't believe a vacation was what was ahead for us.

16

Fly Away Home

The two men in suits whom we had seen come in the helicopter joined Alex and Lieutenant Rowling when they returned to the barn barracks. Once again, Alex told us to sit on a cot. She sat on the one brought closer to us, and the three men stood around and stared down at us as if we were extraterrestrials or something that had just been found in the desert.

"We need your help to understand what exactly happened here," Alex began in a soft, friendly tone.

None of the men smiled. I had the feeling that if she weren't there, they would beat every answer out of us.

"All three of you were sent here as part of the juvenile recovery program, correct?" she asked, thumbing through some pages in a file she carried.

"Was that what they called it?" Teal asked, looking at Robin and me as if we had kept it a secret from her.

"I never heard that term, Teal," I said.

"I thought it was part of the garbage recycle program," Robin muttered.

"Maybe we should conduct this interrogation someplace else," Lieutenant Rowling growled, "like the state's maximum security prison."

Alex held up her right hand without turning to him. She kept her eyes on us.

"Listen to me, girls. People are dead. This is an obvious case of felonious arson."

"*Murder* is a better word," Lieutenant Rowling corrected.

Alex closed and opened her eyes, again without looking up at him. "Before we can take you to more comfortable surroundings and see about your futures, we need to know as much as possible about what transpired here. How long have you girls been here?" she asked, flipping through those pages again.

We looked at each other, and then, after a moment, when no one replied, we all just laughed.

The men again looked ready to pounce and pound us.

"We're not being disrespectful, Alex," I said. "We've all lost track of time. It seems like a very long time, but I imagine it's not."

"When you arrived here, these other girls, Mindy and Gia, were already here, however?"

"Yes," Robin said.

"Is Mindy dead?" I asked. I looked up quickly at Lieutenant Rowling, anticipating his saying again that they were the ones who asked the questions, not us. "We're worried about her. We don't know what to believe."

Alex nodded. "We understand she did attempt suicide. She's at a clinic. A mental clinic, and she is in treatment."

"She didn't die?" Teal asked, then looked at me.

"Why did she get to go to a clinic and not Gia?" I wondered aloud. "Maybe none of this would have happened then."

"Why do you say that? Was Gia angry about Mindy?" Alex asked.

"She told us she was dead. I don't think she was lying. I think she really believed it, so, yes, she was upset about her. When we returned from our picnic in the desert, we found her to be very different. She didn't talk to us very much. She slept a lot," I said.

"What did she actually do?" Teal asked.

Robin and I looked up in anticipation of hearing the gruesome details.

"Did she talk to you girls about doing anything?" Alex replied instead of answering directly.

"No," I said.

"All she did was work, eat, and write in her notebook," Robin offered. "Like us."

"Notebook?"

"Dr. Foreman made us write in notebooks," Teal said. "If we didn't do it, we lost privileges or were punished. After we had done so this time, we were supposed to get our mattresses, pillows, and blankets back," she added with indignation, as if she were lodging a complaint with a hotel manager. "We handed them in and never heard a word."

"Did Gia hand in her notebook, too?" Alex asked.

"No. It's right there, under the pillow." I nodded at Gia's cot.

Lieutenant Rowling, probably frustrated with just standing and listening and not applying some sort of electric torture, lunged at the cot and found the notebook. He opened it, then smirked with disappointment and handed it to Alex. I don't know what he was expecting to find between the covers. Maybe a confession.

Alex read some of it quickly, nodded, and handed it to the shorter of the two well-dressed men. He began to read it with the other man looking over his shoulder.

Alex turned back to us. "Just give me a quick understanding of what went on here."

"Went on?" Teal asked, tilting her head as if she were talking to a complete idiot.

"You had classes you attended. You talked about good and bad behavior. You had therapy sessions with Dr. Foreman, who tried to help you understand why you were getting into more and more trouble. I imagine you had your chores every day, helped with the management of the ranch, the preparations for your meals, am I not correct?"

None of us replied. We all stared at her again.

Then Teal leaned forward, holding her head with that superior air as only she could and looked Alex in the face. "Your understandings are somewhat misdirected," she said in perfect, teacherlike tones.

Alex lost her smile. "Then help me understand correctly."

Teal looked at us. "Shall we help her, girls?"

"Look, Mrs. . . . Alex, whatever," Robin said. "Y'all been given a lot of hogwash it seems. We didn't have any real classes. She threw books and assignments at us and we were left on our own to do them, and if we failed, she gave us demerits, and if we got too many demerits, we lost privileges, and if we got even more demerits, we were sent to the Ice Room."

"Ice Room?"

The two men in suits closed Gia's notebook and turned to listen to us.

Neither Robin nor I was anxious to describe the Ice Room. In fact, Robin just wouldn't say much at all. I explained how I had revealed my fear of rats and how that had been used to torture me into obedience.

"Virtual reality," one of the men in suits said. He nodded at the other. "Pretty sophisticated equipment. Look into that as they sift through the ruins. See what you can find."

The man nodded and left the barracks.

"Tell me about this desert trip," Alex asked.

Robin did describe that. When she reached the point when Teal got bitten, Teal started to cry silently. It was almost as if she didn't know she was crying. She sat there staring and the tears started to emerge from under her lids and trickle down her cheeks.

"I'm sorry, girls. I don't want to force you to relive painful experiences," Alex said, "but we're just trying to understand how all this came about."

"Did you help this Gia with the gasoline?" Lieutenant Rowling demanded, raising his voice with impatience and stepping closer to us.

"Gasoline?" Robin responded.

"No." I looked at Alex. "What did she do exactly? Please tell us already."

"This is ridiculous," Lieutenant Rowling complained. "This girl, Gia, went out and did all this and you three are sitting there and telling us you knew nothing about it. Is that it?"

"Y'all don't have to believe it, but that's true," Robin told him, her eyes just as fiery.

The stronger my friend was, the prouder I was of her, and the stronger I felt myself become.

"Gia was smarter than any of us," I said. "She helped us all get through the schoolwork. Whatever she came up with to do, she didn't need any of us to help her do it or think it up. What did she do?" I repeated with more firmness.

"It looks like she poured gasoline strategically around the hacienda so that the fire and the flames would entrap the inhabitants. She poured it on the roof, around windows, everywhere. The lieutenant believes she might have spread this gasoline over a significant period of time and not have just come up with the idea and done it all at once. That's why he and some others are so suspicious about no one else noticing anything," Alex explained calmly.

"If she was carrying that much gasoline to that house, she would be marching back and forth a number of times from the barn where the tractor was housed," Lieutenant Rowling continued. "Someone would have to see her doing it and ask what she was doing. She would smell from gasoline, too."

"We all smelled from one thing or another around here," Teal said. "You ever clean out a pigpen?" She wiped away a tear.

"Maybe there was some gasoline closer to the house," I suggested. "Besides being in the barn with the tractor."

Teal looked at me. "That big tin drum," she said.

"What drum?" Lieutenant Rowling asked.

"There was a big drum behind the house." I then described how we had spied on the buddies. Confessing about something so innocent compared with what had just happened here and what had been done to us over time didn't seem risky. I told how we had gotten the idea from Gia in the first place.

"So she knew the drum was there," Robin said.

"I don't think there was anything in it then. I didn't smell any gasoline," Robin said, "and it fell over, remember? We would have seen gasoline spill out."

"It just wasn't in it then," I said.

Robin shrugged.

"She might have been sneaking gasoline from time to time and spilling it into the drum until she thought she had enough," Teal suggested.

"I guess that makes sense. That way she wouldn't have to be running back and forth with pails all day and night to spill it all around the house," Robin added. "I guess she did have it all well planned out."

Her look of appreciation for Gia's ingenuity only made Lieutenant Rowling more enraged. "And you are sitting there and telling us you didn't help her and you didn't know anything about it?"

"See that?" Teal said, looking at me. "And you said he wouldn't be able to figure it out."

If the top of Lieutenant Rowling's head hadn't been securely attached to the rest of his skull, it would surely have blown off from the explosion of anger inside his brain.

"Girls, please," Alex said. "I'm trying to get this all over with quickly for you and get you out of here."

"I guess they did belong here," Lieutenant Rowling said. "I guess no matter what was done to them, it wasn't enough to change them."

"Oh, we're changed, sir," I said. "We're changed. We used to be nice people."

Robin laughed and Teal smiled widely.

"I'm sorry," I said to Alex, "but we're tired and we have seen terrible things and terrible things have been done to us, whether we deserved them or not." I glared up at the policeman. "Won't you please tell us what happened to Gia? What happened to Dr. Foreman? Was she in the house?"

"Five people were killed. Figure it out," Lieutenant Rowling snapped. "You're smart enough to add."

"Please, Lieutenant. You have enough information to go forward, don't you?" Alex asked, directing herself mostly at the man in the suit.

He nodded. "Okay. We'll talk to them after you've gathered the information you need and made what arrangements you need to make," he said softly. He nodded at Lieutenant Rowling, who turned reluctantly and followed him out of the barracks.

"Gia and Dr. Foreman are dead, girls," Alex said as soon as they were gone. "And so are the girls assisting Dr. Foreman."

"Gia got trapped in her own fire," I said, realizing.

"No, she went into the building after she began the fire."

"Why did she go into the building after she started the fire?" Teal asked.

"To spread it inside as well, probably," I said.

"No, not only for that. It looks like she went in to prevent Dr. Foreman from getting out."

"How can you tell that?" I asked, grimacing.

"They found a chain around Gia's waist. The chain was around Dr. Foreman's waist, too, and there was a lock on it preventing her from just slipping out of it. She was caught in bed, sleeping apparently. There was a struggle of some sort, but dragging Gia out along with her was too difficult, and by then the fire must have been consuming the hallways, the rooms, and all the exits."

"You're saying Gia wanted to die with her? She sacrificed herself to be sure Dr. Foreman couldn't escape?"

Alex nodded. "It certainly looks that way, I'm afraid. You girls are telling the truth? You knew nothing of this, nothing of her intentions? You didn't know she hated Dr. Foreman that much, enough to be responsible for her death?"

"No, ma'am," I said.

"We all got so we hated Dr. Foreman," Teal told her, "but maybe Gia had reason to hate her more."

"No maybe about that," Robin said. "I guess Mindy was the breaking point."

"Gia wasn't right from the start, was she, Phoebe? She was living in her imagination, creating a girl named Posy. I guess for a while that was her escape," Teal said.

I watched Alex Patterson's face as they spoke, then I leaned forward. "Was it all her imagination, ma'am? I mean, everything in that notebook?"

For a long moment, I didn't think she would reply, but then she shook her head. "No. What she wrote in that notebook was true. It's all very sad." She stood up.

"All of it was true? She was Dr. Foreman's adopted daughter?" I asked.

"Exactly," Alex said. "You're right," she told Teal. "This Posy she created was her way of dealing with all that, her escape I imagine."

"How desperate she must have finally become," Teal thought aloud.

Alex nodded. "I'm going to arrange for the three of you to be taken to a facility in Phoenix. You'll be questioned further there and I'll be on the phone with the various justice agencies you've all been involved with and that have had stipulations as to your dispositions. There is a lot to do, so we'll have to get started soon. I don't imagine you have anything much to gather up and take with you."

We shook our heads, our voices trapped inside our thoughts.

"I should have a car here within the hour. Don't wander too far," she advised.

We watched her leave.

"Wander too far?" Robin muttered.

"We could run away," I said, looking at Teal.

She started to laugh, her shoulders shaking, and then that laugh turned into a sob. We joined her like a chorus, all three of us crying for so many reasons it was impossible to center on one in particular.

Afterward, before the car arrived for us, I left the barracks and went to find Natani. He and his nephew had rounded up the horses and gotten them back into the corral. They were still nervous, the stench of the fires filling their nostrils and rekindling their recent traumatic horror. Wind Song looked at me as I approached the railing. He snorted and patted the ground, but he didn't walk over as he usually did. I didn't blame him for distrusting humans who were supposed to protect him.

I saw Natani's nephew filling the water trough and was about to ask him where Natani was when I heard the drumbeats coming from Natani's hogan. I hurried over to it, knocked on the frame of the door, and peered in. He was squatting on the floor, the drum before him, those magical rocks spread around it. He said nothing, but I saw him greet me with his eyes so I entered and sat across from him.

"What do you have in your healing bag that can fix all this, Natani? Who knows where we're going to end up now?"

He closed his eyes and stopped his drumbeating.

"Once, when I was a young boy, my mother took me

by the hand and made me sit and watch a mother wren care for her newborn babies. She brought me back day after day and I watched how hard the mother worked to feed and care for the newborns, who never stopped demanding.

"They grew quickly. I was surprised at how quickly, and soon they became more adventurous and began to explore the world outside their nest. Everything frightened them though and they returned, hovering beside each other and waiting to be fed and protected.

"And soon they were too big to be in the nest, but they tried to stay. I saw that. I saw the mother drive them out of the nest. She refused to permit them to return. They looked very lost and afraid to me, but after a while, they flew off and my mother had me bring the empty nest down and keep it and think about it until I could answer for myself why the mother wren drove her own babies away.

"I had trouble with the answer for a long time. And then my grandmother died, my mother's mother, and after she was gone, my mother came into our hogan and sat beside me. I was very, very sad. I was my grandmother's favorite.

" 'What has this taught you about the birds?' my mother asked me.

"I looked at her with great confusion at first. How could my grandmother's death teach me anything about a nest of baby birds and how their mother had cared so devotedly for them and then driven them away? My mother waited and waited. I soon realized I knew the answer, daughter of the tortoise. I knew it but I didn't want to know it."

"What is the answer, Natani?"

"The mother bird knew she was much older and

there would be a time, not far off in the earth's life, when she would be no longer and her babies would die with her if they didn't go out and become strong and independent. To turn your own from your door is hard, but it is nature's way.

"I used to wonder if the mother bird ever saw her babies again, and if she saw them and they saw her, would they show it or were the babies so angry at her that they would no longer acknowledge her or care for her?"

"Did they?"

"You never see a bird die, do you, daughter of the tortoise? They die in the dark, alone. You don't look up and suddenly see one topple to the earth. In the morning you might find them, but they have died in the dark.

"It was my father who told me that in the dark the babies gather and thank their mother as they hope their babies will thank them. Before the sun is up, they are gone.

"*Hagoone* is our word for good-bye, daughter of the tortoise, but there is no word for good-bye for children and parents. You cannot say good-bye to that which is part of you or of which you are a part. It is forever with you and with those who come after you. It is the greatest gift of all, this truth, this never saying good-bye.

"What you think is gone, what you think you will never see or hear again, is still with you. Go away with that in your heart. Nothing here has changed that truth nor could it.

"They died in the dark," he said, nodding toward the demolished hacienda. "I saw their spirits go with the smoke to join what has come before them."

He lowered his head and I rose to leave.

"Thank you, Natani. *Hagoone.*"

He looked up at me and smiled. "Remember the tortoise that stayed too long in his shell. Do not stay too long in yours."

"I won't," I promised.

And I left him.

Afterward, the three of us rode away in silence, none of us looking back. All I took with me was the turquoise stone Natani had given me, a piece of the fallen sky. Alex had brought us some clothes to wear. Of course, Teal complained about them, how cheap and ugly they were, but I could see how grateful she was for them.

We dozed on and off. The landscape flowed like a continuous stream of sand, rocks, and desert plants. I saw some rabbits, but we were moving too fast to really see anything else. Alex sat up front with the driver and frequently asked us how we were doing, if we were thirsty or needed the bathroom. Most of the time, we just shook our heads. No one seemed to want to break the silence. Maybe we were all afraid that if we talked too much, we would stop this escape, for that was what it surely was to each of us, a rescue, a flight from someone else's private hell.

Eventually, we were brought to a government building where we were taken to a room and, once again, asked a series of questions about the final events at Dr. Foreman's School for Girls. The two men in suits back at the barracks turned out to be special agents of the FBI, the reason for that, we learned, being that the ranch was leased by Dr. Foreman. She actually leased it from Natani's people so he had more reason than she had for staying and caring for it. Any crime committed on Indian land came under the jurisdiction of the FBI, as well as the Indian agency and their own tribal police.

Teal joked that it was an accomplishment to be interrogated by FBI agents. We had all been arrested at one time or another by city police, local law enforcement, and now we had graduated to the head of the juvenile criminal class. We laughed, but we didn't really think it was funny. We laughed because we were still nervous about what would happen next.

We were fed, given cold drinks, and left to rest in a lounge. Funnily enough, having not had television for so long, we were all bored by what was on and ignored it. Teal was the first to start looking at the magazines. Robin joined her and I soon followed. It was as if we were slowly emerging from a coma, which was what I had felt when I had first been brought to the orientation room. It was all a sleep and an awakening, after all.

Finally, Alex returned and we all looked up with great anticipation.

"I'm not going to go through all the details concerning the various government agencies that have something to say about your futures, girls," she began. "You all know you were sent to this school as a result of a legal decision with guardian approval. The bottom line is you're all still on probation. I'm to make sure you all understand that. Do you?"

"Alex," Teal said with her cute little smirk on her lips, "we've been on probation since the day we were born."

"Yes, well, as long as you understand you still are." Then Alex sighed so deeply I thought she would come apart right before our eyes.

"Teal, you are going home. You'll be on a flight that will take you to Albany via Newark. There'll be an officer from the juvenile criminal division greeting you at the Newark airport and seeing that you get on the right flight for Albany, where your parents will take custody.

There, a division of juvenile justice will see to your counseling.

"Robin, you have a direct flight to Nashville."

"I do?"

"Your mother will meet you at the airport and the same will be true for you."

"Mother darling wants to meet me at the airport? Y'all sure about that?"

"Your families have all been told something about the events that have just transpired, and some of what you have been going through at the ranch."

"Mother darling will probably write a song about it," Robin told me.

I smiled gently, but my eyes were on Alex, who was looking at me.

"Phoebe, your uncle and aunt have refused to accept custody and responsibility for you. I'm sorry. Arrangements have been made for you to be with foster parents in Atlanta. They'll be greeting you at the airport and you will have a direct flight. The same counseling and overseeing will take place there for you. Arrangements will be made concerning your schooling. They are, I've been told, a very nice couple, whose children are all grown and out of the house. They're actually looking forward to taking you into their home. I hope you will respect that and it will work out for you.

"Well, then," she added, standing, "any questions I can answer for you?"

"Yeah," Teal said. "Why were we born?"

"That, I'm afraid, is a question you'll have to answer for yourself, dear. I wish you all the best of luck. There are cars outside waiting to transport you three to the different terminals and the different flights. Why don't you all freshen up, go to the bathroom, and come out in ten minutes or so, okay?"

She smiled and then left us just like anyone who had unloaded a burden would leave us, her shoulders relaxing, her body softening, her mind rushing to think about something pleasurable that awaited her when she returned home from work and could put us out of mind forever and ever. I envied her for being able to do that.

"Anyone want to go to the bathroom?" Teal asked.

"Not me," Robin said. "Phoebe?"

"I'm not used to bathrooms inside," I said, "without something crawling around the toilet."

They laughed.

"You're such an idiot," Teal said.

"And what are you?" Robin asked her. "Besides a spoiled brat, that is?"

Teal pretended to think. "Nothing else. That seems to be enough for now."

We laughed again.

"The first thing my mother is going to ask me," Teal said as we started out of the room, "is what did I do to my hair? It would never occur to her that someone else would have done it to me. I'll be kept locked up until she thinks I look good enough to be out in public again."

"Were you ever good enough?" Robin asked her.

"Oh, listen to her? I hope your mother does write a song about Dr. Foreman's School and sings it to you every night."

"I might write it for her," Robin said.

A man in a suit who looked like another FBI agent waited at the front door of the building. Alex, apparently, was already gone.

He opened the door and began assigning the cars. They were parked in a line at the sidewalk, and the drivers of each looked bored to death. We paused.

It was dark now. There were stars, but they weren't as bright or as numerous as the stars in the desert sky. Streetlights and other lights washed them out.

"You're probably going to be better off than both of us, Phoebe. You'll have people who actually want you," Teal said.

"My daddy wanted me. I think in her own way my mama tried to want me, did want me very much once," I said, smiling.

They looked at me, each of them thinking of times when they had felt the same way about their parents, I'm sure.

"Let's get moving, girls," the man behind us ordered.

Robin pressed her lips together. Her eyes watered.

Teal looked away quickly.

"You know," I said, "I almost feel like thanking Dr. Foreman."

"For what?" Teal said, turning back quickly.

"For ourselves," I said.

"Yeah, well, if either of you see me on a street in Beverly Hills or Worth Avenue in Palm Beach, pretend we never met, will you?" Teal said.

She took a step toward her car, then turned and hugged Robin. They held each other as if they thought when they let go they'd fall into a dark hole.

Teal did the same to me and I held her tightly, too. Then Robin and I hugged.

None of us spoke. We looked at each other as if for the first time ever, then they turned to their vehicles.

Hagoone, I thought as they got into their cars.

Just before I got into mine, a sparrow landed on its

hood, tapped proudly in a small circle, then lifted into the wind, looking like it could fly to the stars.

I watched it.

And then I got into the car, embraced myself, and snuggled into a corner of the seat.

I looked out the window, but I saw nothing but my own face reflected in the glass.

Then I fingered the small turquoise stone and smiled.

Natani's drum followed me all the way to my new home.

Epilogue

Dear Freaks,

I guess you didn't expect to hear from me, especially in the form of a letter, but all that writing experience at Dr. Foreman's School has paid off. Ha! Ha!

Seriously, I actually received an A in English this quarter. I'm doing well in all my classes, even math. Every time I receive a good grade for anything in any class, I thank Gia.

I figured the only reason I haven't heard from either of you was you didn't know my address, especially since I didn't know it myself when we parted. Why else would you have ignored me all this time? Unless, of course, you're both doing time in some maximum security institution for continuing to violate every law possible.

I haven't so much as been reprimanded in

class, and I haven't been late to school or to any class. No one is more shocked about that than I am.

You know what frightens me the most about all this? If Dr. Foreman were alive, she'd claim credit. She'd be telling everyone she did it, then more poor and pathetic girls like us would be sent to her school. Maybe that is really why Gia did what she did. She put a stop to it.

I don't know how it is for you these days with all the time that has passed. Sometimes, I wake up and look around as if I expect I'm back in the barn barracks, and I'm surprised I'm in a real bed in my own room, which is a very nice room, by the way. I'm sure it's not as nice as Teal's, so don't start describing your room again and cataloging all your valuable possessions, Teal. I acknowledge you're a spoiled rich kid.

Just kidding. I'm jealous as always.

Sometimes, often I should say, if I hear a thumping sound, maybe just the bass on a speaker in some guy's car, I think about Natani. I laugh to myself, remembering the looks on your faces when he told us his animal stories or spoke in his mystical way. The truth is I miss him and wish that someday I can go back to see him.

The only thing is, just like you two, I imagine, thoughts about returning to that place make me shudder as well.

I wonder about Mindy. There doesn't seem to be any way to find out about her. For all we know, she might still be locked up in some clinic. Maybe she's too far gone to be cured, ever. I hope not. You ever think about her?

And of course, I think a great deal about Gia, how she kept so much of herself hidden from us, disguised in imaginary people and events. When I think about it, my parents essentially gave me away, too, and I rate my uncle and aunt about the same in the horror factor as Dr. Foreman. You'd have to meet my aunt to see what I mean. The big difference was that my daddy really hoped to have me back.

Well, I guess I'll have to tell you. I've met someone nice. I'm talking about a boy. His name's Ralston Marks. He's on the football team. Actually, he's the quarterback. Teal, don't start bragging about your boyfriends.

Ralston is unlike any boy I have ever been with. He's polite, religious, but not overly so, and he's a very good student. He looks to be a shoo-in for scholarships to important colleges. I don't know why he wants to be with me all the time, but, be still my pitter-patter heart, he does. He says I'm one of the most mature girls for our age he's known.

I guess how I am now is a result of what we all went through. Everything other girls are doing seems to be so silly to me lately. I hate just hanging around malls anymore, and when I hear them gossiping in school, I really do think of Natani's chickens clucking. That's how Ralston first saw me, sitting there with this goofy smile on my face. He asked me what was so funny, and I told him and he laughed and we haven't stopped talking and being with each other since.

I should tell you that my foster parents are truly very nice people. My foster mother's name is

Coco. She's French Canadian. Her parents emigrated there (How do you like the big word?) from a place called Cap Ferrat in southern France where they were in the service industry, a nice way to say butlers and maids. She met Andre in Quebec and they were married in Canada, then came to America and settled in Atlanta because of a business connection Andre had. They now own a big department store, and Coco is the clothes buyer.

So here's the best news of all . . . yours truly models clothes at the store on Sundays, the new fashions from Europe. It was Coco's idea. I almost refused to do it because I remembered Dr. Foreman telling me I could be a model and she would help arrange for that if I was just a good little Foreman girl. Why should we stop ourselves from doing things we like just because Dr. Foreman mentioned them, however?

I might actually continue doing this on a professional basis. A woman who runs a modeling agency stopped in last week. She said she had heard about me and she wants me to come see her. Coco approves. I really love her. She's so up and happy all the time and her and Andre's three children all like me, too.

All this happiness frightens me. I keep thinking someone from my past is going to appear on the doorstep and have reasons why I can't continue. Do you have any of those sorts of fears? When will they stop?

Last week, at Andre and Coco's insistence, I went to the cemetery and visited my daddy's and mama's graves. It didn't seem real to me. I had to

*keep rereading their names to convince myself
that this was where they really were now.*

*Is there really any way to make peace with
your past? I was tempted to crawl into one of
Natani's shells, to avoid the tombstones, but I
didn't. I couldn't.*

*And he was right, I couldn't stand there and
say good-bye.*

*I knew I would be back many times and I would
tell them good things.*

*And maybe someday even bring my own chil-
dren along.*

*When I think of all this, I realize what it is
we've achieved. Again, ironically, what we have
achieved is something Dr. Foreman said we didn't
have, a future.*

We have a future, don't we?

We can hope, and most of all, we can dream.

*Write me if you can, if you want, if it doesn't
bring back too many painful memories.*

*I don't ever, ever want to be the cause of some-
one's painful memories again.*

Love,
Phoebe bird

Dear Phoebe,

*You won't believe this, but I have been after my
big-shot brother to use his connections to find out
where you are. He promised he would and bragged
how easily he could do that. He knew this one in
government and that one, and until your letter
arrived yesterday, he has been able to find out zilch.
That's a new word for your expanding vocabulary.*

I am writing you this letter from my dorm. No, I'm not living at home. My parents, after many intense discussions, decided to put me into this new prep school. I hate to say it, but it's a very good school, and like you, I am doing well in my academic work, and again like you, I haven't been in any serious trouble. Maybe a little trouble. I was almost caught out after curfew, but, and I know you won't believe it, I wasn't doing anything terribly exciting. I wasn't out meeting a boy or carrying on with some other girls or smoking. I was just walking and lost track of the time.

I do a lot of walking alone and thinking. Everyone thinks I'm weird, but I don't care.

My mother has visited me a number of times, more than I expected she would actually. She usually spends the entire visitation talking about her new charity events and planned vacations. She'll interrupt herself to tell me about some fashions she thinks are nice and elegant for me, and then she goes on to talk about some rich people I never knew and couldn't care less about knowing. But I have a new tolerance for her and I smile and look like I'm listening, and you know what, she's starting to talk more to me and look at me. It's as if by not showing her how much I hate what she is, she will start to change. The last time we spoke, in fact, she talked about just her and me going someplace together and getting to know each other better. She wants to take me to places she enjoyed when she was my age. Once, I would make fun of the idea, but now I've decided I would do it.

I guess what I'm saying is nothing can change quickly, and most might not ever change, but it's learning how to live with that realization that makes happiness possible. Otherwise, I return to what I was, always angry, always frustrated, always self-destructive.

Surprised at my self-analysis?

I have this psych course and I'm learning more about myself than I wanted to learn. I've even come to understand things about Dr. Foreman, although I battle back the memories. It's like trying to keep air bubbles from rising in a glass or something.

I'm jealous of you, Phoebe. I haven't met anyone like your Ralston yet. We have these mixers with an all-boys prep school, but it's all too artificial for me. I love spontaneity and I daydream about meeting Mr. Right on some street corner or in a store or in the park, anywhere except a prearranged mixer approved by both schools.

Am I hopeless?

Maybe not. You know how sometimes you can feel something is really going to happen if you're just patient and you keep yourself up and happy? That's how I feel about Mr. Right. He's out there. We're going to meet.

Not that boys are all I think about anymore. I'm not going into modeling, but I have been told by my English teacher that I have a flare—that's the way he puts it, a flare—for writing. He says I capture people and events so well, I should think about working in film. So, I'm enrolling in a film study course next semester. It involves writing scripts. When I'm big and famous and important, I'll cast you in a movie.

I wish my life now was all and only what I described. I still have bad nights, Phoebe. I see snakes. I see the buddies in the fire. I hear the screams. I'm getting better, but it's all not buried deeply enough. It will be someday. Won't it?

I miss the both of you. All my new friends are afraid of me or are obvious about how much they'd like me to like them. I need you two. I need to be reminded I'm not a big shot.

So, here's what I've decided. I'm getting my mother to ask my father to sponsor a trip for both you and Robin for my birthday. You'll both come to my big, rich house and we'll sleep on the floor and go to the bathroom outside, and plant a garden and take ice-cold showers.

Just kidding. We'll have a big, fat time. Will you come? Please. Bring Ralston if you have to. I just think we need to look at each other's ugly face again just so we know we are really here, we really matter. I'll work out the details.

Love,
Teal

Dear Losers,

I photocopied this letter so I would only have to write y'all one. I did it at my mother's agent's office. I don't call her Mother darling anymore. She went ahead and wrote a song called "Mother Darling." She really did and it was a big hit in the country music world.

The good thing is she left the creep she was

*with shortly after I had been sent to Dr.
Foreman's School. Then, she got a lucky break
when a really big agent heard her singing and he
helped her develop her style, got her a great
backup group of musicians, and began to find her
some important bookings. She has two recordings
on the charts as we speak.*

*Now here's the news. One day I was practicing
with her just for the fun of it and her agent heard
us singing together and decided we should do a
song. We worked on it together. We really had
never done anything like that together before, but
she liked my suggestions.*

*I know y'all are going to think it's corny but
here it is. It's called "Mama, Let Me Be Me":*

Well, I've been growing up and I've been doing
    all you say,
I've learned all my schooling and I've worked
    hard every day,
You laid out directions and made me follow in
    your way,
But, Mama, oh, dear Mama, let me be myself
    today.
Let me be myself today,
Let me look a different way,
Let me find a voice that's me,
Let me try to be the woman I was always meant
    to be.
Say good-bye to your baby,
Say hello to someone new,
And maybe then, dear Mama,
You'll see I'm really you.

We do the chorus again and we're adding more verses. The agent likes it. You've got to hear it with music, but I think you get the idea. Phoebe, you wipe off that smirk. I remember how you made fun of country music, but I also know in your heart of hearts, you liked it.

I'm hoping to bring a copy of the taping when I see you two at Teal's party.

Now as to boyfriends. I do have someone I'm sweet on. He's a guitar player, the younger brother of a more famous country guitar player, and his name is not Willie or Boone, Phoebe. His name happens to be Thomas, and not Tom either. He likes Thomas, Thomas Caton. His great-granddaddy fought in the Civil War and not for the Yankees.

Mama said if I marry him, I'll be living on the road or in trailers or whatever, but then I asked her where she's living and she laughed.

I thought you didn't want to be me, she said.

I guess she doesn't know I do in many ways. Maybe she's learning that and that's why we're closer than ever.

Yesterday, I was thinking, when we crossed that desert together and survived, we crossed a lot more than just sand and rocks.

We crossed from one world to another. Maybe someday I'll be able to write a song about it and sing it, with Mama or not. Then I'll know it's finally all put away. There are lots of ways to bury pain, but in my business, you make it work for you.

Don't I sound sophisticated for a country girl? Stop laughing, Teal. Teal, Phoebe . . . how

many, many times I've muttered your names like a prayer.
Can't wait to see y'all.

Love,
Robin

On a summer day Robin and I were flown into the Albany, New York, airport and Teal met us at the gate. We were all too excited to wait for the others to stop talking.

"Wait," Robin cried. "Y'all just got to learn how to take turns. Where's those manners I heard y'all bragging about?"

We laughed and hugged and hurried out to get in the stretch limousine. Teal made it clear we were going to be spoiled and we were to be impressed no matter what or her mother would leave the country.

We couldn't get enough of each other and I thought we would talk ourselves hoarse.

Finally, we were all quiet. Our smiles rested on our faces like tired birds lighting on a branch, and we stared ahead and the limousine continued to sail over the highway.

It really didn't matter where we were going.

We were there already. We were there the moment we all met.

Together again.

Later, Robin sang her song and we locked it forever in our hearts along with all the promises we knew now we would fulfill to each other as well as to ourselves.